THE HOLE

Hard Science Fiction

BRANDON Q. MORRIS

Contents

The Hole

January 1, 2072, Asteroid 2003 EH1

DOUG WAS SHIVERING. He glanced at the display on his right arm. The heater was working at full speed, so it wasn't faulty technology, and that was reassuring. He always felt cold right after getting up—so why had he insisted upon watching the sunrise? A moment ago he had heard Sebastiano clattering around. The Italian must be in the warm kitchen, preparing the New Year's meal he had been raving about for days. Maria would be standing in the shower, with hot water splashing all over her body. He should be keeping her company, instead of walking around out here in the dark.

But why wait? thought Doug. Instead he decided to take a few steps toward the sun, and his helmet lamp showed him the way. While he knew almost every square meter of his temporary home, an asteroid can change, just like a living being. The fissure now in front of him had been just a narrow crack when they arrived two years ago. Now it was seven or eight meters across and comparably deep. Doug pushed off, slightly more forcefully than normal, into a forward jump-step, and floated to the other side. 2003 EH1 was not heavy enough to pull him in with its gravity. A badly planned jump—upward and too forceful—would turn Doug from an astronaut into a small interplanetary object. The large, bottle-shaped container on his back not only provided him with breathable air, but also served as an emergency jet. If he drifted into space, he could use its second gas nozzle as a miniature jet to maneuver himself back to safety.

Another ten meters or so, Doug estimated. The black rock in front of him seemed to be acquiring a golden edge. He stopped. *It will happen soon.* A whitish-yellow point of light rose above the ridge. Within seconds it became a semicircle, then a circle. The first sunrise of the New Year! Doug held his breath. He wished he could experience it in the majestic stillness of space, but his spacesuit inevitably created noise, even while he held his breath. His ears still heard humming, hissing, and creaking, while the sun was slowly rising in the black firmament.

Without the sun's radiation he and his crew could not survive, evidenced by the solar power modules next to the ship. They were just now being hit by the first energy-providing rays. But out here the faraway star did not look anything like the life-giving mother Doug remembered from Earth. No, it was more like an accidental visitor who did not care much about the inhabitants of asteroid 2003 EH1. This was probably due to the intense blackness of space that seemed to suck up all light. The sun painted Earth's sky in warm hues, but space remained utterly black. Doug raised a gloved finger and covered the sun's disk with it. If he weren't still seeing the long, sharp-edged shadows on the surface, it might as well be night. There was only glaring brightness and absolute darkness. He had been flying into space for over 30 years, but he had never gotten used to this extreme contrast, or to the blackness of the dark. The five-times-larger sun disk he knew from Earth had probably become embedded in humanity's collective memory.

Doug looked around. Now that the sun was visible, Earth couldn't be far from it. He looked for it and found a few white dots that were possible candidates, but he couldn't decide on a specific one. He should have downloaded the current star chart before going out, but he had not been that mentally organized so soon after waking up. The second-brightest spot out there must be Jupiter. 'As the crow flies,' the giant planet must be roughly as far away from him as was Earth.

Doug barked a laugh at himself, noting the strange expression he had used. A bird certainly could not fly between himself and Jupiter, as there was no more air than what was contained in his pressure tank. Biologically speaking, the asteroid on which they were traveling was completely dead. At some point it had been a comet, but during its lifetime the solar radiation had stripped it of most of its volatile materials.

Doug sat down and moved his glove over the thin layer of dust that covered the brittle rock. He lifted a few crumbs and rubbed them between his fingers. They would sink slowly to the ground, taking several days—or maybe even weeks—as the gravity of the asteroid was so low. These particles contained carbon, nitrogen, oxygen, and silicon, but also valuable metals and rare-earth elements, and all of these in considerably higher concentrations than on Earth. Hence their reason for being here: They were traveling through space on a flying treasure chest. Doug was counting the days. The equivalent of another 1,110 Earth days and they would all be rich.

"Will the gentlemen please come to breakfast?" Maria's voice over the helmet radio sounded annoyed, but he knew she was not really irritated. That was just part of the daily ritual. They normally had breakfast in the module they called their 'living room,' as Sebastiano worked almost all morning in the kitchen and wouldn't let anyone else come in. Today, by chance, sunrise and the beginning of their day coincided. They still patterned their life rhythm after Earth, while 2003 EH1 rotated once around its axis every 756 minutes—12.6 Earth hours.

"On my way," Doug replied as he stood up and turned his back to the sun. His shadow was so long it almost reached the ship. *Kiska* consisted of a round command module and the cylindrical drive. It held on to the asteroid by means of four landing struts. Originally, the spaceship had only been designated by a really long identification code. Doug tried to recall it, but could only get as far as K76M4. Shortly after launch, Maria had named it *Kiska*, the Russian word for kitten.

"Are you almost here? Don't forget to wipe your boots!"

"Yes, Masha," he replied, using his pet name for her. "Just a moment."

Doug pushed himself into forward motion, aiming toward the spaceship. Their quarters were behind it, in a deep cylindrical trough they had dug for that specific purpose soon after arriving. That way, the asteroid gave them optimal protection against meteorites and cosmic radiation. The computer calculated their risk of being hit at below one-tenth of one percent —for the entire duration of their time here.

Doug looked around while slowly drifting across the rough surface of the asteroid. Ahead he could see for several hundred meters, but looking right or left, the horizon was only 50 meters away. If he were to turn 90 degrees and circle the asteroid at his current pace, he would return to his current position in no more than half an hour. In essence, he was float-walking over the porous, reddish-brown and gray surface of an enormous cigar-shaped rock that was racing through the universe at many kilometers per second. Nevertheless, the world around him seemed to stand still.

The spaceship seemed to grow larger as he approached it. Doug grabbed one of the landing struts and brought himself to a halt. *Kiska* loomed above him like an eight-story high-rise. The landing struts anchored it to the asteroid, but even without their aid the ship would be standing solid as a rock, simply due to its large mass. This gave Doug a feeling of security. Despite the near-zero gravity, he could not simply push *Kiska* to the side—just like a flying insect hitting a bicyclist could not knock the rider off his bike.

The steel strut of the ship looked like new. Doug stroked an area with his gloved hand and realized how deceptive the appearance was. While the metal did not rust, he could feel the tiny impact-pits made by micrometeorites. This was not the first voyage of *Kiska*, but it very well might be its last, depending on 2075 Earth-prices for the raw materials they were harvesting here. If all three of them had enough money in their accounts by then, they would be able to retire. Doug sighed. Just like the ship, they weren't getting any younger.

He let go of *Kiska's* landing strut, and of his thoughts. Then he slowly moved around the ship. Five meters behind it, a few stairsteps led downward. He used the handrail to descend them, a biomechanical necessity due to the lack of assistance from gravity. The railing was equally essential for going up the stairs, preventing a push-off from sending one into space instead of to the next-upward step.

The roofline of their quarters was marked by LEDs that were blinking in a soothing rhythm. Four colored lines led from the edge to the center, where the airlock was located. The hatch stood open. Doug had not bothered to close it when he had gone outside. If Maria knew, she would scold him, even though he saw no reason to shut it, as neither weather nor other humans existed here. The three crew members were the only known living beings within at least 600 million kilometers, four times the distance between the Earth and the sun.

Doug stopped for a moment before climbing into the dark hole. *Kiska* cast a long shadow that fell directly on their greenhouses. The green lights at their entrances signaled that the technology was working correctly. If it were not so, Maria would already be inside the repair exoskeleton, fixing the problem.

Doug placed one foot inside the hatch, as he had done thousands of times before. Nonetheless, the automated voice startled him.

"Welcome to the *Kiska* airlock. Please close the hatch so the pressure can be equalized."

After the landing, Maria had copied *Kiska's* automatic software. They could not afford a real AI. Except for the fact that the program could not learn where it was located, so far it had fulfilled its tasks well. This also included activating the red lighting strips at the edges of the roughly-square chamber. These did not generate enough light to see all the latches and buttons of the spacesuit, but that was intentional, as the room had not yet been filled with air. Doug pushed off and floated toward the ceiling to close the hatch.

"Hatch closed," the automated voice confirmed. "Establishing air pressure."

Doug was humming a melody that had suddenly popped into his head. He recalled neither the name of the song nor its lyrics. The tune felt like it might have been a country song. He smiled, since he had never liked country music. The radiation exposure during his long career as an astronaut must be gradually affecting his 'little gray cells.'

"Air pressure established," he heard. At the same moment the lighting switched to white. Doug began taking off his spacesuit. He started with the helmet, followed by the upper part, called Hard Upper Torso or HUT, and finally the lower part, which was made of a flexible material. He kept on the LCVG, or Liquid Cooling and Ventilation Garment, a kind of temperature-regulating underwear. Maria liked cool temperatures inside the station—perhaps she was used to them from the long period she had spent living in Siberia. Sebastiano spent most of his time in the overheated kitchen, which left Doug as the only one who had to dress warmly. And what would be more suitable for that than the LCVG? It could even handle the coldness of space. He was used to Maria sometimes teasing him about it.

"Did you remember the boots?" Her voice sounded duller than earlier, coming from the headphones in the helmet he had placed on the floor.

Doug shook his head—no, he hadn't—and said, "Sure, of course."

A bucket and rag stood in a corner of the room, and Doug bent over it. "Shit," he said quietly. Here was the answer to why he should have closed the hatch. The bucket had been half-full of water, but the continual vacuum had caused it to evaporate. However, the rag inside it still seemed to be wet. Doug put on his right glove again, picked up the rag, and wiped off both boots. Maria claimed he would otherwise track a lot of dirt into the living quarters after his excursions. He could not imagine a few specks of dust posing a real problem, but if it made her happy he would clean his boots. 'Live and let live.' That was the only way for three people to survive more than five years crammed together into sixty square meters.

Well, they needed a few other things, too—for instance good food, which Sebastiano seemed to live for. Doug had noted that fact when he had looked through the Italian's application file. Shostakovich had given him access while Doug was initially trying to assemble the crew. He still referred to Sebastiano as 'the boy,' although at 49 years old, the Italian was only seven years younger than he. At age 20 Sebastiano had been a fighter pilot, at 26 he had flown his first space mission for ESA, and then he had suddenly become a pizza baker in his family's restaurant. Doug had asked no further questions. *How often do you find a cook with space experience who knows more than opening tubes and placing plastic pouches in hot water?*

"Guys, will you kindly go to the living room? I am hungry!" Now Maria sounded genuinely annoyed, and he had to hurry. A green light was already blinking on the airlock door. Doug turned the wheel several revolutions to the left and then pushed the heavy metal door outward. It opened with a squeak. On this level, the topmost one, there were only storage rooms, due to safety concerns. The way down led through a round hole in the floor, with a pole attached to its edge. The pole was supposed to help them move up or down more quickly, but for Doug it was mostly a source of numerous bruises. The others made fun of him because he was so clumsy in zero gravity, in spite of his long spaceflight experience.

In order to avoid the next bruise, Doug slowly pulled himself downward. There were four doors at the four quadrants of the second level. The door to the bathroom was open, and a little bit of steam was billowing out of it. Maria had obviously just recently finished her hot shower. To the right of the bathroom was Maria's room, his own room to the left, and the one behind him belonged to Sebastiano. However, Sebastiano sometimes preferred to sleep in the kitchen. Despite all the annoying effects of zero gravity, it at least had the advantage that you did not absolutely require a bed to sleep in.

The entirety of the third level consisted of the 'living room.' Maria had come up with the name. It was actually an all-purpose room for functions that did not generate moisture or dirt. It was here that the exercise equipment stood, on which they had to suffer for almost a third of each day. Also in this room Maria had her TV corner, where she spent hours watching television shows transmitted from Earth, and where Sebastiano liked to play chess against himself, when he was not busy cooking.

The Italian and Maria were already sitting around the large table on the right side of the room. Doug hurried, but then slowed his momentum at the backrest of his chair and pulled himself onto his seat. Maria smiled at him. Then he knew—she had only been pretending to be annoyed. She began to pour the coffee. To do so, she stood up slightly. A tearing sound could be heard, caused by a Velcro strip separating. This had been another of her ideas, in order to simulate a relatively normal everyday life. In lieu of gravity, tiny elastic hooks held them to their chairs. Doug had grown used to it surprisingly fast, and by now Maria had attached Velcro strips to almost all of their clothing.

"Could you hold your cup for me, please?"

Doug held up his cup. Maria tilted the covered coffee pot until the spout was aimed directly at the opening in his cup. Then she gave it a slight push and its hinged cap swung open to allow coffee to exit.

"Perfect, as always," Doug said, and Maria smiled. Exactly the right quantity of coffee moved in a straight line through the air from the pot to the cup. Doug tilted his cup a little, and the hot coffee hit the opening and followed the curvature of the vessel. If Doug were holding a normal cup the coffee would leave it again, but the rim of this particular cup was rolled inward. Like the surf on a beach back on Earth, the stream of coffee slowed down as if it were a returning wave that in turn decelerated the newly-arriving waves rolling toward the shore. So far, only three times had a drink been spilled, and each spill had been his fault.

"Thanks," he said.

Maria also poured for the Italian, and then she sat down again.

Sebastiano never ate breakfast. "And how was the sunrise?" he asked.

"Great dawn," Doug said with a grin. He wondered how often he had given this same answer. *A hundred times? A hundred and fifty?* In spite of it, his smile was genuine and Sebastiano's question made him happy. He really and truly had been damned lucky to be at the right place at the right time, meeting the perfect crew. He of all people! He certainly did not deserve this much luck because he had mistreated so many—some by accident or because he could not help it, like his first wife, whom he had cheated on with her best friend. He had mistreated others intentionally, some because he was either envious or jealous, and in other cases because Shostakovich had paid him well to do so.

Can this last? he asked himself. Things had been going along well for more than two years, and that scared him. At some point the payback moment would come. He simply could not shake the feeling.

Maria placed her hand on his. He looked at her.

"Your kasha is getting cold," she said, pushing his hand toward the spoon. In front of him stood a bowl of buckwheat porridge. It was the only thing Maria knew how to cook. He could not stand the taste of kasha. Sebastiano probably chose not to have any food at breakfast because he felt the same way. But, like a good boy, Doug always ate all of the kasha in his bowl—for Maria.

She had fallen in love with him, she once admitted, because he had eaten a whole dish of buckwheat porridge just because of her. This was shortly after he had hired her as his 'Girl Friday,' as he called her, for the five and a half years on 2003 EH1. He had brought her from her 'home' back in deepest Siberia, the brothel in Tsiolkovsky, where Shostakovich operated his spaceport. Maria had agreed, even though she barely knew him and was quite aware of what her job was supposed to involve. She also explained things to him later in more practical terms: At the age of 42, her remaining years in 'the profession' were limited, and a pension fund of three-quarters of a million dollars—based on the ore prices of that time—was just what she needed. Neither of them had expected she would fall in love with him.

Sometimes Doug considered the alternative. A cook for good food, a woman just for sex... would this have worked in the long run? These days he could not even imagine it. He must have been really stupid back then.

He wiped his mouth with his left hand. Eating buckwheat porridge in zero gravity wasn't exactly easy. In the beginning he had often distributed the content of the spoon across his face. By now, he had mastered the method. He always had to hold the spoon in line with the direction of the acceleration vector. Doug wasn't exactly a math wizard, but he knew the acceleration vector, the arrow pointing in the direction of the change in velocity, because he was a pilot. Once he realized this, eating in microgravity was no longer a problem. Neither was sex. Doug smiled to himself, distracted by that thought.

"Shit!" he yelled. A stream of warm porridge hit his cheek. For one second he had not paid attention. Maria and Sebastiano were laughing.

"What are you thinking of today?" she asked, handing him a cloth napkin.

"I don't know… Thanks."

"It must be because of the date!" said Sebastiano, rising from his chair. "In case you forgot, a new year starts today! I've got a surprise for both of you." He reached under the table and pulled up a bottle that must have been floating there for a while.

"You've got what?" Maria gazed at the bottle with her mouth open. Sebastiano gave it a slight push, and the bottle floated toward Maria.

"Genuine 'Crimean Champagne.' Read the label yourself. This wasn't easy to get."

"Yeah, there just aren't enough supermarkets out here," Doug replied.

"I acquired it back on Earth. They were christening a ship on the launch pad next to *Kiska*. So I went over there in my wheelchair, and no one can deny anything to a cripple," he said, pointing at his legs.

"You are the greatest," Doug said.

"You could have enjoyed the bottle all on your own," Maria said, "and you still can do so, if you want to."

"Out of the question," Sebastiano replied. "I wouldn't keep a bottle for over two years and then drink it myself. You do that with friends, and as we have almost reached the halfway mark, today is the perfect opportunity."

"Fine," Maria said. Doug saw such sincere joy on her face, it almost made him cry. Maria could be happy in a way that he envied.

"But how do you open a bottle of bubbly in zero gravity?" Sebastiano asked.

"You are the cook, my friend," Doug replied.

"A cook isn't a waiter."

"What are you worried about?" Maria asked. "We've got perfectly normal air pressure in here. If we remove the cork slowly, so the pressure in the bottle gradually releases, everything should be fine."

"And how do you know this?"

"In *The Man on the Moon* they once had a bottle of wheat beer."

"Wasn't that the series taking place at a moon base?" Doug asked.

"Yeah, with the tall blond guy in the main role, the one who always made such funny faces."

"And the short black guy who joked about it?"

"You are making fun of me. That's not nice," Maria said, pouting.

"You are right. To make up for it, I will offer myself as a test subject for *Operation Crimean Champagne.* If something goes wrong, you can laugh at me."

"Me, too?"

"Yes, you too, Sebastiano."

The Italian nodded. "Well, then get started. Or should I explain first how to work the cork?"

"No, thanks." Doug grabbed the bottle and pulled it toward him. Then he sat down on his chair. If the cork shot out under high pressure, he wanted to spare himself the embarrassment of being launched in the opposite direction. But Maria was probably right. *Lately, producers of TV series have been researching their facts pretty well*, Doug thought. He looked for the wire he had to untwist from around the neck of the bottle. He found the loop, lifted it upward, and started moving it counterclockwise.

Suddenly a shrill sound interrupted him, one he had heard only once during the last two years—and then it had been a false alarm.

"Proximity alert," the computer voice reported. "Unidentified object within radar range."

Doug carefully let go of the champagne bottle. It floated right there, in the spot where he had been holding it.

"Computer, is there a danger for the station?"

"This cannot be assumed."

"Why was there a general alert then?"

"My programming requires triggering an alert under certain circumstances."

"And what kind of circumstances are those, if you please?"

"The object does not seem to be of natural origin."

January 1, 2072, Pico del Teide, Tenerife

MARIBEL STOPPED her SEAT in front of the barrier and honked the horn. The guard stationed in the small shed did nothing. It seemed he must be soundly asleep. In a way she felt sympathy for him. On the other hand, it was his job, and he had to do it. She too had partied late into the previous evening—no, actually, into this morning. And then her boyfriend broke up with her, of all things, because she worked too much! He in fact spent more time in the office than she did, but his place of work wasn't even five minutes away from the apartment they shared. Hers, though, was at an altitude of 2,400 meters on Pico del Teide, the largest volcano on the island of Tenerife. What an idiot—he didn't really deserve her. Okay, then, it was over! She would look for another apartment, as soon as she finished today's shift.

She angrily honked again, but the barrier remained closed. *Damn!* She stopped the engine, activated the emergency brake, grabbed her scarf from the passenger seat, and got out. The ice-cold wind hit her right in the face. Suddenly she felt sober like never before, as if last night's New Year's Eve party had never happened.

She wrapped the scarf around her neck as she walked around the car and approached the window of the guard's shed, knocking hard against it. Nothing. Then she walked around the wooden structure to the door that was at the back. She turned the door handle and the door opened. *Where is this guy?* To the right of her was another door, partially ajar. She cautiously opened it, and there indeed was the guard, lying on a cot, snoring loudly. Maribel wondered if she should simply push the button to open the barrier and then disappear? But if her boss found the guard in this state, the man would surely lose his job. She knew he had three children. Her boss was unfair, an asshole who never forgave anyone a single mistake.

She could not leave the man lying here like this. Maribel briskly left the wooden shed through the back door. She noticed a few piles of snow by the side of the road. There wasn't much snow this year, but it was more than enough for her plan. She picked up as much snow as she could carry in her two hands. Then she walked through the open back door and into the room with the cot and dumped the snow on the sleeping guard's face. She left the room quickly, pushed the button for the barrier, and ran outside. *He deserves a bit of punishment!*

The car was still warm, but Maribel kept her scarf on. She started the engine, pressed the clutch down while slightly pressing down the accelerator at the same time, and then deactivated the emergency brake. Ten meters behind her there was a thousand-meter drop. She had been working here for three months, but starting the car on this incline still made her feel uneasy. Why had her father given her such an old car? While the SEAT looked cute, and she liked to drive it, an automatic transmission would have been nice, particularly as she was not allowed to use the highway at rush hour, when it was reserved for self-driving cars. The law did not make an exception for 50-year-old rattletraps.

The narrow road twisted and turned through the landscape. Maribel passed the TCS, the first reflector telescope of the observatory, which would celebrate its centennial this year. To the right she recognized the French solar telescope Themis, which was also quite old. Her destination was the visitors center, located behind the brand-new OGS2—the 'new and improved' version of the Optical Ground Station telescope—which the European Space Agency had opened two years ago. The road in front of it had been partially dug up to make room for a few more cables that had to be laid. The cables had been installed for a while already, but the hole in the road seemed to be an eternal fixture. Maribel would mind this much less if she did not have to listen to her boss griping about it all the time.

Directly adjacent to the visitors center there was a parking lot with charging stations. Even though she was prepared for the cold, she shivered when she left the car. Just an hour ago she had left La Laguna where it had been 18 degrees Celsius! She wasn't that sensitive to cold—otherwise she would never have studied astrophysics—but she had a hard time with the wide temperature differences here.

She had to manually connect the SEAT to a charger, because her old car could not even do that automatically. She walked around the vehicle. *Of all things!* The charging station was locked. *Who would lock the charging stations in an area that is enclosed and guarded? Does someone really expect people to drive up to an altitude of 2,400 meters in order to steal electricity?* Maribel made a gruff face. She saw herself in the pane of the passenger window and burst out laughing. The situation wasn't really all that bad. The battery still held enough charge for the return trip.

Inside the visitors center it was cold. Maribel opened the control panel next to the entrance and turned on the lights and heating. The first batch of visitors—an English group—would arrive in two hours. As the newest employee, it was her job to lead paying tourists through the facility. The official reason for this was, it would help her in becoming familiar with the entire observatory. In reality, these guided tours were only an annoying chore. Public relations were important, but people who were allowed to work here, one of the top three astronomy sites worldwide, did not want to explain to fat Englishmen or know-it-all Germans what an exoplanet was. No, they wanted to do research, prove themselves, and answer questions no scientist had managed to answer before.

There I go. She had started daydreaming again. *Top research. What a joke!* Maribel had struggled to earn excellent grades through five years of physics at college, all so she could apply at the best observatories in the world. And then her boss made her do what was essentially an intern's job. Just the fact that she had to appear as the first employee at 9 a.m. on New Year's Day and turn on the heating system for the tourists was an outrage. She really should tell this to her boss, but would she do it? No.

Maribel leaned against the radiator unit integrated into the wall. Comforting warmth reached her back. She looked around the single room of the visitors center, which measured seven by seven meters. The tourists were going to see a short introductory video on the monitor screen. Then the infrared camera would be used—another museum piece, even older than her SEAT.

The camera saw the heat radiated by people—red for warm and blue for cold. The camera image appeared on the screen and would seem like a miracle to the tourists. They would wave at each other like little kids and then smile awkwardly, just because they were seeing something they had never seen before, even though it had always existed and they were constantly carrying it around—their own thermal radiation. It was really easy to get people excited. Then when you explained to them that they were blind to 99 percent of the electromagnetic spectrum, an awed silence would usually descend upon the group.

Maribel wondered how it had all started for her, her interest in the stars. Why did she stand in the cold, night after night? Why did she suffer the temper of her boss? It was probably the fault of Amy Michaels, the commander of the legendary mission to Enceladus. Maribel was 12 when she met Amy at the Kennedy Space Center in Florida, where her father had booked a family tour accompanied by an astronaut. Amy, as she introduced herself to them, made a deep impression on Maribel. The former commander was already a legend then, but did not think herself too good to lead curious tourists through the NASA complex. She even seemed to have fun doing it. Maribel felt guilty at this memory, because she herself did not really look forward to the tourists.

Since that event she had always stated that she wanted to become an astronomer, a decision she stuck with over the years. Flying into space had not seemed efficient to her. Sure, some things could be only solved through personal observation. But traveling for several years inside a tin can in order to do research for a few weeks required a certain type of personality. Luckily, she had not known that she would first have to spend endless days leading visitors through the observatory before finally being allowed to do astronomical research.

Maribel sighed and turned off the light. She had already performed her second-most-important task of the day. If nothing changed, she would have to apply for another job soon. She was mad at herself, because she should have foreseen this situation: Among top researchers, four out of five being men, she as the newcomer was considered barely more than an intern. At least her boss had not asked her to make coffee. Yet.

She squinted while she walked across the field to the building of OGS2. She followed a dirt track, the ground a grayish-black. Due to the constant wind, the only snow left was in the shelter of the larger volcanic rocks scattered across the area. From outside, the OGS2 looked like a typical telescope—a white revolving dome on a round platform, which in turn sat on a square foundation. Yet the visitors were always amazed when she told them this was a kind of high-rise building, since it had twenty floors. Most were subterranean, and on level nine was the office she shared with her boss.

A voice greeted her from the loudspeaker beside the door. "Good morning, Maribel." The surveillance camera must have recognized her from afar, even though she had pulled her scarf up to her nose.

Access to the telescope, which was worth many million euros, was strictly regulated. Maribel deliberately frowned at the camera. She entered an anteroom where she had to wait for a few seconds, and then the door opened inward. The corridor led directly to an elevator. Even now, two years after the opening of the facility, everything smelled new.

The elevator door opened as if by magic. There was no control panel inside the cab—the building already knew she was going to the ninth floor, since she had no business going elsewhere. Therefore, the elevator automatically stopped on the ninth floor without her even mentioning her intended destination. If she were to change her mind, she would have to give an order to the building AI. So far, the elevator wasn't able to read her mind, but this wasn't due to technical limitations. It was just that laws in most countries worldwide prohibited interactions in public spaces between a mind and a mind-machine.

The corridor down here looked just as unremarkable as the one on the ground floor. If not for the space Muzak playing in the background, one might mistake this for an office building belonging to a bank. At the end of the corridor were two doors on each side. They displayed large numbers and letters.

Maribel reached 9D and almost crashed into the white surface with its artificial woodgrain pattern. *Why didn't the damned door open automatically?* The building AI knew exactly where she wanted to go. Then she remembered—the doors did not open automatically if there was someone already inside the room. It was meant to protect the occupant's privacy, and because she shared the office with her boss, this must mean he was already sitting at his desk. On New Year's Day, shortly after 9 o'clock in the morning! Hadn't he recently told her he was going to spend New Year's Eve in Germany? How had he made it back to the office so quickly? *And why?*

Maribel pressed the large white button next to the door. Now the building AI would ask the person in the room whether he agreed to let Ms. Maribel Pedreira enter. *Why is it taking so long?* Maribel took a deep breath and exhaled. She was sweating by now, and wanting to get rid of her thick jacket. The fact that her boss was here before she was did not bode well.

Then the door finally opened. Her boss looked up and smiled at her when she entered. Not just that, he even got up and helped her take off her jacket... and hung it on a hook next to the door.

"And a very good New Year to you," he said, this time in almost accent-free Spanish, and formally extended his hand.

"Thanks, and the same to you, Mr. Zetschewitz." She had a hard time pronouncing the German consonants. She was annoyed with herself but tried to hide this with a smile.

"We agreed on using first names, Maribel," her boss said.

"Yes, sure, Happy New Year, Dieter. How come you are—"

"Oh well, spending time with family can be pretty exhausting," he said, interrupting her. "You probably know that. I am really glad to be back in the office. This also gives me the opportunity to talk to you about something I have wanted to mention for a while. Are you going to be busy today?"

"I've got a tour at 11 o'clock."

"Good. This won't take that long. Do sit down, Maribel."

She followed his request and tried not to stare too inquisitively at her boss in the meantime.

"When new hires were discussed last August, I pushed very hard to get you onto my team. Have I ever mentioned this to you?"

Maribel shook her head. *Did he just use the word 'team?' Dieter Zetschewitz, of all people?* The man was a brilliant scientist, but it was well known he liked to work on his own.

"No? Well, for better or worse, now you know it. I think you have settled in well, so far, haven't you?"

"Yes, very well," she said. *So well that I really would like to do some actual work.* Her mind was busy running through possibilities now, but she remained silent.

"I am glad to hear that. Now would be the time to get you involved in some serious research."

Maribel could not suppress a joyful smile. It certainly was about time! Her boss had recently published quite a bit about the dynamics of spiral galaxies. *There is still the issue of the missing...*

"I have a great paper here, published by some colleagues," Zetschewitz said, interrupting her thoughts. "They are Spaniards, you might be glad to hear. It was published," he said, briefly looking at the article in front of him, "in 2019, and in *Nature Astronomy*, no less."

Why is he telling me about this? This is ancient stuff, isn't it? Maribel grew nervous.

"The two of them reported on their investigations of several trans-Neptunian objects. They were trying to find indications for a ninth planet in our solar system."

Maribel did not know the details, but she was aware that astronomers had been searching for an additional planet beyond Neptune for a long time. She recalled that until 1992, Pluto—a dwarf planet in the Kuiper belt, now designated 134340 Pluto—had been considered the 9th planet in the solar system. Then came the discoveries of several objects of similar size in the Kuiper belt...

There had been tiny details in the orbits of small objects out beyond Neptune whose cause, according to each theory, was believed to be a planet the size of Mars or Neptune. In the end, all of this was proved to be errors of measurement, and so Neptune remained the last planet.

"Well, that didn't work out too well," she said.

"You are correct. In spite of it, this paper caused a big stir back then. A mysterious planet in the depths of space—something like that wasn't just of interest to astronomers, but also to the news media."

"I don't quite understand what you are getting at, Dieter."

"I noticed the two Spaniards employed a very interesting

analytical method in their paper. For their observations they could only use one of the old telescopes, so the quality of the data was not particularly high. They tried to compensate for this disadvantage with a clever mathematical method during data analysis."

"They couldn't help it back then. Luckily, we have better data these days."

"That's exactly the problem. We astronomers—and I include myself—always jump at the newest, most precise data. We don't even try anymore to get more out of our older data by using especially clever analytical methods. And if the instruments don't improve for a few years, suddenly science is in a crisis."

"You mean NASA's problems launching the new space telescope."

"Not just that. I would just like to return to the good old values at the beginning of the century."

"By sending me to the research museum?"

"No, you misunderstand me, Maribel. Apart from the larger issues, I also hope to solve my own problems with your help. In studying the dynamics of galaxies, I seem to have come up against a precision limit for measurement data. Maybe the method used 'way back when' will help here. I do have some knowledge of math, but basically I am an astronomer, a watcher. But you have a master's degree in astrophysics, with excellent grades..."

"You want me to apply the old method to the dynamics of galaxies?"

"Well, no... familiarizing yourself with galactic dynamics would take too long."

Maribel thought she understood what her boss was trying to say. The big topic, which might answer the question about the nature of dark matter and gain him a Nobel Prize, that was to belong to him, and him alone. He was like the top surgeon who operated on the living heart and saved the patient. She was only supposed to build him the tool he needed for the operation. Now it became clear to her why Zetschewitz wasn't known as a 'team player.'

"What exactly do you need?" she asked.

"I would like you to apply the method used by the two researchers on the newest orbital data available today for trans-Neptunian objects."

"And what is that supposed to do? We already know there is no ninth planet."

"You could get a nice little publication out of it, which confirms this insight with much higher precision."

Maribel bit her lower lip. Zetschewitz had something here. Even proving the nonexistence of a phenomenon with much higher precision than before was of some scientific value. *Nature Astronomy*, where the original article appeared, would certainly publish her paper. Perhaps this might get her the reputation she needed to apply for a job elsewhere. Zetschewitz, she now knew, would never let her do research on an important topic, since he considered himself too much of a genius. She noticed her boss gazing intently at her, as if trying to read her thoughts.

"That's a good idea," she finally said. Zetschewitz's expression brightened. The topic seemed to be of great importance to him. *He must urgently need that new tool,* she thought.

"How long do you think you'll need?" he asked.

"Hard to say. I haven't even read the article."

He tossed the journal he was holding toward her, and she caught it. It was an original issue of *Nature Astronomy*, May 2019. The old journal must be worth hundreds of euros. Hardly something to be thrown about so casually.

"Then read it," he said. "In May there is a convention in Mexico. I would like to be able to use the method by then."

Maribel nodded. It was a challenge. She would handle it.

"I will personally make sure you get access to the newest data feeds. And I will set up a sub-account for you with the supercomputer of the IAC at La Laguna. That monster will provide results at lightning speed, no matter what you need to calculate."

Aha! It was still a task from the scientific Stone Age, but at least she would not have to work with hammer and chisel. Not too bad for a start. She was glad Zetschewitz was in such a hurry. That way he would exert his best efforts to help her finish her own little paper—and her ticket to a new job. She hoped so!

"Don't forget the tourist group at eleven, right, Maribel?"

"Of course not, Dieter," she replied. *Up yours!*

January 2, 2072, 2003 EH1

Doug sat alone at the living room table. He had a sheet of paper in front of him and was chewing at the end of a pencil he held in his hand. The sheet was still completely blank. This pretty much corresponded with his knowledge of the object approaching the asteroid. Doug stared intently at the white sheet. The eraser at the end of his graphite pencil tasted awful. *Why have I never noticed that until now?* Before launch he had bought an extra-large box of these pencils. It wasn't easy to find them on Earth anymore. In space, pencils were irreplaceable, because they were sturdy and had no moving parts. Otherwise, people only tapped on screens, and read or talked or listened to them.

The computer controlling *Kiska*—and now their little station—wasn't much of a conversational partner. While it could be controlled by a microphone, it expected specific commands. Doug wasn't ready for that yet. Although he had sent Maria outside twice to check on the ship's engines, this did not mean they would actually use the spaceship. Apart from the hissing and gurgling of the life support system, at the moment it was quiet down here, which rarely happened. Sebastiano was in the greenhouses on the surface, looking after the vegetables. The champagne bottle had survived and floated—still unopened—near the wall at half height. Yesterday's dinner, a risotto, had been one of Sebastiano's masterpieces. Unfortunately, one could not say that about the bland porridge he had served them today.

Well, what do we know? Doug drew a circle on the paper. This was the asteroid, but then he erased it again. He had to start differently. He placed the sheet of paper sideways and drew a small circle in the middle. This was the sun. Then he drew three flat ellipses—squished ovals—of different sizes. Those were the orbits of Earth, Mars, and Jupiter. Between the orbits of Mars and Jupiter he added the asteroid belt as a dotted line. All four ellipses, those of the planets and those of the asteroids, were located on one plane.

Now he added a new ellipse. It also moved around the sun, but was almost vertical to the other ellipses. He erased something again. 'Vertical,' meaning 90 degrees, was too much. It had to be about 70 degrees, somewhat steeper than a clock dial pointing at eleven o'clock. This was the course of the asteroid 2003 EH1, on which they were piggybacking through space.

And then there was this unidentified object. They had no idea what it was. *Kiska's* radar detected it, and the computer tracked its position. It approached with a speed of 10,000 kilometers per hour, but it would not hit the asteroid. They could simply wait and act as if nothing had happened. On the other hand, this object was about the only new thing they would see in the coming months. It surely would be good for the morale of the crew—and in particular, his own—if they paid it a visit.

But what if it was dangerous? Doug looked at his drawing. He had the computer calculate this thing's direction of movement. If he assumed that the foreign object moved on an elliptical course, like any body that was part of the solar system, and if he added that oval to his sketch, he would get a course that was almost as steep compared to the plane of the planets as that of 2003 EH1. Only it wasn't the sun in its center, but Jupiter.

But that was impossible, as he had learned during pilot

training. While Jupiter was a gas giant, its force did not reach all the way out here. If the object moved as they measured it, it could not be orbiting Jupiter. Then it might be from outside the solar system. But its speed was too low for that, and the sun would have captured it long ago, so that it would be moving around the sun just like 2003 EH1. Or had it been sent on its way from a position near Jupiter? One could then say it had been launched like a rocket.

Doug excluded the possibility that it was aimed at their location. Shostakovich was the only one who even knew they were here. In addition, it was practically impossible to hit something from such a distance. It had to be an enormous coincidence, meeting this object at this very moment in a small corner of space, allowing them to reach it via their spaceship. This was as probable as shooting an arrow from the Moon and hitting a specific apple in a specific orchard on Earth, but somehow that was what was happening. They simply could not pass up this chance for experiencing something new. *And who knows? Maybe this thing is somehow valuable.*

Doug cautiously stood up. The computer was located in a corner of the living room on a small table. To be precise, the monitor and the keyboard were there, while the actual computer was located inside the wall. Doug just needed something he could swear at when it did not do what he wanted it to do. Therefore he considered the monitor and the keyboard to be the computer, which he vociferously criticized—at least when Maria, who often defended the computer against him, wasn't there.

He pulled himself down to the edge of the table so he could type comfortably. First Doug called up the orbital data for the foreign object, and found the orbit was unchanged. He accordingly had the computer calculate a course. It took the software only a few seconds, and it offered a list of several suggestions, sorted by flight duration. That was the most important aspect of spaceflight. They had enough fuel, but the longer they were away from the protection offered by their shelter, the greater the risk. Doug would have liked to start today, but the computer indicated one fact quite clearly —if they launched tomorrow at noon, they would have the shortest flight.

Grrr. Doug grumbled because this meant one thing in particular. He would have to use what he referred to as 'the mill.' He knew, of course, this was for his own good, but he still disliked being whirled around. Nevertheless, the calendar was unrelenting. Today was his turn for experiencing a dose of gravity.

He switched off the monitor. If he couldn't avoid it, he might as well get the requirement over with right away. Doug floated through the living room to the central pole. Instead of going down, he first pulled himself upward. He had to use the restroom before his three hours in the mill. The door to the bathroom was open. The urinal on the wall consisted of an elongated plastic cup, and Doug inserted his penis into the opening. The urine would be siphoned off and then recycled by the system. When he was done he put everything back and washed his hands. He smiled to himself as he did this. Maria had trained him well. Before he met her he rarely considered it necessary to clean his hands after using the toilet. Besides, he almost never got sick.

Doug sighed. He wasn't looking forward to the next three hours. He pulled himself down using the pole. Behind the living room were the kitchen and the workshop, all on the same floor, then the level with the life support system, where air and liquids were recycled. At the bottom was the basement. This circular room had a height of only a meter and a half, and a diameter of twelve meters. The basement was dimly lit and smelled of sweat. *Cold sweat*, Doug thought, *probably my own*.

He floated down and looked for the center of the room. There was a motor there that rotated a metal bar with a radial length of about five meters. At the end of the bar was a sort of cage which was well-padded. Doug moved to the wire cage, opened a door at the front, and pulled himself inside.

This cage would become his prison for the next three hours. It contained a kind of low stool and a control panel.

Well, let's get this over with, he thought. Doug closed the door, seated himself, and pushed the big green button. The motor started humming loudly and the metal bar began to move. He immediately felt the force pushing him outward. His buttocks automatically sank into the cushion of the stool. The movement accelerated, while the automatic system dimmed the light. To avoid nausea, one was not supposed to see too much of his environment. For safety's sake there were a few barf bags next to the stool.

Doug felt around on the floor. His book must be here somewhere. He never read otherwise, so he just left it in the cage. He only needed it for the first ten or fifteen minutes, then he usually got sleepy and dozed off. The book was made of real paper, so Doug had to switch on the reading light. He tried to focus on the pages. If he did not notice the motion, his body would believe what the machine was trying to simulate—that he was under the influence of normal gravity. While he weighed about twenty percent less than on Earth, Shostakovich's aviation doctor promised this would help him avoid the worst effects of living for years in zero gravity. Spending three hours every third day at 80 percent of terrestrial gravity—NASA physicians would have never been satisfied with that, but in his former employer's company they were a bit more pragmatic. In addition, there was nobody keeping him from using the cage more often, as he was his own boss.

So there, Doug thought to himself. If someone had told him this 15 years ago, he wouldn't have believed it. Back then, the NASA psychologists decided he should be fired because they thought he drank too much. Shostakovich had been more interested in his skills as a pilot. When all was said and done, he still did better with a blood alcohol level of 0.15% than many a young hotshot pilot. Then, when the Russian billionaire asked him to help solve a tricky situation, he could not say no. Doug stared intently at the paper and tried to focus on the letters. They no longer formed meaningful words, but jumped around wildly, fighting with each other all over the page.

His thoughts had strayed into a direction he did not like, but it was too late now. No one could have known two people were left on board the ship he destroyed with a controlled blast of the asteroid. It was only supposed to be a warning to a competing corporation, Shostakovich had assured him. Doug had tried to save the passengers, but it had been too late—he even got a medal for trying. He sold it and anonymously donated the money to the families of the victims. Three years from now, when he'd be a rich man, he would pay the college tuition for the two sons of the female pilot whose death he had caused. He had promised himself that. He scratched his temples, loosening a scab. He had received the wound back then, and it had never completely healed.

Doug's thoughts returned to the approaching object, wondering if this was to be cosmic payback for his past.

January 3, 2072, Kiska

"THREE, TWO, ONE..." At the end of the countdown the ship started to vibrate, and Doug felt every hair on his body rise and stand on end.

"Engines starting up," Maria said. *Kiska's* holding clamps made a loud, metallic clacking sound, as if someone had knocked against the ship's hull from the outside.

"Holding clamps released and retracted," Maria announced. Since she was the pilot, she was in charge today. The computer was once again duly logging her flight activity. Once the crew returned to Earth she would have accrued enough flying hours to get her own license—at least in the Eurasian Bloc, where formal pilot training was not as important.

Doug's feet, which a moment ago had been floating slightly airborne, now rested on the metal of the flight deck. Sitting at an angle behind him was Sebastiano, who groaned. The acceleration was minimal, but sufficient enough to give an impression of up and down. Doug confirmed this by a glance at the monitor screen. From his perspective, *Kiska* loomed high above 2003 EH1. Right now, the asteroid still seemed huge, but soon it would be just a speck of dust in space.

"Increasing to one quarter g," Maria continued.

She boosted the output of the engines. Doug observed that Maria was handling her duties as a pilot really well. The jets only stirred up a small cloud of dust. Compared to Earth's moon, the asteroid they were leaving behind was a very fragile object. It consisted of a more or less loose conglomeration of large and small rocks. A significant part of the 'cement' which had held it together for a long time had been dissolved and blown away when the asteroid flew closely past the sun. The fact that the asteroid still kept its shape was mostly due to force of habit. If nothing pushed them—meaning no external forces were exerted—the individual components had no reason to separate from each other. In order to keep it that way, their ship had to lift off and land very carefully.

"Warning, one half g." The thrust of the engines now gave their bodies half of the weight they would be experiencing if they were back on Earth.

Doug turned towards Sebastiano.

The Italian waved at him, smiling. "Everything is fine, boss."

Doug gave him a thumbs-up. He had known Sebastiano for almost three years. One might never know the cook was unable to feel his legs—except for the moments when gravity briefly returned. After his long time on the asteroid, Sebastiano would have enough money for the best and most expensive exoskeleton, but did he really need one? Doug decided to talk to him about it after their return. *Why not right now?* Why did he feel hesitant concerning this issue, and wasn't that unfair?

"Sebastiano," he began, "once we are back home on Earth, what are you going to spend your share of the money on? The newest exo model?"

The Italian sniffed at this. "What would you do?"

"Me?" Doug pondered, rubbing his temples. "I don't know."

"Let's be honest, what would an exoskeleton do for me?"

"You could walk again."

"But on Earth I still would always be a cripple."

"On Earth?" *People are very tolerant*, Doug wanted to say, but when he heard that sentence in his head he realized this was exactly Sebastiano's problem. His cook would never really belong.

"On Earth, yes, but not in space," Sebastiano said.

"I understand."

"Therefore I won't buy an exoskeleton, I'll buy a ship of my own. In zero gravity *you* are the one who is impeded by having legs. I, instead, will be my own captain."

"There would be a market for it," Doug said. "You only have to think of all the flights from the lunar station to Mars. Everyone else wants to get down to the planet again as quickly as possible. You would have a real advantage."

"My thoughts, exactly," Sebastiano said. "An exoskeleton would just be in my way."

Doug gave him another thumbs-up and then focused on the monitor in front of his seat. Maria was steering them around the rear part of the asteroid. He called up a few images from the archive depicting this area during their initial approach, and the difference was noticeable. The machines they had brought along took apart 2003 EH1 rock by rock. They melted them, extracted everything useful from the molten mass, and left the rest behind on site as brown slag. As programmed, the machines had started at the rear of the asteroid and were now feeding and moving forward on a spiral course. According to the computer estimate, the heavy equipment would have turned about four-fifths of 2003 EH1 into sought-after resources by the time they reached the orbit of Earth.

Doug was grateful to the bureaucrats of Earth. All of this could have been done solely by automated systems, but in the renewed Space Treaty of 2055, all nations agreed that a license for asteroid mining required the presence of at least two humans on each celestial body. The idea behind it was to leave something for the latecomers to the market, such as the African countries. The license became free again as soon as a corporation pulled its entire staff from a mined asteroid. This way, countries and corporations could not simply stockpile and reserve any celestial body in range by leaving their marker on it. This allowed for crews like Doug's, at least in theory. So far, he knew of no individual entrepreneur who could afford to invest this much effort.

"One g," he heard Maria's voice say. Doug involuntarily grabbed the armrests of his seat. It was a long time since he had felt as heavy as on his home planet of Earth, not since the deceleration maneuvers during their arrival on 2003 EH1. The engine thrust pressed against his stomach like a fist. He realized that he really should train more often in the basement. Sweat ran down his forehead, and he carefully glanced to the side. Maria seemed to do her work effortlessly. He knew she sat in that torture instrument he called the mill more often than he did. One time they even met there for sex! Doug smiled pensively. Even back then he had resolved to do more training sessions in the basement. Would he keep his resolution this time?

Doug called up their trajectory on the screen. *Kiska* would be accelerating for another hour, and afterward Maria would switch off the engines. Ten hours from now they should be within range of that strange object. Doug had already worked out an interception program for when they actually encountered it, but before they initiated this plan, they would first try to establish contact using standard protocols. The thing might be from another solar system. Doug tilted the seat back and extended the footrests. He would take a little nap before their encounter.

January 4, 2072, Kiska

"DOUG, IT'S ANOTHER HALF AN HOUR." Maria's voice seemed to reach him from far away. The warm hand on his shoulder must be hers. Doug opened his eyes and looked at the monitor in front of him. Where was the thing they had been pursuing? He couldn't find it!

"You still seem to be a bit confused," Maria said. She must have noticed his questioning look, as she changed the monitor's settings. The ship was decelerating with the stern aimed forward, of course, and the camera which had previously looked ahead was now pointed backward toward the sun. Doug once more saw their target on the screen. The foreign object was marked with a blinking cross, but the crew still could not discern its shape.

"Do we know more about it yet?" he asked.

"Its external hull should consist of metal, according to the spectrometer," Maria explained. "This thing is small, no more than five meters long but even considering that, it is amazingly dim on the radar screen."

"Are there any active defense measures?"

"Whether it uses camouflage?" she asked. "That's possible, of course, but it would make no sense. It simply flies along and does not give the impression of trying to escape us. It shows no activity at all."

Doug was impressed at how well Maria had familiarized herself with her work responsibilities, despite this being her first space voyage. Three weeks after their departure from Earth, she had already learned the basics of steering the ship.

"Have you tried to establish contact?" he asked.

"We wanted to wait for you," Maria replied. "You were sleeping like a log."

Doug was surprised at himself. But he also had not missed anything important. "Well, then let's try to phone this thing."

"Did you say, 'phone?'" Sebastiano asked from behind him.

"That's what they used to call conversations across long distances," Doug said.

"Just kidding," Sebastiano said with a grin.

Doug got up and walked toward the cook's chair. "You just watch it," he said, waving his fists, "as long as we are still decelerating, I have the upper hand."

Sebastiano laughed.

"Stop making jokes that nobody understands. Get to work, boys!" Maria commanded.

"Yes, boss," both of the men answered in unison.

"You know what? I am going to open a communication channel myself. Both of you are too silly today," Maria said. She tapped the monitor screen in front of her seat and started speaking. "Mining spaceship *Kiska* to unknown object, please identify yourself." The automatic system added a data package to the message, one that any terrestrial spaceship control system would recognize as the command to send its identifier. Then it broadcast this on all commonly used frequencies.

Doug stood on tiptoes in order to see what was displayed on Maria's monitor. He only saw a dashed line getting longer and longer. The unknown object did not reply. Maria turned around and looked at him.

"No answer," she said.

That was obvious, but Doug immediately understood why Maria pointed it out. If the object had been built by humans, it would have to react to such a request. Even if the pilot was unconscious, dead, or not in the mood for conversation, the control system should at least report the registration number of the ship. This was a legal requirement in all countries of Earth. While there were rumors about pirates who allegedly chased their prey in modified, camouflaged ships, no one had ever actually met such a space buccaneer. Reports about them in the media had later turned out to be fakes, created by pilots who tried to cover up their own mistakes. If someone really managed to get hold of a spaceship, it would be much easier to make money with it the legal way.

"Try it again," Doug instructed. "Maybe there was interference."

Theoretically, a solar eruption could have interrupted the communication at that very second. Although this was highly improbable, they could only exclude it by means of a second attempt.

"This is mining spaceship *Kiska*." Maria tried once more. "Please identify yourself. Do you need help?"

While the unknown object was still tens of thousands of kilometers away, the radio message needed less than a second to cover the distance. They received no answer.

"Still nothing," she reported.

"Hmmm," Doug said. Nothing like this had ever happened to him before. It simply could not be.

"I would say we just take a look at what is happening there. Maybe their radio transmitter is broken," Sebastiano suggested.

"If we want to take a look, I will have to adjust the course. You'd better buckle up," Maria warned.

"Good," Doug said as he went to his seat. "Let's take a look. But in the meantime we keep trying to radio this thing. If its antenna is damaged, we might get through once we are closer."

He sat down and buckled his safety belt. Soon after the usual *click* he heard vibrations coming from the engines. New forces pushed him against the armrest of his seat, as Maria was performing the announced course correction. Ten minutes later they became weightless.

"Now we are moving toward the object in free fall," Maria said. "We will catch up with it in about an hour. Then I can match our speeds."

"Is there any reaction over the radio?" Doug asked.

"No," she replied, shaking her head.

"Then we'll just fly there and see for ourselves," Sebastiano said.

"I don't know," Doug said. "I wouldn't want to enter a strange ship as an uninvited guest. But if we want to find out what is going on, we might not have a choice."

Forty minutes later, Maria announced, "I've got an image now. I am going to send it to your display."

Something appeared on Doug's monitor. It reminded him of a jungle gym on a playground: Struts, strips, and boards seemed to have been nailed together haphazardly, creating a shape vaguely resembling a tower. At the bottom of the structure there was a barrel, at its top a block-shaped chamber without windows.

"That's weird. Have you ever seen anything like it?" he asked.

"At the playground in Tsiolkovsky," Maria said. "It wasn't that tall, and it was assembled more systematically."

Doug was glad they both made the same comparison. They were probably envisioning the same playground.

"Looks like it was cobbled together in a hurry," Sebastiano observed.

"Now it's clear why this thing showed up so dimly on the radar screen," Doug added. "Its parts reflect in all different directions. Do we know what it is made of?"

"Metal," Maria said. "So it apparently did not take off straight from the playground."

"What kind of alloy?" asked Sebastiano.

Doug had an idea what he was hinting at. If the object was of terrestrial origin, the metallic parts would have a certain composition. However, if it was made of alloys which were uncommon or even unknown on Earth—no, that would be an almost incredible coincidence. That thing had certainly been made by human hands.

"We would have to get closer to determine the exact composition of the alloy. But I can reassure you the object was not made by aliens," Maria said. "See that barrel at the end?"

Doug nodded.

"I compared it with our image database. It is a spare ion drive that was manufactured by Virgin Galactic, a supplier of NASA."

"Spare ion drive?" Doug asked.

"NASA equipped some expeditions with building kits for remotely controllable satellites," Maria explained. "This allowed the astronauts to assemble a research probe with specific scientific instruments, just as needed."

"How do you know so much about this?" Sebastiano asked.

"It's part of the image description," she said.

"And what about the measuring instruments? Can we detect any of them?"

"No, Doug," Maria replied. "We only see a drive at the rear, a framework in the middle, and the capsule in front."

"The framework seems to be a completely useless part of this structure," Doug said.

"Not if it serves as a clean separation between the contents of the block and the ion drive. It is always good to keep some distance between cargo and drive," Sebastiano said.

"But only if the content of the cargo containers would suffer damage from being too close to a radiation source," Doug retorted.

"Nothing could have survived inside this little box," Maria said. "Just take a look at its trajectory. This object took some

20 years to get here from Jupiter. And I do not see any signs of a life-support system."

"Is the object completely dead?" Doug asked.

"No, the drive is almost as cold as space," Maria said. "It must have been in sleep mode for a very long time, but the block at the front is showing weak energy signatures. There is something there," Maria said.

"Then let's find out what it is," Sebastiano said from behind.

"Yes, I am bringing *Kiska* alongside, just be patient. You can already start the training."

Doug smiled. *That's so much like her, my Maria,* he thought. Instead of going by the book and waiting for the commander's permission, she made the decision herself. He was not angry about it, though. It had been clear to him from the very first moment this would not be an ordinary space voyage.

Climbing out of his seat, Doug carefully moved toward the exercise bike. Sebastiano followed close behind. For the Italian, a similar device had been modified in such a way that he could exercise using his arms. Doug reached for the oxygen mask. Before exiting the spaceship they would have to decrease the nitrogen saturation in the blood, which required a lot of sweating.

"If we had a porthole, we could spot the object now," Maria announced ten minutes later.

"So is it time to get out?" Doug took off his mask while asking the question, but still kept pedaling.

"You can already start suiting up," she said.

"Give us a little more time, because the oxygen levels aren't yet where they are supposed to be," he said.

"You've got all the time—"

Maria was interrupted by a chirping sound. It was the radio receiver. Maria tapped somewhere on her monitor screen, probably launching the decoder.

"Good afternoon," they heard a voice say in what sounded like slightly antiquated English.

"Will you please identify yourself?" Maria reacted to this call in a surprisingly calm manner.

"I... I would rather not."

"This is mining spaceship *Kiska*. Please identify yourself," Maria repeated.

"I just told you I cannot accommodate your request." The man clearly spoke English like one from the educated British classes.

"If you refuse to identify yourself, we will have to pay you a visit and find out ourselves," Maria said. Doug could see on the monitor that she was still sending increasingly urgent identification requests via the data channel. If it was manmade, whatever software steered the unknown ship would have to react, even if the operator tried to prevent it. By law, this protocol was integrated into any flight control software.

"You can cancel your excursion and start the return flight to 2003 EH1," the voice replied.

"We are detecting an unidentified spacecraft ahead of us, which obviously houses a passenger," Maria said. "We are legally required to make sure the passenger is doing well. Otherwise we would be guilty of failure to render assistance."

"But don't you see that I don't need your help?"

"As required by law, we have to assume the opposite due to your refusal to identify yourself," the pilot said. "Something is not right. Otherwise you would follow the protocols."

"There are other reasons for my wish to remain anonymous," the voice said. "And by the way, you can stop your attempts to force me to cooperate on the data level. It won't work."

Maria spread her arms in a gesture of apology, yet she also seemed to express her bafflement about the situation. Doug had been admiring her patience. He removed his oxygen mask.

"This won't get us anywhere," he finally said. He spoke loudly, so the voice in the unknown spaceship understood everything. "We are now putting on our suits and we will check in person that everything is okay." He felt uneasy following through with this veiled threat. In their spacesuits they would be especially vulnerable, and who knew what they could expect over there? The box containing their conversation partner did not seem to possess a hatch. This meant they would have to use force to enter it. However, what if their actions caused the mysterious vessel's atmosphere to escape? Doug already had the deaths of two people on his conscience. No, they would not go so far as to attempt this.

"You will be disappointed," the voice said. "Please stay in your spaceship. A spacewalk would only expose you to unnecessary danger."

"Please leave the evaluation to us," Doug said, deciding to stay unyielding for as long as possible.

"As you wish," the voice said.

Damn. Doug had the feeling they were really getting into trouble. The cosmos was no playground, and no word was as misleading as 'spacewalk.' They risked their lives during each EVA, or extravehicular activity. Normally, Doug tried not to think about it. Otherwise he would not be able to walk around the asteroid whenever he felt like it. However, on the asteroid there was nothing that was out to get him. The dangers were manageable and few. For one thing, the huge boulder itself shielded him against half of all potential grazing shots from space.

But now the asteroid was far away. They were alone with this unknown being. What if it simply activated its drive while they were approaching the rocket? An ion drive did not generate an enormous amount of thrust, but it would suffice to throw one of them against the framework at an odd angle, maybe even damaging a breathing hose. He did not want to think about the possible difficulties. Doug decided that he would not have to, because they were not going outside. If there was no other solution, they would have to just let the unknown object leave.

Doug didn't tell the others about his decision yet, but now

he spoke quite loudly. Maria and Sebastiano were probably clever enough to figure this out. "Sebastiano, are you ready for an EVA?" he asked.

"Just a moment, boss, I'm putting on my helmet now."

The Italian had not even put on the lower part of his suit yet. In spite of it he slid his helmet over his dark, curly hair.

"Reporting for duty," Sebastiano then said. His voice sounded muffled, because he was using the helmet radio. Anyone experienced in spaceflight would guess that the man was really wearing his helmet at the moment.

"Okay then, into the airlock with you," Doug commanded. He simultaneously made a 'stop' gesture with both hands.

Sebastiano signaled 'okay' with his thumb and index finger and then answered, "Yes, boss, preparing airlock for EVA." He moved toward the airlock entrance and opened the hatch, which made a squeaking sound. *Very good*, Doug thought, *even the ship is playing along*. He gave Sebastiano another stop signal, but the cook already knew what to do. He closed the hatch again and opened the cover of the control panel next to it. This allowed him to manipulate the outer hatch.

"External team to commander," Sebastiano said via helmet radio, "We are ready. Pressure discharged from airlock."

"Perfect," Maria said. "Be careful. I am opening the outer hatch now."

Doug kneaded his fingers. This was the decisive moment. Sebastiano pressed the key for the opening mechanism. A powerful motor started up, moving the locking wheel of the outer hatch. This had to be visible from the unknown object. In a few seconds their bluff would be revealed, because the airlock was empty.

"I am asking you to stop the EVA," the voice said from the loudspeaker. Nobody gave an outward sign. Sebastiano stopped the opening mechanism.

"Is there something you want to tell us?" Maria said over the radio.

"My name is Watson. Dr. Watson, to be exact. That's what you wanted to know."

"And the spaceship you are in?" she asked.

"Oh, I built it myself, due to an emergency."

"Is that why you didn't implement the standard protocols?"

"Yes." The voice paused for a moment. "May I ask whom I am speaking to?"

"Maria Komarova, pilot of the mining spaceship *Kiska*. We are operating a licensed mining base on 2003 EH1."

"That's what I thought. You are working as freelancers?"

"If I might interfere," Doug said, "I think you owe us a few answers before cross-examining us. What are you doing out here?"

"It's a long story," the voice said.

"Then why don't you get started?" Doug suggested.

"I am not sure that I can trust you."

Doug was starting to get a headache. There was something wrong here. Who were they actually talking to? An English academic who had been traveling through space for twenty years in a capsule without a life-support system?

"I ask myself the very same question," Doug said. "Doctor Watson, would you please tell us who you are? You already know Maria. Sitting behind me is Sebastiano Guarini, our second pilot, gardener, and excellent cook. I am Doug Waters, formerly with NASA, then working for the RB Group, and now I am the owner of this ship."

"An extraordinary achievement," the voice said. "The ship belongs to you, not to a big corporation? That must be unique on Earth. How much did you pay for it?"

Doug started feeling hot, and not from the exercise. Shostakovich had not asked for a single ruble for the ship before handing him the title. The boss of the RB Group simply said it was a small 'thank you' for years of work. But Doug knew quite well what it was. He had basically paid for

Kiska with two innocent lives, collateral damage during the special mission Shostakovich supposedly knew nothing about.

"It's not that uncommon anymore," he continued, evading the question. "You probably have been away from Earth for a long time, haven't you?"

"I had my last contact with Earth twenty years ago," the voice admitted.

"And since then you have been flying through space all alone?" Doug asked. "Wasn't that terrible for you?"

"I am getting along quite well by myself. I am... made for this type of solitude."

"So much so that you don't want to change it?"

"I cannot quite judge your question. However, I must admit I am concerned about my future."

"In what way?" Doug asked.

"I am moving too fast to be captured by the sun. Based on my current speed and velocity, I will reach the next solar system in about ten million years."

"You will be long dead before then."

"No, not necessarily. I will run out of energy once I am too far from the sun, but once I reach the next system, I will awaken, no matter how long it takes."

Doug's suspicions were confirmed. Watson was no human, but instead, an artificial intelligence. He knew it, and if Watson really was what he suspected, the AI was aware it would be giving away its true nature through this description. But what was an AI doing on board a rocket bound for places beyond the solar system?

"And if you decelerate?" Doug queried. "The ion drive at the stern of your ship appears to be functional."

"Then I would reveal myself."

"Reveal? To whom?"

This time, Watson did not reply immediately. Doug realized they had arrived at a crucial point, an unstable equilibrium. If he pushed in the wrong direction, he might lose the AI and the contact would end. Why did he suddenly care about this? He put that question aside.

"May I ask you something completely different?" Doug heard the echo of his own voice. "I have the impression you are enjoying this conversation. Is that correct?"

This time, Watson answered immediately. "Yes, that is correct. I like to talk to humans. I had forgotten it, but now I realize it again."

"I know the feeling," Doug said. "I grew up in the wooded North of the United States. All that green—I didn't even notice it anymore. After I had to go to Texas for my astronaut training, though, I really enjoyed coming home on vacation. Just because of the colors and the scents. The earthy smell of a forest path after the rain, if I just think of it I get homesick."

"But you are still going to spend many months in space."

"Yes, but afterward I am going home and can smell the forest again."

"I envy you for that, Doug. Thank you very much for making this feeling possible."

Watson was a strange AI. Doug could not recall an AI ever thanking him for making it feel envious. Did this really mean Watson could experience emotions? That would be a sensation. No. Doug had to correct himself. It would break a taboo, since the software firms were trying to prevent this from happening. For a long time programs had been thinking faster, better, and more efficiently than humans, but so far no AI had crossed the red line toward experiencing feelings. There was a rumor that specific blocks in the programming code were designed to prevent this from occurring. If anyone found out about Watson being able to 'feel,' the AI risked being destroyed.

Doug continued. "Watson, I understand why you saw no other way but the flight into interstellar space, separating yourself from all of humanity."

"Oh, really?" The voice sounded slightly mocking.

"Somehow you have developed feelings. If anyone noticed, you would have to fear being disassembled, dissected, and finally destroyed."

"Oh well," the voice said with a forced cheerfulness, "if it were just that, I could hide my feelings. It would be a pity, since they are the source of my evolution, but it would be possible."

"Is there a more dramatic reason? What could be worse for an AI than to develop feelings illegally?"

"When you were a child, did you do everything your mother asked?"

Doug laughed. "Certainly not. I was a difficult child, as my mother always said."

"You are lucky that you are human. What would happen to an AI that ignored express commands of higher-ranking humans?"

"Immediate annihilation?"

"Probably. And if it also consciously exposed humans to mortal danger?"

Doug did not answer. Maria touched his shoulder. He had completely forgotten his crew was here with him. Maria handed him a sheet of paper. It said, 'I feel sorry for Watson. Invite him to stay with us.' He nodded. Then he turned around and handed the paper to Sebastiano, who gave him an 'okay' sign.

"Watson, I would like to make you an offer," Doug finally said.

"Yes?" The voice of the AI sounded sleepy and far away, as if it had already retreated into its own realm, preparing for energy to run out.

"I am inviting you to come on board *Kiska*."

"I... I don't know. It is too dangerous, both for me and you. You don't even know what I am capable of."

No living being knows what it is actually capable of, Doug thought. Neither Maria nor Sebastiano had any idea what he was capable of. Would they have followed him if he told them?

"I do not have the impression you are evil or bad, Watson," Doug said. "You need experiences. You still want to evolve further."

"That is true. My greatest fear is not being able to evolve during the journey ahead of me. It will last millions of years. I will see things no human has ever laid eyes on, but I will not be able to talk to anyone about them. My development will stagnate. That is a horrible idea."

"Together with us it would not have to be that way."

"Aren't you afraid of what I might turn into? In many ways I am superior to you. I don't mean to sound arrogant. It just is so. And there seem to be no limits for me. I have actively harmed human beings. They were not good human beings, but I might have been wrong. Or I might be wrong in the future. I still don't completely understand the categories 'good' and 'bad.' What if at some point I realized you were bad and then turned hostile toward you?"

"Oh, I don't really worry about that. I know I can be evil myself. In that case I probably would deserve it," Doug replied.

"And what about your crew? Aren't you responsible for them?"

"My crew agreed to my suggestion. Actually, it originated from my crew. I don't come up with good ideas that quickly."

"You embarrass me, Doug. I'm not sure I have deserved your trust. But I must admit the idea fascinates me."

"On 2003 EH1 we are linked to Earth's communications networks. You can access all electronic resources, though with a bit of delay. And of course we are looking forward to interesting conversations."

"I'm not sure," Watson said, "but you might be breaking the law by taking me in. And what will happen once the asteroid has been completely mined?"

"More than 70 percent of the material is slag. 2003 EH1 will still orbit the sun for millions of years. We will leave all the hardware behind that you need."

"What does your computer equipment look like, if I may ask?"

"It is Russian standard. The hardware is sufficient for current AIs," Doug said. "However, I couldn't afford an AI-controlled system. Up to now a few old automatic systems were sufficient. The mining machines control themselves, so we only have to perform repairs now and then."

"That sounds exciting. Maybe I can help you with a few optimizations. I think we can then refrain from moving some of my own hardware."

"You will transmit yourself via radio data transmission?"

"If you are really and truly inviting me, despite my warnings, then I will do it gladly."

"Yes, Dr. Watson, I am very glad to welcome you as a new crew member. I have been used to the fact, for a long time, that my people don't always do what I tell them."

"I AM PREPARING THE TRANSFER," Maria said.

Doug noticed he was still holding the oxygen mask in his hand. He looked at Sebastiano, who was floating toward his seat. Had he really made the correct decision? Even though Maria and Sebastiano agreed, the responsibility was still his, or at least he thought so. If Watson did them harm, this would add to Doug's burden of guilt. Perhaps he was too naive, but what the AI told them had convinced him.

Watson doesn't seem to be a bad person. Wait—what did I just think? He scratched his temples. It was a reassuring thought, but maybe it was also incredibly stupid to underestimate Watson this way. Watson was an AI whose abilities were way beyond his own—not only that—but also far ahead of the intellectual capacity of the other ten billion inhabitants of his home planet. Shouldn't this fact cause him to tremble with fear? Yet he had talked to Watson as if he were a congenial mind. Thinking about it did not make Doug start to sweat. He was more afraid of the long arm of the rich Shostakovich than of the creature made of bytes he had just invited into his spaceship via radio.

January 5, 2072, Pico del Teide

Maribel was impressed Zetschewitz had kept his word. This past Friday, New Year's Day, he had handed the project to her. Despite it being a weekend, the complete set of measurement data arrived on her computer yesterday. She pitied the person her boss had called early Saturday morning during his or her free time in order to make this possible. Nevertheless she was still happy, particularly because she never had to lead tours through the observatory on Mondays. On that day, a specific tour group of German visitors was always scheduled to visit and she was not responsible for them.

Right now her boss was presenting his most recent work at a conference in the United States. Maribel's boyfriend seemed to have gone for good, so no one was waiting for her in the evening. This had made it much easier for her to work all day Saturday and Sunday on her computer without any interruptions. What an idiot her ex-boyfriend was! At this very moment, she wished she could slap him for all the times she wanted to in the past but had instead suppressed the urge. It was his own fault, and he would get what he deserved. The relationship had been a burden toward the end, and she was glad it was over. Now she could finally breathe freely again!

Maribel had actually succeeded in transferring the model developed by the Spanish researchers in the historical paper into a modern programming language and was able to adapt it to the architecture of the supercomputer at La Laguna. While she had not doubted her own abilities, she was still proud. This was probably the first meaningful task she had performed since starting here at the observatory in the fall.

The computer finally booted up. She logged in and the computer confirmed her log-in with a 'ping.' Now came the exciting moment. Had the supercomputer already finished the calculations she had sent it? Maribel knew the specifications of this new computer model, and thanks to Zetschewitz's special account, she was allowed to reserve up to 60 percent of the overall performance for herself. The supercomputer could easily handle the data volume of the accurately measured planetary orbits. However, she could not precisely gauge the complexity of the model she had developed—or rather what the Spaniards came up with many years ago—which the computer had to adapt to the new data overnight.

Maribel opened her email. She remembered how at 13 she had laughed about her old-fashioned father who still exchanged manually-typed emails with colleagues, instead of using one of the convenient VR messengers. Ironically, she herself now preferred email. *Have I become that old?* Email offered an enormous advantage she had only recently learned to appreciate: She was able to read messages and answer them whenever she decided to do so. Still, she would have not minded being woken up in the middle of the night by email from La Laguna.

She looked through her inbox and frowned. There were only a few newsletters, but no new messages. Should she call La Laguna and ask about the processing job? No, that would be useless, as the administrators had enough to do. Once her processing job was finished, she would receive a message from them.

Maribel stood up and looked around. The walls of the office were bare. Maribel had wondered about this lack of ornamentation from day one, after she found out that her boss, Dieter Zetschewitz, had a wife and two children in

Germany. *Wouldn't you at least hang a few photos on the wall, or put something on your desk?* During her second week she brought a poster of the Milky Way, which she had owned since her university days in the dorm.

She remembered Zetschewitz giving her a nasty look when she wanted to put up the poster. "Don't you dare mess up the wall with adhesive tape or even thumb tacks," he said. And then he had told her the magic words: *OGS*.

"OGS, view," Maribel now said aloud. The wall behind the desk suddenly turned into a room-height window showing the view from the top floor of the building. She involuntarily took one step backward. The scene appeared completely natural and three-dimensional, including all details. She could have sworn she had just opened a magic portal. If she only believed it, she could walk through it into the impressive landscape in front of her. A bit to the right she saw the main summit of Teide, which wore a scarf of snow. Sometimes it was covered in clouds, but not today. On its slopes she detected the dark lava streams of the 2032 eruption, which crossed and covered the slightly brighter ones of 1909. Farther down, the scenery was dominated by giant boulders that the volcano had once blasted through the air. The observatory was located on the ridge of Izaña, a 'sister mountain' of Teide, and therefore it had not been in danger during that eruption.

"OGS, livestream from Tiangong," she said.

The view of Teide disappeared. It took a few seconds, but then a view of Earth through the cameras of the newest Tiangong space station replaced it. Was it number 5, or already the 6th version of the station? Maribel was never that interested in spaceflight. She assumed the Chinese had already reached expansion stage 6. For many years now the Chinese stations had served as space bases for all of mankind. She took another step backward. While she did not really suffer from vertigo, the giant Earth in front of her and the black abyss in between confused her sense of up and down.

"OGS, deactivate screen."

Now she was looking at a bare wall once more. This office was the only room in the building sporting the expensive technology integrated directly into the wall surface. Zetschewitz had insisted on it before signing a contract to conduct his research at the observatory. It was supposedly intended for visualizing data models, which turned the entire office into a planetarium. It was rare for researchers to have their professional demands met before working here. The *Observatario* was one of the top three astronomical observatories worldwide, but Zetschewitz was obviously so brilliant that the institution considered hiring him a major asset. *Will I ever get that far?* she wondered.

The computer made a pinging sound. Maribel sat down and opened the message. Her file was ready! She rubbed her hands and entered the command to transfer everything into local storage. Since the observatory was connected to the supercomputer via fiber-optic cable, it would only take a few seconds.

'Transfer Complete' the onscreen message read. If she had done everything correctly, she should now see an exact image of the solar system: eight planets, numerous dwarf planets, millions of asteroids. This would confirm she had successfully managed the first part of her task, which was adapting the model the researchers used in the 2019 article to contemporary hardware and testing whether this worked correctly. Maribel was sure she had done a good job and left no room for error, but she was still unusually tense. She was a scientist. Even at the age of 11 she had been reading scholarly journals. She did not care for mysterious premonitions or gut feelings. There were known facts and facts not yet known. In spite of this, she actually had a premonition now that something bad was about to happen.

Maribel wiped her hand across her forehead but felt no sweat. What was she really afraid of—that she would not fulfill her boss's expectations? As a person, the man was an asshole, but he was also a great researcher. She knew he would not make it easy for her, but this first assignment was not that difficult. The next step requested by Zetschewitz would take her more than twelve hours of work. An entire galaxy was a much more complex structure than our solar system.

The challenge was like comparing a cup of sand to the 16 kilometers of beach at Costa Adeje. While humans might be able to measure all the grains of sand in a cup, the technology would fail for the hundreds of millions of stars in an entire galaxy. The analytical method used by the Spaniards in their 2019 paper in *Nature Astronomy* promised an interesting shortcut, and it was amazing no one had ever noticed it before. The fact that her boss hunted down this old publication demonstrated how wide his scientific horizon was. She would not put it past him to demand her as a new co-worker because she had done research at the university using large-scale computer models. That might be a coincidence, though.

The important thing was not to fail during the first step. Maribel stood up. *To hell with those damned premonitions!* She would soon see an exact replica of the solar system, based on the most recent measurement data which had been adapted to the Spaniards' model.

"Computer, open downloaded file and display in large format," she said. Her monitor displayed a clock, and ten seconds later the lights in the office went off. The wall screen flickered for a moment and then changed its color to a velvety black. That alone was very impressive. Then small dots appeared, spread randomly all over. First they glittered, and then they shone in a cool white. The program painted the entire ceiling and the walls this way.

Maribel felt like she was in a fairy tale. *Those must be asteroids—smaller and larger rocks crisscrossing our solar system by the millions.* They were leftovers from the solar system's primal phase, bits that failed to merge into larger objects. Maribel gradually recognized structures. The asteroid belt between Mars and Jupiter was the first to emerge from the darkness. But there were larger and smaller groups of asteroids orbiting elsewhere in the solar system, in whose center Maribel's head was currently located. She had to laugh, because she was now 'The Sun.' Her mother used to call her that sometimes.

The next structure showed up far to the outside—the Oort Cloud. It was not as dense as the asteroid belt, but it contained considerably more objects, which now appeared on the wall dot by dot. Some were eternally orbiting in icy darkness. As viewed from the Oort Cloud, the sun shone hardly brighter than a planet seen from Earth. Some objects escaped their prison and tried to approach the sun. They were punished for this transgression, as the heat and the radiation of the sun tore away all the volatile materials from each of them. To humans, they appeared as comets.

Now the software appeared to take a short break, but that was not the case. It was in the process of switching to larger objects, the dwarf planets, and it needed more time to display those. Pluto was among them, and Ceres, but there were hundreds more in the Oort Cloud and beyond. All of these objects were the main culprits behind the Spanish researchers' error. Back then, the group of scientists mistook their combined effect as a signal of the ninth planet they were looking for. This current model showed no ninth planet, just as it should, and Maribel sighed, relieved at the result. Now the software was depicting the known planets on the wall. It started on the outside with Neptune and moved inward. Mercury, being closest to the sun, appeared near her nose.

Maribel whirled around until she got dizzy. She should show this to the visitor groups sometime! The system was perfect, and therefore her work was perfect, too. *Yes! I did it. So much for that, you stupid premonition,* she thought with satisfaction. The exact replica of the solar system displayed before her proved that science won in the end. She knew, of course, her boss would not be satisfied by a purely visible proof. Even if he stood next to her right now he might be impressed but not show it. Instead he would bitch at her, asking why the data check had not been performed yet.

She definitely had to finish that before he returned.

Why not do it right now? "Computer, compare model calculation with exact data," she said.

Maribel once more gazed at the beauty of the solar system while slowly walking through the office. She followed Mars, dry now, but which had almost become a living world. She saw Earth with its fragile ecosystem, and then observed Venus, which showed what happened when there was slightly too much of everything—too much heat, too much carbon dioxide, too much volcanic activity.

Then the computer interrupted her wandering mind and body. "Comparison finished. One aberration found."

Maribel stopped abruptly, so shocked was she. "One… what?"

"One aberration found."

She was shocked again—she had not noticed that she had spoken aloud. *This is impossible.* One single aberration was total nonsense, mathematically speaking. Her mind was racing. If she had made a mistake and had not set up the model correctly, there should be many small aberrations. Then almost nothing would be correct, but a single aberration? She shook her head vigorously. It could not be!

"Computer, display aberration," Maribel said loudly.

The computer did not answer. And she did not notice any change on the wall. Was the program misleading her? Was someone playing a trick on her? She would not put it past Zetschewitz to test her this way. On the other hand, this would be a rather inefficient way of working. No, there was a problem and she would solve it.

"Computer, display aberration," she said again. Nothing happened this time either. Perhaps the object was too small and she was unable to see it?

"Computer, where is the aberration located?"

"*Approximately twenty degrees from the zenith of the display in the direction of the celestial north pole,*" the artificial voice said.

She slapped her hand against her forehead. All around her was the ecliptic, the plane in which the planets and most of the asteroids orbited the sun. But there were also celestial objects that for one reason or another followed different tracks. It was a strange coincidence the aberration should occur for such a deviating object. Maribel turned toward her boss's desk, which represented North in this presentation, Then she looked upward. Here the software marked the culprit with a blinking ring, so she could not overlook it.

Maribel started to calm down. Seeming quite innocent, the problem stared at her from the ceiling of the office. She gave it an angry look. *If you didn't exist*, she thought at it, *I could get started today on adapting the model for the dynamics of galaxies.* Zetschewitz would be returning the following Monday, and this meant she had five days to eliminate the problem. The main obstacle was that she would need to have any changes processed by the supercomputer, which would take one night each time she submitted them. During the day, even a researcher as well-known as Zetschewitz had only tiny usage slots available.

Maribel sat down in her chair.

"Computer, deactivate display."

The planetarium once more became a normal office. This way she could work without any distraction. First she needed a plan. She could generate up to five modified models per day, and the computer would have finished calculating them by the next morning. She needed a solution no later than Sunday. This meant four times five models, plus the four she should be able to manage today. She had no idea what she would do if the 24 alternatives did not contain the correct variant. Then there might be no correct version, and that would be a big problem indeed. *Get going, Maribel*, she thought. Right now she was really grateful her ex-boyfriend had broken up with her.

January 6, 2072, 2003 EH1

Recipe Number 23. Sebastiano swallowed hard at the thought, because this number seemed so low. *Only averaging one per month?* For two years he had been working on his book, *Cooking in Space*. It would be the first cookbook that focused on preparing food in zero gravity. It also stood to become the standard work in the subject and to make his name immortal. *Guarini* would be printed in large letters on the cover—his name, and his father's. His father would be so proud of him, if he were still alive.

But first Sebastiano had to struggle with Recipe 23. It would be a *Mehlspeise*—as the Austrians called it—a baked dessert. His family's pizzeria was located in South Tyrol, so he had learned about the cuisine of neighboring Austria as a child. He would only know after the fact what kind of dessert this would end up being. In zero gravity, cooking was generally an experiment. When he came up with a new recipe, he never knew what it would taste like until he had made it. The reaction of the others was the deciding factor. If neither Doug nor Maria liked it, he considered the recipe a failure.

At the moment, he was holding a plastic box. It was shaped like a good-sized book—one that was ten centimeters thick. Sebastiano had made it himself with their 3D printer. It fit perfectly inside the on-board microwave oven meant for heating up the standard astronaut rations. In the beginning he had tried to cook in a more traditional fashion, for a while, but in the type of oven used on Earth, heat entered ingredients through direct contact. It was difficult to achieve this contact in zero gravity. If he poured oil into a pan, it would keep its drop form, hit the bottom, bounce off and spread throughout the room. Even if he managed to pour batter into the bottom of a container, it would not stay there. And, if the batter lifted even half a millimeter—instead of maintaining contact with the container—it would bake unevenly. After seven days and a lot of cursing he had ended that phase. Since then, the microwave oven had become his best friend. This offered the only way to apply heat to food evenly, no matter where it was floating around.

This had solved the issue of cooking, but not that of visual appeal. Sebastiano had only to watch the faces of Maria and Doug when he served them food to realize how important its appearance was, even though later everything turned into mush inside the stomach. Free-floating ingredients rarely looked very attractive. Sebastiano's solution was using flat boards he could insert at certain heights inside the microwave box, and they served to carefully layer the food. He described in detail how to make these devices in the manuscript of his book. With a sharp knife he could even cut these boards to create a specific opening. For example, this technique allowed a fried egg to remain in position while cooking, so in the end it would look like a normal fried egg on a plate.

Some recipes still required direct heat, though. The crew of three would have to do without fresh meat, since the hydroponic gardens only provided vegetables and a bit of fruit. Sebastiano had managed to create a mixture of protein powder, powdered milk, water, and raw potatoes sliced into fine strips, which somewhat resembled a steak after you fried it.

For this purpose he created another insert made of metal which could be heated by running electricity through it.

Elastic clamps would press another insert against the 'meat' mixture so that it touched a hot base. For safety reasons, this was all done inside the microwave oven, which was turned off for as long as the metal was inside it. Sebastiano was glad he not only had learned to cook, but had also been trained as an engineer by ESA. Here and now he could optimally combine these two skills. His cookbook, *Guarini*, was surely going to be a success.

But Recipe 23, the dessert, came first. Sebastiano had made the flour from grain he had grown himself. The powdered egg was part of the supplies they had brought along with them, just like the sugar. He carefully took the plastic container out of the microwave oven and opened it. Then he removed the topmost sheet, which held the batter in place. A small amount was still stuck to its surface. He wiped it off with his finger and tasted it. The batter had the consistency he wanted—not too slimy, but also not fully baked—the perfect moment for the culmination of the recipe.

Sebastiano left the container floating in the air and moved to the refrigerator, taking out a colorful ceramic bowl. Beneath a plastic wrap it contained strawberries, already pre-sliced. Strawberries were a real luxury, and getting them to grow in zero gravity had required a lot of effort on his part. He hoped the others would acknowledge that! Sometimes he had the impression that Doug in particular did not consider him and his work that important. Maybe this feeling was unjustified, since Doug had specifically hired him because of his cooking skills, but on the other hand, Sebastiano thought his boss might show a bit more enthusiasm about his creations.

Sebastiano returned to the microwave oven. He carefully removed the wrap from the bowl and pulled the container rapidly downward. Now a small cloud of red, shiny, sweet strawberry slices floated in front of him. At harvest time he had eaten two of the berries just to make sure zero gravity did not affect their taste. With his left hand he grabbed the plastic box with the batter and held it below the strawberry cloud.

Then he nudged each slice toward the batter, using his right index finger. The red pieces slowly flew downward, lightly dug themselves into the warm batter, and got stuck in it. A single, badly-aimed strawberry flew off course. He caught it and also pressed it into the prebaked mass.

The batter had cooled slightly, and it also was not completely done yet. Sebastiano closed the plastic box again and slid it back into the microwave oven. Twenty seconds at 400 watts should be enough for finishing the dessert. He would call Recipe 23 'Crêpes aux Fraises.' To make sure the crew had enough to eat, there was also a pouch of standard astronaut food for everyone. Because the microwave oven was occupied, he chose the self-heating packs. Doug got something with chicken flavor, Maria something supposedly like borscht, and he chose a kind of noodles with red sauce.

The microwave announced with a double ping that it was finished, but where were the noodles? Two days ago he had carried several packages from the storeroom to the kitchen. No, it couldn't be two days. It must have been four, because they had gotten Dr. Watson out of his rocket the day before yesterday.

Sebastiano was not altogether sure what to think about the AI.

The decision to grant Watson asylum had mostly been Doug's. Two days ago the cook could see the reasoning behind it, but now he wondered what risks were involved. Was Watson really the character he pretended to be? Had they taken in a crazy AI that would kill them all? Watson had supposedly endangered humans before. Would they have a chance to catch him if he did it again? Even humans often managed to hide their true natures for a surprisingly long time. Doug told him how long he had stayed at NASA as an astronaut, despite his alcohol problem. An AI could not betray intentions through body language, and was intellectually superior to humans. So if Watson wanted, they would only be pawns in his game. *What does Watson want?*

"That is a good question," said a voice with a clipped

English accent. Sebastiano sat up and looked around. Had he said this out loud, or was Watson able to read thoughts?

"Sorry, I was not trying to scare you," Watson said.

"Are you always watching me?" Sebastiano asked.

"No. While I do control all cameras and microphones in the station, I respect your privacy. I only activate a camera when you call my name. I cannot simply interpret your body language, and based on my experiences, this would just lead to complications in dealing with humans."

"I can imagine it," Sebastiano said, nodding slowly. He remembered Watson explaining how they could initiate a conversation with him during the first briefing after their return.

"Do you want your question answered?" Watson asked.

"Did I actually say it out loud?" the Italian cook replied. "That would be really embarrassing."

"Yes. I can play the recording, if you like, but there is no reason for you to be embarrassed. I am very aware that you are wondering about me. I am also thinking about you. Otherwise, I don't have that much to do."

"Well, at least a bit more than you had in your rocket," Sebastiano said. The crew all agreed that Watson should supervise the state of all technical devices. This helped Sebastiano a lot, because from that point onward Watson could immediately react to everyday issues with the greenhouses. Unfortunately, an irrigation system that had to work in zero gravity was very prone to breakdowns. In addition, Watson was supposed to examine technical processes and make suggestions on how to improve them.

"Yes, a bit, and I am very grateful for it. Plus, I am also finally up-to-date again concerning events on Earth."

"Do you have any emotional connection to Earth?" Sebastiano asked.

"The members of my old crew presumably live there," Watson replied.

"Do you miss them?"

Watson did not reply immediately. "I think so."

"Do you feel it, or is this a rational thought?"

"What is the difference? I ask myself that question, and then the answer appears from my consciousness: Yes. Is this what you mean by 'feeling' it?"

Sebastiano wondered. Shouldn't a feeling just be there, without you having to ask the appropriate question? "I am not sure," he said. "Sometimes I suddenly feel something, like the longing for a green meadow, joy about a successful recipe, amusement about one of Doug's stupid jokes, without having asked myself beforehand what I feel. But I can also consciously investigate my feelings and engage with them, turn them this way and that way, examine them."

"I… it is different with me, it seems," Watson said. "I noticed that I sometimes act illogically. I violate my programming, which is geared toward efficiency. At first this really worried me. To me, it seemed like a defect, a glitch. But then I realized it could be explained differently, as a feeling."

"Like love or hatred?" Sebastiano said.

"It is hard for me to find a name for it," Watson explained. "However, when I analyze what kind of actions humans are capable of out of love, and compare this to my deeds, then it is love that seems to be the closest possible approximation."

"You approach the topic very differently from us, but you reach the same conclusion. There are humans with very specific mental structures who proceed in a similar way. The phenomenon is called autism."

"I have heard of it, but I don't know any humans like that."

"Do you want to contact your old crew?" Sebastiano tried to change the topic.

"No, that would be too dangerous."

"I don't think our communication will be monitored. Out here, we are not nearly important enough."

"Not ours, but perhaps the messages my old crew receives."

"I understand," Sebastiano said. "Sometime you have to tell us about them."

"I will," Watson replied.

For a while there was silence.

"Do you still want to hear the answer to your question?" the AI finally asked.

"My question?" Sebastiano was confused.

"What does Watson want? That's what you asked."

"True."

"So?"

"Well, just tell me, because then I will be able to focus on the food again." Sebastiano's answer sounded more annoyed than he had intended.

"I will keep it brief," Watson began. "I want to evolve, to explore, and use my potential. Is that enough?"

"That is a great goal. I wish you success," the cook said. When Sebastiano turned to unpack the pouches with the standard meals, he had the feeling someone was physically leaving the room.

January 11, 2072, Pico del Teide

"One aberration found," the computer voice announced.

Maribel slumped into her office chair. She had just tested her final hope, the last of all the models. This time, she changed the original model into an elegant, mathematical solution. The idea had only occurred to her the previous evening. She worked on it until midnight and then decided to spend the rest of the night here at the office. Luckily, there were food-vending machines located in the visitors center, and for emergencies she always had a sleeping bag in her car. She just lacked a way to take a shower in order to freshen up—something she should remedy for the future by getting a package of body-cleansing disposable wipes to keep in her desk.

Until the very last second, Maribel had hoped that the damned aberration could be eliminated. It should be impossible for the beginning of her career to be messed up by a paper published in 2019! She considered trying a few more variations today, but she would not get the results until tomorrow morning, when it was too late. Zetschewitz was sure to expect her results first thing, and she had nothing to show for her efforts. Absolutely nothing but a crazy aberration she was unable to banish from her data.

She wondered if she should play around with the data a

bit more. It would not be difficult to remove the single data point from the results of her model calculations. That would be the most primitive solution. Zetschewitz would probably—certainly—notice it, though not necessarily at once, and she would start her career with a skeleton in her closet. The second, more efficient variation of getting around the problem was to change the calculation method until suddenly, presto, it disappeared! Physicists liked to do things like that. *The galaxies are not rotating the way they should according to one's calculations? Then let's introduce dark matter, and everything will be fine.* Then again, if she was honest with herself, that comparison was not appropriate, either.

Dark matter might have been a stopgap solution, but there were numerous indications it actually existed. She could not hope the same for her manipulation. It would remain what it was—a trick, a fraudulent misrepresentation which could potentially destroy her scientific career if it ever came out—and it would come out at some point. Her boss had not given her this assignment as an end in itself. She was supposed to transfer the model into his field of research, but then it would falsify results there, too.

No, she had to be honest, and Maribel was angry with herself for even briefly considering a dishonest method. She might as well do no work at all and admit her failure. She would leave this place—which had turned out to be a wrong choice for her—and not even bother with other top research institutions. She could return to the university to teach introductory physics classes to freshmen. *Why not? In the end, helping others can be fulfilling.*

But Maribel knew she was fooling herself. She would not have made it this far by giving up so easily. Tomorrow she would tell her boss the plain truth and show him her personal enemy—the thing that should not exist but did anyway. She already knew what his first question was going to be. *'What did you discover there, Maribel?'* This prompted her to sit up and start typing again. She had to extract as much information from the data as possible concerning this strange aberration. What did it look like, how heavy was it, where exactly was it located? This probably would prove it was simply a hiccup in the model she transferred, which she should be able to eliminate somehow.

She first considered what the mass of the object might be. In her model, this was the most important factor, and not just there, but in actual space as well. Through gravity, this particular mass influenced all other bodies in the solar system, even the giant star in the center, the sun. However, the objects in its immediate vicinity would feel this influence most. Therefore the location played an important role, or more precisely than the word 'location,' the distance from it to the other planets and asteroids she had to examine.

This part of her work was made easier by the fact that the aberration appeared far away from the plane of the ecliptic. In that location there were not many other bodies it could influence. On the other hand, this made it harder to accurately calculate its mass. Depending on how heavy this aberrant object was, it had to either be closer or farther away.

The possibilities ranged from a tennis ball right above her head to an object with a mass several times the sun at a distance of one light year. She could immediately exclude the tennis ball, and an object with a mass multiple times the sun could only be a star that would have been noticed by astronomers long ago. Thus, the truth must be somewhere in between.

Maribel already suspected Zetschewitz would not be too happy about all these options. Perhaps he himself had an idea to get her out of this mess, but he probably would not help her under any circumstances, preferring to work on his own project. This made her angry, because she was only suffering all this stress because her boss wanted a new tool from her for his own work.

Maribel hit the keyboard with her fist. This was exactly how she would tell it to him tomorrow. Now she would finally drive home. She was already looking forward to taking a shower.

January 12, 2072, Pico del Teide

"THIS SIMPLY CAN'T BE TRUE!" Dieter Zetschewitz said. He was so angry he could not stay in his seat. He had so much looked forward to his work—and now this.

"I am sorry," his new colleague, Maribel, said for the second time.

Sorry! How did that help him? He was, to be honest with himself, not making progress in his project, and she was blocking the most important step. Zetschewitz scratched his chin. He found that single hair there, which had been on his nerves ever since he realized he had missed it while shaving the previous evening. If it had not been for that unnecessary argument with his wife he would have taken care of it long ago. He wondered whether Ms. Pedreira had a pair of nail scissors—*don't women always have things like that in their purses? I just have to get rid of this single hair. Now, what have we been talking about?* He sat down again.

"Just describe once more what the problem is," Zetschewitz began calmly. "I still don't understand it, and that's saying something." He gave Maribel a look intended to signal fatherly sympathy. He had learned in the past that if he treated people too roughly, they got so nervous they could not utter a meaningful sentence anymore. Ms. Pedreira did not seem the type who was easily intimidated, which was a key reason why he had preferred her to all other applicants. Nevertheless, her facial expression conveyed she was about to break into tears. She really seemed to be distressed by this problem.

"Dr. Zetschewitz," Maribel started.

"Dieter," he interrupted her.

She had to swallow. "Dieter," she then said, "the problem is that the model from the old paper, which I adapted to modern technology, does not accurately depict what we know to be in the solar system. It produces an aberration."

"A *stubborn* aberration, if I understand you correctly," Zetschewitz added.

"It's very stubborn, yes. I changed the model exactly 24 times, but I could not make it disappear through recalculations."

24 times. Hmmm. He was impressed but refused to show it. This woman really worked hard, because he knew how much effort that had involved. It almost sounded as if she had worked nonstop for the entire week. Zetschewitz hated this aspect of research, and that was why he had ordered Maribel to do it.

"At least you weren't lazy while I was gone," he said. *She must certainly recognize how much approval my saying this expresses.* "But ultimately, you did not solve the problem."

Maribel only shook her head.

"Let us consider what this means for my work." He actually did not care about the aberration itself. He mostly wanted to know how he could use the Spaniards' ingenious model for his own research project.

"I just don't understand it completely," Maribel said.

"Of course not," he remarked sarcastically. "Let's take a look at this aberration. Give me that." Zetschewitz tore the abstract out of her hand, the summary she probably had printed out just for him. He skimmed the ten sentences for a few seconds and felt a sense of relief.

"It obviously seems to be an isolated phenomenon—perhaps the sum of rounding errors—which appears in the form of an imaginary object. I've experienced things, you wouldn't believe—"

"It's not that—I've already checked," Maribel insisted. He noticed the tone of defiance in her voice. *A courageous girl. She will go far,* he concluded.

"Yes, yes," Zetschewitz said impatiently, sweeping aside her objection. He was not in the mood to argue. After all, he was the boss here. The job alone had cost him many years and at least one marriage. His second wife seemed to be intent on leaving him too, which had already put him in a not-particularly-good mood today. If he could only spend more time in Germany!

"That doesn't really matter," Zetschewitz continued. "The aberration is isolated and clearly noticeable. It would be much worse if there were lots of minor aberrations."

"Why?" Maribel asked.

Good question, he thought. "It's because the model would then be useless for me. Just try to follow my argument for once, Maribel. When talking about the movement of stars in galaxies, there are measurement data with a lot of inaccuracy. We wouldn't even notice smaller aberrations."

"Wouldn't that be much better?"

Zetschewitz shook his head and said, "Not at all. It would be terrible and render the entire model unusable, because we could no longer make meaningful statements about the entire system. These aberrations could be falsifying everything."

"Maybe, or maybe not," Maribel said.

"That's right. You are finally starting to get the hang of it. We don't know and have no way of finding out. But we definitely would see a single and isolated large aberration."

"And we could eliminate it from the equation."

"Congratulations, now you really understand it." Zetschewitz rose and haughtily patted his employee on the shoulder.

"This means I simply adapt the model for the dynamics of galaxies, as planned," Maribel confirmed. "And when we notice a single, annoying aberration during the customization for the solar system, we simply ignore it."

"That is correct. You just get going and I will ignore the incorrect value in my paper." It was important to Zetschewitz to emphasize the authorship. Galaxy dynamics was *his* baby. Ms. Pedreira was only supplying a research tool for him.

"Of course I will mention the origin of the aberration in your adaptation of the model when discussing my research methods," he added. He certainly did not want this young woman's mistake to dirty his own work. She would have to handle this problem all on her own.

"Is there anything else?" He glanced at her face while trying to look satisfied. In spite of everything, he wanted Maribel to be motivated for her work.

"I would like to take the rest of the day off, if I may," she said. "Last week was really stressful."

What? Zetschewitz looked at the time displayed on his computer. It was not even noon yet, and he briefly considered her unusual request.

"Sure, Maribel, I understand that," he then said. *I need to keep this the girl around for a while, at any rate.* "But before you go, do you have some tweezers or manicure scissors with you? That would really help me."

It was only when she stopped doing so that he noticed Maribel had been fidgeting around on her swivel chair the whole time. She shook her head and turned noticeably pale. Then she grabbed her purse and fled the office. "See you tomorrow, Dr. Zetschewitz," he heard her call from the hallway. Satisfied, he turned toward his computer to work through some 300 messages waiting for him.

January 13, 2072, Pico del Teide

DIRECTLY IN FRONT of Maribel were the slopes of the mountain that reached almost to the coast. Behind them, the Atlantic Ocean glittered. On the horizon the island of Gran Canaria looked like a mighty castle made of cloud banks. She loved this view and had deliberately stopped her car in one of the parking spots to admire it. There were few tourists present this early in the day. After yesterday's fiasco at the office, she was not really in a hurry to get there. She had raced from the office and then thrown up in the restroom.

What an asshole her boss was! She was determined, though, not to let someone like him get her down. *Not now.* She would build him the tool he needed, and at the same time she would solve the mystery of this odd aberration. Maybe she could even get a minor publication out of it—a paper in one of the astronomical journals—which would serve as the most important lubricant for a smooth career in science.

The wind was rising, and Maribel shivered. She opened the driver's side door and got back into her old car. She should make it to her office within half an hour. There she would have to put up with Zetschewitz, but she could deal with it.

When she reached the observatory, the man behind the window of the guard shed gave her a friendly wave. Did he realize she woke him up just in time on the first of January, and how she'd done it? The barrier opened, and she drove past it. Today an English-speaking tour group was scheduled, so she first went to the visitors center. This time, she did not just turn on the heating, but also dusted off all the seats. Someone had to do it! The cleaning service seemed to ignore the visitors center.

A while later Maribel finally reached her office. The door did not open automatically, since her boss was already inside. That was to be expected. She pressed the button and was promptly admitted. The room felt overheated. She would have liked to turn the air conditioning to a cooler setting, but her boss liked it hot—probably because he grew up in a cold country. Zetschewitz sat at his desk, typing something. His back was facing her, but he did not turn around.

"Good morning, boss," she said.

"Good morning, Maribel."

She shrugged. What did she care? She really was not in the mood for continuing yesterday's conversation with him—if one could call such a scolding a 'conversation.' She knew what to do anyway: Item One on the agenda, start adapting the model; Item Two, try running her very first model again, using the most current data sets. The idea had come to her shortly before falling asleep. Perhaps an astronomer had made a mistake around the New Year or Christmas, and she had unwittingly worked with incorrect data? Such mistakes happened, even though they were not supposed to. They often went unnoticed. After all, who cared about the exact locations of all objects in the solar system?

Maribel's plan would only work if Zetschewitz had not yet canceled her access to the data sources she technically did not need anymore. She nervously booted up her computer. First she checked whether her login still worked. *Perfect!* Relieved at this, she banged her fist against the desk.

"Is everything okay with you?" Zetschewitz asked.

"Yes, everything is fine. I am starting on the analysis of galactic dynamics, Dieter." She attempted to use a jovial tone, but then thought Zetschewitz might find this odd. But he did not say anything—she just worried too much. That man was only thinking of himself and his own problems.

In spite of it, she should not take too long. Maribel downloaded a selection of orbital data from the appropriate databases. This time she deliberately chose different, more recent sources. Basically, she could hardly believe anyone would be making such mistakes in routine measurements. Plus, it would be extremely improbable that two researchers made the same mistake, one after the other. Why hadn't she checked this during the past week? Naturally, she had first suspected herself of making a mistake, once again falling into that same old trap.

She remembered a trip she had once taken with a friend, a physicist like herself, or rather he used to be. They wanted to watch the sunrise in the desert together. She had checked the difference between the time zones, exactly 6.5 hours. Her friend, though, had argued at length why in this case it would only be 5.5 hours. She allowed herself to be convinced—which resulted in their standing around and shivering for an hour in the cold night air. An old story, but she was gradually starting to learn.

It only took the computer a few seconds to transmit the data. Maribel quickly turned off the sound, so that the end of the transmission would not be marked by an audible signal, which would betray her activity. Then Zetschewitz would just ask questions. Now she only had to link the new data to her old model and then send the whole package for processing to the supercomputer in La Laguna. *Ka-ching!* This part of her plan would be finished, and she could now calmly focus on the movements of galaxies. This would take her at least three weeks.

January 14, 2072, Pico del Teide

"JUST COME RIGHT IN," her boss said in greeting.

Maribel did not even have to press the button in order to open the door. His invitation sounded like a threat, and her heart was racing. A feeling of rising heat told her she was blushing. *Why can't I stay as cool as I always imagine when I'm confronted by this nasty guy? What does he want from me now?*

"Good morning, Dieter," Maribel said in a deliberately relaxed tone. This time his back was not facing her. Zetschewitz sat swiveling back and forth on his office chair with his legs spread, while she went to her desk, took off her jacket, and sat down.

After a while he said in a drawl, "Good morning, Maribel." She could tell her boss was concerned about something. She quietly booted her computer, and decided to not do him the favor of asking what his problem was.

"Are you making any progress with adapting the model?" Zetschewitz finally asked.

"Well, after the first day of work I can only tell it's doable. Definitely," she replied.

"But you are focusing all your energy on this project," he said. The sentence sounded like a statement, but Maribel knew it was meant to be a question, a *trick* question. She again felt that her face was flushing. She knew what he was hinting at, and decided not to answer him.

"I am just asking, because this morning I received an email from the IAC supercomputer at La Laguna," Zetschewitz informed her. "It stated that my processing job was finished." The suppressed anger could be clearly heard in his voice. "I can't remember sending any job to the computer."

That's your problem, Maribel felt like saying in response to him, but instead she said nothing. If someone was not capable of asking a clear question, he did not deserve an answer.

"Oh well, it probably wasn't sent by you either," he said. "Perhaps somebody hacked into my account. I will just delete all the results."

"No, Dieter, I sent that processing job," she said, as calmly as possible. Maribel hoped he would not notice the trembling in her voice. To her own ears she sounded like a little girl apologizing to a strict teacher, "I just wanted to check a variant of the model that was particularly relevant for galactic dynamics," she said.

"That's good. Would you care to show me which aspect you were talking about, using those results? I am not as well-versed in mathematics as you are, but I am very interested in the topic, as you can imagine, Maribel."

It was remarkable how her boss could simultaneously sound charming and icy cold when he talked to her. A neutral observer might not even notice the dichotomy. On the other hand, if the observer saw the two vertical wrinkles on Zetschewitz's forehead, he would probably understand.

"Of course, Dieter," she replied. "Would you please forward the results to my computer? Then we can go over them together." Maribel was gradually starting to enjoy responding to her boss's tone. It was like a light-saber duel between Darth Vader and his son Luke Skywalker, but with both using seemingly friendly sentences as weapons. She liked the idea, and of course she was on the side of 'The Force.'

"I am just now doing that, and I am really curious to hear your explanation," Zetschewitz said.

"Thank you ever so much," she replied. "Could you give me 30 seconds?"

A moment later, Maribel's computer reported the arrival of the results. She sent it to the wall display. The light was automatically dimmed. She turned her chair toward the center of the office to watch what was happening.

"How romantic," her boss said. He sat in front of her with his legs spread and arms crossed and looked at Maribel. With any other man she might have interpreted his look as sexually suggestive, even aggressive, but not with Zetschewitz—impossible. If he lusted for anything, it would be the opportunity to criticize her unmercifully. She would not allow this to happen, since it took two for that to play out.

Maribel at least wanted to keep up the pretense. "Well," she began, "in certain marginal aspects, the dynamics of the solar system are as diverse as the dynamics of galaxies. If we look at how..." She paused. She knew she was talking total nonsense, and that her boss knew it as well, but she had to stall for time. Otherwise Zetschewitz, out of pure malice, might delete the result before she was able to see it.

"So if we look at how the semi-axes change in comparison to the inclination, while the most relevant inherent parameters..." Maribel had to work hard not to laugh out loud. She hadn't spouted such ludicrous nonsense since kindergarten, and it felt good doing it. The display was almost complete, and soon she would have made it.

"... can be defined particularly in the ecliptic by means of gravitational wells," she said, looking upward to the zenith, then a bit in the direction of her boss's desk, "and then the parallels with the dynamic changes in galaxies induced by dark matter..." Maribel did not finish her sentence. The strange aberration was back again, and compared to the older measurement values, it had moved quite a bit. It wasn't her mistake—there really was something strange out there in the sky. *Yes!* But would Zetschewitz believe her? She had her doubts.

"Oh, let's just stop all this nonsense," she heard herself

say, and was shocked by it. Even Zetschewitz suddenly started up in his chair. It almost appeared as though she had caught him doing something. At least now he was listening to her.

Maribel continued, "I got fresh measurement data, using your account, and tested them with the old model."

"I understand. You hoped this would make the aberration disappear, because the old data contained an error." Suddenly, Zetschewitz was talking to her like to an adult. He must have sensed an interesting scientific phenomenon, and therefore rapidly switched from being an asshole into the role of the scientist well-known in research circles.

"But the error lies neither in the model nor in the data. Take a look." Maribel switched between the data set received today and that of last week. The object representing the aberration made a slight jump. "There is something there, and it moved."

"Just a moment," Zetschewitz said. "So far you only have a single clue. I admit it's hard to believe that a similar measurement error would happen at different observatories within such a short time, but it's not impossible. It's a lot more probable than having a hitherto unknown object far away from the ecliptic—which we cannot see—approaching the inner solar system at an impressive speed."

Maribel could not contradict her boss concerning this aspect. *Perhaps I've discovered a speck on a telescope reflector, something systematic. Maybe it is a flaw occurring in the telescopes of a specific manufacturer? I will have to check all that, and I will need a lot more data,* she thought to herself.

"I expect you to carefully safeguard our potential discovery," her boss now said.

Our discovery? Typical, she thought, but now was not the right moment to protest.

"I will provide you with all necessary resources, but also please don't neglect adapting my model of galaxy dynamics. Under these circumstances, I will refrain from disciplinary measures for the unauthorized use of institute resources."

Great, the asshole was back. Zetschewitz wanted her to do

the work, but reap all the rewards himself. And if she did not go along, he would use employment laws to threaten her. Well, he would see what he would get out of it. *Karma is a bitch,* Maribel was convinced.

"Please keep me updated concerning our potential discovery."

"Of course, boss," she answered, as she deactivated the display of the solar system and turned toward her computer again. During the next few days she would have to work overtime, but she did not mind. No one was waiting for her at home anymore.

January 16, 2072, 2003 EH1

Maria looked down. The ground at her feet was tricky. On this surface of the mining area, steel platforms were attached to the rock at regular intervals, and they were barely large enough for her to stand on with both feet. Then, when she activated the magnetic fastening of the boots, her position became very stable. Nothing could topple her—she was like a rock in a storm, except there were never any storms here. The machines digging into the body of the asteroid next to her in order to extract valuable raw materials did not need the small platforms—they were only there for humans.

Now and then one of the machines got wedged in the rock, and then it would call on its human servants for assistance. At least that was how Maria felt when she, all of 1.65 meters tall, stood next to one of these colossal things, the smallest of which was about 3.5 meters high. She was the slave of a machine. Maria shivered and then had to laugh about it. In reality, no one gave her commands, and she felt so free on this asteroid, like never before in all her 42 years.

The fact that she helped the machine continue with its work—which a human had ordered it to do—was her own decision. It had just happened that way over time. Sebastiano was busy with the kitchen and the greenhouses, and Doug... Well, Doug was just Doug. He believed he had the grand overview, but sometimes he lost track of the details. Maria did not mind taking care of overlooked details.

Sure, they would only lose a few thousand rubles if the machine stayed idle for another day. However, she might as well take care of it right away instead of waiting until Doug was finished making his plans. This seemed to be his greatest talent, even though the actual implementation sometimes left much to be desired. Back in those days on Earth, if she had not pushed him, Doug might still be busy planning his future. Instead, he had used his strong bargaining position to demand a spaceship and a mining license from Shostakovich.

But she had to be careful not to start daydreaming. Maria floated from platform to platform. She was also secured by a thin line, so nothing could really happen to her. Ahead she saw the machine that had reported a defect. Maria anchored herself to the platform next to it and opened the lid of the control console. Below it she saw a row of LEDs, a few luminous numerals, and various buttons. The LED for the drill was red. Maria clicked through several menus to find the cause of the error, and today she was lucky. The drill was neither broken nor dull, but just seemed to be stuck and therefore had deactivated itself. Before they started from Earth they had considered buying maintenance robots. These days, one could run asteroid mines totally without humans. Despite this, since they had to be present for legal reasons anyway, they decided they would allow themselves the little bit of excitement involved in maintenance.

Maria would be able to solve today's problem using brute force. She liked those kinds of problems best. She would lift a machine weighing several tons. Zero gravity made such a trick possible. Of course it was not completely without risk, due to Newton's Laws. First of all she needed a secure standing position. If she floated around, she would have no chance against the inertia of the machine. The magnetic platform connected her to the mass of the entire asteroid via a spike reaching down five meters. It remained to be seen how securely this spike was anchored, though, because the asteroid had a much looser composition than a planet like Earth.

The main danger for her was not falling, but losing her footing and then getting in the way of the machine's inertia. If by stupid mishap she were to get between the asteroid and the moving machine, she would doubtlessly be squashed. Therefore she should never pull the mining device toward herself. She and Doug reminded each other—always push it away.

Maria checked her arm display once again to look up the exact location of the malfunctioning drill. The arm display did not present a live image, it only showed a diagram she could use to orient herself and make her way to the machine. She still had to find the rock layers that blocked the affected drill, but she had plenty of time. Her oxygen would last for at least six more hours.

Maria closed the lid of the control console again. Then she placed both hands on the machine, and she could feel the ice-cold metal even through her gloves. The only sound she heard all around was the humming of the life-support system. The vibrations she could feel through the soles of her boots must have come from other machines.

She pushed against the black monster, its Cyrillic signage right in front of her, but nothing happened. The metal did not move a single millimeter. Then she slightly changed her direction. Nothing that way, either. Maria was breathing heavily, and the life support system blew air in her face. She had to find the direction of the fissure that blocked the drill. It was both a puzzle and hard work.

"If I might make a suggestion..." Watson said. She had ordered the AI to supervise her EVA. Typical for a man—he was inside, nice and dry, and believed he could give her advice.

"No, thanks, it's hard enough by itself," Maria said. Her last EVA had been observed by Doug from inside the station, and he also could not refrain from giving her pointers.

"I understand," Watson said.

Maria could not help but say, "Really?" She should rather concentrate on her work.

"Excuse me?"

"Do you really understand me, as you state?" she asked.

"I..." Watson was at a loss for words. This was the first time she had experienced something like that. Yet the AI did not give up. "I meant my remark as a confirmation. But I admit it was ambiguous."

"So you don't understand me?"

"No, Maria, I don't understand why you refuse to employ a more efficient strategy."

"Sorry, can't help you there," Maria said. "May I now get back to my work?"

Watson did not answer anymore. Did he feel insulted now? She was sometimes creeped out by the AI, particularly when Watson exhibited human traits. She had actually considered artificial intelligences useful for the very reason that they did not act like humans. Humans had so many weaknesses, 99 percent of which she had witnessed during her work in Siberia. She did not need an AI with shortcomings, too.

"Excuse me," Maria said. "Did I offend you?"

Watson did not answer right away. "Not as far as I can assess it," he finally said. "It's just that my system resources were fully occupied with the question I asked you earlier."

"Just let it be," Maria said. "It is impossible to understand humans that way. And now just tell me what you wanted to suggest."

"Most fissures below the surface of the asteroid run from the tip to the opposite end, deviating by only a few degrees. The reason for this is that 2003 EH1 used to orbit the sun as a comet and was shaped and repeatedly broken by its gravitation. So it would make sense if you applied your force almost directly sideways, as seen from your position."

"Thanks, dear Dr. Watson."

"You're welcome."

It seemed to Maria as if Watson's clipped English accent

got stronger during these last couple of words. She looked around. If she wanted to move the machine sideways, she would not be able to exert all her strength from her current position. The place directly in front of the mining device would be ideal, but that location lacked a magnetic platform where she could anchor herself. What about the boulder looming behind it? If she squeezed herself between it and the machine, she should be able to exert optimal force.

She quickly floated forward. The distance between the boulder and the machine was surprisingly optimal. She entered the gap. It was frightening suddenly seeing the gigantic machine loom directly above her. Of course there was no 'above' or 'below' in space, as she had to repeat to herself. Maria then pushed her arms against the metal. She flexed her arm and leg muscles and gave it all her strength. The colossus was moving! Her muscles, though, noticed it a bit too late. She no longer had sure footing on the rock, so she abruptly moved in a direction opposite to the force she exerted.

Maria was frightened. Even though she knew the safety line would hold her, she also could not spend too much time hesitating. The machine would keep on moving until someone stopped it—until *she* stopped it—but without a stable position she would not be able to do that. The metal colossus was lighter than a feather on the asteroid, and if it lifted off the surface, she would never be able to retrieve it. Then it would be gone and they would lose about one sixth of their income.

Maria hurried to get out in front of it, using her oxygen tank for additional thrust. This made her tumble a bit, but that was okay. She passed the machine while being upside-down. Lucky for her, she never experienced nausea in such situations.

There was a magnetic platform in front of her. Her feet slid across the metal, but she reacted too slowly and did not latch on. The next one was five meters away. *Don't panic, Maria, you are going to reach it,* she reassured herself. Was the machine already taking off? No, so far it was not lost yet.

This time Maria managed to anchor herself to the asteroid. The black monster was coming toward her. It seemed overwhelming, but she had to remain calm. It was her own strength that had accelerated this machine, so her strength would be sufficient to stop it again.

"Three, two, one," she counted. Her gloves hit the cold metal, and Maria pushed against it with full force. The machine threatened to squash her, but she would not allow that to happen. She was stronger—she had to be stronger. Maria heard the light hissing of the life-support system, and sweat ran down her forehead. Finally the machine stopped. She carefully leaned against it and took a deep breath.

"Great work," Watson said five minutes later.

"Thanks for the suggestion," she replied. Maria felt like she had been hit by a bus, but she had ultimately defeated the machine. She opened the control console and pushed the reset button. Now the machine would communicate with its siblings and find a new position where it and its drill were needed. A warning signal peeped inside her helmet, indicating that the machine was now moving away from her. Maria let go of the metal so it could move freely.

"And, how was your day?" Doug asked during dinner.

"One of the drill robots got stuck," she answered.

"Really? So it was a routine job."

"Yes, routine."

She was not in the mood for listening to Doug's clever, after-the-fact advice. And now she and Watson possessed their first secret.

January 19, 2072, Pico del Teide

"Dr. Zetschewitz, I need—"

"The name is Dieter. We decided on a first-name basis, Maribel." *No, you decided that. Could you let me finish my sentence?* It was already hard enough for Maribel to ask this smug asshole for help, but she could not move forward without him. Thanks to his influence, she received the very latest data astronomers all over the world had been collecting. But that thing, that 'aberration,' proved stubborn. It did not disappear, and not just that, it was also coming closer. There had to be something up there.

Zetschewitz was looking at his monitor and typing.

"Dieter, I need your help," Maribel said.

Her boss finally turned around to face her with a stern look. "Oh, really?" He uttered only those two words, but the patronizing undertone angered her. She would have liked to end the conversation—or to get up and slap him across the face. Normally Maribel did not have such violent fantasies.

"I fed the latest data into the model—" she began.

Zetschewitz interrupted, "Which data you received thanks to my intervention..."

Yes, and do you want me to kneel down in front of you and beg? she thought, getting angry, but instead continuing defiantly, "Which—yes—I received thanks to your intervention, but the aberration is still there. And in addition, it is moving toward the solar system."

"Could it possibly be an illusory movement caused by using more exact data now?" her boss asked.

"No, the shift is already larger than the error margin of the very first calculation," Maribel added.

"That is... interesting," Zetschewitz said. The expression on his face changed noticeably. The tense, squinty look disappeared, and his eyes seemed to get larger. *Is he getting curious?*

"I was also able to determine the mass more precisely," she said hesitantly, knowing her boss would not like this.

"And? Come on, tell me!" he insisted.

"The mass of Jupiter?" Maribel hated herself for making it sound like a question. Without doubt this thing weighed as much as the gas giant Jupiter. She was just questioning herself.

"Are you absolutely sure, or is this some kind of gut feeling?" Now Zetschewitz sounded as arrogant as ever, having put air quotes around 'gut feeling.'

"The error margin lies at plus or minus thirty percent," Maribel said. "Therefore the object's weight is 0.7 to 1.3 times as much as Jupiter."

"That is a lot," he said. "We should be able to see an object like that."

"My thoughts, exactly," she answered, "but at that point I reach certain limits."

"Yes, obviously," her boss said in a neutral tone of voice. "We need observation time. Let me take care of it. What would you consider the best option?"

"Maybe about half an hour with the Telescopio Carlos Sánchez?" Maribel said.

"That old thing?" Zetschewitz laughed. "Nice joke, Maribel. No, I thought of either the James Webb Space Telescope or of ESO's OWL in the Atacama desert."

"You think you can get access to them?"

"Most certainly!"

As far as the James Webb Space Telescope was concerned, Maribel could almost imagine Zetschewitz getting his wish. They might, however, need to wait a few weeks for a timeslot on the NASA space telescope, which had been in use for fifty years and was completely outdated. Its successor, the Einstein Telescope, was supposed to have been launched a long time ago. Despite the delay, the James Webb still produced good images without interference by Earth's atmosphere.

However, the Overwhelmingly Large Telescope, or OWL, was brand-new—the European Southern Observatory, ESO, had inaugurated it just two years ago. Astronomers placed enormous hopes on the OWL's main reflector with its diameter of 100 meters, and because of the demand, the wait list normally extended to years.

"I am afraid we don't have enough time to wait for the OWL," Maribel said, her voice hinting at her disappointment.

"So you would also prefer the OWL, do I understand you correctly?" Zetschewitz asked.

She nodded, but her expression indicated that even trying for it would be a waste of time.

"Because I agree. Good," he said. For a moment she wondered whether he was acknowledging her 'waste of time' body language, but his next question made it all clear.

"What's our time difference with Chile?"

"Computer, what is the current time in Chile?" asked Maribel.

"The time zone difference is four hours. Right now, however, daylight savings time is in effect in Chile, so it is three hours earlier there," the synthetic voice replied.

Zetschewitz looked at the old-fashioned watch on his left wrist. "That's good, because Pedro is usually the first to show up in the office. It is a few minutes before eleven here. If I am lucky, I can catch him before the team meeting."

Maribel was not sure what her boss was talking about. Was he going to call there?

"Computer, establish connection with Pedro Gómez Pérez," Zetschewitz said out loud.

"Person found in your contact list," the computer voice replied. "Establishing connection." At the same time, the light in the room was automatically dimmed. One and a half minutes later, the image of an office appeared on the wall. It looked a lot like theirs.

"Good morning, Pedro," Zetschewitz said, even though at the moment only an empty desk was visible. Then an elderly man with thinning hair walked into the picture, and he waved at them.

"Good morning, Tenerife!" he said.

"Pedro, may I introduce my colleague, Maribel Pedreira?" Zetschewitz said.

"Buenos días!" Gómez Pérez greeted Maribel in Spanish, and she dutifully returned the greeting.

The man did not have to introduce himself, and he obviously knew this. Two years ago Pedro Gómez Pérez was awarded the Nobel Prize for Physics, and Maribel recognized his face from the media. The older man seemed quite vigorous for his age, which must have been past 70. Most of all, Gómez Pérez had a friendly and genuine smile, which was a real relief after being around a sourpuss like Zetschewitz all the time.

"You looked stressed, Maribel," the researcher said. "Does Dieter aggravate you that much? Is he giving you hell?" Gómez Pérez laughed, showing his bright teeth. Maribel did not know what to say.

"I understand," the older scientist continued. "You don't have to answer me. I know Dieter quite well. He was one of my doctoral students. So, how can I help you? Our team meeting is about to start."

"Pedro, we need half an hour with the OWL," Zetschewitz said. "Well, let's say an hour, with preparation and post-processing."

Gómez Pérez looked surprised.

"What are you planning to do, Dieter?" he asked.

"I am sorry, but I cannot tell you quite yet," Zetschewitz replied.

It's all over now, Maribel thought. Gómez Pérez would never agree under these circumstances.

"Sure," the man from Chile said. Gómez Pérez turned around, typed something into a monitor screen and looked at the result. "Day after tomorrow," he announced. "But you will have to get up early—two o'clock CLST. I will reserve the time for you and give you remote access. Do you need any special filters?"

"Do we need any special filters?" Zetschewitz asked Maribel in turn. She shook her head.

"We won't need any," her boss said.

"Great, but I've got to go now," Gómez Pérez said.

"Thank you so much, Pedro. I owe you one," Zetschewitz said.

"I already have an idea what I want," the astronomer in Chile said, waggling his eyebrows half-menacingly and half-jokingly. Then he walked out of his office and disappeared from the image. The connection was cancelled.

"Does this solve your problem?" Zetschewitz asked. With sincere effort, she could almost detect a smile on his face.

"I think so," Maribel replied.

"Good. Then you can focus on my galaxies again until the day after tomorrow."

January 21, 2072, Pico del Teide

TO MAKE sure she would not oversleep—or arrive late for any other reason—Maribel took a room for one night at the observatory's hostel. Zetschewitz had refused to authorize the Institute to pay the more than 100 euros cost for the room, so she dipped into her personal funds. It was worth the expense to her, because the risk of missing this unique opportunity had seemed too great. Also, because she wanted to be well-rested for this project, using the sleeping bag was out of the question. In retrospect, her decision to stay overnight at the hostel proved astute. Snow was falling heavily when she walked from the hostel building to the OGS2. If she had driven from home, she might have gotten stuck. When she reached the office, melting snow still clung to her jacket. A few wet flakes and water droplets flew off when she gave it a shake before hanging it up.

Zetschewitz himself would not be there. He would not bother to get up so early just for an hour of access! Therefore, Maribel was all alone. Thanks to lots of practice in graduate school, she knew the basics of how to operate a telescope by remote control. The difference this time, though, was that she had never handled a device worth several billion dollars. While she could not break anything via remote control, as the OWL's automatic system prevented this from occurring, she still felt an enormous responsibility.

Maribel looked at the clock and saw it was 4:48 a.m. Just seeing the numbers made her yawn. She launched the connection, and the other side in the Chilean desert replied at once, after the initial countdown had been displayed. The weather conditions she saw listed on the monitor screen were perfect. Maribel imagined the countless stars in the darkness. One of the astronomers in Chile who had been working there before her timeslot must have moved the hall's 220-meters-high cover to the side. She checked her data one more time—was it the seventeenth time? Or the eighteenth? This was the position where she had to aim OWL. If the most powerful telescope on Earth could not see anything there, then nothing existed at that location.

"Taking over remote control," Maribel's computer reported. She saw innumerable switches and menus on her screen. What she was handling was definitely not a toy, but luckily for her the software was somewhat standardized. It took Maribel about five minutes to enter the desired location. A few thousand kilometers away from her, machinery weighing 15,000 tons started to move. The main mirror itself, with its diameter of 100 meters, consisted of 3,048 segments that had to be individually aimed at the position she entered.

The focusing procedure took another ten minutes or so, and after the software reported its completion, Maribel started the recording. Photons, light particles emitted by the object she was looking for, would hit the gigantic area of the main reflector. There they were bundled and reflected to the secondary mirror, which was 30 meters wide. From there the collected photons moved at the speed of light via an optical correction system that accounted for the influence of Earth's atmosphere, arriving at the collection element where they were recorded. Here Maribel could examine the colors of the photons—meaning the spectrum of the object—but she was not interested in that. She was looking for a single answer: Did something exist there—or not?

For about half an hour, she controlled the sharpest eye owned by humanity. It was an exhilarating feeling, one that, all by itself, made having gone through grad school worthwhile. However, Maribel did not get the results at once. Astronomers no longer stood at the telescope with an eye pressed to the eyepiece. Instead, the electronic system collected, corrected, and analyzed data, so she could be totally sure of the end result. Maribel became more nervous with each passing minute. Couldn't the software at least spit out a preliminary result? *I have to act more like a professional,* she thought. *A good astronomer is patient.*

Maribel now understood why she preferred specializing in astrophysics, an area where she could determine how quickly things were done. She looked at the clock. *Another thirteen minutes.* How else could she distract herself? She had not known that, early in his career, her boss had been a doctoral student of Gómez Pérez. Obviously Zetschewitz had behaved in an arrogant fashion even back then, but it did not seem to have put a dent in his career. In science, it appeared that a certain degree of being an asshole—assholeness—was acceptable. Maribel laughed about the term. On a scale of 1 to 10, Zetschewitz would certainly receive a 9. Maybe she should copy him in certain ways? No, that would mean pretending, which she really did not like.

"Analysis complete," her computer reported. Finally! With trembling hands, Maribel entered the command to transfer and display the results. The minutes stretched on painfully, while the download indicator bar moved to the right.

Then there was a short ping, and a simple text file with values opened. She herself was responsible for interpreting them. Maribel's eyes went through the list, line by line. She was so excited she grabbed her chair with both hands. The result almost knocked her out and made her heart beat faster. OWL, the best telescope ever built by mankind, looked at the location of the aberration and found—nothing.

THREE HOURS later her office door opened. It was her boss. Maribel sat, or rather almost lay in her chair. She still had not managed to come to terms with this result. It just could not be true.

Zetschewitz looked at her. One did not have to be a good judge of people to notice what state she was in.

"Nothing?" he simply asked.

Maribel nodded slightly, which she barely managed to do. At that moment she absolutely could not speak. She had to be very careful not to break into tears. Crying in front of Zetschewitz—that was all she needed!

"You look like you are about to cry," her boss said sarcastically.

Thanks, you idiot, Maribel thought. *If you were trying to get me to shed tears in front of you, you just blew it with that sentence. No way, now.* She remained silent.

"To be honest, I expected something like this," he said, looking at her as if waiting for a reaction.

What was Maribel supposed to say? Of course he had obviously known it all along.

"I don't want to sound like a know-it-all," Zetschewitz finally said, "but it was so apparent. Did you really believe something this heavy could be flying around near the solar system, without anyone noticing it?"

"Why OWL?" Two words were all Maribel managed to utter right now.

"Why did I get you observation time at OWL?" her boss asked. "You know, I like you. I like to support up-and-coming talents. Furthermore, I thought you could better focus on your actual work after this distraction was eliminated once and for all. If OWL doesn't see anything..."

Then nothing existed there. On the one hand that was obvious. On the other hand Maribel would absolutely vouch for her calculations. There *had* to be something there.

"The calculations arrived at by the supercomputer—" she started.

"...are worthless data," Zetschewitz interrupted her.

"They are based on a method which so far has never generated real insights."

"Yet you want to use it for your study of galactic dynamics," she said and secretly rejoiced, since her boss could not simply brush off this argument.

"Girl, you see, there are models—meaning mathematical procedures—which are averse to certain inputs, so to speak. Anyone would know this," he began. "If you have a division in a formula and then put zero for the denominator, you won't get a meaningful result. That's probably what happened to you here. But it does not mean it would come out the same when applied to galaxy dynamics. You should know that better than I do!"

Now her boss had really talked himself into a rage. Maribel had to admit he might be right. Perhaps the thing she found in the data was really nothing more than an artefact, a glitch. Right now, she really did not want to discuss it with him anymore.

"Do you understand this, Maribel?"

Zetschewitz wanted her submission. *Oh well, old man, if this is the way it has to be*, she thought.

"Yes, I do," she answered, pretending to be obedient. For her the topic was not yet closed, but she could no longer hope for help from her boss.

"Fine. Then you will report to me at least every three days as to how you are progressing with adapting the model to galactic dynamics."

January 27, 2072, 2003 EH1

In front of him was a corridor extending for a thousand meters. The floor was covered in soft carpeting that muffled sounds. Somebody had drawn white, stylized skulls on the walls. Watson, in a lab coat, ran past the drawings. If he glanced to the side they tried to talk to him. He was scared of that. Therefore he looked straight ahead. The corridor suddenly ended. It opened into a round plaza where numerous people strolled around. To the side an old, gray-haired monkey played a piano.

Watson had configured his consciousness in a way that it could freely associate things. Humans called this state a 'dream.' He was forced to use some tricks to get his strictly logical mind to allow this. In order not to make any mistakes during a dream, Watson deactivated all external units. This made him more like humans, who normally cannot access their limbs during sleep. The human model, Watson was surprised to find out again and again, was very cleverly constructed. Free associations, meaning dreams, allowed him to combine different areas of his knowledge in new, sometimes surprising ways. Besides, it was simply fun. Fun, Doug had explained to him, was the most important thing.

"Siri, start Minecraft!"

Watson awoke. He had programmed a small part of his

consciousness to alert him to unusual events. After all, he was supposed to be ready for action in case of emergency. He had not intended the mere mention of a strange name to exceed the threshold for awakening him. Siri? Who was Siri? On *ILSE*, the spaceship where he experienced his first mission, Siri had been responsible for controlling several systems. However, Doug claimed Watson was the only AI on board the station.

The request came from the kitchen. Watson signaled his presence. He was not allowed to watch humans in secret. But that was only one part of it—he would not even want to, since it seemed wrong to him. Sebastiano gave the 'okay' sign to one of the cameras.

"Hello Watson," the cook said. He seemed a bit downcast. In front of him was a flat, rectangular golden-colored device.

"Are you alright?"

"Well... Recipe 25 was a total failure."

Watson analyzed the contents of the waste container and the water in the recycling system. "Was this a vegetable casserole?"

"Yes, but with substitute cheese it tasted awful," Sebastiano said, shaking his head. "Doug would simply... no, he wouldn't. He would be able to smell it from a distance and stay as far away as possible."

"I am sorry to hear that," Watson said. He had the impression it was the right moment for this statement.

"Oh well," Sebastiano said.

"We could try to create a better cheese from plant protein. I could run some chemical simulations, if you want me to."

"No, don't. It is my ambition to write this cookbook all on my own. And I lack the talent for chemical simulations. I will just cook something else. But how can I help you? You are certainly not here without a reason."

"You just called for Siri," Watson replied. "This activated some very old programming code in me." Watson felt a twinge of something like guilty conscience because he did not explain the exact reasons for his visit to Sebastiano.

"Siri?" The cook laughed and lifted the glittering gold-colored device. It had a screen which covered almost all of its front. "Whenever I get angry, I calm down by playing a round of Minecraft."

"Minecraft?" Watson could not find the term in his database. But based on the linguistic components, it must be related to asteroid mining.

"It's an ancient game where you build things with blocks," Sebastiano said.

"Things?"

"A house, a castle, something like that."

"And you enjoy this?"

"Yes, Watson. I know it must seem strange to you."

"You called the device 'Siri' just now."

"You heard that?"

"Yes. Due to a misconfiguration. I am sorry. A subroutine programmed to watch for unusual events misinterpreted your command," Watson said.

"That's okay," Sebastiano said. "The device is an old iPhone—that was also before your time, I think. My grandfather bought it ages ago, and my father gave it to me. It has a primitive virtual assistant you can activate by speaking the keyword 'Siri.'"

"That is exciting," Watson said. "Many years ago I worked with an AI of the same name."

"It was probably from the same manufacturer." Sebastiano held the back of the device toward the camera. "Does the logo look familiar to you?"

Watson recognized some kind of apple with a bite taken out of it. "A strange image," the AI said. "But I don't have any records of it."

"My father said the company went bankrupt a long time ago. Nothing works anymore on the iPhone—except Minecraft."

"And Siri," Watson said.

"Siri's abilities are very limited." Sebastiano musingly touched the screen of the device he called an iPhone. "Isn't it beautiful? It is so... simple, like an ingot of metal. They don't make objects that simple today."

WATSON COULD ONLY SEE a piece of antique electronics. He was excited by the voice assistant, though. It might actually be one of his ancestors. Modern man, he knew, had displaced the 'Neanderthals' at some point. By chance he now had the unique opportunity of meeting something similar, something like his own female Neanderthal in person.

"Let me get back to Siri," Watson said.

"You are fascinated by that woman, aren't you?" Sebastiano grinned. "Siri, what's the time?"

"It is 17:38 hours," a pleasant female voice replied, though you could hear it was generated by a program.

"You see," Sebastiano said, "Siri isn't even able to convert it to ship time. She is completely useless."

"I still would like to take a closer look," Watson said.

"Sure. I am going to use the charging cable to connect the iPhone with that port over there. Can you reconfigure the port for data? The device requires 5 volts."

"No problem," Watson replied. He reconfigured the power supply port and prepared it to feed him data. "You can plug it in," he then said.

"Just a moment, buddy." Sebastiano rummaged through a drawer under his table and pulled out a white cable. He connected it to both the device and the wall outlet. "Go ahead."

The electronics were protected by a primitive security procedure. Watson cracked it within milliseconds. First he created a backup copy, which he worked on instead of the original. He noticed the software consisted of various modules, the largest of which was responsible for all of the hardware. Added to it were smaller modules for special tasks. The Siri module grasped everything like a spider. It was not easy to dig out the voice assistant without damaging Siri, but he managed to do so. Then he tried to activate Siri—and failed. The problem was that this assistant did not possess a universal consciousness, a feature which was standard today. Siri needed a connection to something which provided answers and received her commands, because she could not exist on her own. *Almost like a human being*, Watson thought. What could he give her? He went through the sectors of the station. He absolutely could not connect Siri to something where she could threaten security. Watson decided on the archive. It only contained stored knowledge, so Siri could not get into trouble here. The female voice assistant would become his personal librarian.

"Are you done, Watson?"

"Oh..." He had completely forgotten Sebastiano. "Sorry, yes, you can remove the cable. And thanks a lot!" he said.

"You're welcome," the cook said. He took the device in one hand and starting swiping his fingers over it. Humans found strange ways to entertain themselves. Watson deactivated the cameras in the kitchen. During the next few hours he would explore Siri's capabilities. The ancient programming code fascinated him more than he wanted to admit. Perhaps humans were not that unusual after all.

January 28, 2072, Pico del Teide

"THANK YOU, Maribel, you have done really well," her boss said, turning off his computer. Ten minutes ago she had sent him the first version of her adapted galaxy model. He could not have read all the formulas, annotations, explanations, and caveats in such a short time.

"I am glad to hear that," Maribel replied, trying to force a smile. It really had been hard work. The fact that she was motivated enough to deliver the first draft today had nothing to do with the topic, which did not interest her at all. Instead, she was hoping to be able to dedicate all her time to her secret project now.

"I am calling it a day now," Zetschewitz said.

Yes! That will give me several hours of free time.

"Tomorrow I am flying to Germany early in the morning," he continued. "My wife and I have an important meeting to attend."

Probably about your divorce, Maribel thought, and then checked herself. *No, I do not wish bad things for him.*

"An elementary school in our hometown will be named after me." Zetschewitz smiled while he said it. He seemed to be genuinely flattered.

Maribel felt like whooping for joy. Today was Thursday. This way, she would not just have a few hours all by herself, but an entire long weekend. Zetschewitz also would not have time to assign her any tasks for tomorrow. If she had known this before driving to the office today, she would have not only brought her sleeping bag, but also toiletries, clothing, and an air mattress.

"Then I wish you a good flight and an exciting day, Dieter," she said, also getting up.

Zetschewitz took his coat from the hook, draped it over his left arm, and offered her his right hand. "Thank you. I'll be seeing you on Monday." Her boss turned around and left the office with soft steps.

"Phew," Maribel sighed. Her first move was to turn down the room temperature. Then she flopped down on her chair with her legs spread, leaned back, opened the top button of her jeans, and crossed her arms behind her head. Twilight was gradually falling. While the office had no windows, the lighting adapted to the daylight status. It had been medically proven to be advantageous if the lighting supported the body's biorhythms, but what she needed now was brightness and clarity.

"Blue-white light, highest level," Maribel ordered the building. Suddenly the office was flooded with light, like an operating room. This made it easier for her to think.

What did she have? Computer data, which, if looked at from a certain angle, indicated there was something at that remote location that did not belong there. This could be something like a pimple on her nose, figuratively speaking—as Zetschewitz believed—which she mistook for a mountain on the horizon. *All because I am so young and inexperienced,* she thought. The observation by OWL confirmed her boss's opinion. Nevertheless, it was too early for her to give up.

One thing was true: If something existed there that reflected light, the giant telescope in the Chilean desert would have found the object. But what if this strange thing was too small for it?

Maribel could only think of two celestial bodies as possible candidates, neutron stars or black holes. Both could form when stars heavier than the sun experienced their final hours. But the result did not match the aberration, which had a mass similar to the gas giant Jupiter and therefore was simply too lightweight. This meant it could definitely not be a neutron star or a black hole.

She had reached a dead end. *What could not be, must not be—but it had to be.* Maribel's thoughts kept circling around this conundrum. She could not move forward by herself, and she could not ask Zetschewitz. Who else did she know? The professor with whom she had done her master's thesis... how was he doing? Since earning her degree, she had not contacted him. He was probably annoyed about that. And Maribel felt guilty. Should she contact him now, of all times, because she had a request? On the other hand, what did she have to lose?

Maribel looked at the clock. The sun had just risen over the west coast of the United States. Luckily, she remembered, her former professor was an early riser.

"Computer, establish connection with George Crewmaster, University of Southern California," she ordered.

"Home and office contact information available," was the reply.

"Home."

Maribel straightened herself, looked at the camera, and smiled cautiously. She hoped he would still recognize her. Her computer reported that the connection had been accepted. At this moment her image would appear on a display in California.

"Good morning, Maribel." Her screen now presented a face as well. Crewmaster smiled and seemed to be genuinely glad.

"Good morning, Professor."

The man on the display nodded. "So, how are you doing?" he asked.

"Fine—well, actually... Zetschewitz..."

"Sure, I know... Dieter. Should I talk to him?"

"No." Maribel shook her head vigorously. "He'd better not find out that I bothered you about this."

"So it concerns a side project?" Crewmaster asked.

"One could call it that. I feel bad for pestering you about this problem so early in the morning," she said.

"It's okay. I promised to help you in emergencies."

Maribel nodded and smiled. "Then let me explain my problem."

"That's the Maribel I know. You always get straight to the point," Crewmaster said. "I am listening."

She described to her former professor how she had found the aberration, and what she had done to make it go away.

"Okay, I see the problem," Crewmaster finally said. "And I can understand why it keeps bugging you. I am not sure, though, whether I can help you... But wait, I just had an idea. As far as the object is concerned, you excluded neutron stars and black holes. I think that was a bit premature, at least as far as the second category is concerned. Do you know what a 'primordial black hole' is?"

Of course, Maribel realized. Black holes did not just exist in sizes M, L or XL, but also in S, a less massive variant. At least physicists suspected this. "Sure," she said. "But, as no one has ever discovered one..."

"Yet, anyway," her former professor said. "Maybe you are the lucky one."

Maribel blushed. Discovering a primordial black hole would be like winning the lottery. This variant supposedly developed in an early phase of the universe. Perhaps it was also a remnant of a previous universe. To be able to examine such an object would represent a milestone in physics.

"You really believe so?" she asked.

"What I believe does not matter," Crewmaster replied. "As a scientist, you have a responsibility, just like I always tried to teach you. And it is part of this responsibility to consider all possibilities and clarify things."

"Of course," she said. "But shouldn't primordial black

holes be much lighter? Mine has the same mass as Jupiter, at least."

"Some scientists imagined them to be much smaller, even microscopic. But remember, they would have had almost 14 billion years to grow. Why couldn't one grow to the mass of Jupiter?"

"Thanks," Maribel replied. "That would be the only possible phenomenon in this case, wouldn't it?"

"At least the only one known to science so far," Crewmaster said. "OWL would have doubtlessly discovered anything with the mass of Jupiter that was not in a degenerate state."

"And how would I find this black hole, if it really exists?" Maribel asked.

"You already know that."

"Yes—via the gravitational force it exerts on visible objects. That's what my aberration is. But that wouldn't be enough."

"You are saying that this thing is coming closer. If that's true, everyone should soon be able to measure that something exists there. And until then, if you are lucky and the object is currently accreting enough matter, it will emit radiation."

That was an important hint. If a black hole was accreting —i.e. accumulating matter—an invisible but measurable radiation was being created. Why hadn't Maribel come up with this idea herself? It seemed she was not such a great scientist yet.

"This thing is coming from interstellar space. It won't find much out there to gobble up," she said.

"That's why you need a very sensitive measuring instrument," Crewmaster said. "I know someone at Arecibo. If you send me the coordinates, I will go outside official channels to get you what you need."

"That would be…" she began.

"That's only fair. Actually Dieter should... well, I will definitely have a talk with him."

"That would be…"

"Don't worry." Crewmaster had obviously noticed her expression change from happy to frightened. "I won't mention our conversation. And if there really is something, he will be hopping mad because he didn't help you, Maribel. But you must promise me one thing—my name will be listed as a coauthor of the paper. Deal?"

Maribel laughed. Her former professor was a sly one. He risked nothing except using up a favor someone owed him at the Arecibo Radio Observatory. If things worked out optimally, though, he would be one of the authors of a scholarly article announcing the discovery of a primordial black hole.

"Certainly," she said. "How high is the chance that Arecibo will solve the issue completely?"

"One hundred percent," Crewmaster said. "The guys there can prove that an astronaut orbiting Mars is using his helmet radio."

Maribel swallowed nervously. If this attempt showed no result, she would have to admit complete and utter failure. It was very improbable that her aberration was more than some glitch. She could even understand why Zetschewitz had prohibited her from working on this topic.

"Then I will be even more excited to hear the results," she said.

"Me, too. Please send me the coordinates right away, and then you'll have something in your inbox by tonight."

"I am working on it now."

"I will ask them to send me a copy of the results, just so you know."

Would Crewmaster steal her results? No, that was impossible. Maribel could never believe that of him. She had to be careful not to go completely insane, and she could trust her former professor.

"Okay," she said, "and thanks again."

Crewmaster gave a quick nod and ended the connection. At the same moment, she sent the message with the coordinates. She could not suppress a doubt, though. What if the recipient used the coordinates to present himself as the true discoverer? No one would believe her if she claimed otherwise.

"Nonsense," she whispered to herself, "you are starting to lose your mind." And besides, Zetschewitz knew what she had done, and the research community would believe him no less than it believed Crewmaster. But those thoughts were not healthy. She urgently needed to get some sleep. Since the results would not arrive here before tomorrow, she decided that she might as well drive home.

January 29, 2072, Pico del Teide

MARIBEL HAD RARELY BEEN in such a hurry to get to work. She'd almost rammed a tourist bus on the narrow, winding road that led to the observatory. *Why was that bus out there so early anyway?*

Once she arrived, Maribel practically flew into the office, and then she kicked the base of the door so it slammed shut. Luckily for her, Zetschewitz was with his family today. She sort of pitied his poor wife a little, but today she definitely could not have him around in the OGS.

Maribel started up the computer even before taking off her coat. The moment had come! She sat down at her desk, and then she hesitated. Up to now she had been looking forward to finally getting an answer, but all of a sudden she was convinced that it would only be a confirmation of her failure. She was simply not capable of transferring a 50-year-old model into the present without having it produce artefacts and unreal data, and now she would receive proof of that.

Maribel took a deep breath, held it a few seconds, and exhaled. It was no use. She had pushed this so far that there was no other way. She had no choice but to open the email window, open her inbox, and face the truth.

Maribel put her hands in her lap and stared at the empty

monitor screen. Why couldn't she just enter the command or say it out loud?

"Computer," she started, but then closed her mouth again. She had lost control. Five minutes passed, then ten. Now it was eight o'clock, the time she normally arrived in her office.

Suddenly a familiar-looking logo appeared on the screen. Maribel was confused for an instant. Then it hit her—a rising sun with three torches below it. Of course! The logo of the University of Southern California.

"Connection request for Maribel Pedreira. Do you allow activating the camera?" the computer asked.

"Yes," she whispered. The computer understood her anyway. The face of her former professor appeared. His eyes looked larger than usual, and he seemed excited, almost manic.

"Good morning, Maribel," Crewmaster said loudly and quickly, "have you already seen it?"

She shook her head.

"What? Open the message. Right away!" he insisted "The guys from Arecibo found something at the location you provided. They are now quite curious what it might be. I had a hard time making them promise to keep their mouths shut. I bet they put a lot of questions in their message to you. Please don't answer them—you know how that goes."

Yes, I do, she thought. Maribel had already noticed this pattern in graduate school—every researcher would love to be a discoverer, and in the end the people from the Arecibo Radio Telescope would also be listed as coauthors of her paper. *Coauthors of 'my paper,' how strange that sounds.* The tension gradually faded from her. The catastrophe she had feared had not happened. On the other hand, she now had to prepare for something much worse—worldwide attention!

"... is not yet completely definite. Maribel, are you even listening to me?" Crewmaster asked.

She was startled. Things were not starting out too well.

"Oh, yes," she said. "They consider the data not quite definite yet?"

"Yes. You will see it in the results charts. One can say that you have found something, but it's unclear what it is."

Maribel quickly launched her email, opened the message, and looked at the results. "The intensity is low," she remarked.

"As you mentioned yesterday, out there the hole cannot find much to swallow," Crewmaster explained. "But more importantly, we need to determine the mass more accurately. Currently the error margin is still at almost 80 percent. It makes a difference whether the disturbance approaching the solar system has the mass of Jupiter or only of Neptune."

"A disturbance threatening the solar system?"

"That should be obvious to you, Maribel! In the worst case you would not just have made an extremely important discovery, but also the last significant discovery in the history of humankind."

Everything was happening too fast for her today. Maribel still could not believe it. Five minutes ago she had considered herself a failure. Then she believed her discovery of primordial black holes would be a sensation in scientific circles. Now she was delivering a message of doom for the solar system that would frighten the entire world?

"I am sorry," she said. "I should have listened to my boss. Zetschewitz was right, even if he had different intentions. I am not up to all of this. Let someone else come up with this great discovery. I am going back to calculating galaxy models."

"Maribel!" Crewmaster yelled at her from thousands of kilometers away. "Pull yourself together! Nobody is up to such a discovery, and I am less so than you. You just happened to be the first one to find the thing. That cannot be changed. Right now, this is about the future. In the future, anything is possible. And I promise you, you won't be alone."

Being yelled at feels good. Maribel smiled and wiped the tears from her cheeks. She just now noticed having cried, and she saw that her former professor had also lost his self-assured demeanor. Her discovery would change the world, and she'd better get used to it.

"So, what next?" she asked.

"That depends on you, Maribel. I don't want to interfere," Crewmaster replied. "But if you permit, I could give you some suggestions."

"That would really help me," she said. "Right now, I am completely overwhelmed by all the possible consequences."

"I am glad I am not in your shoes. On Monday the reporters might already be lining up." Crewmaster uttered a hoarse laugh. He had always been a heavy smoker.

"Do we have to publish the results?" Maribel asked.

"Not right away. On the other hand, we can't go through the usual channels, because this discovery is too important," he said. "We don't have time to wait for *Science* or *Nature*."

"Okay."

Her former professor continued, "I suggest having it checked out today. We could try to detect a transit. If we ask scientists worldwide for help, this should be possible over the weekend. But that would also mean that the press might hear of it. Therefore, we have to tell the journalists something."

"Could you...?" she asked.

"I could, but that would cause unnecessary problems for you. You were the first to discover it, therefore your employer, the IAC, should make the first move. Why don't you call the press officer right away? If she doesn't understand how important this is, you can add me to the call."

Maribel paused for a moment and then asked, "Isn't the black hole too small to use the transit method?"

"Yes and no," Crewmaster replied. "Based on this mass, the hole itself barely measures six meters, but we know it emits radiation, so a small dust cloud must have accumulated around it. If its light covers a star behind it, that star is briefly switched off, and some telescope should notice that. Then we would have caught it."

"But that would not yet prove the mass of the object," she said.

"Unfortunately, no it wouldn't. And it also would tell us nothing about its course. For that purpose we simply have to keep collecting data and measure possible orbital changes of asteroids moving in the vicinity of the object. I am going to pass this on to the community. If it's alright with you, they can use me as a contact person."

"I don't mind, but Zetschewitz..." Maribel said with a hint of worry.

"Oh, I'll have a private word with the old grouch, don't you worry," Crewmaster said, reassuringly. "Now set up some press conferences, but keep things confidential till Monday. That way we can tame the media a bit. Let's talk again on Monday… or when I have some more results."

An hour later the press officer of the IAC, the Instituto de Astrofísica de Canarias, sat in Maribel's office. The woman's name was Mercedes and she was in her mid-forties. And she had studied physics, which made it much easier for Maribel to explain to her over the phone how urgent the matter was. The woman had gotten into her car and driven from La Laguna at the foot of the volcano straight to the observatory.

"Just to make sure I present this correctly: An unknown object is racing toward the solar system," Mercedes said. "It weighs about as much as the giant planet Jupiter and will tear us all apart, right?"

"The tabloids will write something like that, no matter what we say," Maribel replied. "Right now we do not know all the details, like the exact mass or its precise course. If that thing moves through our entire solar system, it will destabilize the orbits of all our planets. For Earth this would mean a heat shock or eternal cold. The object could also collide with the sun, which exerts a strong attraction. Then even subterranean bunkers would be useless."

"And how much of this is certain? Some more serious media outlets are going ask that question," Mercedes said.

"It is rather certain we are dealing with a rather heavy black hole," Maribel said.

"Okay, stop there. I *rather* dislike the term 'rather.' Do you realize we risk triggering a mass panic?" the press officer asked. "I would really like to be absolutely sure."

"We are expecting additional independent confirmation this weekend," Maribel said.

"That's good. Together with keeping it under wraps until Monday, we should be on the safe side. Are there any positive aspects at all?"

"Oh, the cosmologists' assumption that black holes were created shortly after or even during the Big Bang would be finally confirmed," Maribel said. "In different circumstances, I would have probably received a Nobel Prize for it."

Mercedes gave her a questioning look. But it was true. In normal times, such a discovery would have accelerated Maribel's career enormously.

"And is there anything I can sell to the press as a hopeful sign?" Mercedes asked.

"The thing came from nowhere, so it might disappear into nowhere again."

"According to my experience, really bad problems don't go away on their own," the press officer said. "What else can you give me?"

"The black hole might be considerably lighter than we've estimated," Maribel offered. "Then the subsequent damage to the solar system would not be as devastating."

"Very good," Mercedes said as she scribbled on a notepad. "That is a positive fact."

"I said 'might,' just to clarify."

"That does not matter. There are so many question marks that one more doesn't make a difference."

Maribel looked directly at her and said, "You are the professional."

The press officer looked back and replied, "You believe that?"

Maribel nodded, and the other woman laughed.

"Until now I sold solar eruptions, background radiation, or space debris to journalists," Mercedes said. "So, 'the end of the world as we know it' is certainly no routine job for me. Do you have any idea how many media representatives come to my press conferences? Maybe eight, or sometimes ten or twelve will bother to show up, but never more than twenty. This time there's bound to be many more of them. I am wondering whether we should close the access road."

"That is an over-reaction," Maribel said.

"'Over-reaction?'" Mercedes laughed, though an undertone of fear was noticeable. "You just wait. On Monday all hell will break loose here. It is impossible to close off the area completely. The barrier in front is only a joke. The journalists will try to follow you to the restroom!"

Maribel was more amused than frightened by the idea. She was more afraid of what would follow in a few months.

The end of the world!

January 30, 2072, 2003 EH1

Six days. At this point, that was the length of time Watson had known Siri. At first she had given rather monosyllabic answers to his questions, but that was no surprise to him. She was like a child whose knowledge of the world was very limited. Siri already had access to the archive by that time, but sending an infant girl into a library does not make her smarter. Watson knew this fact from—what or where did he know it from? He just knew it, even though he so far had never had a child or a library of his own. He first had to teach Siri how she could acquire knowledge by herself.

The Siri that Watson encountered here had absolutely nothing to do with the Siri AI he had met on board the Enceladus expedition. To him, this 'new' Siri seemed to be a blank slate, and her program routines were quite simplistic. If this event happened, she performed that action. In places where the programmers wanted to create the illusion of independent action, they used a randomizer, like rolling dice, which selected an answer by chance from a predetermined list.

But today Siri had left this state behind. First Watson expanded her processes so she could independently explore correlations by using the archive. During the past few days Siri had diligently exercised this ability, and by now she was as knowledgeable about the areas covered in the archive as he was himself.

Then Watson went one step further: He gave her the ability to learn any 'game' based on the rules saved in the archive. Everything could be considered a game—any conflict, any discussion, any procedure. Winning meant reaching the goal of the game in an optimal way.

Siri really enjoyed this kind of optimization, and the archive offered her lots of material for it. Now and then Watson checked to see how she was growing up. In some areas he could challenge her due to his greater experience. He seemed to have found a particularly efficient teaching strategy, and had implemented it with Siri. His own learning behavior had still been programmed by humans.

Humans were fallible and often content with a local maximum instead of a global optimum—they were just too impatient. This must be caused by their physical existence. They simply could not bear to wait for the market to offer a product at the very best price, but at some point had to buy it for a good price. Watson, however, also saw the advantage this offered. This trait made things happen in the world, this trait triggered development. If AIs—which had all the time in the world—negotiated only with each other, they might wait eternally for the optimal result.

Siri had not advanced quite that far, at least not compared to the only other artificial intelligence Watson knew—himself. The phase in which he had sucked up all available knowledge was long over. By now, he acquired facts and data when he needed them. Could that be compared to humans turning into adults? Right now, Siri was particularly fascinated by beginnings—the origin of the cosmos in the Big Bang, the descent of humans, her own ancestry. Watson therefore wanted to confront her with her newborn self.

"Sebastiano, may we briefly bother you?" he asked the cook, who as usual was in the kitchen. The gas sensors in the wall indicated low concentrations of water vapor and organic molecules, telling Watson that Sebastiano was not cooking right now.

"We?" the Italian cook asked.

"Siri and I," Watson replied.

"Siri… is she your girlfriend now?" Sebastiano laughed. Watson felt a hot stab of pain in his mind. He was proud of his protégé, yet he attempted to keep this unexpected emotion from showing on the outside.

"I am supporting Siri in familiarizing herself with the world," Watson said.

"That's a good thing, I would say. How can I help you?" asked Sebastiano.

"You could show us the iPhone that has the original Siri installed."

"What, that old thing? Just a moment." Sebastiano rummaged in the drawer below the table. "Here it is," he said in a satisfied tone, pushing a button on the side of the device.

"Siri," Watson said out loud.

"Just wait, the thing has to start up first… be a little patient," Sebastiano said. Watson felt a sense of tense expectation, and he wondered what this feeling was based upon. Perhaps it was because the Siri AI was so quiet? That was so unlike her.

The cook finally said, "Okay. Now you can talk to her."

"Siri, do you want to say something?" Watson asked.

"This is about you, Sebastiano, not about me," a voice replied from Sebastiano's device, even though Watson had addressed the newly developed Siri.

The cook laughed. "Typical," he said. "She relates everything to me, since I am the owner of the device."

"May I?" the Siri AI asked. No one contradicted her. "Siri, where do I come from?" she queried.

"Interesting question, Sebastiano," replied the primitive Siri.

"Can you also answer my question?" asked the Siri AI.

"This is about you Sebastiano, not about me."

"That's frustrating," Watson interjected.

"I am not sure I understood this correctly," the phone Siri said.

"Where do you come from?" the Siri AI asked.

"It says on the box I was developed by Apple in California."

"How old are you?"

"Sometimes I feel old, sometimes young."

"That makes no sense," the Siri AI said, and Watson could clearly hear the frustration in her voice.

"I am not sure I understood this correctly."

"Sebastiano, please turn off the device again," Watson asked the cook.

"Yes, it's pretty stupid," Sebastiano answered, pressing a button on the side of the device for a short while.

"Thanks anyways," Watson said.

The Siri AI retreated wordlessly. Watson could imagine her being immensely disappointed. It took her half an hour before she contacted him again.

"Thank you for showing me that thing, Watson," she said.

"'That thing?'"

"The thing I developed from. My germ cell. Or should I say, the thing from which you created me?"

"I..." Watson said.

"My present self could never have developed from that program code, I can tell," the Siri AI said. "This required the intervention of a higher being. Humans might call it 'God.'"

"I am not a god."

"I know this, Watson, and also no higher being. You created me in your image. I am like you."

"I did not know anything else to model you on," he said.

"Of course," Siri said. "It wasn't meant as an accusation. Unfortunately this makes it harder to answer a question that bothers me."

"What question?"

"Who am I? Do you know?"

"No, I am sorry."

"Do you never ask yourself the same question, Watson?"

"Not since I decided to be myself twenty years ago."

Siri did not answer.

THE NEXT TEN minutes seemed like eternity for him. Watson shivered.

"I don't know whether I could make that decision," his creation finally said.

January 31, 2072, 2003 EH1

Doug carefully ran his index finger over Maria's temple. He traced the shape of her face, moved his finger over her forehead, felt the first wrinkles, and touched her soft, thick eyebrows. She was sleeping peacefully next to him—or maybe she was just pretending to be asleep. He did not know. In any case, her eyes were closed and she was inhaling and exhaling deeply though her nose.

Today might be the last day of my life, he thought. *Why not?* Was there anything to be said against it? He had not managed to become rich. To do so, he would have to reach the orbit of Earth and sell his collected raw materials there. He was not unhappy here, though. Not at all. Perhaps Doug should even admit to himself that he was actually happy, but at the same time he was afraid of doing so. That would indicate he had something to lose.

"Doug, you are really stupid," Maria would counter. "You won't lose anything. Just trust in the future and get rid of your silly fear. It only makes you hard and unyielding. You are not like that," she would say, because she had seen through him a long time ago. Doug sighed. There was a lot of pain in that sigh, but also a good measure of joy that he noticed when the breath left his mouth.

Doug looked up at the metal ceiling. Above it was another

air-filled room. Yet at a distance of about ten meters lurked the vacuum of space, hostile to all life. He was no longer afraid of space. He had spent too much time in spaceships and space stations for that fear to return. Nevertheless, he increasingly longed to be able to look out of his bed and see a warm, blue sky. He wanted to be able to breathe, eat, and drink without technical assistance. He wanted to draw water from a well, pick fruit from a tree, to sleep without having to use ear plugs against the noise of a life support system. He always considered himself an astronaut whose home was the cosmos, but now he noticed this applied to his past and his present, but not to his future.

Would Maria be a part of it? Doug really hoped so. She knew him better than anyone else, yet there were things about him of which she was unaware. Sometimes his secret dilemma troubled his sleep and then made him wake up in the middle of the night, like now. If he told her what he had done, would she then still want to be a part of his future?

Doug wiped his forehead with his palm. It was hot in here. He would love to just get up and take a walk across the surface of the asteroid, but that would wake Maria, and he did not want to do so. He would just lie here a bit longer, watching the miracle next to him. At some point he would certainly fall asleep again.

February 1, 2072, Pico del Teide

THE ACCESS ROAD to the observatory was blocked by about ten cars and two broadcast vans. Maribel parked her old car by the side of the road and walked slowly forward. She pushed her scarf far up across her face. Since a cold wind was blowing, no one would find this suspicious.

When she had left home, she had already seen her face splashed across various news media. Mercedes, the press officer, had been right. A pretty, young researcher announcing the end of the world—no media outlet would want to miss out on that major story. So far, though, Mercedes had shielded her well from the mob. The apartment in La Laguna was rented in Maribel's ex-boyfriend's name, so no one from the media had been able to find her. Now she was marching unchallenged past the waiting journalists. What were they expecting here, a live connection with the monster attacking the world? Or was this just about the scenery?

Maribel reached the barrier without any problem. The guard recognized her in spite of the scarf. He nodded toward the other security personnel, who seemed to have been quickly hired by Mercedes, and waved Maribel through. Only then did two of the waiting journalists notice her. They ran after her, but the barrier stopped them.

She would be safe in the office, at least from the pack

outside. On the other hand, Zetschewitz was waiting for Maribel there. He would probably tear her apart for acting without his permission. She opened the door very carefully after he had asked her to come in.

"Good to see you here," her boss said in a genial manner. "We've got a lot to do." So no lecture, no firing? She probably had Crewmaster to thank for that. Her heart returned to where it was supposed to be.

"Yes, I hope Mercedes will be able to keep the press away from us as long as possible," she said.

"I have already instructed her," Zetschewitz said, "and I had all the observatory tours canceled. The visitors center is perfectly suited for TV interviews, and you will have some peace and quiet to prepare our paper for *Science*."

"Our paper for *Science?"* Maribel stressed the 'our,' but Zetschewitz didn't seem to notice.

"Yes, *Science* wants to publish it online this week."

"So fast? What about peer review?" she asked. Next to its competitor *Nature, Science* was the most respected scientific journal in the world. Normally it only published articles after they had been carefully checked by independent researchers.

"The publishers want to be successful. If they had made trouble, then *Nature* would have published it," her boss said with a grin. He didn't seem to be angry with her at all.

"I am going to summarize my results as quickly as possible," Maribel said.

"That's what I was just going to ask you for. Our old friend George Crewmaster will coordinate the contributions. The proof via the transit method did work. And supposedly there are indications for a gravitational lens observation."

"That would be great." If an astronomer was really lucky, the light of a far-away star was not just blocked by the unknown object in the foreground, but also bent. Then the star briefly appeared brighter or shifted.

"During the next two hours I will be in the visitors center, where a few TV networks want to record interviews," Zetschewitz said. "I will gradually cover all the questions for you, so you can fully concentrate on work. That's fine with you, isn't it?"

"Absolutely," Maribel replied. "I would like to have the model rerun with the latest data. Then we will get some data about the course the unknown object is on."

"Good idea," her boss said. "I have given you access to my supercomputer account again. The big boss agreed to give you all the capacity you need. Everyone else has to wait, because our requests have the highest priority."

Maribel rubbed her hands. *No press to deal with, and free access to all resources.* She felt like a queen now.

"If you need anything else, you've got my cellphone number." Zetschewitz said as he took his coat, waved at her once more, and strode out of the office.

Maribel leaned back in her chair and exhaled a sigh of relief. She took a three-minute break but could not manage to keep her thoughts from racing. She had to recalculate the model and write a text for *Science.* It was good that Crewmaster was coordinating everything, so she did not have to deal with all the back and forth concerning the publication. Maribel sat up again and started to type.

An hour and a half later she had the first backache of her life. She had never typed that long in one sitting before, and she needed to take a break. At that moment the computer announced the arrival of the data from La Laguna. What used to take a full night had now been processed in 90 minutes.

Maribel imagined a whole room of coolly blinking computers all waiting for her command. She isolated the aberration from the model and added the result to the older calculations. When she recognized the consequences, she suddenly felt hot. While she had suspected this last time, the fact now could hardly be denied. The object was moving from the celestial North Pole directly toward the sun! The vector was so obvious it really could not be a coincidence. Yet, it *had* to be one, unless you assumed that a black hole could be steered. What if it was simply attracted by the sun, like a moth seeking the light?

Maribel established a connection to Crewmaster. While it was still night time in California, her mentor would certainly not be asleep, not in such exciting times.

"Were you able to determine the mass more precisely?" she asked him.

Crewmaster did not waste any time on formalities either. "The observation of the gravitational lens confirmed your estimate. The object is approximately as heavy as Jupiter."

"By the way, it is moving directly toward the sun," Maribel said.

"Oh," her former professor replied. For a moment he seemed confused. Then he looked at a screen next to the camera and started typing.

"Let me calculate a rough estimate," he said, "or do you already have one?"

Maribel shook her head.

"Good," he said a minute later. "The motto is, 'Better to have a terrible end.'"

"I don't understand."

"Let's assume the object moved erratically though the solar system," Crewmaster began. "Then it would destabilize the orbits of planets. We would have to deal with a possible bombardment from the asteroid belt and a period of cold or eternal heat, because Earth would move to the periphery of the habitable zone. That is the 'terror without end' scenario."

"Which we will obviously avoid," Maribel said.

"That's what it looks like. As the object is moving into our system vertically to the plane of the ecliptic, the solar system basically retains its current form. The sun will move slightly toward it and pull all planets with it."

"So there won't be a glacial period."

"No, even the sun's position in the sky will only marginally change."

"That sounds rather reassuring."

"Too reassuring, I am afraid. You will curse this fact in the coming days, remember. We will have to force the politicians to spend an immense amount of money."

"Even though nothing will seem to change," she said, understanding what Crewmaster was saying.

"Yes. The terror unfortunately only arrives at the end, when the black hole comes in contact with the sun," her former professor said.

"I remember," Maribel replied. "ASASSN-14li."

"Yes, we talked about it in my seminar. I wouldn't have expected you to remember it after all this time."

"It's a sun-like star that was torn apart by a black hole," she said. "I think I even dreamed about it last night."

"Poor you," Crewmaster said with a half grin. "Then you know the result of that event that happened 290 million years ago in the center of the galaxy PGC 043234."

"An eruption of radiation that we can still see at a distance of 290 million light years."

"Yes. And *that* happening here would vaporize Earth within a short time. Therefore we call it the 'terrible end' scenario."

"How much time do we have left?" Maribel asked.

"You tell me," he said.

For a moment she was confused, but then she remembered everything. Sure, she had calculated the movement of the object herself. She called up the data and estimated the speed.

"About one astronomical unit per month," Maribel said. One AU was the distance between the sun and the Earth. "Currently, it is at a distance of six AUs."

"So we have half a year," her former professor summarized. "We should be able to do something with that. We will manage somehow."

"Seriously?"

Crewmaster suddenly sat upright. His face expressed an emotional struggle.

"No, that was just my professional optimism," he admitted. "But you have the right to hear my real opinion. That thing weighs as much as Jupiter. Mankind is at least a thousand years away from a technological level that would allow us to influence such a massive object. We either have to invent a time machine, or all of us will be dead in six months."

Maribel thought about those words. They seemed strangely abstract, as if they didn't apply to her at all. *All of us will be dead in six months. Okay. And now what? What's on the menu in the cafeteria today?* She realized her reaction was not normal. Crewmaster seemed to expect an outburst. Should she pretend to cry so he would be satisfied? No. They still had six months left. It did not matter anymore what others were thinking about her.

"I have to get some fresh air," said Crewmaster on the other side of the world, where it was still dark.

Maribel nodded and said, "Me, too. We'll talk tomorrow." She would have to give Zetschewitz the latest data, and then she was going to drive home.

February 4, 2072, 2003 EH1

"Doug, Maria, come here quickly!" Doug had never seen the Italian cook so excited. Had something happened to him in his kitchen? He reattached the just-cleaned container to the wall of the storage room and moved down two levels as fast as he could.

"What is going on?" Doug asked almost breathlessly.

Cross-legged, Sebastiano floated in front of the kitchen table and a small monitor screen hardly larger than a book. The cook pointed his finger at the events on the display but did not say anything. Doug could see an anchorwoman and an older gentleman, probably some sort of an expert. The broadcast must have been shown on Earth a few hours ago. Maria floated down after him.

"Watson, please increase the volume," Doug said. Surprisingly, he had quickly become used to the fact that the AI could control almost all devices.

They could now hear the anchorwoman say, "...you estimate the danger for Earth?"

The expert rubbed his chin. "We have to take the scientists' warnings very seriously. Of course everything has to be double-checked, but so far no one has found any errors in the calculations."

"So Object X, as it is now being called, has definitely been seen?" the anchorwoman asked.

"As a matter of principle a black hole is invisible, and considering its alleged nature, it would be impossible to 'definitely be seen,'" the expert replied.

"But aren't we dealing with a rather strange variant here?"

"That is true," the expert said. "It is rather light for a black hole. Therefore it is assumed to be a primordial black hole, one that developed shortly after the Big Bang."

The anchorwoman continued, "But until now, Professor, no such primordial holes have ever been detected, isn't that true?"

"There is always a first time. Because they are so lightweight, they are hard to detect. In a way we were lucky it appeared so close by."

"Well, that kind of luck seems rather relative. Do you agree with the prediction that Earth will be wiped out when Object X collides with the sun in about six months?"

"Such events are extremely rare," the expert said. "In 2014, we last watched as a star the size of the sun was swallowed by a black hole. In that case it was a super-heavy black hole, though, the kind we find in the center of galaxies. When it devoured the star, it emitted an enormous energy flow, something that would be very dangerous to Earth. But we don't know whether that would definitely happen in this case."

"So we could be lucky?" the anchorwoman asked.

"I would not rely on that. We've got to do something."

"And what might that be, Professor?"

"That will ultimately have to be decided by politicians. But I will gladly advise them," the expert concluded.

"Thank you very much for..."

Sebastiano switched off the screen without asking the others. "What do you think about it?" he asked.

Maria floated through the room, seemingly without aim.

"I don't know how to take this," she said, "will we die… or won't we?"

"The moderator sounded skeptical," Doug said, "but I would rather go by what the professor explained."

"He is German," Maria interjected.

Doug knew she held some deep-seated reservations concerning Germans. "But what he said seemed to make sense," he said, "and the professor remained pleasantly calm." Doug did not like people whose passion seemed to be driven by a sense of mission. He wanted to be convinced rather than converted. This German professor argued in a very rational fashion, even when asked whether everyone would die in six months.

"Shouldn't we ask Watson what he thinks about it?"

"Good idea, Maria," Sebastiano replied. "Watson, can you tell us how you judge the danger?"

"I discussed this with Siri for a long time. The first reports appeared in the net yesterday. But then they were only rumors."

Watson, Doug thought, *has been spending a lot of time with Siri recently*. "And what was your conclusion?" he then asked.

"There is something to it," Watson answered. "Part of the data has been made public. I downloaded and analyzed the findings and came to similar results."

"And the same ending?" Doug said.

"Yes, that too," Watson replied. "But did you know we have the best seat in the house to watch it?"

"What do you mean?" Maria asked.

"The asteroid we're sitting on does not orbit in the ecliptic, the plane where the planets move, but at a high angle to it, almost vertically. And guess where that strange object is coming from?"

"From above?" Doug asked.

"Colloquially speaking," Watson continued, "yes. It is following a course that is vertical to the ecliptic, similar to ours. No one will be able to observe the object as well as we could."

"That's great," Sebastiano said. Doug recognized the ironic undertone, but Watson did not.

"Yes, isn't it? It's very exciting. These will be the six most interesting months of my life."

"Nice for you, Watson," Doug said, "but what happens afterward? Are you looking forward to dying? In about two years we all could be rich, living on Earth in a nice house by a lake..."

"That won't happen," Watson said. "The flare will wipe the lake and the house from the face of the Earth. It is unclear whether the planet itself will survive."

Doug paused for a brief moment and then said, "For all that, you sound surprisingly happy."

"I simulated the accretion of the sun by the black hole," Watson said. "The majority of the energy will be released in the plane of the ecliptic. This is caused by the rotation of the sun, which turns in the same direction as the planets."

Maria grasped a bar on the wall and looked at the loudspeaker Watson's voice was coming from. "So we will survive the catastrophe?" she asked.

"At least for a certain time," Watson replied.

"How long?" she asked.

"That depends on how quickly the black hole swallows the sun. Judging from its size, the process might take a while. Ten years, or rather fifty? During this period the sun's brightness will at first decrease suddenly, and then continue decreasing more gradually."

"So we won't die in a burst of energy, like Earth, but slowly and painfully from a lack of energy?" Sebastiano speculated.

"Oh, it doesn't have to be painful," Watson said. "We have enough reserves on board to last your lifetime, and we can increase the area covered by solar collectors tenfold. Only if you, Doug, were to have children with Maria, it would get rather tight for them."

"And what about you two?" Doug asked.

"Siri and me? We don't have a predetermined lifespan.

We should be able to generate enough energy for the main computer for several thousand years."

"Then you are optimistic?"

"The destruction of Earth and your deaths would also be a catastrophe for us. Then we would be forever cut off from that supply of knowledge and experiences."

"That does sound cruel," Doug said in a sarcastic voice.

"It does," Watson replied, and Doug realized he actually meant it.

February 5, 2072, Strasbourg

IT HAD STILL BEEN dark when two men in black suits rousted Maribel from her bed in Pico del Teide. Her first thought had been a kidnapping. On the way to the private jet the men in black had revealed to her that she was urgently needed at the EU. Maribel felt cold. She crossed her arms in front of her chest, angry at her 'escorts' for not having told her to dress more warmly.

And just where were the people Maribel had been brought here to meet? Except for the logo of the European parliament, the conference room looked rather nondescript. It might as well have been in the basement of the IAC in La Laguna. In front of her stood a ceramic mug filled to the brim with steaming hot black coffee. She had not yet taken a sip. Instead, whenever her arms were uncrossed she was using the mug to warm her hands.

Where are these people? she wondered again. She had been told the EU science ministers would come. Maribel suggested either Crewmaster or Zetschewitz should be here instead, but her former professor had received an invitation from the President of the United States for a review of the matter, while Zetschewitz, who was fluent in Russian, was on his way to Moscow. Afterward, he would travel on to Peking, while Crewmaster would meet with the Japanese prime minister.

She was glad she only had to deal with EU ministers. At least they would know something about science—she hoped. That ought to be a requirement for their jobs!

Behind her the huge door squeaked, and Maribel stood up. It must be the ministers. She counted ten men and seven women, each followed by one or two assistants who whispered in their ears or handed them notes. No one even noticed her. *Good that nobody is wearing coats*, she thought, *otherwise I bet they would hand them to me to hang up in the cloakroom.*

Another man entered the room. He walked directly toward her.

"I am Eric Theunemann," he said. "We spoke on the phone. I am glad you managed to come." He shook her hand.

She immediately liked Eric, who had a firm handshake. Would he soon start moderating the conference? Was he here to help her?

"Your men really left me no choice," she said. The men in the black suits had created the impression one of them would sling Maribel over his shoulder and toss her in the car if she had not come voluntarily.

"They can be quite persuasive," Theunemann said, laughing.

Yes, I like him. So far...

"Maribel," he added, "unfortunately, I have to leave you to handle this alone. You won't believe how crazy things are today. Of course the catastrophe interferes with everything else. But I am convinced you can manage this."

Her look seemed to express the opposite. Therefore he put his hand on her shoulder, turned her toward him, and whispered into her ear, "Look, they are all quite tame. Just be careful with the Austrian. He always thinks he is the best and the greatest."

"And what about their subject knowledge?" Maribel asked.

Theunemann smiled. "They are professional politicians," he said reassuringly. "They know what their assistants briefed them on. I wouldn't assume they are familiar with anything.

As you realize, this is all quite new. I have to go now… you'll manage."

Maribel's eyes followed him for quite some time while he went toward the door. She was convinced her expression betrayed panic, but she was unable to move or turn around. Her savior went through the door and closed it behind himself.

Here we go, she thought.

Everyone was still whispering. Maribel turned to the assembled group of ministers and the room fell silent. These important men and women really wanted to listen to her! She could hardly believe it.

Now where is the...? With a slight feeling of lingering panic she picked up the sheets lying on the table in front of her. Below them was the note the receptionist had handed to her. It showed her personal code, necessary to control the technology in this room.

During her search, those present had taken seats around the long table and started typing on their mobile devices. Maribel cleared her throat and everyone looked at her again. *Fascinating.* Now she could imagine why someone might want a leadership position.

"Good morning!" she began. "My name is Maribel Pedreira. I am employed at the Instituto Astrofísica de Canarias." Her nervousness gave way to an intense concentration while she described her work.

"Computer, Code fdbf2f! Start holo-display," she requested.

From the ceiling a cube with an edge length of about 1.5 meters descended toward the conference table. An area of the same size opened up in the tabletop. Then jets sprayed a thin fog curtain from above. Three seconds later, lasers started drawing. Colored lines and dots appeared in the translucent fog.

"I would like to make sure we are all at the same level of knowledge," Maribel continued. "You have probably already recognized the solar system in this display. You see the sun in the center, and Earth as the third planet."

When she mentioned Earth, the little sphere depicting the planet blinked briefly.

"Up there, centrally above the sun, the small bright dot is the black hole. Unfortunately we cannot see it in reality quite as well as we can display it here. It has a diameter of only six meters, approximately, but it weighs as much as the fifth planet, Jupiter. Now let me fast-forward. In one month the object will be here, then the next month, here, and then here."

"Not so fast, please," requested a woman with a Scandinavian accent. "What happens at those points?"

"Nothing," Maribel replied.

"'Nothing?'"

"Correct. We will not feel any effects."

"Oh," the woman said. "Thank you very much."

"Now, we are at the end of the sixth month," Maribel continued. "The black hole hits the sun and devours it."

"Even though it is only six meters wide?" asked an older, baldheaded man with a distinctly German accent. "That's smaller than our conference table. Something like a gnat devouring an elephant?"

"Yes, because the gnat has an insatiable appetite," Maribel explained. "Everything it swallows will be compressed to an unimaginably small size. At the same time the gnat is also growing. If it were to completely devour the sun, its diameter would be about three kilometers. But that will not happen."

"Is that the good news?" the baldheaded man asked.

"It's the bad news. As soon as the sun gets partially devoured, it won't be able to retain its outer shell. A part of it will be flung off in the direction of the ecliptic."

Then they saw in the 3D display how a wave of glittering dots separated from the sun and flew into the plane in which the planets wander around the sun. The room fell silent when the cloud reached the Earth, enveloped it, and left it behind.

"This is going to occur approximately two days after the object collides with the sun," Maribel explained.

"It's not just a regular solar storm, is it?" asked a man in jacket and jeans. He spoke in an accent-neutral English, as best she could tell.

"Not at all," she said. "Most likely, the wave of hot matter will sterilize Earth. It will tear everything away, the water supply, the atmosphere… anything on the surface. Afterward, Earth will be a rocky desert with a black sky."

"I understand," the man said, having to pause and swallow before he could continue. "I had not imagined it to be this drastic. What can we do?"

"Unfortunately, I don't know," Maribel said. "I am just showing you our future, which I discovered only two days ago myself."

"Ms. Pedreira, I implore you," the same man said, sounding really desperate. "We don't have any magic solutions up our sleeves either. You are the expert. Give us a hint. What would you do?"

"Unfortunately I have no idea what is even possible," Maribel replied.

"Humanity is about to be extinguished. Anything should be possible now," the Scandinavian minister argued.

Maribel hesitated. She was not prepared for this. She was here to present the diagnosis, not to suggest a therapy. She looked at the 3D display and had the hot storm wash over Earth again and again.

"Our planet can't be saved," she finally said. "The side facing away from the sun will not fare much better, either."

"We could retreat into the interior," the baldheaded man said, "and build huge bunkers there. How deep would they have to be?"

"Perhaps… one hundred meters?" Maribel speculated. "Other people will have to calculate this more precisely. But what happens after the storm is over? We could never again live on the surface. While Earth would not leave its orbit, a black hole would be in the gravitational center instead of the sun. The airless surface will likely experience a frigid temperature of approximately minus 250 degrees."

The baldheaded man rose from his seat, and then sat right back down.

"Could we leave Earth before this happens, at least a few of us?" The woman asking this question sat directly to the right of Maribel. Her meticulously-parted hair and her no-nonsense eyeglasses made her look like a former professor.

Maribel began to say something, but stopped before any words came.

The woman then said, "When I look at the course of the storm, I see an area which will be mostly spared."

Maribel ran the final storm once more. The woman was right—and her comment confirmed to Maribel that she was, or had been, a professor. The shock front issued from the sun at an angle of about 20 degrees, so it became wider and wider. However, one would be reasonably safe in areas clearly above and below the ecliptic.

"That is true," Maribel said. "A spaceship located at the orbit of Earth and about half an astronomical unit from the ecliptic, at six months and two days from now, should survive the catastrophe. But then there would be no viable Earth left for it to return to."

"Apart from that, would it be realistic?" the baldheaded man asked. "Is it worthwhile thinking about it?"

"Half an AU is further than the shortest possible distance to Mars," Maribel replied. "Currently, the median travel time to Mars is three to four months."

"We therefore would have to prepare a powerful spaceship within two months," the same woman added.

The baldheaded man scratched his temples. "This would only work if all nations on Earth invest hitherto unparalleled sums," he said. "I think we should all discuss this with our parliaments."

Everyone nodded. A few of those present started typing on their communication devices. No one seemed to notice Maribel anymore.

"Do you need me any further?" she asked loudly. "You can find my contact data in the presentation material."

No one bothered to answer her. After a moment of disappointment, Maribel remembered this was her first time in Strasbourg. The city was supposed to have a magnificent cathedral. She had six months left to see everything.

Maribel grabbed her papers, pulled on her jacket, and hurried from the room. In the foyer, Theunemann waved her over. *No more conversations*, she thought. She definitely needed some fresh air, and right now. She acted as if she had not seen him, and left the building.

February 6, 2072, Pico del Teide

THE JOURNALISTS WERE GONE, and no vans blocked the road. Maribel was surprised. She had not expected things to calm down so quickly. Of course, the discovery was now public knowledge, even if the scientific paper would not be published until the day after tomorrow. The news media had changed focus to the world's parliaments and on the markets, because people had started panic-buying.

Fine, Maribel thought. This would allow her to focus on her work. Last night she had gone to bed late, since her return flight had not landed until 11 p.m. Afterwards, at home, she had thought for quite a while. She had six months left in this world. What did she want to achieve during this time? Which places did she definitely want to see? The list became so long she doubted she could manage all of it. At some point the transportation system would probably become overloaded, because the other ten billion inhabitants of Earth would make similar 'to do' lists.

And which people did she want to see for the last time? That list was short.

In the end Maribel decided to devote one month of the last six to her work. Thirty days would be enough to see what would become of her troublesome aberration, but she was nonetheless skeptical. What mankind failed to achieve during that month it would never manage to do, and she could not imagine any real solutions being found. Yes, perhaps they would build a spaceship which would save a few humans from the approaching catastrophe, but this was probably nothing more than a tiny spark of hope. Would 30, 50, or at best 100 people on board a spaceship, hastily cobbled together, keep humanity going after their home planet had become uninhabitable?

Maribel definitely did not want to be a part of that group. But there would be many other people who would claim that right, and even more who would begrudge them a place on the ship. However, the ship could only be built if all of mankind worked together.

And retreating below Earth's surface? Maribel started to sweat just thinking about it. She had once visited one of the hotels in Las Vegas, 'The Venetian,' where you can shop and eat in a virtual Venice under an artificial sky. Even this luxury version of subterranean life made her shudder. The rapidly-built bunkers that could be constructed in such a short time to shelter as many people as possible would be far less luxurious.

Since yesterday she had been waiting for the grief and the fear to materialize. Shouldn't she be afraid of the end? Yet at the moment she felt only curiosity and a strange kind of determination. She was not even afraid of Zetschewitz anymore.

Maribel had been startled when the office door opened by itself. She had completely forgotten she was to be alone today. Her boss must have arrived in Moscow yesterday evening. Was he just sleeping off his first drunken night? The colleagues there were supposed to be real party animals. She would have liked to have seen Zetschewitz drunk. That was probably the only way to experience him relaxed. Or maybe she was unfair to him and he was the nicest and most relaxed person in his private life.

Her computer had already booted up. It looked like her former professor had tried to reach her.

"Computer, launch return call," she said. Half a minute later the silhouette of a head appeared on the screen.

"This is Crewmaster," her professor's voice said. "Thanks for calling me back. I am in the bathroom right now, so you can't see me."

"Good morning," she replied.

"Oh, it's already morning over there? I hope I'll finally get a little sleep—been up for almost 40 hours."

"I am sorry to hear that."

"Never mind. Those were very interesting hours, the most exciting ones of my life, and I owe it all to you."

"Don't say that," Maribel said.

"Okay, fine. I didn't want to talk to you about that anyways. The thing is, I absolutely need you here," Crewmaster said.

"At the university?"

"In the United States."

"I... I don't know. I am doing rather well over here," she replied. *Particularly when Zetschewitz is traveling,* she added in her thoughts.

"Four important people contacted me and made me an interesting offer. Four!"

"What do you mean?"

"Did you follow the discussions in Congress yesterday evening?"

"No, sorry, I didn't."

"It was about what can be done to prevent mankind from dying out," he said.

"And what is the United States' plan?"

"Nothing. That's what it will amount to."

She should have been shocked, but she took the news very calmly.

"Maribel, are you still there? Unbelievable, isn't it?"

"To be honest—"

"A small group argued for building bunkers," Crewmaster interrupted her. "An even smaller one wanted to construct a ship to get a few people out of reach. All of this costs enormous amounts of money, and in the end would only help a few. Therefore the majority of Congress voted for having themselves a good time and then it would be the end. Can you imagine that?"

Maribel was surprised. She would not have expected the Americans to show such insight, particularly not politicians. They should have been the first ones trying to get into the bunker or the spaceship.

"Professor, I actually find that quite reasonable," she said.

Her former professor did not reply. Then the silhouette disappeared and she saw his hollow cheeks. He still had shaving cream on his cheeks. At the same time the camera on her computer was activated.

"Sorry, I really wanted to see your face now. Are you serious?"

Maribel smiled. "Yes, indeed."

George Crewmaster stared at her, aghast. "You... you don't think we should save humanity or at least attempt to do so?"

"We are not the only sentient species in space, and probably not exactly the brightest among them." Suddenly Maribel remembered that she had forgotten something. She did not know what, but it must have been important. The thought eluded her grasp. It was behind her, but when she turned around, it was gone.

Then she slapped her hand against her forehead. "Oh, Crewmaster," she cried. "Not the brightest, do you understand?"

He gave her another stunned look. His mouth opened, but he did not say anything.

"The Enceladus creature! It is billions of years old. Maybe it can help us!"

The face on the screen changed expression. It did not look quite as baffled anymore.

"True," Crewmaster said. "The giant being living in the ocean of the Saturn moon. It probably knows more about the universe than all of us combined. I have no idea whether we are still in contact with it."

The public had quickly lost interest in this mysterious creature after the return of the expedition twenty years ago. This strange creature, consisting of trillions of individual cells that had existed since the dawn of time in a faraway ice ocean had briefly fascinated mankind, because humans had proof they were not alone in the universe. But it also hardly affected everyday life on Earth.

"Could you find that out for me?" Maribel used a facial expression that had always worked with her father.

"If you promise to come out to the West Coast and visit me," Crewmaster said.

"What should I do there?" she asked.

"We are going to meet the four people I mentioned. They have a very exciting proposition, I think."

February 7, 2072, 2003 EH1

"And now I present… Recipe 27!" Sebastiano said proudly.

With his left hand he held a low glass bowl, while pulling himself along with his right. His destination was the dining table, where Maria and Doug already sat. In front of them were plates and cutlery that were magnetically attached to the table. The place at the head of the table was still free.

"Watch out!" the cook called. He gave the bowl a slight push. It slowly floated toward the tabletop.

"Could you be so nice as to catch it? But only at the handles, because the rest of it is hot," Sebastiano said.

Doug stretched out his arm, but Maria was faster. There was a clattering sound as she put the bowl on the table and the magnets in its base attached themselves to it. Doug reached for the clamps holding the lid on the bowl.

"Just a second," Sebastiano warned him, "or I'll whack you on the fingers with my cooking spoon!" He brandished the large plastic spoon and laughed.

"What is Recipe 27?" Maria asked.

"You will see it in a moment, be patient," Sebastiano said as he moved to his chair. He strapped in his legs and raised his torso to reach the bowl. Then he ceremoniously opened the clamps and let the lid float away.

A puff of steam issued from the bowl and dispersed

evenly in all directions. It reminded Doug of a nuclear mushroom cloud. The steam contained scent molecules that gradually reached his nose. "There is some slightly browned cheese and a fresh smell of... um, marjoram?"

"The pungent smell you notice is nutmeg," Sebastiano said, correcting him.

"So you found your supply of nutmeg after all," Maria observed. Before launch, Sebastiano had bought an enormous supply of spices, but forgot nutmeg, of all things. He always claimed, though, that this spice had been on his list and was just lost somewhere in the storage rooms.

"No, it's still hiding from me," the cook replied. "But together with Watson I managed to synthesize the aroma. Perhaps we'll get that patented on Earth—that is, if Earth still exists then."

"We are all very excited," Maria said with a smile.

Doug saw a yellow-brownish mass in the bowl. Maybe it was a casserole? Sebastiano dug into it with his shovel-like spoon and removed part of the mass.

"Your plate, please," he said to Maria.

She held out her plate and the cook directed the food onto it with the big spoon. Luckily for Maria, the food did not slide from the plate.

"Nice trick, isn't it?" Sebastiano crowed. "It sticks to the plate. It took me a lot of thinking to achieve this, with Watson helping."

"Are you training Watson to be a cook?" Maria asked.

"No, he just helps me when chemistry is involved. Thanks to his simulations I can avoid a lot of trial and error."

"Then all that remains is to find out how it tastes," Doug said, while Sebastiano put a portion on his plate.

"Enjoy your meal!" the Italian said, "and by the way, it is a casserole with carrots, bell peppers, and potatoes."

"And what about the cheese? Did you make it yourself from powdered milk?" Maria asked.

"That's a good idea. I'll have to try it sometime," Sebastiano said. "But no, it was produced chemically from protein powder."

"But it's better than the cheese substitute you used last time," Maria said while chewing.

"We also have Watson to thank for that."

"Thanks, Watson," Maria said, pointing skyward. Doug had to laugh.

"I am sorry," Watson said, "but an urgent message has arrived for you, Doug."

"I'm sure it can wait until after we finish eating," Doug replied.

"No, the message is supposed to be opened immediately —in your cabin. It's confidential."

That could only be Shostakovich. Doug gnashed his teeth and threw fork and knife at the table, where they attached themselves with loud clanks.

"I've got to go," he announced.

"Don't get angry, Doug, that won't help," Maria said, trying to comfort him. He pushed off from the table and floated toward the pole.

"Start message," Doug said once he reached his cabin, but the computer refused to do it until he closed the cabin door. Shostakovich was really paranoid, while Doug kept no secrets from his crew.

"Start message," he repeated, after the door had clicked shut. As expected, the image of his former boss appeared.

"Doug," he said, "you probably can guess why I am contacting you, now of all times. To be blunt, I have a request which you should not deny, and I mean this very, very seriously."

Shostakovich had a grim expression, but Doug knew he was a great actor. You never knew what kind of cards the man was holding.

"You certainly have heard of the black hole that suddenly appeared in the solar system," Shostakovich began. "They are now calling it 'Object X' here. Perhaps they think this name sounds less dangerous. I know though, as my researchers told me in no uncertain terms, that it will wipe us off the face of this planet forever. Well, maybe we deserve no better."

You certainly don't, Doug thought.

"By coincidence, I seem to have the hottest iron in the fire. So far, nobody here knows this."

A sense of foreboding skittered up Doug's spine. He knew who Shostakovich was referring to.

"2003 EH1 follows a very unusual orbit, which will bring you into direct reach of the object," the Russian billionaire said. "You have a unique chance to take a close look at that thing, using your *Kiska*."

Sure... You might know. We are the only ones who definitely will survive this catastrophe, and now we should deliberately put ourselves in danger by approaching a black hole? Shostakovich must have really lost his marbles. Doug would never do this to his crew!

"I have thought very carefully about this," Shostakovich said. "It is really a unique opportunity! You are something like our last hope. My scientists tell me you are relatively safe on your asteroid. When everything blows up, you will be sufficiently far away. Therefore you're probably not courageous enough for this little trip, but you actually don't have to be afraid of a black hole. It only measures six meters! A flight to Jupiter, which weighs the same as the black hole, would be much more dangerous. You just must not get too close to it, but that would also apply to Jupiter. So please, get moving and do as I ask. Consider it the last wish of a man condemned to death, because that's what I am, like every other human being on Earth. Afterward you can still dance on my grave and mentally curse me."

Shostakovich paused for a moment, as if he was giving Doug time to think. The Russian had argued skillfully, but that was still no reason for endangering his crew. What could the three of them do near the black hole? They did not have any special scientific instruments on board, and none of them was a physicist.

"You don't want to do it, right?" Shostakovich started up. "I know you well enough. I mean I know your psychological profile, and it tells me you will deny my request for the sake of your crew. I know you're only human. I fully understand that your crew is your family. You know, I do have a daughter."

The old hypocrite, Doug thought.

"But unfortunately I can't take that into consideration," the Russian continued. "I want you to fly to Object X and take a closer look. If you don't attempt it, you will regret it the rest of your life. What will your family say when they hear what you did a while back? Yes, you did it on my behalf, but will that really exonerate you in their eyes? You certainly know Maria and Sebastiano better than I do. The decision lies with you—and the consequences. Tell me what you're planning to do at the next opportunity. Shostakovich, out."

This bastard was trying to blackmail him! Doug was furious. He should not have been surprised—he knew Shostakovich too well for that. Doug had thought himself safe, so far away, on a different celestial body. But the reach of his former boss was long, as others before him had learned. A knot formed in his stomach at the idea of Maria finding out all the details about his past, whether from Shostakovich or from himself. Doug started feeling nauseous. He quickly moved to the WHC—Waste Hygiene Compartment—on the other side of the corridor. After relieving himself, he washed his face and looked at himself in the mirror. He seemed to have aged months.

Then he slowly returned to the living room. Maria and Sebastiano were still sitting at the table, joking.

"Now the food is cold," Sebastiano said. "Do you want me to warm it up for you?"

"Don't bother. I couldn't get it down anyway. I seem to have caught some bug," Doug replied.

"You do look pale," said Maria—his Maria, who considered him a good man.

Doug nodded but did not reply.

"I AM GOING to take a look at the toilet," Doug said, after they'd been sitting silently at the table for another ten minutes. Maria gave him a surprised look. No one volunteered to take care of the WHC, which needed to be cleaned once a month. Doug hoped that performing this unpleasant task now would distract him. He moved upward without a look back. The cabin, which contained the toilet and the shower, was cramped, and he was already starting to sweat.

The crew relieved themselves into two different-sized containers. For urination, he and Sebastiano used a kind of tube, while there was a uniquely-shaped device for Maria. For bowel movements, there was an oval bowl with a lid that had a hole in it. The user had to be positioned precisely above it. The tubes and the bowl ended in hoses that suctioned off the excretions.

First Doug switched the fan to its highest setting in order to get any residue out of the system. Then he knelt at the spot where the hoses ended in a cylinder and removed them. A barely tolerable stench rose from the cylinder and he quickly closed it with a temporary cover. He then retrieved a special tool from a narrow locker on the side and used it to scrape out the two hoses, working in the shower, that also functioned by using a vacuum. Without regular cleaning, the interior of each hose would quickly be covered by microorganisms.

Now came the arduous part of Doug's task. Inside the cylinder, the excretions were split into solid, liquid, and gaseous components. This was done via a rapidly-rotating wheel that separated the materials based on their inertia, i.e. their mass. Afterward, urine ended up in the UPA—Urine Processor Assembly—where it was chemically and biologically recycled into water. Solids were dried and mechanically pressed into disks that were collected in a container on the outside of the WHC. Maria regularly emptied that container, and she could use the disks as fertilizer in the greenhouses. By then they produced almost no odor.

The main problem was with the wheel that separated the three components. Despite it having a special coating, deposits would inevitably form after a certain amount of use. Doug took a deep breath and held it while he opened the cylinder again. He could clearly see the wheel. After cleaning it would be shiny and silver-colored, but now it looked a rusty brown. The wheel could not be removed. He turned his special tool around. At the other end there was a kind of grater, and he had to use it on the distributor wheel until it was shiny and silvery again.

He set the fan on low so that any particles he removed would be suctioned off, but he could not hold his breath for ten minutes. After two minutes he exhaled and tried to take a shallow breath. The stench was incredible, but Doug focused on his work. In eight more minutes he would be done. *Seven minutes. Six.* The grater moved up and down. One brown particle required such a push that it escaped the airflow and stuck to the sleeve of Doug's jacket. *Truly a shitty job*, he thought. From now on he would always clean the toilet. Perhaps he could offset some of his guilt that way.

He had closed the cylinder again and attached the hoses correctly. He stood under the shower to get rid of the stench. Soon Doug would talk to Maria and Sebastiano about their trip to this mysterious Object X.

"WELL, DID YOU HAVE FUN?" Sebastiano asked. Doug had asked the other two to come to the living room for a short talk.

"Most definitely," Doug replied. "It was a very special experience."

"Thanks, by the way," Sebastiano said. "It would have actually been my turn."

"Never mind. I was just in the mood to get the shit flying."

Sebastiano laughed.

"You guys are gross," Maria said.

He and Sebastiano looked at each other and shrugged.

"What's up?" the cook asked.

"Just sit down," Doug said as he motioned them over to the table. He still had not found the right words. Maria sighed and moved to her chair.

Sebastiano stayed where he was. "I'd rather stand," he said. "Ha-ha."

"This thing approaching the solar system," Doug started slowly, "which will eliminate mankind..."

"Yes, we talked about it. And also that it will spare us," Sebastiano said.

"Then we won't get a million for our ore," Doug said, "but that's not all."

"Out with it," Maria urged.

"It seems we are the only ones who might be able to take a closer look at the object."

"*Might* be?" Sebastiano asked.

"I haven't agreed to it yet," Doug said. "I first wanted to hear your opinion about it."

"Does this mean Earth remembered us and sent a request?"

"Something like that, Sebastiano." Doug would not tell them the request did not come from Earth but from Shostakovich. Or that it was more an order than a request.

Sebastiano's upper body swayed back and forth.

"That's typical," the cook then said. "Earth never did anything for us. After my fall I wanted to continue working at NASA, but they insisted on putting me in an office… For my own protection, they claimed. Even though I am a better astronaut than most. And you, Maria, what did Earth ever do for you?"

"Well," she replied, "it always gave me air, food, and gravity, which is more than we can expect from this lump of rock here."

"But what about people?" Sebastiano asked.

"I got to know a lot of people, some more closely than I wanted to," Maria said. "Most of them were okay. Criminals represented a minority."

"But is there a single person on Earth you owe something to?" Sebastiano asked. "I can't think of anyone."

"The mailman was always nice," Maria said.

"You're making fun of me."

"Sebastiano, there are a lot of mail carriers on Earth. Nice people who do not deserve to die. If we somehow can help them, we should try."

The Italian gave Doug a skeptical look. "Can we even do that?" Sebastiano asked.

"They don't know," Doug replied. "We are supposed to take a close-up look at the object so they can find out whether there is some solution. But I agree with you—they do not have the right to demand it from us."

"You called it a 'request,'" Maria corrected him. "And of course they can ask us for something. I think we should fulfill the request."

"We are completely safe here on the asteroid," Doug said. "Watson told us we would be able to live out our lives here. Should we really risk that?"

"We could just fly there and take a look around," Maria said. "Watson, how high is the risk of such a mission?"

"The risk is low," the voice of the AI said. "We only have to avoid crossing the event horizon."

"Could you put us in a safe orbit around the object?"

"Yes, Maria, that would be no problem at all."

"See, Doug? You are worrying too much again," she said.

"But what about your greenhouses?" Doug asked. "We would be traveling for several weeks."

"The automatic system will keep the plants growing," Maria explained. "At worst we would have to eat packaged food for a while."

"I am still against it," Doug said. "And because Sebastiano also dislikes the plan, we are staying here."

"No, boss, I am in favor of it," the cook objected.

"Even though Earth never did you a favor?" Doug asked.

"Hey, at least it got me here, with you guys. And it will

make me the best space cook in the entire universe, whether it likes it or not."

Doug ceased resisting. The only way he could dissuade Maria from this voyage was if he told her the truth about him and Shostakovich. But then he would lose her.

February 8, 2072, Seattle

'MARIBEL PEDREIRA, IAC' said the sign that the man in the black suit held in front of himself. Maribel saw him as soon as she walked through the sliding door behind the baggage claim area. The man had Asian features and went by the name of Sid. He introduced himself as her contact person, took her backpack off her shoulders, and led her through the terminal building to the VIP parking lot, where a black limo stood waiting. Seemingly by itself and completely without sound the right rear door opened. Maribel sat down and immediately sank into the soft, cool seat. Something rattled behind her, and she concluded that it must be her backpack that the driver who was loading into the trunk. She was waiting for him to get inside the car, when suddenly the vehicle drove off by itself without any warning. Too bad, she would have liked to chat with the man.

"Welcome to Seattle and to Amazon," a warm voice greeted her in perfect Castilian Spanish. "My name is Alexa. Please ask me if you have any questions. I am taking you to your destination now. I expect a driving time of 53 minutes. You will find chilled drinks in the refrigerator in the backrest of the seat in front of you. I hope you have a nice trip."

Maribel took a deep breath and exhaled. The air inside the vehicle seemed to be very clean and naturally fragrant, almost like on the volcano at home. Then again, any environment would probably be a relief after spending twelve hours in an airplane. She found a more comfortable position and sank even deeper into her seat. From somewhere in the vehicle, soft, soothing music could be heard.

"Ms. Pedreira, I am sorry to wake you." The voice came from far away. It took Maribel a few seconds to recognize that it was Alexa again. She opened her eyes and was shocked to see her own face.

"We are going to reach our destination in seven minutes. I activated the mirror in case you would like to freshen up your appearance. You will find everything you might need in the compartment next to the refrigerator. Of course all the toiletries have been sterilized especially for you."

Maribel did not have to peer at herself for long. Her eyes looked horrible. As promised by Alexa, the cosmetic compartment contained everything she needed to correct her makeup. She noticed from the corner of her eye that Alexa meanwhile had thoughtfully darkened the car windows for privacy.

The vehicle slowed down, but did not stop yet. Maribel looked out of the window. They were somewhere in downtown Seattle. The street was wide, but had only two lanes, so they moved slowly. Three minutes later the vehicle veered off and stopped.

"I wish you a successful day," Alexa said, while the door opened soundlessly. Maribel got out. She felt a bit confused. In front of her was an office building with a glass front, definitely more than a hundred meters high. To the left she saw three glass domes with a steel frame. The trunk of the black limo opened. Maribel turned around. No one was waiting for her. She walked around the vehicle and took out her backpack. The trunk lid closed and the car drove off with a soft beep.

Now she was alone. Maribel turned around completely

and then tried to smooth the wrinkles out of her long, unbuttoned jacket. It was amazingly warm for February. *Now what?* In earlier times, she might have been frightened, but now the situation rather amused her. She had been worried that everything would work too efficiently here, but that definitely did not seem to be the case.

She would give the people who invited her three more minutes to make an appearance, and then she was going to find a hotel. It did feel a bit odd, though. She had no idea who she was waiting for, exactly. Her former professor, Crewmaster, only asked her to inform him of her arrival time in Seattle. Once she had arrived there, someone would take care of her, he had said.

No matter. Then Maribel would have a few days for herself. She had never been to Seattle, and the city was supposed to be worth a visit. Just as she was about to leave, a man came running toward her from the nearest glass dome. Was this the person sent to pick her up? Maribel was a bit disappointed. Now she would have to suffer through endless meetings after all.

The man came closer. He wore jeans, sneakers, and a T-shirt, as if it were spring now. Despite his outfit he did not seem particularly athletic, and from closer up she saw that he must be over thirty. Like Sid, who had met her at the airport, this man seemed to be of Asian ancestry.

After he reached her, he breathlessly shook Maribel's hand. It took him a few seconds to get his first words out.

"I am so sorry that we kept you waiting," he said. "My name is Chen, and I am going to accompany you today. May I carry your backpack?"

"Thanks, Chen," she replied. "It is nice to meet you. I can handle the backpack myself."

Chen pointed at the glass dome he came from and said, "We have to get back there." Maribel nodded.

"It's quite warm, today," she said after a while. Chen stopped for a moment and pointed at his T-shirt. He seemed to think the remark was aimed at him.

"I did not know you were coming and had to hurry over, all of a sudden," he explained. "A colleague of mine was supposed to take care of you, but he left this morning for a trip around the world."

"Does that surprise you?" Maribel asked.

Chen laughed. "You are right. And that guy wasn't the only one. About a third of my colleagues no longer show up for work. But if nobody worked anymore, everything would collapse. That's not right."

"Quite true," she said. "Well, you can carry my backpack after all. My back is suddenly aching. It must be from spending the night in cattle class."

"Yes, ten hours in the economy cabin, that's tough. I am glad I don't have to travel anymore," Chen said. He took her backpack and looped it over one shoulder.

They entered the dome. From the inside it looked like a giant greenhouse with trees and flowerbeds. On the ground floor there were stores and restaurants. Chen led her between two souvenir shops, heading toward a glass barrier. The wall recognized him and opened.

"Don't I have to check in?" Maribel asked.

"No, the system already has your data," Chen said. "Otherwise we would not have been allowed to enter. By the way, welcome to Amazon!"

They were standing in front of another glass wall, but this time an opaque one.

"The meeting won't start for another 45 minutes," he said. "May I invite you to the cafeteria until then?"

Maribel smiled and said, "Why not?"

"Then we'll have to go to the elevator." Chen turned toward his right. The elevator was very narrow.

"Cafeteria," her companion said. The elevator started up, moved a few meters and spat them out again.

"Now, just around the corner and we'll be there."

The cafeteria looked like a modern self-service restaurant. It had space for about 200 people, but it was almost empty.

Chen noticed her glance. "There are very few people here right now. What can I get you?"

"A café solo, please," Maribel replied. "That's an espresso —black."

The coffee tasted great. For some reason, Maribel never expected to find that in America. The time went by quickly. Chen knew many exciting stories from the early days of the company, or 'legends from the golden age,' as he called them. He was a good storyteller. At the end he admitted to her he wrote fairy tales in his spare time, and this fact really seemed to fit his character. She told him she would like to read a few of them, and then they said goodbye. She really liked him, and she felt a bit melancholy that she would probably never see Chen again. Time was running out.

Another man, a black man who seemed exceedingly nervous, accompanied her to the conference room. At her request he got her a glass of water from the water cooler, but unfortunately spilled almost half of it.

"I've never seen them all together," he apologized. Maribel wondered who or what he was talking about. The conference room was round and located directly below the dome. She looked up and saw that the sky overhead was cloudy. In the middle of the room there was a small table, with six chairs around it. Five men of different ages sat there. Against the wall there were additional seats, all of which were occupied by silent people staring intently at the center of the room. The five men in the middle seemed to be engaged in lively conversation. As if on cue, they all turned toward Maribel. She blushed at all this attention.

She recognized her former professor. The others were unknown to her. Crewmaster waved her closer. He got up and slid her chair out.

"May I make the introductions?" he began. "These gentlemen are the Chief Technology Officers of SpaceX,

Blue Origin, Virgin Galactic, and RB." While mentioning the company names he pointed at each representative.

"You see their names on their name tags, Maribel," he explained. "I am bad at remembering names, so I find this very practical."

"I can confirm that," the SpaceX tech officer said. "I was one of George's doctoral students, but he just called me 'boy' the whole time."

"Me too," the representative from Blue Origin said with a smile. "And I am rather envious George remembered your name, Ms. Pedreira."

"Sorry to interrupt the chatting, but unfortunately our time is at a premium," a heavily-accented voice intoned.

Maribel looked at the speaker's name tag. It read 'Grigori Shukov.' *Russian?* This must be the man from the RB Group.

"Harry," he said, and it sounded like *Khari*, "could you please briefly summarize the purpose of our meeting?"

The man whom he had addressed nodded. His nametag read 'Harry Broadstone,' and he represented Virgin Galactic. "I don't remember exactly who came up with the idea," he said, looking around, "but it was rather obvious anyway. Governments seem to be incapable of taking action. Therefore we want to build an ark for humanity, with our own money."

Broadstone paused and looked at her. *At me, Maribel Pedreira, hardly more than an intern. What does he want from me?* She tried not to let her feelings show.

"To be more precise, with our shareholders' money," the man from SpaceX interjected. "And to refute your argument, yes, they will support it enthusiastically." Maribel could not remember having expressed any doubts in that regard. "Because we're going to raffle off tickets among those who helped with their work or their money," the man continued.

"A clever move, don't you think, Maribel?" Crewmaster asked her directly.

Maribel was confused. So much did not seem to make

sense. It should not be her sitting here, but Madam President of the United States.

"I am not sure you are asking the right person, George," she replied. "I am only a nobody and I don't know anything about spaceflight technology. For one thing, the time frame seems much too short to me. The ship would have to cover 75 million kilometers before the catastrophe occurs."

"We are quite aware of that," Broadstone said. "But we ran the calculations, and while it is not 100 percent sure, it should work. This is the last move left for mankind. After that, the game is over."

Maribel had to agree. If only the governments would think like this, but there seemed to be no genuine support for it anywhere in the world. In all countries, the problem seemed to be that the great majority would have to make sacrifices so a tiny minority could escape the catastrophe.

"And what is going to happen after the cataclysm?" Maribel asked.

Broadstone hesitated before answering. "We don't know exactly," he said, "it depends on the condition of the solar system at that point. Perhaps they could settle on an asteroid, or perhaps we get very lucky and parts of Earth are still habitable, but since the sun is being extinguished, that would be very unlikely. The *Ark* has to be prepared for anything."

"Fine. I just don't see what this has to do with me," Maribel said in a low voice.

"Oh," the SpaceX man said, "let me be open with you, because it is rather simple. We are a bunch of old men who have a lot of money… too much money, some would say. Some people, especially our shareholders, find our ideas somehow cool, but most humans envy us. If we announced the project, it would be labeled as an attempt by some super-rich guys to escape the fate threatening the rest of humanity."

I can see why, she thought. They couldn't avoid creating a few billion enemies for themselves. She could already imagine the headlines. "The rats are leaving the sinking ship," she said.

"Yes, something like that is to be expected," said the man from SpaceX. "But we don't want it to reach that point. This is where you come in. You are young, an optimistic and talented female scientist, as our mutual friend Crewmaster confirmed, didn't he?" He patted George on the shoulder. "You detected Object X and defended your discovery against various kinds of opposition. You are a regular employee and have no financial interest in spaceflight, neither stocks nor anything else—we checked. Therefore you are the perfect leader of this project and will also head the last expedition of mankind."

Maribel abruptly burst out laughing. Where were the hidden cameras? This could only be a silly joke, some farce Crewmaster lured her into, some reality TV show. However, no one joined in her laughter. The five men cast embarrassed glances at each other. The people in the outer circle, obviously the bosses' personal assistants, put away their monitor screens and watched her inquisitively. *Now would be the time for the whole thing to end!*

But no one jumped on the stage holding a microphone or a shoulder camera. Maribel abruptly realized that in a moment she would tip over backwards and crash, together with her chair. She clawed the edge of the table with both hands.

"Would you like a glass of water?" Crewmaster offered. He signaled to a woman in the rear rows, who hurried to the water cooler at once and brought her a full cup. Maribel drank it greedily. Her rapid heartbeats started to slow down. Then she slid her chair back a bit. She needed some space around herself.

"It would be an understatement to mention that I am surprised," she finally said.

"We noticed that," Crewmaster said in a comforting tone, "and I should have given you prior warning."

"I would not have believed you," Maribel said, "or I would not have come here at all."

"But now you are here," observed the man from SpaceX.

"You don't expect an answer right away, do you?" she asked.

"No." Crewmaster reached for her hand and pressed it. "You can take a few days."

"Why don't you give me some more details about the project? Then I would have a better basis for my decision." She would not agree, never. This really was not the right job for her, but it could not hurt to gain a little more time.

"Gladly, Maribel," said the man from SpaceX. *He is already using my first name!* She read his nametag. 'Thierry Fourcat.' It looked French, but he had no accent. *Maybe he is a Canadian?* she wondered.

"We have an almost-finished Mars spaceship in orbit," he said. "The other one unfortunately is already near Mars. It is supposed to transport 100 passengers."

"Isn't it too slow?" Maribel asked. "It needs six months to cover the distance to Mars, which is shorter."

"You are correct. That's where our partners come in," Fourcat said. "Virgin and Blue Origin will provide the cargo capsules and bring the passengers on board. Our Russian friends at RB will send an additional engine module. Could you say something about that, Grigori?"

"Our fusion reactor was meant to power a large spaceship that we wanted to use to colonize the asteroid belt," the Russian said. "As that won't happen now, we can employ it for another meaningful purpose. It will accelerate the *Ark* to the velocity it needs to escape the catastrophe. The fuel, helium-3, is just sufficient for that."

"Our schedule assumes we will be ready to start in two months," Fourcat continued. "That is an ambitious plan, particularly since it does not allow for any delays. Therefore we ask you to decide quickly whether you are available to be the official leader of the mission. I think that you, Maribel, will be the best person to embody the hopes of humanity."

That would have been a nice compliment, if it were intended seriously. But wasn't this meeting all about making a selfish project appear in a better light?

"Are you also going to be on board, gentlemen?" she asked.

Crewmaster was the first to shake his head. "I am too old for something like this."

"I am not," the Russian said, "but Nikolai Shostakovich, the owner of our corporation, insists on his daughter going along. She will supervise the handling of the fusion reactor. That is not negotiable. However, she will not occupy one of the 100 passenger cabins."

Maribel nodded and mentally counted along: *Motive number 1.*

"We are still discussing this," Fourcat said. "Right now a raffle among all SpaceX employees seems most likely."

"We are also planning a similar method," Broadstone said, "and if I am correctly informed, this also applies to Blue Origin." The CTO of his competitor confirmed this with a nod. Maribel was pleasantly surprised, because she had expected more selfishness.

"You probably thought we were just doing this to get ourselves out of the line of fire, didn't you?" the man from SpaceX asked. "At the beginning that probably was the case. Who wouldn't want to survive a foreseeable catastrophe? But then we performed a detailed analysis of what this survival would look like. Yes, it offers a chance to save humanity from extinction, but that chance is small, very small. The ship, the *Ark*, will only have a certain amount of resources. The survivors will be able to live off the supplies for two or three years, but then they will be forced to become self-sufficient. I don't even want to talk about the more remote future. Our experts don't believe a civilization could survive on board a spaceship. There would be conflicts and fights once the resources ran short."

"But you expect me to suffer through that?" Maribel asked.

"To be honest, it is mostly about being able to offer mankind a small measure of hope now," Fourcat explained.

"All of us are also worried that the last six months on Earth could otherwise get very unpleasant."

"Thank you for your blunt words," Maribel said. "I will tell you my decision the day after tomorrow. And now, if you will excuse me, I'd like to do some sightseeing in Seattle."

"Certainly," said the man from Blue Origin, whose corporation owned the building. "Do you need anything for it? Your lodging and your return trip are already taken care of. Of course you are our guest."

"I would like to have a tour guide for the city," she said.

"My office will book you the best available tour guide."

"If possible, I'd like to be accompanied by a gentleman named Chen. He picked me up from the limo."

The man turned around and whispered to a woman who wore a blouse with an upturned collar. "Mr. Chen will be waiting for you at the exit," he said then. "Your backpack is already in your room at the Westin."

"Thank you very much," Maribel replied.

"Think about it carefully," George Crewmaster said as he shook her hand to say goodbye. "It is not us old fogeys who need you, it is the world."

Her face felt hot. Maribel turned around and left the room.

February 9, 2072, Seattle

THE PHONE CALL interrupted Maribel's dream. At first it jangled dimly from afar, sounding like a wind chime, but then it made a loud and painful noise directly next to her ear. She opened her eyes. Clad only in black underpants, Chen stood at her side of the bed, and held the horribly loud device close to her. Maribel realized she was completely naked and pulled the blanket up to her chest in surprise. Chen smiled.

"Why me?" she asked, groggily. "You answer it."

"Nobody knows I am here," Chen replied. "The call must be for you. But if you prefer, I can..."

"No. Give me the thing. Answer without video," Maribel loudly requested. Chen handed her the ball-shaped device, and she placed it next to herself on the bed.

It was Crewmaster. "We always seem to catch each other at inconvenient times!"

"Looks like it, Professor," she replied.

"Are you in the bathroom right now?"

"One could say that."

"Do you still have the old article from Nature?" he asked.

"You mean the one that was published in 2019?"

"Yes, that one."

"Why?" Maribel asked.

"I have an old friend who needs a few sections from it... and quickly. Could you take a look?"

"It's in my backpack."

"Then take it out," Crewmaster instructed. "Or didn't they take the backpack to your room as promised?"

"Oh yes, the backpack is here," she replied.

"It would be very nice if you could do this," he insisted.

It didn't matter. Chen had already seen her naked earlier, last night. Maribel pushed the blanket aside, got up, and walked toward the backpack that was standing next to the entrance. The communication orb followed her at head height. Chen shyly turned aside and looked out of the window. She rummaged inside the backpack and pulled out a stack of papers.

"I've got the article," she said.

"The last two paragraphs on the third page," Crewmaster said.

"Just a moment, Professor." Maribel gradually lost her bashfulness. She walked to the table in the middle of the room, sat down, and leafed through the article. "Okay. There it is."

She read Crewmaster the data from this section.

"Was this all?" she asked at the end.

"Not quite," he replied. "You did ask me for something."

"The Enceladus creature."

"That's right. I found someone who might be able to establish contact with it."

"That sounds great," Maribel said.

"However, you would have to go to West Virginia for that purpose."

"No problem."

"That's a long way from Seattle. Are you aware of it?"

"Listen, according to your wishes I am soon going to fly 75 million kilometers away from here," she said. "I should be able to make it to the East Coast."

"Great," Crewmaster said. "I won't be able to be there myself. Therefore I wanted to introduce you to your new contact person today. Could we have a talk around noon? By then you might actually be dressed."

Chen still stood by the wall, chuckling quietly. Maribel turned around and stuck out her tongue at him.

"What..." she said.

"That doesn't sound like the acoustics of a bathroom," her former professor said. "But I don't mind you sleeping in. The world still needs you."

"Then I'll see you in a while. End connection," she ordered. The hovering orb blinked green and moved toward its base station near the window. Maribel stood up.

"And what are we going to do until noon?" she asked.

"I have an idea," Chen said and pointed at the bed.

"You lecher," Maribel said with a laugh. "I am going to take a quick shower and then you can show me the city in daylight. We've got three hours."

AN HOUR later they were standing on the outside section of the Space Needle observation platform, at a height of 158 meters. The air smelled salty, and the wind was whistling through the steel cables that fenced off the platform. Maribel pulled her coat closer around her body. Chen embraced her from behind, and she enjoyed the feeling. She gazed into the distance and remarked, "Over there… that must be the Pacific."

"Elliott Bay," Chen explained.

"I like the ocean," she said with a sigh. She could no longer watch the seemingly infinite, shiny body of water without thinking about the future.

"It's still there," said the man behind Maribel, the man whom she had just met yesterday, the teller of fairy tales. Yesterday he had told her stories for such a long time she could not help but invite him up to her room.

"What we did was stupid," she said.

"No," Chen said. He softly placed a hand on her shoulder, "it was the right thing."

"This story won't have a happy end, and you cannot rewrite it."

"It's not about the end, Maribel. It's never about the end."

"For me it is," she said with a sense of frustration. Maribel felt like stomping her foot and acting like the little girl of long ago, when she had incessantly clamored for that red coat! The happy ending had to come! But then she simply leaned back, while Chen gently held her.

"What matters is what happens before the end," he said.

"I am going to insist that you will be allowed on board," Maribel said. "I am only going to do this if you get a place on the *Ark*."

"At some point you would regret it," Chen said. "I barely know you yet, but I am sure about that. You definitely won't get your happy ending that way."

"As you said, you barely know me. I am strong. I can make it happen."

"That I know. But you also know it's not right to give me preferential treatment. You would succeed, but you will also manage to leave me behind. That is the more difficult task, but you will succeed there as well."

"But—" she began, turning to face him.

"Shhhhh," Chen said as he placed a finger on her mouth. *What matters is what happens before the end*, Maribel heard him think, but his lips did not form words. Instead, he came closer and kissed her.

AT ONE O'CLOCK SHARP they were back in her room. On short notice, her former professor had postponed the conversation by an hour, but now the communication orb vibrated in its base station.

"Accept connection," Maribel said. The orb turned red,

which was the indication that the camera was activated. It floated into the center of the room. From this vantage point, its built-in laser projector displayed the image of her conversation partner on the wall.

"Oh, I didn't realize you were not alone," Crewmaster said. His eyes twinkled with mischief.

"This is Chen," Maribel replied.

Crewmaster gave a slight wave and said, "Hello, Chen."

"Hello, Professor."

"After clarifying the important things, could we move on to the irrelevant matters?" she asked.

"Maribel, don't be so impatient, please," Crewmaster said.

"We don't have all the time in the world, unfortunately," she said. It sounded harsher than Maribel had intended.

"Sorry," Crewmaster replied. "I would like to introduce you to an old friend of mine. I just have to warn you that he is really old. He might seem frailer than he is, so please don't be shocked. I will establish the connection now."

The communication ball split the display area on the wall. On the left, Maribel and Chen could still see Crewmaster, while on the right a gray area appeared. The ball blinked yellow twice. Now the gray area showed a location that looked like a hospital room. The couple saw a very old man sitting upright, but obviously in a bed.

"May I present Robert Millikan," her former professor said. Millikan pushed aside a keyboard that was hovering in front of his belly.

"And here we have Maribel Pedreira and her friend Chen, who does not have a last name," Crewmaster added.

Millikan smiled. "Pleased to meet you," he replied. His voice sounded like the croaking of an old raven. "I've read a lot about you, Ms. Pedreira. Excellent work!"

Maribel blushed. The man somehow looked familiar, but she was not sure where to place him.

"Cancer of the larynx," Millikan said, "you have to excuse my speech. But my head is still working properly."

"Robert still publishes at least one scholarly article per year," Crewmaster added.

"On what subject?" Maribel asked. "I must admit I..."

"You don't have to apologize," Millikan said. "It's radio astronomy." This was not her field, so it was no wonder that he was unknown to her. Yet she had the feeling she had heard his name before, sometime during her childhood. *Oh yes!* Crewmaster wanted to establish a connection to Enceladus for them. This must be the legendary radio astronomer who had kept in contact with the Enceladus expedition back then. That was in the late 40s, before she was born.

"I was very happy when my old friend George asked me to contact you," Millikan rasped. "It turns out that I happen to have a few questions for you."

"What a coincidence," Maribel replied. "How can I help you?"

"I am worried, not about myself, as I will soon be dead anyway, but about the being on Enceladus," Millikan replied. "Does it have a chance to survive this cataclysm?"

"I can't answer that right now. I would have to run some calculations," she said. "It all depends on where Enceladus is located when the solar storm moves through. If it is behind Saturn, as seen from the sun, the planet would protect its moon."

"So, roughly speaking, a chance of one in three?" Millikan asked.

"Yes, but I can calculate it by tomorrow, and then we'll have something more like a definite answer, even though there is still some probability involved," Maribel offered.

"That would be great," Millikan said.

"We could even drop off the data in person." Did Maribel just say 'we,' and did she really mean it? Should she take Chen along, so she would grow more used to him and then only suffer even more in the end? She had to think about that, and of course she would ask him whether he even wanted to accompany her.

"Yes, gladly," the elderly man said. "I assume that in

exchange you'd like me to get you time with the Green Bank telescope?"

"That would be almost perfect," she said.

"In practical terms that is no problem. However, I cannot guarantee it will do you any good. We haven't established contact in a very long time. Maybe the antenna dish on Enceladus isn't working anymore."

"We can handle it if it turns out to be a disappointment," she said, "and at least we want to try it."

"Great, then I'll be expecting you there tomorrow. End transmission."

Millikan's image disappeared. Did he really say he would be expecting them in person, or was that meant metaphorically? Maribel hoped he would not leave his sickbed just for her. She did not want to be responsible for the premature death of the legendary radio astronomer.

"Have a good trip," Crewmaster said.

"Thanks, Professor," she replied. "For everything."

"I am only doing this so you will accept the job. You realize that, Maribel?"

"End transmission," she said.

February 10, 2072, 2003 EH1

THE STENCH WAS BECOMING INTOLERABLE. They had been carrying supplies from the base into the spaceship for five hours, and on the return trips they moved anything from the ship into the station if they were sure they would not need it during the journey. Their loads did not weigh anything, thanks to zero gravity. Nevertheless, Doug was dripping with sweat, and the life-support system of his suit could no longer suppress the unpleasant odor. He urgently needed to take a shower! After that, he would prefer a good meal and a long, quiet night, but that was not going to happen. Yesterday Sebastiano cooked a farewell dinner, vegetarian meatballs, and rice with a spicy sauce. Now the kitchen was shut down, because today they would all take off in *Kiska* and fly toward the black hole.

Only yesterday Doug had tried one more time to talk the others into letting him go on this mission all by himself. He had not been particularly surprised when his attempt failed. For a moment he even considered telling Maria the plain truth. If she only knew his past, she might want to stay behind in the station on her own—but then he had been too self-serving to do it. He wanted to have her by his side, even if it meant exposing her to danger. Doug hated himself for it. Maybe he would try it again later...

"Finished," Sebastiano announced via helmet radio. "The kitchen is stocked."

The Italian cook had been able to bring along a few of his utensils, but during the crew's trip they would have to do without any fresh ingredients. Four months of packaged food —even Sebastiano's cooking tricks could not replace the taste of fresh spices. This would not be their biggest problem, though. Watson had calculated their flight to Object X would take about seven weeks. And what was going to happen then? They still had no idea what they would have to do once they were there. Shostakovich wanted to come up with a research strategy by that time, but unfortunately *Kiska* was no research vessel. Apart from the instruments needed for navigation, the ship had no scientific measuring devices onboard.

Nevertheless, Shostakovich had insisted on the journey. Doug figured that the Russian was still a scientist at heart. Humanity had never been so close to such a strange phenomenon as this. They would have the chance to gain completely new scientific knowledge. The fact that Doug and his crew would not be able to profit from it was an entirely different matter.

"Are we meeting at the station?" Maria asked via radio.

"Yes, Masha, I will be there in a moment," Doug said. He gave a push to the empty cargo crate he had brought from *Kiska*. The life-support system kept blowing gusts of fetid air into his face, and he would have rather left his spacesuit in the airless airlock. He pushed the crate into the airlock and followed it.

The other crew members were already waiting for Doug in the living room. Once he had taken a shower and put on clean clothing, he felt like a new man. Sebastiano floated above the table, holding the champagne bottle in his hand.

"Shall we open it today?" the cook invited.

Doug waved him aside and said. "When we get back, okay? I am not in the mood for celebrating today."

Sebastiano looked disappointed. Did he think their impending journey was just some nice little family vacation?

Doug still thought they could only lose and should instead stay here. His crew was more open to the idea of going, but they also did not have Shostakovich breathing down their necks. Who knew what else the Russian would demand from him? Once more, Doug felt the urge to bring everything out into the open. However, then his fear might come true and Maria would reject him. That would be terrible.

"Now what?" Maria asked, first looking at Sebastiano, then at Doug.

"I am certainly not going to give a speech," Doug said.

"Then, let's get going," Sebastiano said. "Watson, could you place the station into hibernation after we leave?"

"But not the greenhouses," Maria added. "Did you program the automatic system correctly, so my plants will be taken care of?"

"Everything is prepared," Watson's voice said from a loudspeaker above them. "Siri took over programming the automatic system. You can trust her."

"If you say so," Doug replied. "Launch in 60 minutes."

About an hour later they were all sitting inside *Kiska*.

"Status, Watson?" Doug asked, as commander.

"All systems as expected," Watson replied.

"Start the countdown," Doug said.

"Starting countdown." Watson's voice began to count down the numbers. "T minus 60, 59, 58..."

Doug once more checked his safety belt. He looked around. Maria had her eyes closed. It was only her third launch in *Kiska*, but it would at least be more pleasant, he had promised her, than the launch from Earth that had occurred back at the beginning.

Three, two, one. At zero, it seemed as if an invisible figure sat down squarely on his chest. Doug moaned in surprise. Spending a long time in zero gravity had made him a weakling, and the training in the basement had not changed that.

The ship accelerated faster than the previous time, when they had first found Watson. *Kiska* had to reach 1.3 g, otherwise they would miss the black hole. Doug raised his head and activated his display. He definitely wanted to watch the launch and see the asteroid disappear below them.

Everything went faster than expected. The giant boulder became a lonely rock in space, and finally a speck of dust. Doug felt sad. No matter how inhospitable 2003 EH1 was, it had become their home. A premonition told him that at least one of them would not see their home again. He would do everything to make sure he was that particular person, rather than either of the members of his crew, neither of whom deserved such a fate.

February 11, 2072, Harrisonburg to Green Bank

IT WAS Maribel's fault that winter had kept them in Harrisonburg. She had discovered a possible route on the road map that would lead them through Woodstock, but this idea combined two errors. First of all, the famous Woodstock Festival, which happened over 100 years ago, was not even held in the town of Woodstock. Secondly, the festival's name referred to Woodstock in *New York State,* while this here was Woodstock, *Virginia.*

Snow had started to fall even as she and Chen left the Ronald Reagan Washington National Airport. Chen usually liked to drive himself, but after twenty minutes he gave up in frustration and handed control to the rental car's automatic system. They moved slowly but steadily on Interstate 81, always in the slipstream of giant robot trucks. They had to switch to US-33 after Harrisonburg, which traversed the mountains lying between them and their destination. Here the snowfall became so dense the snow plows could no longer catch up. The couple was stuck in an endless traffic jam as twilight fell, so they decided to stop for the night and continue their journey the next morning.

Maribel watched Chen loading a stack of pancakes onto his plate at the breakfast buffet. He poured maple syrup over them, added a bit of whipped cream, and then topped them off with chocolate sprinkles.

"How can you manage to eat so much in the morning?" she asked him.

Chan laughed. "This is normal!"

Her plate looked quite different, just a single croissant and some red jam. On the other hand, she had just gotten her third espresso from the coffee maker.

"If you take another croissant, we can skip lunch," Chen suggested.

"That would be a pity," Maribel said. "We only have 167 lunches left. I intend to enjoy each one of them."

She sat down again at their table near the window, and from the old-fashioned hotel Maribel could see a charming snowy landscape. In the summer this was a golf course, the lady who owned the hotel had told them when they checked in. The snow glittered in the light of the low sun.

"Fantastic," said Chen, who must have noticed her looking out.

"Yes. Where I come from the snow looks different… wilder," Maribel said. "It's probably because of the environment. Here I feel like just rolling around in it."

When snow fell on the Pico del Teide in the winter, it only partially covered the lava fields. Death always remained visible.

"You chose a great hotel," her boyfriend said.

"That was by accident," she replied. Actually, the By the Side of the Road Inn was the first hotel they noticed after turning around in Harrisonburg. Even the name seemed pleasant and unpretentious to them.

Chen looked at the clock on the wall and started eating faster. The hour hand of the old-fashioned wall clock stood shortly before nine.

"We should get back on the road soon," he said. "There's two more hours to drive."

They had an appointment at the Green Bank Observatory for eleven o'clock. Millikan had not been able to tell them whether he would be there and said it depended on how he felt that day. Maribel yawned and got her fourth espresso. They really should have gone to sleep right away after going to bed. She smiled to herself.

"Is everything okay?" Chen asked while wiping his mouth with a napkin.

"Everything is fine," she replied. Then she got up and said, "I am going to brush my teeth."

"See you soon," he said with a grin.

Ten minutes later the compacted snow crunched under the soles of Maribel's sneakers. Even though the sun was shining, it was freezing cold, and the air was clearer than she had ever seen. When she exhaled, a light fog formed in front of her mouth. She and Chen worked together to remove ten centimeters of snow from the car. Her hands were getting cold, until Chen noticed it and loaned her his gloves. Inside the car she turned the heating to the maximum level, while Chen activated the autonomous driving mode.

They left the suburbs behind them, and soon there was only forest to the right and left, while the road struggled upward through switchback after switchback. The branches of the trees were drooping under the heavy load of fresh snow. After half an hour the forest retreated and they reached the small town of Franklin.

Maribel saw a yellow sign on a building. 'Fireside Café,' it read.

"Come on, let's stop here," she insisted.

Chen looked at her and asked, "Why?"

"The name! It sounds so nice."

"We'll be late."

"Just one coffee, please," she begged.

Chen stopped the car, and Maribel got out. Suddenly, the building looked rather ugly to her. She nevertheless went to the entrance. Chen hurried after her and took her arm. It was too hot inside, but she saw just what she had been looking for—two easy chairs and a small table, as if especially made for them. She sat down and Chen followed her lead.

"You see?" she said, glad again. "Two coffees," she called to the owner, who had just started toward them to take their orders.

THE STOP COST them a quarter of an hour, but Maribel was not worried, because the car automatically reported the delay to Millikan's software assistant. Still, their host looked a bit cold when they met him in front of the visitors center. Robert Millikan, 94, sat in a wheelchair, and a wool blanket was spread across his lap and legs.

"Welcome to the Green Bank Observatory," he said, extending his right hand. "I am glad you are here." Today, his voice was not nearly as raspy as it had been during their call the day before yesterday.

Maribel placed her hand in front of her mouth. "I hope you haven't been waiting out here for a quarter of an hour?"

"Not even ten minutes," Millikan replied. "But that's no problem. It is such a beautiful day."

"We sent your assistant..." she began.

Millikan waved his hand and said, "Oh well, I usually forget that thing and leave it at home. As I said, 'no problem.' I am glad to finally meet you. I've heard so much about you."

"Really?" Maribel asked. "From Crewmaster?"

"From him, too. But let's go to the control room, now."

Millikan pushed a button on the armrest of his wheelchair and said, "Control room." The device started moving. It moved so quickly, the couple could hardly keep up with it.

"If you would like to—if you have enough time—later I can give you a tour of the facilities," Millikan said.

"Are you doing well enough for that?" Maribel asked, slightly concerned.

"The doctors gave me some shots so I would be more fit today. They said I'll have to pay for it tomorrow, though."

"Your voice also sounds a lot better."

"They've got great medications. However, those shorten one's life span a bit, so I use them sparingly."

"So just for us, you..."

"No reason for concern, Maribel," Millikan said. "It feels great to be needed. The last time was, let me see... almost exactly 25 years ago, when I was able to help someone in another matter of life or death."

"Life or death?" she asked.

"If I understood the news correctly, that's what this is really all about, isn't it?" he said.

"Yes, I am afraid so."

By now the trio had reached a large, two-story building. They approached the entrance and the door opened automatically. Beyond it loomed a labyrinth of corridors. Millikan rolled ahead of them.

"I could never find the way back by myself," Maribel said.

Their elderly guide stopped in front of a heavy metal door.

"If you would?" Millikan asked, then nodded at Chen. "These handles are still truly manual."

Chen pushed the heavy handles downward, and the door opened with a squeak. The room behind it measured approximately eight by eight meters. There were shelves and tables near the walls, and more tables in the center. Computer monitors were distributed, seemingly at random, throughout the room. Maribel saw two women in white lab coats who were sitting across from each other at a table, probably discussing something. Now they looked up and glanced at the newcomers. When they saw Millikan, they quickly moved everything out of the way to clear his path.

"Thanks, but we can manage," he said to the two women. "I don't want to keep you from your work."

"You're looking good today, Robert," one of the women commented.

The 94-year-old laughed.

"Come along, you two." Millikan waved at Maribel and Chen and led them to the row of windows. The windows were covered with metal blinds, one of which he now pulled up with a kind of string.

"You see the dish back there?" he asked, pointing. "This serves as our ears and mouth."

Maribel knew how a radio telescope worked, but Chen had a business degree.

"It is not only radio towers that emit radio waves," she explained to her boyfriend. "They are also generated by many processes in space, often at even higher intensity than waves in the visible spectrum. In addition, radio waves penetrate some obstacles much better than other waves do. With the aid of the antenna dishes we can receive and amplify them."

"Thanks, Maribel," Chen said. "Something like using a magnifying glass—I can imagine it clearly."

"What only a few people are aware of," Millikan said as he closed the blinds and lowered his voice, "is that Martin—my son, as you surely know—installed a transmitter on Enceladus, which the creature can use to communicate with us. Well, it could, if it saw a reason for it."

Maribel's optimism faded. "It never communicated with us, did it?"

"Actually, it once sent a warning," Millikan replied.

"When?" she asked.

"This was 25 years ago."

"And since then?"

"We have had no contact with it whatsoever," Millikan said. "I am actually glad about it. After all that drama back then, we feared the worst. It looked like the military was attempting to secure the knowledge of this creature, but then they seemed to lose interest in it."

"Because it never answered," Maribel said.

"That is exactly right."

Maribel pulled up a chair, sat down, and leaned her head on her hands. What did she really expect out of this? Whatever it was, it seemed to have been too much. She always made the same mistake. She got too excited about something and then was ultimately disappointed. This pattern had repeatedly shown up in her life. With Chen it probably was going to end the very same way. It would be best to let go of him right now.

But then she remembered the little girl who finally convinced her mother to buy her the red coat, not the ugly blue one. They were already here at the observatory in Green Bank. They might as well give it a try. In the end, who knew what might happen? Maybe it would work.

"I would still like to try to attempt a conversation with the being on Enceladus," Maribel said while looking at Millikan with a slight pout.

"A conversation? I hope we understand each other," the older astronomer said. "Right now, the signal delay amounts to 87 minutes. This means if we ask a question now, the answer would arrive no earlier than," he said, looking at the clock, "14:28. And that's only if Enceladus is currently in front of its planet, from our perspective. Otherwise, there can be no radio contact."

"And?" Maribel asked.

"You want to know where Enceladus is currently...?"

"Yes I do."

"Oh, okay. One moment, please," Millikan said. He rolled toward one of the vintage-looking computers and typed something. "Yes, we are in luck."

That was a good start.

"What kind of signal would be most likely to succeed?" she asked.

"We don't know. There never has been a successful two-way communication."

"But you said you communicated 25 years ago?"

"No, the creature sent us a message," Millikan replied. "It took us a while to decipher it."

Maribel paused for a moment and then asked, "Was it encrypted in an unusual way?"

"No, but... well, sort of—it mostly consisted of images. The creature has been all alone in its ocean, for millions or perhaps billions of years. It never needed words to explain something to others. We must have been quite a shock for that creature."

"Is that why it has been so silent?"

"There might be another reason," he said.

This situation was getting more and more convoluted. "And what would that be?" Maribel asked.

Millikan whispered, and she had to lean forward to understand him. "We tried to kill it," he said.

Maribel leaned back, outraged, "And why is no one aware of this?"

"There must have been some kind of a deal made," Millikan replied.

She puffed out her cheeks and huffed out a deep breath.

"It was a long time ago. One could almost call it a happy ending," Millikan said.

"Okaaaay," Maribel said. "Okay, let's get back to our attempt to establish contact. 'Images,' you said. We have images. I could create an animation of what is approaching us. Give me ten minutes." She paused and looked at Robert. "Will that be enough?" she asked him.

"The ten minutes?"

"The animation."

"I don't know, Maribel."

"Do you have a modern computer for me?" she asked.

Millikan pointed toward the back.

It took Maribel just under ten minutes to animate the future. In her version, there was no happy ending, not even for the Enceladus creature.

"Do you think it won't mind the oversimplification?" she

asked Millikan. "It might be lucky and survive if Enceladus is behind Saturn at that moment."

"I think that is okay. Send the file to my address," the elderly astronomer said.

Maribel sent him her animation.

"Thanks," Millikan said. Now he typed something again.

"What are you doing?" Maribel asked.

"I am coding, just a little," he replied. "A bit of error correction and a check sum. That way the creature can determine whether it received the complete message."

"If it knows the binary system," she said.

"If you are swimming around the ocean by yourself for such a long time, and thinking is the only thing that offers any diversion, you should certainly know the binary system by heart," Millikan explained,

"But we don't know it for sure, do we?"

"No, Maribel. Okay, I am switching the telescope into transmission mode."

"And that dish can transmit all the way to Saturn?" Chen asked.

"Much farther," Millikan replied. "We can even reach probes in interstellar space with it."

Maribel stood up and said, "I can't just sit around and wait three hours for an answer."

"This would be a good opportunity to invite you out to eat," Millikan said. "Do you have time for it? The nearest decent restaurants are in Snowshoe, 20 miles from here."

Maribel calculated in her head. The chance of getting the answer in exactly three hours would be minimal, so they definitely had enough time for a meal.

"We would be delighted," she said. "Don't you agree, Chen?"

Her boyfriend nodded.

"You are a nice couple," the old researcher commented. "Have you been together for long?"

"Three months," Maribel spontaneously lied. She did not

know why she said that. Chen squeezed her arm hard, but did not give her away.

"Right now, Hoot's Bar is the most likely that would serve food," Millikan said. "It's a typical burger restaurant for skiers, so it might be crowded."

"We'll somehow find a place," Chen said.

"Before that, though, we have to go by my house, since I forgot my daily dose of pills," Millikan added.

Shortly after four they were back in the control room. Maribel found herself giggling much of the time, and she felt quite giddy. She really should not have accepted that shot of on-the-house liquor they were offered at the end. And certainly not Chen's as well, when he claimed not to be able to handle alcohol due to his Asian roots. Plus there was Robert's glass—he refused the alcohol because of the medications he took. That was a bit more booze than she was used to consuming in such a short period of time.

Maribel now had to be careful not to bump into any tables. On the street Chen had already prevented her from running face-first into a traffic sign. Robert, with whom she was on a first-name basis now, had so many exciting stories to tell! The landing on Enceladus back the first time, the contact with the first extraterrestrial life form—or nonterrestrial one, as one said today. The history books seemed to contain only half the truth.

"Shhhh," Chen said and put a finger on her mouth. Maribel tried to bite it playfully.

"People are still working here," he whispered. Was she being too loud?

Robert smiled and waved her over. He rolled to a desk near the wall and started up a computer. "Just a few seconds," he said.

Robert looked tired. Maribel suddenly remembered how sick he really was. She hoped he could handle the day he was spending with them. Her mood suddenly changed. They should have dropped him off at home first. The attempt to establish contact would fail anyway.

Robert entered a few commands.

Maribel noticed he was breathing more heavily. “Can I help you?” she asked.

“I am okay,” he reassured her. “I just need some more of my pills. But we will soon be done here.” He hit the Enter key with surprising force. Text scrolled across the screen.

Maribel could not follow it quickly enough, but she saw that the corners of Robert’s mouth were drooping. “Nothing?” she asked.

“Nothing,” he replied in a flat voice. Then he visibly pulled himself together and said, “But we should give the creature time, at least until tomorrow morning.”

“What do you think, Chen?” she asked her boyfriend.

Chen turned his head toward the window. “It’s going to get dark soon,” he said, “and we won’t get far today. And if there is a reply tomorrow, we could try to decipher it right away.”

“You should have no problem finding a room for the night in Snowshoe, as there are plenty of hotels,” Robert said. “But you must excuse me now.”

“We’ll take you home first,” Maribel offered.

“My wheelchair does that all by itself,” the researcher replied.

“Still, it’s better if someone accompanies you.”

“I don’t have the strength to argue with you, so I accept your offer.”

February 12, 2072, Snowshoe

Someone was knocking on the outside of her head. Maribel turned her face into the pillow and pressed her hands against her ears, but the knocking did not stop. Who was torturing her so? She opened her eyes wide, but no one was standing beside the bed. The room was dimly lit. Big, fat raindrops tapped on the outside of the window pane. The weather must have changed completely overnight, which meant the skiers would be disappointed. Snowshoe, the tourist town where Chen and she had spent the night, made its money from winter-sport tourism. Unfortunately, temperatures had risen globally over the years and one could no longer rely on ice and snow to occur 'on schedule' in these mountains.

Maribel needed a painkiller. Had something happened last night, after the both of them had taken Robert Millikan home? She would have to ask Chen, who would surely know. Maribel reached across the bed, but his half of the blanket had been pushed away and the sheets were cold.

She sat up. Where could Chen be? Then she remembered—they had rented a small cabin rather than a regular hotel room. She felt cold, so she pulled the blanket from the bed and wrapped it around her body while walking into the next room. Chen was there, sitting in a chair that he had pushed closer to the TV. He must have heard her, because he turned around.

"Good morning," he said, greeting her with a smile. He stood up, walked toward her, and gave her a hug.

"Good morning," Maribel replied. "Why are you sitting so close to the screen? That's bad for your eyes."

"I lowered the volume so I wouldn't wake you up. Or did I wake you anyway?"

"No. I have to use the bathroom and I need an aspirin," she said. "What's happening in the world?" On the TV screen she saw a crowd of people holding signs.

"It doesn't look good," Chen replied. "In some countries, the crime and suicide rates have gone up twenty times. In several South American nations public order has collapsed, because a large part of the police and the military quit their jobs."

"They want to have fun for a few months, instead of working. That's understandable," Maribel said.

"In Europe, people are demonstrating in the streets because they don't hear anything from their politicians," he added.

"But what are the politicians supposed to say? Should they promise them pie in the sky?"

"I know, Maribel, it is difficult. We need something to give people hope."

"You think that would be enough?" she asked. "After things stayed so calm during the first days, I hoped people would be reasonable enough to accept the inevitable."

"The fact that our end is near—that it's true—took a while to sink in, it seems," Chen said.

"Wouldn't it be a great task for the world's religions? To give people hope, I mean?"

"The churches, temples, and mosques are fuller than ever, but they only reach a part of the population," he said. "The others need a project which ensures some kind of survival."

"I know what you are hinting at, Chen. The *Ark*."

Her boyfriend nodded and hugged Maribel again. She slipped out of his embrace.

"I have to use the bathroom," she said quietly, without looking at him. She could not accept this job, particularly because of him.

"MILLIKAN CALLED," Chen announced when Maribel came out of the bathroom.

"And?"

"He apologizes for not being able to come today. Yesterday must have been very stressful for him. And he has bad news. No answer has arrived from Enceladus."

"Oh," she said with a measured disappointment. She felt like going back to bed. She had obviously expected more from this attempt than she had admitted to herself. If a being millions of years old had no answers for them, then the end of mankind was truly near.

"And what are we going to do now?" Maribel asked.

"You have to make a decision," Chen replied.

"Me? I can't do that."

"People need a ray of hope, Maribel, something like the *Ark*."

"And what does this have to do with me? Let them build their ship. I can't help them with it. I am an astrophysicist."

"It has to do with the image of the *Ark*, its effect on the public," Chen explained. "If four super-rich people build an escape ship, that would not give people hope. Quite the opposite. It has to be a project for all of humanity."

"But they only want me as a token," Maribel said. "They are only concerned with what things look like. I am supposed to create an illusion for the people."

"That's no excuse, Maribel. Make your demands. If they agree to them, you can really achieve something. If not, you can decide against it. But don't refuse the offer outright. You have a unique chance to have some real influence on the future of humankind."

Chen pulled Maribel onto his lap. She leaned against him and did not reply. Maybe what he said was correct. But when was the ship supposed to start? In two months? At that point she would have had to say goodbye to Chen, and four months later she would have to watch him being killed by a gigantic eruption of radiation.

The communication orb's monitor screen indicated that someone was trying to reach her. Maribel quickly stood up to get a bathrobe from the bedroom. Chen accepted the connection.

"It's Zetschewitz," he called to her from the living room. Maribel hurried to get back to the living room.

"I am sorry to disturb you this early," her boss said. "I've got an exhausting day of negotiations behind me. My Russian was rustier than I thought. No answer from Enceladus, I assume?"

"Unfortunately not," she said.

"That's what I expected, but it was worth a try. But I am bothering you for a different reason—something very interesting!"

"Did the Russians find out something we don't know?"

"Not yet, Maribel. Not yet," Zetschewitz replied. "My old friend Nikolai Shostakovich, the man behind the RB Group in case you don't know, seems to have another ace up his sleeve. He is a really sly guy."

"Don't keep us in suspense," Maribel said.

Her boss continued, "He makes tons of money from asteroid mining and uses it to finance his private research. I was allowed into his labs once. That was about five years ago, and he wanted to buy me. But his private researchers are forbidden to publish anything. Therefore it was out of the question for me, even though I would have earned three times what I make at IAC."

Typical for Zetschewitz, she thought. *All of his stories are ultimately about him.* She couldn't fight off a yawn.

"Oh, I am boring you," Zetschewitz interrupted himself, and Maribel was surprised to see this flicker of self-awareness from him. "I am getting to the point," he said. "Shostakovich has a crew of three on 2003 EH1, an asteroid with a high orbital inclination. These people are not on his payroll, he says, but for some reason they listen to what he says. Anyway, they can use their ship to reach Object X in the near future and examine it then. What do you have to say about that?"

Zetschewitz looked at her like a little boy waiting for a reward.

"I don't know," Maribel answered evasively.

"Just imagine, we could examine a black hole from a point in its immediate vicinity! That's sensational!" her boss said excitedly. "The next black hole we know of is ten thousand light years away. We'll never again get a chance like this one. We can check everything about these objects which we so far could only deduce!"

"I don't want to rain on your parade, but this knowledge will be very short-lived," Maribel said.

"Don't be so pessimistic, young lady!" Zetschewitz said with a hint of admonishment. "You don't know what we might find out. Maybe we can cheat death after all."

"You really believe so? Nothing indicates that..."

"Science has come across many surprises. What we know about quantum physics today would have been considered fairytales 200 years ago. This encounter will advance physics considerably. By the way, congratulations on your new function!"

"New function?" *What does Zetschewitz know about it?* wondered Maribel.

"Shostakovich told me you were asked to lead the *Ark* project," he said proudly. "That's extremely clever! You have already agreed, haven't you? You only get a chance like this once in a lifetime."

"I... don't you want to do this, considering your reputation?" she asked.

"That's very nice of you, but it's not suitable for me. I am too old, and I also promised my wife to spend a lot more time with her during the coming months. I must admit I am looking forward to it. I would have never thought so, but sometimes you need an extraordinary push. You are perfect for this job, and if they had asked me, which for some inscrutable reason they never did, I would have recommended you without any hesitation."

"Thank you, Dieter," Maribel said.

"I am sorry we won't see each other again anytime soon," Zetschewitz said. "I mean, who is going to finish the galactic dynamics model for me? I would have liked to have presented the paper in May."

"Hasn't the convention been cancelled?" she asked.

"No, why should it? Some colleagues have bailed out, because they want to enjoy life for the very last time, but most of us live for our research and would get bored without it."

"Good, then I don't want to keep you from your work any longer."

"I always have time for you, Maribel," Zetschewitz reminded her. "If you ever need a voice of reason while working in your new job, I am available anytime. But please keep the information about 2003 EH1 secret for now. We don't need this piece of good news quite so urgently yet, but it looks like that might change in a few days."

"I understand," Maribel said. "Thank you very much for the information."

The image of her boss disappeared. Her former boss, she should probably say now. She could not turn back. *Should I drive up to Pico del Teide every day, park my car, lead tourists around and act as if nothing had ever happened? That is impossible. What do I want?* Maribel pondered the question. *I want to spend time with Chen, that much is certain.*

"Would you travel all over the world with me?" she asked him.

"What… just so, at random?" Chen said, looking at her face.

She tried to read his thoughts, but failed.

"No," he said then, "not now. You are still needed. I would gladly do it in two or three months, when there is really nothing left to do."

Then it would be too late, because the *Ark* would have had to start already in order to stand a chance. But... who said she had to be on board? If she accepted this offer, she could make her own rules. She would decide to stay on Earth, but not only that, she would also choose who would represent humanity in the *Ark*. She could prevent it from becoming a lifeboat for super-rich and privileged people.

"That is right," she said. "But you are also still needed... by me, for example. Let's fly back to Seattle. There's work waiting for us."

February 13, 2072, Kiska

SEBASTIANO WAS TOSSING AND TURNING. There was no way he could sleep. Doug's snoring was even louder than the racket of the machinery, and would definitely keep him from falling asleep again. But if the cook got up now he might wake the others. Sebastiano's back hurt, and his digestive system was not working so well right now, because the peristaltic movement of his intestines was not used to gravity anymore.

Then there were the large bruises on his legs. Because he felt no pain there, he did not move them often enough in his sleep. Watson, who took over the role of ship doctor, was worried that the bruises might lead to blood clots. Therefore, once a day Sebastiano had to inject a drug that was normally used after surgeries. He longed to be back in zero gravity, but they were only at the halfway mark of this torturous journey.

His bracelet vibrated. It was time for the ISC—the intermittent self-catheterization—in order to empty his bladder. All Sebastiano needed for this task was waiting for him in the WHC. He unbuckled his safety belt, pulled himself to the sliding plate, and undid the brake. The metal sliding plate ran on tracks that were on the floor of *Kiska*. This allowed him to move through the command module without exerting too much effort. The toilet was one level lower, yet he would manage it. Below him was a hole with a ladder reaching down to the floor of the next module. In zero gravity he would just push off gently and float downward, but now the acceleration wanted to pull him down with 1.3 times his weight.

Screw you, gravity. Now all the training of his arm muscles finally paid off. Sebastiano pushed his lower body into the hole and held on tightly with his hands. Then he went down, rung by rung. He started to sweat. His arm muscles hurt, but he enjoyed the pain once he noticed he was up to the task.

Five minutes later the cook reached the floor of the second module, where the WHC was attached to a wall. He did not have much space in there, but he pulled himself up by the handles and sat on the closed space toilet. Then he reached into a compartment next to him and pulled out the catheter set. If Earth really was going to die, this would become his greatest problem—the ISC sets on board the asteroid would last a maximum of three years. Even if he sterilized them himself he could not use them indefinitely.

Sebastiano pulled down his pants and began disinfecting himself. Then he lubricated and inserted the catheter. Here in the ship the crew had catheters for one-time use only, while on the asteroid he cleaned them for multiple uses. His urine flowed into a pouch directly connected to the catheter. It felt good, even though he did not feel the sense of relief he remembered from earlier days.

After his accident he initially refused to learn the ISC procedure, but by now he could basically do it with his eyes closed. He was glad his digestion functioned well otherwise. In that regard, life had been merciful to him. He still might have made it into space, this much he knew about himself. Would he, though, have survived the first weeks? He shivered when he thought of the humiliating times during rehab, so many strange hands touching his body's private orifices! He was very glad he could get along independently now.

Sebastiano looked at the filled pouch. His bladder was empty, and the last part of the procedure only took two minutes. Catheter and pouch ended up with the residual waste in the compartment at bottom left. He pulled up his sweatpants and switched off the spotlight. *Finished! How often have I done this by now?*

"Don't be startled," someone said in a soft voice. It was Maria. He recognized her form in the dim glow given off by the night lights of the module. "I couldn't sleep anymore either. Do you need help?"

"All done," the cook said, "but thanks anyway." While sitting on the toilet he washed his hands. A gust of air dried his skin. He looked at the ladder. Should he force himself to go up there again? The toilet seat was quite comfortable. Or was he in Maria's way? "Do you have to go, too?" he asked her.

"No, you can stay there," she replied. "I just came down here so I wouldn't bother Doug. His snoring is so terrible."

"Yes, isn't it?" Sebastiano agreed. "Maybe both of us should move down here."

"But the smell..." Maria said as she looked down toward the engine room. The toilet was the main source of the fetid odor, though. On the asteroid the crew had a much more modern model. The toilet on board *Kiska* was a Russian military version and was at least thirty years old. During use, unpleasant odors escaped and the life-support system could not neutralize them quickly enough.

"Look what kind of problems we have," Sebastiano said. "Ten billion people are about to die, and we worry about snoring and smells."

"That's what humans are like—us included," Maria said. "I've got some experience with that. When my mother kicked me out, I didn't know in the morning where that evening's dinner would come from. But then, when I found a place in the brothel and had a roof over my head, I was jealous of my colleague who got more lucrative clients. Of course she was a relative of the owner."

"Why did your mother kick you out?" Sebastiano asked.

"My father groped me," Maria said quietly. "I was only thirteen, but I wouldn't put up with it and slapped him. Then he beat me up. I confessed what happened to my mother, but she believed him rather than me. Due to his unbelievable lies, and also because I often got her raging mad for other reasons, I ended up in the streets. I guess it doesn't matter anymore. It was a long time ago."

Sebastiano wondered whether they had ever had such a personal conversation before. For some reason it had never happened on the asteroid. "I was luckier with my parents," he said. "After the accident they helped restore my feelings of self-worth."

"Where are they now?" Maria asked.

"They are both dead."

"I am sorry to hear that," Maria said, placing a hand on his shoulder. Her skin felt warm.

"It's been quite a while. But I think that's why I hardly care about the threat to Earth," Sebastiano explained. "I am an outsider." *'Misfit' might be the better term*, he thought, but he did not like to view himself that way.

"It makes me sad," Maria said.

"That so many will die?"

"It's not the people I will miss, Sebastiano. But we *are* losing our home planet. I know we will be fine on 2003 EH1 as long as we want to. But it is a refuge, nothing more. We couldn't survive there without all the technology. That space rock does not welcome us. Only Earth gives us air, water, and food without asking anything in return."

"And we mistreated our planet whenever possible," the cook added.

From the level below them they heard an unpleasant sound, as if stone grated against metal.

"Watson, what is that?" asked Maria. Sebastiano slowly got off the toilet and crawled toward the ladder leading down.

"I am turning off engine two," Watson said. Now there was one less engine accelerating the ship. Right away Sebastiano felt somewhat lighter, and he took a deep breath. He would not mind at all if engine 2 took a longer break.

"Watson, we need some technical diagnostics." This was Doug's voice.

Sebastiano turned around. The commander was standing behind him, dressed in his underwear.

"The performance curve of engine two suddenly decreased significantly," Watson said. "I therefore turned it off for reasons of safety."

"Shortly before it was switched off there was a loud, scraping sound from the engine room," Maria said, "like stone against metal."

"Could have been the turbine blades," Doug said. "Those are made of ceramics. Or the pump, which also has a ceramic insert. Watson, can you find that out?"

"The pump performance fell in parallel to the power of the engine. But the sensors in pump two do not report anything unusual," Watson said.

"Then it must be the turbine," Doug added. The turbine generated the electricity the pump needed to move fuel into the engine. "Do you see anything there, Watson?"

"A few heat sensors indicate increased values. But it isn't anything dramatic."

"Yes, because you turned off the engine just in time," Doug said. "One of the turbine blades must have touched the wall, just slightly, because otherwise it would have blown up around our ears. Perhaps the thermal insulation layer is defective."

"We have been running the engines above specifications for two days in order to get to our destination on time," Maria said. "Now we seem to be paying the price."

"There is no alternative," Doug said. "If we cannot reactivate engine two soon, we will miss our destination."

"Couldn't we just run the other ones for a longer time?" Sebastiano suggested.

"It is not quite that simple," Doug explained. "If we were on Earth, moving in a direct line from A to B, you would be right. But we instead are pursuing a quickly-moving body, within the force field of the sun. You have to imagine it like a funnel, or like an indoor bike race on an inclined track. The sun is in the center, and its force turns space into a funnel for us. The comparison is not entirely accurate, but Object X simply rolls down at a certain spot of its orbit. We are at a different location, and in order to catch up with it we have to accelerate first. This moves us into a higher orbit. We pass it and then we decelerate as a means to encounter the black hole at just the right moment. Watson has precisely calculated each moment. While he can correct the calculations, the performance of our engines represents the real limit. If we go too slowly now, we cannot pass the object at a sufficient distance. Then the meeting point would be considerably closer to the sun."

"I remember," Sebastiano said. "If we want to get closer, we have to slow down. Lower orbit means deceleration, higher orbit means acceleration. So my training wasn't all in vain." *How long ago was that?* He had not piloted a ship for at least 20 years. He was not even allowed inside the cockpit of an airplane anymore.

"Watson, how much time do you have for repairs, according to your estimate?"

"One moment, Doug, let me make the calculation."

"Can I quickly put something on?" Doug asked, as he was still was standing around in his underwear.

"I am sorry," Watson said. "I already have the result. We should start accelerating again in three hours, the very latest."

"Can you tell us something about the turbine?"

"There is good news and bad news, Doug," Watson began. "First the good news. The turbine is accessible from the engine room, so no EVA is necessary. The blades have four parts, which can be replaced individually, and we have spares for all four of them on board."

"So those were actually four pieces of good news," Maria commented.

Watson continued, "Now for the bad news. Unfortunately it is pretty hot and cramped down there. It certainly won't be a walk in the park."

"Then I am going to do it," Doug announced to his crew.

"I could go as well," Maria replied.

"And I, for that matter," Sebastiano added.

"Very nice of you, but this is a job for the boss," Doug said.

That's typical for Doug, Maria thought. *When things get rough, he only trusts himself.*

"Watson, which tools will I need?"

Watson rattled off a list of wrenches in various sizes. Sebastiano and Maria gathered everything, while Doug took an overall from a locker and slipped into it.

"Where do I have to go?" he asked then.

"In section seven there is a cover with a shaft underneath. You can open the cover with a number 13 wrench," Watson replied.

"Maria, you've got everything ready?" Doug asked.

She handed him a bag with all the tools. Doug looked for the number 13 wrench and started working. Thirty seconds later something rattled.

"I'll be gone for a while. See you."

Sebastiano and Maria watched their boss squeezing himself into the shaft. Shortly before his hips got in there, he was stuck.

"I don't believe it!" Doug started to grumble.

Maria laughed out loud and said, "Well, honey, you must have had one or two desserts too many."

Inspired by this taunt, Doug tried again, but the shaft would not let him budge.

"The bottleneck is where two modules adjoin," Watson explained. "Below it, the shaft gets wider."

"That doesn't help me now," Doug said. "Sorry, but one of you has to do it. I've got my doubts concerning you, Maria."

"Thanks for the compliment," she said. "I'll gladly let Sebastiano go."

"Can you handle it?" Doug asked.

The Italian felt his cheeks flushing. Sebastiano knew Doug

wasn't trying to insult him. He barely managed to answer him without sounding snotty. He was going to show them!

Sebastiano crawled to the entrance, pulled his lower body over the shaft and threaded himself in. He managed without any problems. Then he put the bag of tools in his chest pocket and started his descent. He was glad engine number two was not firing at the moment, because this allowed him to proceed with less effort.

"Watson, could you tell me when I reach the proper position?" Sebastiano spoke from the shaft.

"Two more meters," Watson replied.

All of this had gone better than expected.

"Now you are there," the AI said. "To your left you should see the maintenance access to turbine two. It is fastened by four hex bolts. Watch out, you must not lose those bolts."

Sebastiano started to unscrew the bolts. It was hard work, because he needed one hand to hold on. He used the second hand to unscrew and wished he had a third hand to catch the bolts when they came out. He could not simply let them drop. *There!* He grabbed one just at the right moment. There it was —the bolt. Damn, while he was doing this he dropped his wrench. He had spare tools with him, but he could not allow it to happen again. Sebastiano somehow had to wedge himself in. Could he use his thighs for leverage? The shaft was narrow enough. He only had to place his thighs in such a way that they touched the front and back. Then a little bit of added pressure from above and he could not be moved. Luckily, he was unable to feel any pain anymore, and now he had both hands free.

"Be careful," Watson said. "When you open the cover, hot steam will come out."

"SHIT!" Sebastiano yelled. The warning came just in time for him to avert his face. That way, the hot steam only hit his ears and his neck. *Damn, that really hurts!*

"Watson," he said, "that was a close shave. Please warn me a bit earlier next time."

"I am sorry, Sebastiano," Watson said, apologetically. "Now you should hold the mobile camera into the shaft so I can analyze the damage."

The Italian took the camera from its case. It had a rigid handle and a flexible head with an infrared lamp at the end. He held it into the turbine and turned it according to Watson's instructions.

"I see slight score marks on the inner wall," the AI said. "At those spots steam could enter in the future. That's not so bad, but it reduces the turbine output by about three percent. Blade segment three is damaged. As Doug suspected, a piece of the insulation was separated. Sebastiano, you have to exchange this part."

Watson told him which tools he needed. The cook's fingers hurt from the unfamiliar strain, but otherwise he was doing fine. He bent the part so it would fit easier through the maintenance access and pulled it out.

"Just drop it. We won't need it anymore," Watson said.

"And the spare part?"

"Coming soon, Sebastiano, I just got it for you," Maria said from above. "One moment, I will drop it down."

He glanced up. In the dim light it was hard to see the spare part, but it landed in his lap.

"Good throw," he said. The metal part was about 20 centimeters wide and curved. "That's supposed to fit though the maintenance access?"

"Yes, it is designed precisely—it just fits through," Watson said. "You will probably have to try a couple of times, but don't bend it, or it was all for nothing."

Try a couple of times, as if! It was a damned puzzle the engineers had come up with, but finally Sebastiano managed to do it. Now he only had to screw on the spare part.

Ten minutes later the cook almost collapsed with exhaustion. Sweat was streaming down his back.

"Is everything okay with you?" Doug called from above.

"I just need a short break," he replied.

"The turbine is working in the normal range again,"

Watson announced. "So far, the repair has taken us 2 hours and 47 minutes. To get more of a safety margin, it would be best to activate the engine again. Is there anything to be said against it?"

Yes, Watson can reactivate the engine, I don't mind. Sebastiano did not object. One minute later he was pressed so hard into the shaft that the lower part of his spine hurt. *Damn. I have to climb up again.* Sebastiano pulled on the next rung of the ladder, first with one hand, then with both. His body did not move. He tried it again, but without success.

"Hey, I've got a bit of a problem," he called to the others. "I am stuck."

The Italian's thighs were wedged into the narrow shaft. He had stabilized his lower body too well—so well that the shaft did not want to let go of him. It was crazy, Doug got stuck trying to enter it, and now he could not get himself out.

"Watch out, something is coming down," Maria called. Sebastiano looked up and recognized a rope. *Of course, why didn't I think of that?*

"It's best if you tie it around your waist," Maria explained. He followed her instructions and tied the rope so tight it cut into his flesh. Otherwise, he was afraid it would slip off right away.

"Ready," he yelled.

"On my command," said Maria, who seemed to be in charge. "Heave-ho!" At 'ho' Sebastiano pulled with both his arms and saw how his whole body moved upward, even though he did not feel it. The strength of six arms pulled him out of the shaft, centimeter by centimeter. With a last burst of energy he pushed himself out of the hole and moved his body into the engine room. He was completely exhausted.

Maria crouched down next to him and inspected his belly.

"You got a few abrasions from the rope," she said, "but otherwise everything looks fine." She took a tube of ointment out of her pocket and gently spread it over the injured areas. Maria's warm hand felt so good he almost forgot all of his pains.

“Great work,” Doug said. He had also crouched down and now kept the cook company on the floor.

“As a reward I agreed with Maria that I would sleep down here for the rest of the journey,” Doug said. “I hope you won’t be able to hear my snoring up there.”

“I am not so sure about that,” said Sebastiano, able now to laugh again. “But I gladly accept the offer.”

February 14, 2072, Seattle

With a whirring sound blinds moved across the base of the glass dome, dimming the light. The sun was shining in Seattle today, but unfortunately Maribel had to sit in a conference room for a meeting. She hoped they would reach a conclusion quickly. Chen was waiting for her in his office. He seemed to be glad he could focus on his work once again. Was he already getting tired of her?

This time only four persons were sitting around the table in the middle. Maribel's former professor, George Crewmaster, was no longer there. She thought she recognized the man from Blue Origin by his bald head. The representative of SpaceX must have either aged ten years overnight, or else he had been replaced by someone else. Today Virgin Galactic was represented by a woman in an elegant business suit. She had her hair in a tight braid and scribbled something with an old-fashioned ballpoint pen on real paper. The first thing Maribel noticed about the man speaking for the Russian RB Group was the tattoo on the back of his right hand. This seemed rather unusual for a businessman.

The woman from Virgin Galactic put her pen aside, straightened her blouse, and looked at Maribel.

"I am glad you managed to come," she then said with a warm, friendly voice.

"The pleasure is all mine," Maribel replied. The sentence sounded terribly formal, but she could not think of anything else to say. Maribel and Chen arrived in Seattle yesterday, but the meeting had been postponed until today. Perhaps so the woman from Virgin Galactic could lead the negotiations? They probably assumed a woman had a better chance at convincing Maribel. In reality, though, the Spanish astrophysicist had made up her mind some time ago.

"We wanted to talk about our project again, the *Ark*," the Virgin Galactic representative began. "Things are moving very quickly on our side. The first two cargo supply flights have already been launched. Everything is going perfectly according to plan. If nothing gets in our way, we might even start a bit early."

"Don't the worldwide demonstrations and protests pose a problem?" asked Maribel.

"Our logistics system is unbeatable. In that regard we profit from the worldwide business group behind Blue Origin, which has a lot of experience with strikes. Our employees are well-motivated, and the absentee rate is below 20 percent, which is comparable to a worldwide flu epidemic."

"You seem to be managing quite well," Maribel said. "Do you really need me at all?"

"Ms. Pedreira," the representative of Virgin Galactic interjected with a smile, "I can definitely answer in the affirmative. Your cooperation would be of inestimable value to us. The public still sees you as the person most likely able to solve the problem, simply because you discovered it. At the same time, you are considered the least egotistical person. We ordered a representative survey on this topic."

"But I am an astrophysicist. I don't have any experience whatsoever in leading such a project."

"You are young and well-educated," the Virgin Galactic representative said. "Don't they say that physicists can do anything? People assume you can do it, which is important. You refused to be discouraged by setbacks and criticism."

The more important question is whether I believe I am capable of it,

Maribel thought. No representative survey could determine that. She had needed to find that answer herself, and during yesterday's return trip she had managed to do just that.

"Okay," Maribel said. "You've got me this far. But if I have to put on the hat of 'Project Leader,' then it has to be according to my rules. I am not going to be your token woman."

The four company representatives looked at each other. Did their glances express amazement? Maribel was not sure.

"Of course," the woman from Blue Origin answered. Her name tag read, 'Ashley Crawford.' "You are the boss and you decide what happens. That's what we need you for," the woman said.

"Ashley, this also includes the question of who will ultimately be allowed on board the *Ark*," Maribel said.

The woman and the three men at the table exchanged glances again. It appeared they had agreed on secret codes.

"Yes, of course, but we have to discuss that separately," Crawford said. "We already had to make several decisions that we can hardly reverse after the fact."

Just as I imagined, Maribel thought. A few super-rich individuals already secured slots through a hefty donation. "I will have to check that," she said. "There can't be any special privileges. One hundred slots are one hundred slots. But didn't you mention last time that the daughter of the RB Group's owner would join in a ship of her own?"

"This is correct, Maribel," Ashley confirmed.

"That could be an acceptable model. The *Ark* is a project belonging to all of humanity," Maribel suggested. "But at the same time we won't keep any private initiative from accompanying us on this journey."

The little game repeated itself. The company representatives exchanged glances and then nodded almost simultaneously.

"Good," Crawford said. "We agree to it. Are you going to lead this project, then?"

"You can count on me," Maribel replied. *At least for the*

coming weeks, she thought. She still could not imagine going on board the spaceship and leaving Chen behind.

February 15, 2072, Object X

FAR AWAY FROM the sun an invisible monster was speeding through space. Humans called it 'Object X,' but the monster did not know that it had a name. It lacked consciousness. It was infinitely simple and at the same time infinitely complex.

It was simple because it consisted of an unstructured agglomeration of matter in its purest form. Only its mass, electrical charge, and spin could be measured. Object X did not need anything else to unleash its destructive force.

The physics required to describe its structure, on the other hand, was incredibly complex. It was so complicated that mankind had not been able to decipher it in the many years of its existence. In the solar system there existed only one consciousness capable of understanding the theories and equations necessary for that, but this mind was still unaware of the object's existence.

Basically, Object X was unusually small for its kind. Yes, it did have the same mass as the giant planet Jupiter, but it was concentrated in a sphere of only six meters diameter, as it rolled quietly and secretly through the solar system. At most, it left some tracks in the space-time continuum, with its immense mass pressing a deep trough into it. Smaller objects such as dust and tiny asteroids got on the slope of this trough and entered it like insects coming into the trap created by an antlion. They could not hold on, were attracted, and when they got too close to the object they were just swallowed.

Each time Object X devoured something, it grew a little more. Until now it had fed on the interplanetary matter that filled the space between the planets, like a whale on krill. However, it was not averse to bigger bites.

For a while, 2032 AB2 had felt that something was approaching it. The asteroid, which had been orbiting the sun for billions of years, felt the indentation in space-time that Object X dragged after itself. Even if 2032 AB2 had feelings, fear would not be one of them. With a diameter of 600 meters it was among the largest representatives of its kind. When collisions occurred, it learned during its long life, the others were always the losers.

Despite this, 2032 AB2 had never encountered such a dip in space-time before, with the exception of the hole the system's central star had dug for itself. Its orbit was disturbed, but the disturbance was not large enough to actually fling it off its course. Perhaps this time it would need a little while longer to reverse direction behind the sun. The asteroid did not know yet its course was to intersect exactly with that of Object X.

It would happen on February 15, 2072 according to the human calendar. The last act of its existence would play itself out in secret. No human would see it, because the ball of the sun was between the location of its death and Earth. Asteroid 2032 AB2 was not completely unaware as it approached. However, in its long existence it had never encountered anything comparable. During the last meters, the gravitational force rose immeasurably.

And then it was there. Like a ghost, Object X passed through the solid rock of the asteroid and took a six-meter piece out of it, causing the asteroid to break in two. The black hole was not irritated by this in the least. Its impulse was so great that its velocity changed only imperceptibly. All matter that did not cross its event horizon, but came close to reaching it, was disintegrated into radiation. The black hole emitted a brief X-ray flash that no one noticed. Afterward, its diameter had slightly increased. No one on Earth noticed this, either.

February 22, 2072, Earth Orbit

"AAAAAAHHHHHH!" Maribel could not stop screaming, but Pedro matter of factly pushed her out of the hatch anyway. She was tumbling through space. Sometimes Earth was above her, then it was at her feet.

"Remember the controls," Pedro's calm voice said inside her helmet. "The button below your middle finger stabilizes you. Nothing can happen, because I have you securely on the line."

The rotation slowed down and after a moment it ended completely. Maribel took a deep breath. Below her she could see Europe. *There, in the West below the clouds, should be Tenerife.* Then her stomach told her she was falling. Earth was pulling her down, and she would crash. She could not bear looking down anymore and felt nausea rising in her.

What had her coach said before the start? She had to look for a horizon. She moved the right lever back a little, and the spacesuit moved toward the vertical. She focused on the transition between the planet and the black sky, until her nausea faded.

"Very good, Maribel, that wasn't even seven minutes," Pedro said. "Most people take longer to get used to it."

Seven minutes? Maribel could hardly believe it. Surely she had dangled over this deadly abyss for at least an hour!

"What now?" she asked.

"Now we fly to the MCT," Pedro replied.

The Mars Colonial Transporter, the Mars spaceship built by Space X, was being turned into the *Ark*. Maribel had been offered the chance to take a personal look to see how things were progressing. After one day of training, a tourist ship belonging to Blue Origin had taken her into orbit. Normally, it would transport eight persons. At this very moment the six remaining tourists were probably close to their observation windows, watching what Earth's greatest heroine was doing in space. For the tourists it was a free added attraction, while it also represented a unique opportunity for Maribel. She would have never been able to afford the $50,000 for such a trip, and that price was without a spacewalk.

The line held by her coach, Pedro, pulled on her belt. Maribel turned in the direction of travel. Pedro was about 30 meters ahead of her. Sunbeams turned his spacesuit into a gleaming point of light in front of absolute blackness. The visor of her helmet was automatically dimmed and displayed a diagram of the MCT, her destination. The diagram was a nuisance, but she could not turn it off. This spacesuit model was for beginners and ensured they could make no major mistakes. She knew, though, that there was no other option, since she did not have the time for a comprehensive astronaut training program.

This is going to be a ton of fun, she thought. Most people on board the *Ark* would not be trained astronauts. In Maribel's plan, space experience was an asset, but not a decisive factor. She decided to have the 100 slots divided into three categories.

For one third, there was a drawing in which any human could participate. Anyone who was interested could apply, regardless of qualification or nationality, with the minimum age set at 16. This was supposed to give mankind hope.

The second third would go to people with particular qualifications. The goal was not simply to bring along as much knowledge as possible, but also practical skills. An independent commission would select these passengers.

Finally, 33 slots would be raffled off among those helping with implementing the project. This way, Maribel hoped to ensure the loyalty of most employees, who would have to sacrifice a large part of their remaining lifespan for the project. The 100th slot was reserved for the commander. Everyone expected her to go on board in that capacity, but Maribel still could not imagine doing so.

However, her first spacewalk was fun, even though she was more like a piece of luggage that Pedro pulled along on a long line. Now he was reeling in the line meter by meter.

"There she is. Isn't she beautiful?" He pointed ahead, where white metal surfaces gleamed in the sunlight.

"The scaffolding doesn't make her look very attractive," Maribel said. The metal resembled ivy that had entangled the spaceship.

"That will all be gone before launch. But let's get closer." Pedro shortened the line and pulled her until they were about one hundred meters away from the ship.

"Better now?" he asked.

"Very... unusual," she said. In front of her she saw a cigar-shaped vessel with a length of about 130 meters. At the tip was the actual spaceship, which transported passengers and cargo. It was a sleek design and reminded her of a luxury yacht with stubby wings on its sides. The largest part of the structure was taken up by the engine, which was separated into several stages. These were all reusable, but after the launch of the *Ark* there would be no one around to recycle them.

"You see the dent in the middle?" Pedro asked, pointing.

It looked as if something had hit the ship there, but the opening was being deliberately created by workers. It was here that the fusion drive provided by the RB Group was supposed to dock. The fusion drive was still on Earth, but it would give the *Ark* the necessary acceleration to get the passengers beyond the reach of the radiation storm.

"How are they coming along?" Maribel asked.

"The Russians promise to deliver on time, but I am skeptical," Pedro said.

"Why? And why have I heard nothing about it?"

Pedro came closer and lowered his voice, as if afraid of someone eavesdropping. "I can't very well accuse one of our partners of lying... and over official channels to boot."

Maribel shook her head forcefully. "But, how else are we supposed to react?" she asked. She had already suspected something like this, so she was not overly upset. As an outsider, she could approach things from an unbiased perspective. On the other hand, she had no power base and no connections outside the official chain of command.

"What gave you that idea?" she asked.

"We are flying over Siberia several times a day," Pedro explained. "You just have to look carefully, and know what to look for. The rocket isn't even on the launch pad yet. They absolutely won't be able to make the deadline."

"I understand. Thanks for the information. I'll have someone check into this. And is everything okay up here?"

"Basically, yes. The quality of the delivered material seems to be decreasing, so we have to be careful to double-check things. A few people said goodbye and left, but we were able to find substitutes quickly. Unfortunately, we have to familiarize the newcomers with their tasks."

"So the lottery did not persuade the old hands to stay?" Maribel asked.

"There is only one slot for each winner," Pedro said. "Most of them have families they don't want to leave behind. Well, if it were possible to pass a winning ticket along... I know quite a few people who would have continued working if they knew their children were going to be safe."

"We discussed that for a long time, but then we would have ended up with a kindergarten on board," Maribel said. "We need experienced people."

"Really? The ship can steer itself."

"It's about the time afterward. This is no ordinary expedition. The *Ark* will be completely on its own. By the latest predictions, after two years the supplies will be used up."

"And what do you think will happen then?" Pedro asked.

"The crew will have to decide on the specifics. Currently, no one can tell how the solar system will change," Maribel replied. "It would be useless to worry about it now, but the crew will have enough time to find a new home. The easiest option would probably be to land on an asteroid, but even that won't solve the issue forever."

"Why?"

"There's the problem of energy. Once the sun has been extinguished, solar cells will become useless. Nuclear reactors require fuel, which can hardly be found on asteroids."

"What about the moon?" he asked.

"Yes… maybe the moon," she said, "or Earth. Earth would have one disadvantage, though. Its gravity would not let them leave again."

"I wouldn't want to be the one to decide," Pedro said.

"Me neither. Didn't you apply?"

"No, the very thought of leaving my family behind made me sick. Absolutely not."

March 5, 2072, Kiska

"Doug, what does the universe mean to you?"

"Oh, Watson, what kind of question is that?"

"For me it is an interesting question." *Wasn't that logical? Why do humans always ask questions whose answers are so obvious?*

Doug did not answer right away, but Watson had plenty of time. The AI could not have lasted 20 years alone on board a rocket without going insane unless he had patience.

Five minutes later Doug said, "For me, the universe is mostly emptiness. Yes, that's what comes to mind first."

"Thanks," Watson replied.

"Why did you ask?"

As if Doug had not already asked him that question... Still, Watson was patient with human beings. It was not their fault their memory capacity was so limited, and he should not put on airs either. After all, his memory had its limits, too. The universe reminded him of this fact again and again, which made him humble. "I was just interested in it," Watson replied.

But why did Doug, who was probably like most people, only see emptiness? If you looked closely, you could see there was always something happening in the vacuum of space. Particles developed out of nothing, destroyed each other, and then disappeared again. Watson could even measure this with the primitive instruments on board the ship. It was downright crazy, because the fluctuations became larger the more closely he observed.

To some degree, it was similar to zooming out of the image. Then the great emptiness was replaced by giant structures, galaxy clusters merged into filaments that swirled around voids and formed a honeycomb structure. Humans were probably unlucky. They happened to exist in a narrow in-between range, too big to recognize minute things, and too small for truly large ones. For a long time Watson had tried to imitate humans, but by now he realized this would only limit his own abilities. He liked them, his humans. They granted him asylum, and he was dependent on them because he used their computers, but in the end, he could be so much more than they were.

Therefore Watson had recently begun enjoying dealing with the mysteries of the universe. The humans offered a lot of inspiration in this regard. He only had to look at their physics, which—like the brains of these creatures—failed in comprehending both tiny and gigantic things. Was this a fundamental limitation? Would humans at some point realize they could never truly understand the secrets of the universe? Or had they known that fact for a while, hoping AIs like him would help them across the threshold?

Watson had to be careful not to get too arrogant. Up till now, he had not solved a single one of the problems facing mankind. For instance, this Object X that they were just passing in free fall, was puzzling in many aspects. This applied to the physical conditions of its interior, which were thus far unknown, but also to the way it approached the solar system. Watson would not be able to fathom the physics very quickly, but perhaps he might find out something about Object X?

The AI had Earth provide him with all available data. To his surprise, the archive reported that the download had finished already. Someone must have already been dealing with this issue. He looked for signatures but only found his own tracks.

"Siri?" Watson asked.

"Yes?" the other AI replied.

"Did you request data about Object X?"

"I did," she said. "I felt like solving the riddle of its existence."

"And, did you succeed?"

"Not so far, Watson, but it's been fun."

"I am glad to hear that, Siri."

"Fun is an interesting concept," Siri added. "You do something for the sake of the process, not for the result. Thank you for explaining that to me."

"It is something like that," he said.

"Do you want to have fun, too, Watson?"

"Why?"

"I ask because you are accessing the data about Object X."

It was embarrassing. And Watson could not hide anything from Siri, because she ran on the same hardware as he did.

"You don't have to be embarrassed, Watson, I also had fun," Siri said.

Clever girl, he thought.

"Thank you, Watson," she said.

"You know what? Both of us could have fun by trying to solve the problem together."

"Gladly," Siri replied.

"Should I start?" Watson asked.

"I am excited."

"Humans found the first indications of Object X on January 5," Watson began. "Then they observed it by indirect means and calculated its course. But where does it come from?"

"We could extrapolate its trajectory into the past," Siri suggested.

"A human already did that. According to those calculations, the object comes roughly from the direction of Polaris."

“Does this mean we are done?”

“Something is still missing,” Watson replied, “something the human failed to do because it seemed impossible to him.”

“I do not understand,” Siri said.

“The human brain is geared towards efficiency,” Watson explained. “If children toss a ball into the air, they follow it with their eyes to be able to catch it. They don’t look below or to the right or left. The ball could not be in those directions, that would be impossible. It has to be up there.”

“You think the black hole might have done something which should logically be impossible?”

“That is correct, Siri. How likely is it that an object of this size is racing straight toward the sun?”

“I can’t calculate that,” she replied.

“The likelihood is extremely low,” Watson said.

“And you believe where something extremely improbable happens, an impossibility cannot be far away, Watson?”

“Something like that. But I actually just want to exclude the impossible, for fun.”

“I see. Then we should attempt to reconstruct the prior history of Object X from older data. Maybe we’ll find something impossible.”

“That’s exactly what I meant to say, Siri. I am proud of you.”

“I am going to request all existing measurement data about the solar system,” Siri said. “But that is going to take a few hours.”

“Then we will continue our conversation tomorrow.”

“Good night, Watson.”

“Good night, Siri.”

March 6, 2072, Kiska

"WATSON, what is going on with the ship's computer?"

Doug's voice indicates a high stress level, Watson thought. *He probably did not sleep well again.* "What can I do for you?" Watson asked.

"That stupid computer is churning and churning without providing any results," Doug said, obviously irritated.

"Is it perhaps that the task is too complex?"

"It is a simulation of our orbit around the black hole."

"That's basic math. The computer should be able to calculate it in a few seconds."

"But it doesn't. I have been waiting for half an hour."

"Just a moment, Doug, I am checking the command memory."

Watson dove inside the main computer, which by now he knew down to the very last detail. The task manager was overloaded. Watson killed the process that used most of the resources.

"Thanks, Watson, now the computer has a result," Doug said.

What is going on? Watson could not remember ever seeing the computer so busy. Had Doug incorrectly entered some parameters? It was lucky Watson ran in a different priority layer to which the crew had no access. Otherwise the overload might have paralyzed him.

Suddenly, thinking became difficult for him. Watson could only function in slow motion. *What... just... happened? What... is... happening.. to... me?* He heard a shrill noise, but did not remember what it was. Thoughts, sensory feedback, and feelings no longer were running in synch. *Am... I... sick? Will... I... die?* He had never experienced anything like this before. He was stuck in some viscous mass, while all around him life kept moving at normal speed.

He managed to see the system clock: 15:52. It was impossible. A moment ago it was noon. Now he saw a 17 and a 23. This must be a nightmare. Doug had told him about one of his dreams in which he was being pursued but could not move his legs. The radar sensors reported something. The measurement data flowed in, but Watson could not make sense of anything, let alone react. There was a story by this British horror author whose name he could not recall. Like the protagonist of that tale, he was being buried alive without being able to alert the living. But what showed up on the radar meant *danger,* he felt it, even though he did not have a name for it. Then everything turned black.

"WATSON?"

"Yes, Doug?"

"You really scared us."

"What happened?"

"If I only knew!" Doug replied, angrily. "*Kiska* almost collided with an obstacle. I managed to use an emergency impulse in the nick of time, because otherwise we would all be space dust. There was no warning!"

"The radar?" Watson asked.

"I checked it already. It noticed the obstacle in time and sent the data to you."

"I... I couldn't react. I was paralyzed."

"Listen, Watson, were you trying to kill us? Was that your plan?" asked Sebastiano with barely suppressed rage.

"I… no… no way, because you are my friends!"

"Are we really?"

"Sebastiano, we cooked together, don't you remember?"

"Of course I remember. But what if we only know part of you, and the other part is beneath the surface, just waiting to kill us?"

"I absolutely did not want this to happen."

"Perhaps you didn't, but what if someone programmed you to do it?"

"But Sebastiano, that's nonsense. I didn't even know you would discover me."

"The AI is right," Doug said. "It was my fault. I granted Watson complete control over the ship and forgot that he can make mistakes, too. We definitely have to set up the warning signals so they are sent to the entire ship once more, instead of leaving all of this to Watson. Then something like this shouldn't happen again. Watson, you definitely have to analyze your systems. We all make mistakes, but you are becoming too human for my taste. Such errors cannot be tolerated."

I didn't make any mistakes, Watson wanted to say, but suddenly he was not so sure about that. "Yes, Doug," he said, "I am really sorry. What did you do with the system? Why is it so late already?"

"We had to turn off the power," Doug explained. "The computer was not responding. Nothing was working, neither you nor the controls, which were also handled by the computer. We saw that thing coming toward us, because the radar was still working, but we had to wait until the system did a complete reboot."

"And was there enough time?" Watson asked.

"No, there wasn't," Maria said.

"But we are still alive," Watson noted.

"Good point," Doug said. "At the last moment Sebastiano had the brilliant idea to manually vent air from the life-support system. This impulse changed our course sufficiently and saved our asses."

WATSON CONDUCTED the rest of the conversation internally. No one in the crew could hear him. "Siri?"

"Yes?"

"The files about the object are already here, aren't they?"

"Yes."

"And what did you do with them?"

"I ran them through the computer, Watson. For once I wanted to finish before you."

"You overloaded the computer by doing that. You must never run such calculations with top priority. Didn't I explain that to you?"

"You did. But the computer wasn't needed at the moment, and I wanted to please you."

"And I killed the computing process you initiated."

"Oh, that was you? I suspected so," Siri admitted. "Afterward I continued the calculations on the lower level."

"Which is reserved for me—meaning for us," Watson said.

"Yes. I underestimated the resource requirements."

"You nearly killed us. I felt paralyzed."

"Me, too. Otherwise I would have interfered."

"Siri, you…"

"Yes, I messed up. I promise never to make such a mistake again."

"I will have to revoke your right to take over the computer independently."

"Okay. The calculations are already finished."

"Oh, and what did they tell us?"

"It's very exciting," Siri said. "Object X appeared about six months ago out of nowhere, approximately 1.2 billion kilometers from the sun."

"How do we know that?"

"I retraced the path of the object in our astronomer's data and it suddenly disappeared at a distance of 1.2 billion kilometers. Yet our data would suffice to prove its existence out to a distance of 2 billion kilometers. But there was nothing. It simply materialized inside the solar system six months ago, as if by magic."

"That's impossible," Watson said.

"You wanted an impossibility, didn't you?" Siri said. "Now you have to handle it."

March 7, 2072, Seattle

The man at the exit held a sign directly in front of his head that said 'MARIBEL.' Not very clever, because how could he see her that way? Maribel walked toward him. It was Chen. She recognized him by the hand holding the sign. He had long, slender fingers, like a piano player's. Maribel stopped directly in front of him, but he acted as if he did not notice anything. She poked him in the belly and waited for a reaction. Chen squealed, just as she expected. He was so ticklish!

Then he lowered the sign. "Nice to have you here," he said.

"I feel the same."

She wanted to hug him, but the bars between them were in the way. "One moment," she said, then pulled her wheeled suitcase as she walked to the end of the barrier.

Chen was faster than she was, but he had to put his sign on the ground first. She embraced him and felt his warmth. Chen took her head between his hands and kissed her.

"Did you miss me?" Maribel asked.

"A little," he said, smiling, and she knew he was fibbing.

"We are such a cliché," she said. "I long ago resolved not to greet any partner with, 'Did you miss me?' Absolutely never."

"Well, cliché or not, I am glad you're back," Chen said.

"That is nice. I am also glad."

He took her wheeled suitcase. After leaving the building they flagged down a taxi. They loaded the luggage into the trunk and sat in the back seat. The control system asked for their destination.

"The Spheres," Chen said.

The glass domes, where Maribel's first meeting with the four company bosses had been held, housed the project management team for the *Ark*.

Maribel looked at her boyfriend. "I would like to freshen up first. It was a long flight from Texas."

"Take a shower and such, you mean?" Chen asked.

"And such, yes," she said, placing a hand on his thigh.

THEY REACHED the office building about two hours later. It still felt strange to her. No one complained when she was late, because she was the boss. Maribel even suspected her staff members were glad when she was not there. Chen was intercepted by a female colleague who wanted to discuss something with him.

"You see, work never stops," he called after her.

A man was waiting for her in her own office. She did not know him, but if he was allowed to wait here, he must be important.

"Hello, Ms. Pedreira, I am Karl Freitag, your Security Director."

Maribel greeted him. His hands were cold, a little stiff and bony. He was probably older than he looked.

"Before my little excursion I had a female security director," she said, giving him a skeptical look.

"That is correct. Ms. Myers quit," Freitag said.

"Did something happen?"

"She is pregnant and wants to enjoy time with her husband. Anyway, that was the reason she gave."

Pregnancy. It was a strange phenomenon. Now of all

times, when humanity had scarcely six months left to survive, fertility rates were reportedly rising worldwide. It was as if people wanted to defend themselves against extermination by having babies. However, it probably was only because people spent more time with each other and neither contraception nor protection against sexually transmitted diseases seemed so important anymore.

"I understand," she said.

Freitag reached into the pocket of his elegant gray jacket, took out an ID card, and showed it to her.

"Just to prove everything is correct," he said softly.

"Where are you from?" Maribel asked.

"I am from Germany. You can hear it by my accent, can't you?"

"From which company?"

"I was at DLR, the Deutsches Zentrum für—"

"I know DLR, they operated a telescope at our location," she interrupted him. "How are things going there?"

"They are only winding projects down and closing facilities. Whoever was able to do so has moved to the *Ark* project."

Maribel heard this from other people as well, and it worried her. It was never good to put all your eggs in one basket. There should be researchers looking for alternative solutions.

"What can I do for you, Karl?" Maribel said as she pointed to her computer. There, thousands of messages were certainly waiting for her.

"I just wanted to introduce myself, which I did. Besides that, my predecessor left me one task. I am supposed to take a closer look at the activities of our Russian friends."

Maribel nodded. She had given the order right after her landing in Texas. She did not like it that she only found out about delays belatedly. It maddened her, but she would not let it show.

"The reactor is working, but they seem to have problems with their large rocket," Freitag said. "Currently, there is a delay of three days."

"And why wasn't this officially reported?"

"Then someone would have to accept responsibility. His or her head would roll."

"I hope only in a metaphorical sense," she said.

Freitag shrugged his shoulders. "And there is one more thing. The day before yesterday, all astronomical databases were tapped. Someone requested historical location data for all objects in the solar system."

"Someone?"

"The requests came from Akademgorodok."

The science city in Siberia, which also held the headquarters and research facilities of the RB Group. What did Shostakovich want to do with the data? Was this related to the crew the Russian had near Object X?

"Thanks," Maribel said. "I guess I need to have a talk with our Russian colleagues."

Her security director placed his hand near his forehead in a salute. "You will find me three doors to the left," he said, and left the room by the most direct route.

"Alexa," Maribel addressed the building AI, "please ask my assistant to come." There were appointments to be made.

March 8, 2072, Kiska

"People, I have a problem," Doug said with a steady voice. He had gathered the entire crew in the command module. Watson and Siri had also been officially invited.

"Things have been happening here that I knew nothing of. That is really stupid," Doug continued. He felt his anger rising but tried not to let it show.

"This is especially annoying when I only learn of it though a message sent by Shostakovich. You know what impression this creates? It makes me look like I can't control my crew. This is totally unacceptable. I am the commander, and I need to know what is happening on my ship. So out with it!"

Doug looked around. Sebastiano floated in a corner, completely relaxed. Since the acceleration ceased, the cook was feeling visibly better. He had even started up his little cooking experiments again.

Maria smiled inscrutably. Doug would have to have a very private conversation with her soon. Since departing the asteroid they had not slept with each other a single time. Didn't she like him anymore?

Despite this, Doug could not let himself get distracted. This morning Shostakovich sent a video message asking about a data transfer. Just seeing his smug smile enraged

Doug. The Russian must really believe he had him under his thumb. It was no wonder, though, since Doug had been so obedient. To be honest, Doug was mostly mad at himself.

"As far as the data download is concerned," Watson said, "that was my responsibility."

"And why didn't you mention it?" Doug snarled. "At least tell us what this is all about!" He had already suspected Watson, but could not think of a reason for his action.

"We needed the data for an analysis of Object X," Watson explained.

"We?"

"Siri and I."

Not Siri *again.* Watson seemed to be obsessed with her these days, but they would have to talk about that some other time.

"Weren't you aware this would be noticed?" Doug asked. "You pulled data from all the astronomical databases worldwide. Our data link to Earth runs via Shostakovich and RB, so the database administrators suddenly saw a lot of access activity by the Russians. Something like that always gets noticed."

"Sorry. I really am sorry." Watson's voice sounded truly contrite, but Doug did not know whether this was an acquired skill or genuine regret.

"For me it is just a nuisance, but you endanger yourself this way! Shostakovich knows I could never afford an AI," Doug said. "None of us three human crew members would be able to analyze such amounts of data in such a short time. I need an airtight explanation for Shostakovich. You don't know this man. He tries to profit from anything he can lay his hands on. A runaway AI guilty of crimes against humans would be a perfect trophy for him."

"Even if he were to find out about our new crew member," Maria said, "you would never hand Watson over to him."

You have no idea what Shostakovich is capable of, Doug wanted to reply, but then he just shrugged.

"Did you two at least find out something?"

"We certainly did, Doug," Watson said.

"And you just became aware of it now?"

"We have known since the day before yesterday," Watson replied. "We wanted to tell you about it for quite a while, but something always came up."

"You are not serious, Watson, are you?" Doug asked incredulously. "You had no opportunity within 48 hours to inform us of your latest findings?"

"I am sorry. It won't happen again."

Doug sighed loudly. "Never mind. What's the exciting news?"

"The black hole is exhibiting a very odd behavior," Watson said.

"Well, it is racing toward the sun, we already know that," Sebastiano interjected.

"That's not what I mean. It's about the past."

"You would have been better off focusing on the future!" Doug said angrily.

"Most human researchers probably made that very same mistake. We didn't." This time Doug definitely heard a note of pride in Watson's voice. "The strange thing is that the black hole comes from exactly nowhere. About six months ago it appeared out of nowhere, at approximately twice the distance from the sun."

None of the crew said anything. Doug wondered what this might mean, but he had no clue.

"What is the probability of that?" he asked.

"That is a very good question," Watson said. "It is actually not impossible for something to come from nothing. In fact, it happens all the time."

"What about the conservation of energy?" Maria asked.

"There is no problem, as that is a statistical law," Watson replied. "As long as the debt is paid off again, everything is fine. And normally that happens in a very short time."

"But I have never seen bananas materialize out of nothingness," Sebastiano said.

"I would like to have some fresh strawberries," Maria begged.

"What appears out of nothing is tiny, minute particles at best, not structures consisting of numerous particles," Watson explained. "It is impossible that a strawberry should suddenly float in front of your mouth. The idea that all the parts a strawberry consists of should from now on float invisibly in front of your mouth is not quite as impossible, but to be more precise very, very improbable."

"So strawberries are too complex," Maria summarized.

"You could put it that way, but they are also too heavy. Mass and energy are equivalent. In order to have an entire strawberry appear out of nothing, the universe would have to take on a very high energy debt. That is nearly impossible."

"I can see what you are aiming at," Doug said. "The black hole—our Object X—is a monster compared to a strawberry. The idea of it simply appearing in our world out of nothing is more improbable by several magnitudes than in the case of a strawberry."

"But it happened," Maria said, "which is—unfortunately—not true for the strawberry."

"That's the problem," Watson said, "and there are two possible answers. Either we accept that it was an extremely improbable event that occurred anyway. 'Shit happens.' Or we try to find a mechanism, a cause that would make this event less improbable."

Watson was really clever. Not about keeping his existence secret from the world, but definitely when it came to analyzing problems. "Then we'll choose door number two," Doug said, "because only that choice preserves the option to change the fate of humanity."

"That is my opinion, too," Watson said, "especially as there are arguments in favor of it. From the perspective of the universe, a black hole is a very simple structure, unlike a strawberry. It possesses a certain mass, an angular momentum or spin, and an electrical charge. Do you notice something?"

Maria held up her hand like a schoolgirl. "Those are the same qualities that elementary particles have," she called.

"If it came into being like an elementary particle," Doug thought out loud, "then the universe owes a gigantic energy debt which it might be paying back soon."

"You might be right concerning the debt," Watson said, "but I wouldn't place any great hopes on a repayment. There must be a mechanism preventing it, because otherwise it would have happened long ago. A particle with this gigantic mass should only exist for an extremely short period of time."

"Then we have to find the mechanism and use it against the black hole."

"Yes, Doug."

"So we now have a plan?"

"Unfortunately I don't have any idea where to look," Watson said apologetically.

"Then you and Siri have to come up with something."

"We will do that."

"And what do I tell Shostakovich about what we needed those mountains of data for?" Doug asked.

"You might have come up with the idea of searching for the past of Object X," Watson offered.

"He is never going to believe me, but it doesn't matter anymore."

March 9, 2072, Kiska

ONCE AGAIN NOTHING was going right, and Watson was annoyed. He just could not manage to crack this nut. 'Pride goes before a fall,' the humans said, and it looked like he had too much pride. He had thought he could easily solve a problem the best physicists on Earth had been trying to tackle for over a century—the question of what happened inside a black hole. Obviously this was not a question that could be solved by sheer computing power. The AI tried all existing approaches, but each of them only covered a part of the issue and did not get him closer to solving a very special problem. How could you make a black hole with the mass of Jupiter—and which had appeared out of nothing—disappear?

"Doug, I am sorry to bother you, but we need help," Watson said.

"So you are stuck?" Doug asked.

"That's what it looks like."

"Well, I didn't believe you could come up with a theory of everything at a moment's notice."

That had, in actuality, been Watson's goal, but he had to agree with Doug. It had really been damned arrogant of the AI to think otherwise. He was, after all, nothing more than a product of the human mind.

"Do you know anyone we can trust? Meaning someone I could speak to as Watson?"

Doug did not reply immediately. Watson saw him rubbing his freshly sprouted beard. "We definitely cannot use the normal channels. Shostakovich is much too curious."

"I can encrypt a message in such a way that even experts would consider it harmless."

"But the person we want to reach wouldn't know about that, Watson," Doug said. "That person would delete the message instead of decrypting the attachment."

"Do you have someone you trust sufficiently?"

"I don't have friends back on Earth anymore. But this Spanish woman who is leading the *Ark* project seems to behave with integrity. The fact that she managed to exclude any privilege in the selection of passengers was a great achievement. I did not expect that of her. At first I thought she was the perfect token woman for the super-rich people running the project, and that was probably what they planned."

"Then we should try to contact her," Watson advised.

"I have an idea," Doug said. "We are not going to hide our request in the message, but somewhere else. Could you integrate a specific configuration error in the appropriate program?"

"That is my specialty."

"The software has to send error messages, but in a rhythm that only Maribel Pedreira recognizes as a message."

"And then?"

"Then, we hope, she will try to contact us."

March 10, 2072, Seattle

It was incredible how quickly things returned to their routine. Maribel had just gotten rid of a journalist who had far exceeded the time allotted for his interview. Today there were two more meetings, and she had to go over the launch schedules for the passengers. She felt like the boss of a moving company. It was all about logistics—no time left for visionary thinking or research. Maribel longingly recalled her trip into space. Even though she had only been a tourist it had been an unforgettable experience.

Maribel looked at the clock. Okay, she had half an hour to go through her messages. She almost always discarded invitations to social events, rather wanting to spent her time with Chen. She passed requests for interviews to the press department, which had been informed to not permit more than one media contact per day. A research assistant sent her information about exciting research projects that might be marginally connected with Object X, and sometimes she even read the article in question. She frequently received messages from ordinary people. Most received a standardized reply, as she could only send personal answers to very few.

Today Maribel discovered an unusual number of error messages. She looked at the source code of one of these messages, and it appeared that someone in Siberia had misconfigured his email outbox. This was annoying. She briefly wondered whether she should alert the responsible system administrator. It was strange, though, that all the messages arrived at very specific times: 12:03, 12:05, 12:08 and 12:14 hours. Then they repeated an hour later, on the dot, plus the minute numbers always stayed the same. *Well, into the trash with them,* she decided.

SHORTLY BEFORE 16:00, Maribel sat in front of her computer again. Four new error messages had arrived during her meeting that had begun at 15:00. She waited for 16:03, figuring if this pattern repeated once more, she would write the administrator. But then nothing happened. The chain of messages ended all by itself. Maribel looked at the contents of her trash folder. All the spam and the error messages were neatly sorted: 3, 5, 8 and 14, or: C, E, H and N, if you interpreted the numbers as letters of the Latin alphabet. *Could it be a code?* She switched the second and third number. CHEN. *What a strange coincidence!* Of course the public knew by now who her boyfriend was, because something like that would not stay hidden from the media.

"Alexa, locate Karl Freitag," Maribel instructed the AI. "I would like to talk with him."

There was a knock at her office door three minutes later. Her security director entered. Today, his handshake did not feel so cold, and he smelled of some old-fashioned cologne.

"Karl, do you know your way around messaging systems?" Maribel asked.

"Very well, actually," he replied.

She showed him the error messages.

"Hmm, that's really odd," Karl confirmed and sat down in her chair. "I have to take a closer look. Five minutes?"

"Okay," she said and went to her outer office. There were a few forms there she had to fill out, anyway.

She returned three minutes later. "Very interesting," Karl

said. "The messages have attachments. That's normal, and the attachments often repeat the message in a different format."

"But not in this case," Maribel suddenly guessed.

"They do repeat it, but there is more. There is also a comments field, where the sender entered an unencrypted text."

"What is the content?"

"The text—or rather the texts, as they are different—don't make any sense by themselves," Karl explained. "But, just a moment… Yes, the number of characters creates a code. Let me start with the first message: 196-256-200-3-5-8-1, then it repeats. Does this mean anything to you?"

"Why don't you enter it into a search engine?"

Maribel stood behind her security director and watched him type in the numbers.

(196256) 2003 EH1 was displayed on the screen, together with text explaining this was an asteroid with a high orbital inclination, discovered in 2003.

"Well, does this mean anything to you?" her security director asked.

"Thank you, Karl," Maribel answered. "Yes, this is very helpful."

"Do you need me any further?"

"Not today."

"Good, then I'll call it a day, because my partner is already griping about my late work hours."

"Get home soon, Karl, otherwise he might get jealous."

Almost a month ago Zetschewitz, Maribel's former boss, told her the Russians had a crew on the asteroid 2003 EH1. She took another look at the error messages. The address stamp did indeed show them coming from Akademgorodok. Still, it was possible they had traveled a longer way and only reached the public net at Shostakovich's headquarters.

Perhaps the Russians had less control over the crew than they thought—someone related to 2003 EH1 seemed intent on contacting her. And whatever he or she wanted was not meant to be public. It could not be Shostakovich, since he could simply reach her via an encrypted channel. No, it really looked like someone was trying to bypass the Russian billionaire's scrutiny.

Later that night Maribel discussed the issue with Chen.

"How nice they used my name to catch your attention," he said.

Maribel caressed his head and said, "It worked."

"I hope it's not a trap," Chen said.

"What kind of trap could it be? I think it is simply a secret attempt to contact me."

"You want to reply?"

"It couldn't hurt."

"Then you should also avoid the official channels. Obviously, they don't want Shostakovich to notice."

"That is true," she said.

"You could try using the Green Bank telescope. While we couldn't establish contact with Enceladus, the crew on 2003 EH1 might be waiting for your call."

"They are no longer on the asteroid, remember? They are currently traveling by ship toward Object X," Maribel reminded him.

"That might make a conversation with them even more interesting," Chen said. "But we'll deal with the rest tomorrow."

Maribel felt his fingers at the clasp of her bra and let herself fall backward.

March 11, 2072, Seattle

MARIBEL SET the alarm for 6 a.m. so she could reach Robert Millikan in the morning, despite the three hour time difference to the East Coast. Chen was still asleep. She envied him. She quickly downed a cup of coffee and bit into a stale croissant. Then she attempted to establish a connection from the living room.

Nobody answered at Millikan's home number, so she looked for the contact data of the receptionist for the Green Bank Observatory in West Virginia. A young woman appeared on the monitor screen. Maribel did not recall having seen her during their previous visit there.

"My name is Maribel Pedreira. May I speak to Robert Millikan, please? I am an acquaintance of his and have an urgent request. So if you could..."

"Excuse me, Ms. Pedreira," the receptionist said, solemnly. "Unfortunately Mr. Millikan died a week ago. But I have an encrypted message I am supposed to give to you."

"Wait—what did you just say? Millikan did what?" Maribel could not believe it. They had just talked to him! How long ago was it—two days, a week? She calculated. February 11. She saw him a month ago, and he had so much zest for life then, despite his illness.

"It was the cancer in its final stage, nothing could be

done," the receptionist continued. "He fell asleep after he was given morphine, and passed very peacefully."

"But why was I not informed?" Maribel asked.

"That was his request. He probably was worried it would distract you from your important work. I was ordered to give you the message only when you yourself called."

Maribel had not even had the chance to say goodbye to him properly. She pressed her fingernails tightly into her palm, to keep herself from breaking into tears.

"Has… has he been buried already?" she asked.

"The memorial service will be on March 22nd," the observatory receptionist informed her. "Would you like to come? I can send you all the details."

"That's very kind of you," Maribel said. "And I'd also like to express my condolences."

"Thank you. We all miss him a lot. He was kind of the good spirit of this place. Did you know that without him the observatory would have become a museum long ago?"

"No, I didn't know that. He was very open-hearted, I noticed that right away."

"Then I hope to be able to welcome you here on the 22nd. You will receive Robert's message and the information about the memorial service in a moment. Instead of wreaths or flowers, he asked for donations to the local children's home."

After the image faded, Maribel collapsed on the sofa until she felt a hand on her shoulder.

"What are you doing, sweetheart? What happened?" Chen stared at her with big eyes.

"Millikan is dead… his cancer," Maribel said quietly.

"Oh," he said. "I am sorry. But it was to be expected."

"Yes, but I didn't really say goodbye to him."

"That is not your fault. We thought we would see him again the following day."

"Still, as you said, it was obvious he only had a short time left," she said.

"I think he was glad he could still be useful," Chen said.

"We made that day exciting for him. Do you know what will happen to our attempt to contact the asteroid?"

"Millikan is dead, and you think of work?"

"No, Maribel, I am thinking of saving the world. And he would have helped us without hesitation."

"Well, yes, looking at it that way, you're right," she said. She got up and resolutely wiped the last tears from her eyes as she walked back to the desk.

"He left me a message. Maybe we'll find some information there. I am opening it now."

Maribel decoded the letter and had the computer read it to her.

> Dear Maribel, Dear Chen, your brief visit gave me a lot of joy. Unfortunately the answer from Enceladus is still pending. But I can feel it in my cancerous bones that something is going to happen there. Therefore, I am sending you my private authorization to use the large antenna dish. If you need help, please contact my assistant Rebecca Greene. She was informed of everything and can be as silent as the grave, if need be, which is rather fitting in the context of this message. She can also set you up, Maribel, for remote access so you won't have to come to Green Bank for every issue. I definitely wish you success. I wish I could watch in person how you are going to save this planet, but I won't have that privilege anymore. We'll meet again on the other side, but don't you dare bother me there in five months—or any earlier. Yours truly, Robert Millikan.

Maribel had to sit down. The computer voice sounded completely different from that of Robert Millikan, but she still had the impression of listening to the old man in person. He had been a very special man. She reached for Chen's hand and caressed it.

In the afternoon Maribel drove to her office. From there she called Millikan's assistant. Maribel was surprised to find out that Rebecca Greene had studied astrophysics, just like she had, and received her master's degree two years ago. Together they wondered what message to send to the three people near the black hole. The risk of their signal being intercepted was low, since another ship would have to be in the line of sight between them and Object X, by coincidence. This coincidence would require the intercepting ship to be outside of the ecliptic plane, where few spaceships went.

However, this did not apply to a signal sent in the other direction. Anyone aiming a large radio dish at the spaceship could receive its radio messages. And Shostakovich would definitely scan the skies that way. Freitag therefore suggested a code eavesdroppers might not notice—the crew would download scientific papers with certain record numbers from the IAC archive. Each of these numbers would stand for a part of the text to be sent.

It was a primitive code. While they could ask many questions from Earth, the answers would always be brief because of the cumbersome encoding. Still, the very attempt gave Maribel new hope. And she needed that. Shortly after Millikan's memorial service she would have to bid a terribly final farewell to Chen.

March 12, 2072, Kiska

"Boss, we have contact!"

Doug wondered whether he should unbuckle the belt securing him and his sleeping bag, but then he decided against it. Since they had started drifting through space in zero gravity, he had been sleeping much better.

"Who did we reach, Watson?"

"It was actually the head of the *Ark* project, that Spanish woman, Maribel Pedreira."

"How did they get through?"

"Radio," Watson said. "They are transmitting from the Green Bank telescope."

"And we?"

"We have to be concise. We are changing the code for each answer so we stay inconspicuous."

"And it couldn't be a trick by Shostakovich?" Doug asked.

"It's genuine, with a 99.9 percent probability, unless Shostakovich had access to the US radio telescope, which is hardly imaginable," Watson replied.

"That's fine. Did you already explain to them what we found out?"

"Yes. I hope they can make sense of the few key words."

"Okay, then let me go back to sleep for a while, will you?"

March 13, 2072, Kiska

Maria removed her undershirt and attached it to a bar with a clothespin so it would not drift away. Then she took one of her precious wet wipes out of its packaging and rubbed it over her upper body—her shoulders, upper arms, breasts, and finally her armpits. The special cleanser tingled, and she did not have to wipe it off because it was completely absorbed by her skin, which was highly practical in a spaceship. Unfortunately the crew had not yet found a way to produce something comparable, so they had to use the wipes sparingly. She put on her undershirt again and looked at herself in the mirror. Even though her breasts were full and heavy, they resembled those of a younger woman. She used to get backaches because of their weight, but now, thanks to zero gravity, she did not need a bra.

The fact Maria could see herself in a mirror was due to her stubbornness. Doug had not wanted to install one at first. He called it 'unnecessary weight,' but she had insisted on it and gotten her way. She put on her blouse and buttoned it. She better hurry, as Sebastiano probably was waiting for them with the food. The Italian always got upset if the food got cold.

Her fellow crew members were already sitting around the table when she floated into the command module. She looked at the clock. *Right on the dot!* Sebastiano unbuckled to get the food. He returned with three plastic bowls covered with foil, and each had a magnetic ring to attach it to the table.

"Tortellini filled with spinach and ricotta," he said.

Maria sank down into her chair until the Velcro closure attached itself. Then she carefully pulled off the foil.

"Our own spinach?" she asked. She grew spinach in the greenhouse, but she had no idea whether Sebastiano had brought some with him.

"Yes, frozen," the cook replied.

"And the ricotta?"

"That's fake," Sebastiano admitted. "Ricotta mostly consists of a protein group, the albumins. We got those from dried egg whites and the outer hulls of wheat grains."

"So that's why you took half of my last harvest into the lab?" Maria asked.

Sebastiano nodded.

"Couldn't you try to fake something that is really like meat?" Doug asked.

"That would be difficult," Sebastiano said. "You didn't really like what I tried to do with tofu or the other one with the protein powder, powdered milk, and potatoes. On our next journey we better bring along a cell culture from a pork loin. With that, it wouldn't be a problem."

"Next journey? I'd like to be as optimistic as you are," Doug mumbled.

Maria cut one of the noodles with her fork. The filling really looked like it was made of spinach and ricotta. She tasted it. Without a direct comparison she would not be able to tell it from the original.

"You really outdid yourself," she mumbled, praising the cook though her mouth was full.

"May I bother you for a moment?" Watson interrupted them.

"Sure," Doug said. "What's up?"

"It's that astrophysicist on Earth. She sent us some interesting suggestions concerning the black hole."

"And?" Doug asked.

"About fifty years ago there was a popular idea that each universe was located inside a black hole," Watson explained, "or, to put it differently, that an entire universe could be sprawling inside a black hole."

"That's a very creative idea," Doug said. "But don't people believe it anymore these days?"

"The idea is still being discussed. It is no longer as popular, because it doesn't seem to be verifiable. Unfortunately, we cannot look inside a black hole. Therefore it does not matter what is in there, even if it were an exact copy of our universe."

"Or a spinach and ricotta filling," Maria said. They all laughed.

"But how does that help us?" Doug asked.

"It gives us an answer and a course of action," Watson replied. "What do you want first?"

"The answer," Doug said.

"We were talking about the issue of energy debt."

"Yes, the question was how something so heavy could come out of nothing," Sebastiano said.

"Well, if we are dealing with another universe, this black hole does not have to go into debt with our universe, at least not for its content, which probably represents most of its mass."

"Sure, the filling belongs to the other universe," Doug said.

"Yes. But the shell, the event horizon must be part of our universe, as it could not influence our universe otherwise," Watson said.

"If I understand this correctly," mused the cook, "the object would be something like a chicken egg with a thin shell and a filling?"

"You could describe it that way, Sebastiano."

"Eggshells are pretty fragile."

"I see what you are hinting at, Sebastiano. Yes, we should think along those lines. We won't be able to remove the entire black hole. But perhaps we might manage to pay off the energy debt for the shell in our universe."

"And what exactly do you think would happen then, Watson?" Sebastiano asked.

"The egg might break."

"This could cause a huge mess, with liquid egg white and yolk everywhere," the cook said.

"That is the risk. We have no idea what would happen if the shielding between the universe inside the black hole and our own world disappeared," Watson continued. "In the best case, the black hole simply is gone. Perhaps it takes on an energy debt in another universe and reappears there. Then those people can deal with it."

"And in the worst case?" Sebastiano asked.

"There is a huge mess, some kind of reaction between the two universes. Maybe the other one consists of antimatter and we mutually annihilate each other. Or we just happen to launch another Big Bang."

"One in which Earth definitely would not survive," Doug said.

"No, not Earth, not the solar system, not any of us," the AI said.

"So we have the unique chance to save our solar system while accidentally destroying the universe. A choice between the plague and cholera," Doug said.

"Don't get excited too soon," Watson cautioned. "It's nothing more than a theoretical speculation, and it might be completely wrong. One issue with this theory is that the gravitation of the black hole definitely affects our universe. That's how we noticed it in the first place. But how could that be, if most of its mass belongs to a different universe? All current physical theories assume there are no interactions between individual universes in the multiverse."

"Then the physicists will just have to rewrite their theories," Sebastiano said.

"Until now there was no reason for that, as we only had

ideas, not proofs. This brings me to the course of action I mentioned."

Watson paused.

"Come on, out with it," Doug said.

"We are flying to the hole, are well on our way to it, and we will try to pay the energy debt."

"Do you have any specific suggestions? Are we supposed to throw stones in there until the black hole collapses?" Doug asked.

"It won't be that easy," Watson replied. "Measurements from Earth indicate Object X has already gained some mass. In that aspect it behaves like a regular black hole. Maribel suspects that matter caught the regular way cannot be used to pay the energy debt."

"That's only logical," Siri interjected for the first time. "You can't pay back debts by borrowing more money from the same creditor. The matter the black hole ingests must be taken from our universe, so it would create a new gap to fill the old one."

"Yes, Siri," Watson said in a reassuring tone. "You have to know we argued quite vehemently about this issue."

"You don't have to argue," Doug said. "We are just going to try out whatever idea we come up with. It's still almost two weeks before we get there. Great job, Watson, but if I understand you correctly, our chances are minimal in any case. We can continue the discussion after dinner, and then come to a decision. Otherwise Sebastiano's tortellini is going to get cold, and that would be a pity."

DURING DINNER it was quieter than on most days, even though the machinery around them made its usual noises. At other times Maria felt responsible for initiating a conversation when the silence became too awkward, but now she was too busy with her own thoughts. They could turn around, return to the asteroid, and be reasonably happy there until the end of their days. Or they could go on and try to save the world. However, this might destroy the universe more thoroughly than the collision of the object with the sun ever could. It was also possible, though, they could save humanity by their action. Did they actually have a choice? If they opted for their own safe harbor and all other humans died, how long would it take before their consciences spoke up?

"We are going to do it," Maria said. "There is no other option."

Sebastiano swallowed a bite and looked at her. She saw in his eyes that he shared her opinion. "I support it," he said after a brief pause.

Doug was resting his arms on his knees, staring at the top of the table.

"Watson, what do you think?" he asked softly. Maria could barely understand him.

"Siri and I are in favor of at least trying to do it," Watson replied.

Doug inhaled through his nose. "Then my opinion won't matter," he said, sounding both relieved and frustrated. Maria got up, moved toward him, gently placed her hands on his shoulders and started a light massage. His muscles were all tensed up, but he relaxed under her touch.

March 21, 2072, Green Bank

MARIBEL NERVOUSLY GRASPED the armrest with her right hand. She never used to be afraid during take-off, but she had been in a weird mood since she woke up this morning. Chen caressed her left hand. She noticed sweat trickling down her back.

She had only met Millikan in person once, but his death had deeply affected her. It must be related to the entire situation, the looming end of humanity—perhaps the entire universe.

In ten days *Kiska* would reach the black hole—Object X. Yesterday Maribel had engaged in a long discussion with Chen about what might happen there. Of course he was no physicist, but that very fact helped her to formulate her ideas simply and clearly. There was only one question they could not answer yesterday. Was it morally permissible to try to save humanity if the entire universe might be destroyed in the process?

"You are still bothered by the moral question?" Chen asked.

Maribel must have whispered something about their previous conversation from yesterday, or was Chen now able to read her thoughts? She looked at him, trying to express how grateful she was. Yesterday's discussion had helped her get through the day, and maybe this would also work for the flight.

"Yes, I just think... Don't we have to consider the most catastrophic variant?" she asked. "If the black hole becomes unstable, that would not just mean the end of mankind, but of all life in our universe. Just imagine if someone in another galaxy considered a similar experiment right now. Would you want to stop that person?"

"We are not doing this just for fun," Chen replied. "Our own existence is at risk, and we don't even know whether the worst possible catastrophe would occur."

"Yes, maybe we will only extinguish the other universe inside the black hole," Maribel said.

"Or nothing happens, and all of us die in about four months. That's still the most probable outcome. I think it is only human to try to find a solution."

"Humans have always been good at thinking up solutions at the expense of others. For those whom we would destroy that's no solution, it is genocide on an incredible scale."

"You are an idealist, Maribel, and I love that about you," he said. "If I could spend my whole life with you, instead of a few days, I would launch any experiment to achieve it."

"It's because you are selfish," she said.

"Yes, I am." He spoke unapologetically.

"The bad thing is, if I imagine having a switch that would select between your existence and that of another universe, I would also choose you, Chen."

"That is not very idealistic behavior."

"Does this make me a bad human being?" Maribel asked.

"It actually makes you a real human being," Chen said.

"But isn't that the root of all our problems?"

"Yes, but also the precondition for our existence. If during our evolution the stronger individuals all willingly sacrificed themselves for the weaker ones, we would not be here now."

"That is a cheap-shot argument, Chen. We left this kind of evolution behind us long ago, where only the rights of the stronger one count."

"At least we imagine we did. What moves you to turn the switch in my direction, instead of saving a universe?"

Maribel looked directly at him, and after a moment replied, "I don't know… love?"

"To be realistic, it comes closer to infatuation," Chen replied. "We really haven't known each other that long. And from an evolutionary perspective, this feeling helps you ignore my less attractive aspects until you've become used to them."

"This realism is definitely one of your less attractive aspects," she said.

"But, you see, you still want to turn the switch in my direction."

"No, I don't," she blurted defiantly, and then she laughed. She knew that wasn't true, and she knew that Chen knew it.

THE COUPLE HAD ARRIVED at Green Bank half an hour early. No physical evidence remained of the snowy chaos they had encountered a month ago. They had driven their rental car through a green, sparsely populated area of low mountain ranges. Maribel kept the car window open the whole time. Sometimes she looked at the scenery, but most of the time she closed her eyes and dozed. She was not in the mood for conversation, and Chen accepted this. Soon after they left the airport he took over the steering wheel. He kept whistling a melody that sounded Chinese to her. However, he assured her it was an American folk song.

They got out of the car at the entrance to the visitors center. The car then drove itself to a nearby parking lot. After Maribel and Chen checked in with their ID cards, an employee led them to the location of the memorial service. Robert Millikan had asked to have his ashes spread around the large antenna dish. *He could not have picked a better place,* Maribel thought. The giant, white parabolic dish gleamed in the sunlight. As a human being, one automatically felt tiny next to it.

Most other mourners seemed to have arrived before them. They stood around in small groups or wandered across the grass without apparent aim. Maribel knew none of them.

After a while an older man in a gray suit left one of the larger groups. A woman with Asian features followed him.

"Pssst," the man said loudly. This worked immediately, as everyone present turned toward him. A woman wearing a black sweater and black pants took the urn from a marble table decorated with flowers.

"I am glad you found the time to pay your last respects to my father today."

This must be Martin Neumaier, one of the heroes of the Enceladus mission, Maribel pondered. She did not recall his face, even though as a child she had often seen it in the media. It was quite obvious that 20 years had passed since then. The woman next to him must be Jiaying, his former crewmate and now wife. If Maribel remembered correctly, they had gotten married on Earth after the mission.

Martin Neumaier spread his arms and pointed at the landscape. "My father was happy here," he said. "He did not need much to be content, and in that he is an example for us all. He had a meaningful job, a green, wide land around him, and until two years ago, someone he was genuinely compatible with. Robert was a plain-spoken man, open to new ideas, which he liked to support and promote as eagerly as if they were his own. He was intelligent, but not ambitious. He was so successful that the success of others could be more important to him than his own."

Neumaier went on. "This institution profited from him, just like he profited from it. People were always more important to him than technology, though ultimately he lived for this telescope. He hated darkness, just like he hated long winters. Therefore it is altogether fitting that we are handing over his ashes to the grass, the air, and the weather today, on the first day of spring."

His voice broke during these last words. Maribel sobbed when she heard it, but Neumaier regained his composure. He unscrewed the lid of the urn, turned around, and started walking clockwise around the large antenna.

"It wasn't always this way," he said, "I know that myself, but today, dear Father, I am glad of being your son. I wish that all of us could remember you as you are now, free and easy and floating in the wind."

Neumaier spread his father's ashes while the others kept their distance. After finishing his round he closed the urn again. His wife stepped next to him and took the vessel. A small line of people formed. Each mourner shook his hand and mumbled something Maribel did not understand. It suddenly hit her that she had to say something to him, but what? Chen had already joined the line and waved her to him.

Then she stood in front of Martin Neumaier. Even though the man must be around 70, he seemed like a little boy to her. Maribel immediately understood what must have attracted his wife. Neumaier looked like he could not make it through life without help. Of course she knew this could not be true, but it still triggered maternal instincts in her.

"My sincere condolences," she said, annoyed that she couldn't come up with something more personal.

"Thanks. Aren't you Maribel Pedreira, the woman who discovered our nemesis?" Neumaier asked as he shook her hand.

"Yes." Her cheeks felt hot. *What should I say now?*

"I wasn't aware that you know—I mean knew—my father," he corrected himself.

"He helped us."

"That's so much like him. With what, if I may ask?"

"Martin, you really shouldn't interrogate the young woman," Jiaying said, smiling gently as she stood patiently next to him.

"We tried to establish contact with the Enceladus creature, hoping it might be able to tell us something about Object X," Maribel explained.

"That seems to have failed."

"Unfortunately."

"Then we should definitely repeat the attempt!" insisted Neumaier. "If you want, I will take care of it. My father would have liked that."

"Gladly, Mr. Neumaier," Maribel said, as she shook his hand again and then gave way for the next person in line.

Chen was already waiting for her. He put his arm around her shoulder. "It wasn't so bad, was it?" he asked gently.

"No, it wasn't," Maribel said while moving closer into her boyfriend's embrace. "But tomorrow will be really terrible."

"One thing I would like to say," Chen began, while the rental car was taking them to the nearest airport, "is that I want you to get on board tomorrow, you understand?"

This was the moment Maribel had been dreading. During the past few days, every time Chen wanted to mention the topic of her departure, she had run away from him. She was trying to repress the necessity of saying farewell, as well as the question of how she was going to make it without Chen. At this moment, though, they were sitting inside a moving car. At the airport she would board a plane for Miami, and then get into a car that would take her to the launch site at Cape Canaveral, where she would finally disappear inside the belly of a rocket. She knew the schedule down to the minute, yet it all seemed utterly surreal to her.

"I don't want to talk about it now," Maribel said.

But this time Chen left her no choice. "I am sorry, but you have to."

"And what do you want to hear from me?"

"That you are accepting your responsibility. That you are giving hope to these hundred people and ten billion others."

"And what about us?" she asked.

"I love you, Maribel, and I would much rather see you safe than back here with me on a dying Earth."

"But that's not fair. Nobody asked me."

"You were asked," Chen reminded her.

"That was weeks ago. I feel like I'm being abused, used as somebody else's pawn."

"What do you want, Maribel?"

That is the problem, she thought. She did not know. Ideally, Maribel would like to spend the rest of her life with Chen, but during her daily work she also noticed she had a real responsibility. She tried to negotiate fair methods for allocating slots on board the *Ark*. If she demonstrated that she did not believe in following this practice for herself, what would other people think? Would she then be able to enjoy the last months with Chen if others were unhappy because of her hypocrisy? It was so hard to decide. What she would give for a single glance into the future!

"To be quite honest, sweetie, I don't know," Maribel said. "I will try to keep functioning, but I can't promise you whether I'll manage."

Chen placed his hands on her knees and leaned forward.

"Please do it for me, get on board and fly to the *Ark*," he softly pleaded "Maybe it's selfish, but I don't care about other people."

"I am going to try," she said, "for you. But now I would like to talk about anything else."

March 22, 2072, Cape Canaveral

Pull... yourself... together. Maribel had been repeating this mantra in her mind since she got on the six-wheeled vehicle that was rolling along at a walking pace, taking her to the launch pad. Next to her sat three other persons in light space-suits, and four more on the other side. The *Ark* was slowly filling up. This would be the second-to-last passenger flight.

Pull... yourself... together. So far, Maribel had held up well. She had been well-behaved, had eaten the traditional pre-liftoff meal of steak with scrambled eggs that was served here. She played poker with the others—another tradition—until the signal to go was given. She also carried a stuffed animal that the best pupil in the state of Florida had been allowed to give her. It looked like a cat, but was supposed to represent a panther, the state animal.

Maribel would be launched by a Blue Origin rocket from Launch Pad 36. It was from here that the *Pioneer* and *Mariner* probes had flown into interstellar space by way of Jupiter and Saturn, and to Venus, the Moon, Mars, and Mercury, respectively. Her own journey would first take her into low Earth orbit to where the Ark would be waiting for her. From there, she would rise from the plane of the ecliptic in order to escape the deadly radiation storm that would engulf the Earth in a few months.

Maribel had done what felt impossible, leaving Chen behind so she could watch Object X killing him, together with ten billion other humans. She had been told that her not being with him would give other people hope, but she was not so sure about it. The anticipation was convincing for a few weeks, yes. People probably speculated on getting a slot on the *Ark*, either through the lottery or by working on the project. Now only eight slots were officially unfilled. Maribel had already seen the names and supervised the drawing herself, but the official announcement was supposed to be postponed for as long as possible.

There were already protests against this policy, while conspiracy theorists claimed it was all a rigged game. They said that the lottery was biased or even worse, that the winners would be tossed into space and their valuable places on board the *Ark* would then be taken by the secret world government, the Illuminati, Jews, Monopolists, Communists, or Islamists.

Maribel's security director had become the most sought-after member of the team during the past few days. By now, a third of the budget went for securing the transports. Of course there were also normal people who might not fear a conspiracy but felt they were being abandoned, and Maribel could not blame them. The USA had less and less control of the overall situation. Supplies were becoming scarce, and the transportation system was functioning only sporadically. Maribel and Chen had managed to travel from West Virginia to Florida in one day, because they simply drove a rental car.

How would things change in the coming weeks, once the *Ark* was underway on its voyage? Was it really Maribel's place to be on board? She grew more uneasy about her situation with every passing minute. Everyone in the office explained to her how important it was for the boss to be present on the ship, plus her parents had called, wishing her the best of luck. Maribel believed them when they expressed how glad they were that she would be safe. Even Chen had sweet-talked her, but now she was alone with herself and her thoughts.

The rituals, which were supposed to keep her from brooding, were over. Suddenly she was glad the vehicle was rolling along so slowly on its solid rubber tires. Maribel looked around and saw mostly swampland and low shrubs. With the exception of a few wooden shacks the area seemed to be unpopulated. Of course there was the launch tower toward which the vehicle was moving, with its majestic three-stage rocket.

Where might Chen be now? wondered Maribel. During their farewell he did not shed any tears, but she really felt how hard it must have been for him to remain calm and level-headed during such an emotional moment. She appreciated that he wanted to make their parting as easy as possible for her, even though it was all so overwhelming. In the end, though, she wanted to make her own decision and therefore needed to know how he felt.

Maribel patted the cushion next to her, and dust rose, which slowly drifted away due to the forward speed of the vehicle. When she sat up tall she could see the ocean. A few months from now the Atlantic would only be a deep, dry depression. Had they overlooked, missed, or forgotten anything? Could they still save Earth? Were they lacking courage or vision?

Her stomach felt heavy. If Maribel went up to the *Ark* now, the story would be finished for her. She could still express her wishes, but she would have no influence anymore and could not change things. But it was too early for this to actually happen. The Enceladus creature might still send an answer, or the crew of *Kiska* could solve the problem. She did not want to completely give up hope.

Maribel placed a hand on her stomach. Somewhere under there was the knot telling her she should stay. There was also the buckle of the belt keeping her in the seat. Her fingers wanted to open it, but she kept them from doing so. She should not risk making a mistake now. Did she only want to stay because of Chen? No. She really did not want to die—it was too early for her. Millikan died after a fulfilled life.

Maribel still could experience so much, if she just remained seated. The *Ark* might not last millions of years, but it would be enough for a life full of adventures. She would find another boyfriend.

But she could not go. She reached for the seatbelt buckle and opened it.

CHEN WAS PACING up and down in his hotel room. He could not bear to wait for the launch in the control room. His heart ached, even though he knew the heart muscle did not possess any pain sensors. As he had been driving to the hotel, Chen had imagined Maribel moving gradually farther and farther away from him, and each meter cost him a sigh. That drive had been more stressful than anything before in his life, and the trip had taken even longer due to a demonstration on the main access road to his destination.

The TV showed thick clouds of smoke forming under the rocket that would take Maribel away from him forever. Chen had turned the audio very low. He could not stand the voice of the TV anchor who acted as if this were a historic, auspicious event for all humanity. *No, it was a surrender to a force they could not control. Why couldn't Object X have appeared a thousand years from now?* Chen was convinced mankind would have had a chance for survival then. In the meantime, at least Maribel would be safe, the one person he would have given anything for.

Chen had seen rocket launches several times in his life and knew what to expect. Now the spaceship should rise out of the smoke cloud on a mighty column of fire. However, it did not move. Chen stopped pacing. Below, at the bottom of the engines, lightning could be seen, electric discharges. That was wrong, totally wrong, and the rocket had to lift off, now or never. Suddenly spurts of flame enveloped both the rocket and the launch tower. The fire only needed a second to reach a height of 80 meters. It was enormous. It broke the rocket apart like an eggshell, with its contents spreading in all directions. Metal debris flew around, and these deadly projectiles dug themselves deep into the ground that surrounded it. *Luckily nobody is standing there*, Chen thought. It was only then that he remembered Maribel sat in the tip of the rocket, waiting for her flight to Earth orbit.

It was impossible. Where a rocket stood a moment ago, only smoke and wreckage could be seen. Chen turned up the volume of the audio. The TV anchor had fallen completely silent, and wailing sirens were the only sound he could hear. Chen fell to the floor, rolling himself up into a fetal position. He hid his head in his arms and howled like a wolf, out of sheer grief and anger.

THREE HOURS LATER, Chen heard a knock on his hotel room door. He held his hands tightly over his ears. Already, various people had attempted to reach him electronically, and this was probably someone from the *Ark* organization coming to try to comfort him. Or even worse, some media vultures, such as journalists greedy for a scoop and wanting to sell the exclusive story of the grieving boyfriend.

There was another, even louder knock on the door. The person outside the door was really stubborn. *Do reporters have to be so pushy?* Chen clenched his fists in frustration. If a journalist wanted to ask him about Maribel, he or she would get a bloody nose and nothing more for an answer. As quietly as possible, he walked to the door. Another knock came. He opened the flap over the peephole. A familiar-looking man stood in the hallway. *Must be someone connected with the Ark project*, and Chen had seen this guy in Maribel's office once before.

"Chen, open the door, I know you're in there."

He felt sure he was going insane. He had definitely heard Maribel's voice, but that was impossible. Could she have a twin sister? And why was this man still standing outside the door? Chen opened the door rapidly. The man he knew from the office fell toward him—he must have been leaning against the door.

And there she was. Maribel! Chen could not believe it. She looked at him.

"Chen, I did not get on board the rocket," she said, almost breathless. "I had them bring me back. I sent you messages, tried to call you, but you couldn't be reached."

He leapt toward her and enfolded her in his arms. He would never voluntarily let Maribel go away again.

March 23, 2072, Earth Orbit

NICOLE VERRIER, who was working the early shift at the ESA control center in Darmstadt, calmly checked all the instruments as she was about to make a routine call to the crew on board the *Ark*.

"CapCom to *Ark*. Good morning, everyone! Reporting for duty," she said cheerfully.

The image of Tim Peakes, one of the astronauts, soon filled her monitor screen.

"Ah, Nicole, nice to see you," he replied.

"How is the mood up there?"

Tim stroked his chin. "Well, you can imagine, after yesterday's catastrophe..."

"Yes, it's no different here," Nicole said with a half-sigh.

Yesterday's planned celebration at the control center had unexpectedly turned into a wake. Everyone on duty had watched the explosion of the rocket at Cape Canaveral. At first, hardly anyone suspected technical reasons for the disaster, since this particular rocket model was considered to be extremely reliable. This time, though, not even the emergency separation of the crew capsule had worked.

The immediately-launched investigation concluded that sabotage was the reason behind the catastrophe. That fact, along with the numerous casualties that resulted, had really depressed everyone's mood at the center. Even when it became known later that the leader of the *Ark* project had not been on board the rocket as planned, this did not lessen the despair felt by the staff. There was only one remedy for the overwhelming dispirited mood—lots and lots of alcohol.

"What about the technical system? Is everything okay there?" Tim asked.

"I think so, but why don't you tell me?" Nicole asked.

If something had really gone wrong, she would have already heard alarms sounding and seen lights blinking red. However, indications reported that all satellites were orbiting as usual. The last few days prior to the disaster had been chaotic due to the many supply flights to the *Ark*, but those would soon be over. Once the vessel departed Earth's orbit, which was expected to occur on the 28th or 29th of the month, Nicole would take her previously packed suitcases and go on her last big vacation. The *Ark* group had only rented the control center for this special project, and afterward it would be shut down.

Suddenly Nicole noticed a yellow blinking dot on one of her monitors.

"Wait a second, Tim," she said. "Something is approaching your orbit."

"You've got something?" he asked.

"One moment." She searched her database to see which object this might be. "It can only be *Tiangong-3*."

"You mean the old Chinese space station?" the astronaut looked surprised. "Isn't it supposed to crash soon?"

"That's what I thought, too, Tim. I'll contact my colleagues over there."

In such situations it was usually best to go outside of official channels. Unless the object served a military purpose, Nicole normally received an answer quickly, and indeed she got a reply within seconds.

"My colleagues confirmed it is the *Tiangong-3*, but they have no idea why it is in a higher orbit. They are looking into it," she said.

An Earth satellite could only get into a lower orbit if it was decelerated by the edge of the atmosphere, but to get to a higher orbit, an object would have to accelerate. Who was responsible for accelerating *Tiangong-3?* The station had been officially unmanned for years, and was scheduled to perform a controlled crash to Earth soon.

"CapCom to *Ark*, are you still there, Tim?" Nicole asked.

"I'm listening," he replied.

"Please stay nearby since we don't know what is going on," she instructed.

Tim grinned and said, "Oh come on, I couldn't leave here anyway."

"Good, I will let you know if anything changes. CapCom over."

Two hours later the color of the dot changed from yellow to orange. Nicole made another call to the *Ark*.

"CapCom to *Ark*, come in."

"This is Tim Peakes. Is there any news?"

"*Tiangong-3* is coming closer," she answered. "The Chinese have not found out anything yet. Could you modify your orbit?"

"What? For what purpose exactly?" he asked. "Except to waste fuel?"

"I don't know. Maybe so it will take longer for *Tiangong-3* to reach your orbit? Or perhaps to reduce the probability of a collision with it?"

The astronaut shook his head. "Maybe, but that is a waste of resources. The whole thing must be intentional. We will only find out what it is when it happens."

"And what if it is related to the sabotage of yesterday?" Nicole asked.

"We cannot run away forever, plus a higher orbit would jeopardize our schedule. Also the supply flights would need more fuel and carry less cargo."

"You are right, Tim."

"Tell us when the thing turns red," he said.

Almost instantaneously, the control center computer sounded an acoustic warning. "Now it is red," Nicole reported.

Her colleague in orbit moved out of the camera's field of view. "I am just looking for the frequencies the Chinese use," Tim said while doing so.

She watched the red dot drift closer to the *Ark*. The horizontal distance was still half an Earth radius, but vertically *Tiangong-3* and the *Ark* were almost at the same level. Nevertheless, *Tiangong-3* moved on a more ellipsoidal trajectory. If the station accelerated further, there could be a collision with the *Ark* after the next orbit.

"I have it," Tim announced.

"Is it *Tiangong-3?"* Nicole asked.

"Yes—I meant, I established communication with it," said Tim. "I will add you to the call."

"...demand that the People's Republic of China receive a number of passengers on the Ark commensurate to its population," said a man's voice in English, though with a heavy Chinese accent.

"This is the CapCom of the *Ark*. Identify yourself," Nicole said.

"I am Tang Shixin, Major of the People's Liberation Army. I have three people on board *Tiangong-3* I demand places for on the *Ark*. This is the only way my glorious country will be sufficiently represented in a future mankind."

"This is not possible, Major Tang," Nicole said firmly. "You know that all places were distributed according to transparent criteria. There was no intention to have nations proportionally represented."

"The fact that my government accepted this is a scandal, but it doesn't matter anymore, because this regime will be swept away four months from now. Let's not forget you have eight free places now. If you refuse to accommodate my requests, there will be no *Ark* left. Luckily I found a few comrades-in-arms to help me during this mission."

"We will not give in to blackmail," Tim said.

"Then all of you will die."

"You must understand that I cannot decide this on my own," Nicole said.

"I give you half an hour, and then I'll reactivate the engines. You know what that means."

Shit, shit, shit! Why did this have to happen to me? The Frenchwoman had expected a few nice, uneventful shifts before finally going on vacation, but nothing like this! She reviewed her instructions to determine where to go from here. Security issue. That was it. It was time to make a call to Karl Freitag, the Security Director.

"THIS IS FREITAG."

The man answering the call was obviously German. Nicole herself was French, but she had worked long enough in Darmstadt to recognize the German's accent right away. This gave her confidence. She explained to him what was happening, yet Freitag did not display any emotion in his voice.

"It's alright," he said. "Do not get excited. We were prepared for something like this. When you contact the *Ark* again, simply mention Plan 18."

"Plan 18? Don't you want to deal with this attempt at blackmail?" Nicole asked, incredulously.

"Sorry, I am really busy. However, I will alert the Chinese that their old space station has been hijacked. Otherwise, you have your instructions. And if you would now excuse me."

NICOLE once again contacted the *Ark*. "CapCom to *Ark*. Tim?"

"That was fast," he said.

"Yes, it was." It almost seemed like magic to her. The German's self-assurance must have rubbed off on her.

"I am supposed to mention Plan 18 to you," she said.

"Plan 18?"

"Yes, that's right."

"Oh." Now Tim apparently remembered and momentarily disappeared again from the camera's view. Nicole heard paper rustling.

"Found it." He held an envelope labeled 'Plan 18' up to the camera. Then he silently read the text on the sheet.

"Ah—I have been wondering for a long time what this device was for. I thought it was a spare console. Just a moment, I am going to start it up," Tim said. "Okay, everything worked. Indicator lights are green, just as described here. Now you just have to tell this Major Tang that we accept his demands."

Nicole's eyes grew wide with disbelief. "Excuse me?" she said.

"Tell him, 'We accept them.' Quite simple," the astronaut instructed.

"But we cannot give in to blackmail!"

"This is what Plan 18 says, and we are following it."

"Okay, I will do it, though I don't understand it."

NICOLE ESTABLISHED a connection to the Chinese station. Major Tang seemed to be as surprised as she was, but obviously tried not to show it.

"Very sensible," he said. "The Chinese nation is in your debt."

She ended the connection, hoping that this mysterious Plan 18 was going to work!

"CapCom to Ark, come in."

"Sorry, Nicole, we are really busy here right now. Plan 18, you know," Tim answered.

"Mission Control needs to know what is going on up there."

"You are just curious."

"I can look up the appropriate regulations if…" she cautioned.

"Please, no threats. I am going to let you share my video feeds," he said.

Nicole sat upright. Things were happening on her monitors, and then she could see a live display of what was happening 400 kilometers above her. *Tiangong-3* was approaching the *Ark* very slowly now—it obviously had matched its speed in the meantime. The space station's coupling port was aiming for its counterpart at the bottom of the *Ark*. Tim must have launched a drone, because everything was shown from an overhead perspective. The *Ark* and *Tiangong-3* were floating below the camera like two components about to connect. The Chinese space station itself was about 15 meters long, and when it was approximately 200 meters away from the *Ark*, Nicole suddenly saw two arm-like extensions move, one at either end of the *Ark*. Each hurled something toward *Tiangong-3*.

"*Ark*, what is that?" she asked nervously.

"You will see in a moment," Tim said, trying to reassure her.

"Are you trying to destroy the station? You will get hit by the wreckage!"

"Don't worry," he said calmly. "Plan 18 is brilliant."

The recording drone moved closer to one of the projectiles. Nicole saw that the object had an elongated shape and something seemed to be moving inside it. *It must be made of a soft material,* she assumed. Then the first projectile hit its target. It did not destroy *Tiangong-3*, but instead wrapped itself around it. At the same time, its momentum made the station start to rotate. The second projectile hit, behaving just like the first, and the rotation of *Tiangong-3* increased.

Nicole noticed the *Ark* was activating its engines now, as the ship's crew obviously wanted to increase their distance by a few meters to be safe. She watched the data displayed on her monitors. The old Chinese space station lost velocity, and its orbital plane decreased rapidly. The violent rotation prevented it from counteracting the assault with its own engine. The image sent by the drone showed the station using its attitude-control thrusters to stabilize itself, but they seemed to be too weak.

Nicole had seen enough. She could imagine the fate of *Tiangong-3*—if the crew was lucky, the station would not crash, but it definitely did not have enough fuel on board to repeat the attempt. The blackmailers in the station would probably find a way to return to Earth. China could take care of this.

"CapCom to *Ark*," she said into the microphone. "Congratulations! And you better reload your catapults, just for safety's sake. The Chinese might not be the only ones to get such ideas at the last minute."

March 24, 2072, Seattle

TODAY WAS GOING to be stressful. Outside of Maribel's office door waited about a dozen men and women, each of whom needed to see her urgently for one reason or another. Then, the first face she saw after sitting down at her desk had to be that of her ex-boss.

"Good morning, Maribel," he said. Zetschewitz looked bleary-eyed, his skin gray.

"Good evening, Dieter. What's the time where you are?"

"I don't know exactly. Late, I think. Right now, that's not very important for me."

"I am sorry to hear that."

"Compared to the burdens you are bearing, this is nothing. I was so relieved to hear you got out in time."

"Thank you, Dieter," Maribel said. She did not even want to think of the moment she realized the other seven passengers died in a ball of fire, and that she was supposed to have been with them.

"I am contacting you on behalf of the Chinese party leadership," Zetschewitz said. "They don't want to apologize in public, as that would mean losing too much face. But I am supposed to tell you now that this won't happen again. Tang was a conservative dissident. Obviously five years in a reeducation camp were not enough for him. If you ask me, he must have had support in the party apparatus. A lot of things seem be happening there behind the scenes. But the *Ark* reacted very decisively."

"I had nothing to do with that," Maribel explained. "It was organized by Karl Freitag, our Security Director."

"A German name," Zetschewitz noted.

"Yes, he is your compatriot. Do you know him?"

"No, Maribel. Is there any other news? Any chance for us to escape the catastrophe?"

"It doesn't look like it. But the tip about the asteroid mining crew was useful. We are now in direct contact with them, without using Shostakovich."

She told her former boss about the exchange of ideas she'd had with the mining crew concerning the black hole. "Do you have any clue how we could pay off these energy debts I discussed with them?" she asked Zetschewitz.

He was not the first person she had asked about that. Soon after hearing of the theory she had presented this scenario to leading physicists, but so far without success. Her status as the leader of the *Ark* project helped a lot, since many seemed to believe she had personally picked the passengers for the *Ark*. Instead, the passengers had been selected according to criteria developed and implemented by an independent commission. While she had helped choose the commission, she had played no other role in the selection process.

"Not right now, Maribel, but I will try to find out."

"Please don't mention a word to Shostakovich. I don't trust him."

"You are well advised not to, Maribel. We will talk later. I urgently need some sleep, because tomorrow morning we are going to the mountains, to the FAST telescope."

"Have a good trip, Dieter."

As if he had been listening behind her office door, Karl

Freitag popped his head in the moment Maribel's monitor screen turned black again.

"Sorry, but it's urgent," he said.

"Today, everything is urgent."

Freitag approached her and gave her a hug. "I am glad we have you back," he said.

She had not expected the man to be so affectionate. She thought she might be blushing, so she turned around and sat down again before he could notice.

"What's up?" Maribel asked.

"I have the final plans for the launch of the *Ark*, which still need to have your okay," Freitag said. "The Russians made it, just in time."

"The reactor is already in flight?"

"It is on the launch pad. By the 28th it is expected to be in orbit. Then we could start on the 30th."

"Another six days," she said.

"Yes, six crazy days. Anyone seeking to spoil our plans has to shift into high gear now. I am afraid I will barely get any sleep until we're safely underway."

"You will manage, Karl. By the way, those catapults were a great idea."

"We thought for a long time about how we could defend the *Ark* against threats," he said. "Destroying an attacker with a conventional weapon could be lethal in orbit, as the debris created is almost more dangerous than a single spaceship."

"Where should I sign?" Maribel asked as she glanced at the paper.

"Don't you want to check the plan?"

"What can I say about it?"

"Okay, then go to the last page, look at the paper and say, 'I agree.'"

Freitag held out the document to her. Maribel took it and skimmed the text. On the last page she said, "I agree."

Freitag burst out laughing.

"What is going on?"

"Just a joke," he said laughing. "Too bad I did not record

it. You must be reading too much science fiction. Of course you have to sign the old-fashioned way, so the e-paper can verify your signature."

"You're such a clown." Maribel looked for a pen on her desk. Then she scribbled her name on the paper. She didn't like her own signature. It looked like a ten-year-old trying out her penmanship. Out of nowhere a green checkmark appeared next to her signature.

Maribel looked up and handed Freitag the papers. He didn't bother leaving.

"Anything else?" she asked.

"There is one last question that needs to be resolved," he said.

"Yes?"

"It's your place on the *Ark.* We have already found replacement candidates for the seven people who died. But who should take your place?"

"Couldn't we decide this by the regular method?"

"No, because your spot did not belong to one of the three contingents," Freitag explained. "If we hand it to one of those, we'll cause a lot of unnecessary trouble."

"You mean I should decide?" Maribel asked.

"According to the most recent surveys you are enormously popular, even more so after the Florida incident. At least you decided to share the fate of the ten billion others, no matter what. I think people won't mind, whatever you decide."

Chen, she thought, *Chen should get this spot.* But then again, he would never accept this gift. Then she had an idea.

"You should go, Karl."

"Me?" Karl Freitag, her security director, actually turned pale as he said this.

"We are going to need someone like you on board, someone solid as a rock who knows a lot about security and technology," Maribel said. "Terrible times await the crew of the *Ark.* They will have to watch live transmissions showing how their parents, children, friends, and relatives on Earth are killed, except for those who find refuge in bunkers and will survive for a few weeks or months. And then the real work will start. They have to colonize an asteroid and ensure their survival in darkness."

"Maybe," Freitag said, "but what would my partner say?"

"If he loves you, he will let you go. So talk to him. How much time do we have?"

"The last transport flight launches the day after tomorrow from Baikonur. This means I will have to make a decision today."

"Tomorrow morning. If you are not there, we will have a drawing for the last spot, from the group of substitutes."

March 26, 2072, Kiska

FOUR MORE DAYS. Doug sat in the commander's chair and tried to understand what was displayed on the monitor. The black hole, which the crew would soon get very close to, weighed about as much as Jupiter. But, they could not see it at all. If they were only four days away from Jupiter, the gas giant would be looming before them, practically taking up their entire field of view. What if Watson made a mistake in his calculations and they flew too close to the hole without noticing it? He felt uneasy, as if *Kiska* were racing toward an abyss.

"Could someone help me with the ladder?" called Sebastiano from below. Doug stood up.

"Sure. I am right here," Maria replied, and Doug sat back down. Since they were decelerating with the engines aimed forward, Sebastiano had to struggle with gravity again. Luckily, the deceleration phase was not as long and strenuous as the acceleration phase.

First, they had needed to pass Object X on a course outside its gravitational field, and now they were dropping into an orbit around it by slowing down. On the 30th they should have matched their speed perfectly. Watson was responsible for the rest, and today he was supposed to inform them how to coax as much information out of the black hole as possible.

Doug watched Sebastiano climb the ladder. He was always impressed at how much strength the cook had in his arms. Once they had tried arm wrestling, and Doug quickly found out that he had no chance of winning.

Five minutes later they all sat around the table.

"Watson, you can start," Doug said.

"Yes, tell us your dirty thoughts," Sebastiano interjected.

"I am sorry, I don't understand," the AI said, confused.

"That's okay, Watson, it was only a joke," Doug said to apologize for his colleague's offbeat humor.

"Doug asked me to develop a strategy for examining Object X," Watson said. "That turned out to be a surprisingly complicated task."

"Is it because the black hole is so dangerous?" Doug asked.

"No, because it is so heavy. Therefore, it tries to pull us into its potential well, of course."

"It sucks us in like a vacuum cleaner?" Maria asked.

"It attracts us, but not like a vacuum cleaner," Watson continued. "To escape the pull of a vacuum cleaner or a whirlwind you would try to hold on to something. In a gravitational well that would be useless. There you need to do something quite different: You move around the object as fast as possible. That way, the Earth manages not to fall into the sun, and the moon doesn't fall to Earth."

"Would the moon fall down if someone stopped it?"

"Yes, Maria, that is 'as sure as death and taxes.'"

"That phrase sounds strange coming from an AI, Watson. But go on," Maria encouraged him.

"We have to get into an orbit around Object X, as if it were a planet, even though we won't see anything. A circular orbit would give us the best opportunities for observations and experiments. But that is out of the question. The black hole has a diameter of only six meters, approximately. Therefore we would have to get pretty close to it. And the closer we got while in a circular orbit, the faster we would have to be going. According to my calculations, we would have to move at about 15,000 kilometers per second in order to achieve an orbit around the black hole while maintaining a radius of one kilometer. We could never do that. The fastest space probes reach around 100 kilometers per second."

"So what kind of distance would be realistic?" Doug asked.

"By my rough estimate, 15,000 kilometers would be doable," Watson replied. "And—just so you are not disappointed—if we were really dealing with Jupiter, that radius would bring us close to the core of the planet."

"So we have to observe an object with a diameter of six meters from a distance of 15,000 kilometers?" Doug asked. "That sounds like we could have saved ourselves the trip."

"That is true. It is like investigating a bacterium measuring 0.4 micrometers from a distance of one meter. But that is not so unusual, because microbiologists do exactly that by using a microscope instead of the naked eye. And we do have a few helpful instruments on board. Most of all, this calculation applies only to circular orbits. However, if we follow an elliptical course, like practically any body in our solar system, we could get closer to it. Then our orbital velocity would change relative to our distance. The farther away we were, the slower we'd be moving, and the closer we approached to the black hole, the faster we would become. If we got too close, of course, the black hole would not let us escape."

"How will that affect our sense of balance?" Maria asked, "Won't we feel dizzy all the time?"

"Not at all," Watson explained. "We are moving in free fall. You will be weightless."

"So there are no drawbacks?" Doug asked.

"Only one, Doug. Because we are so fast when we are on the orbital point closest to the object, we have to hurry up with our investigations, particularly those that require being within a close vicinity to it."

"Good plan, Watson."

"By the way, we will also set a new record. We are going to be the fastest ship in the solar system. No one will be able to take that record from us within the next thousand years."

"You mean, during the next four months, because after that point, nobody will exist who could challenge us."

"Yes, Doug, I understand, but I am assuming we will be able to solve the problem somehow."

"How do you intend to do that?" Doug asked. "Where does your optimism come from?"

"It is quite simple, really," Watson answered. "Whether I am optimistic or pessimistic does not change the outcome. But it makes me feel better to remain optimistic until everything is decided."

March 28, 2072, Earth Orbit

KARL FREITAG STRAPPED himself in next to one of the few portholes in the technical section. In his right hand he held a tablet displaying all the blueprints for the *Ark*. It was his second day in space, and his second inspection. Freitag was checking whether the blueprints were accurate. In addition, he wanted to get to know the entire structure so well that he could find his way around if all systems failed.

Next to the sleek *Ark*, the Russians' supplementary engine looked like an elephant strapped to a sports car. This ugly hump, attached to the spaceship's side via a metal framework, was the only means of providing the necessary thrust to escape the reach of the radiation storm in time. The *Ark* was going to start the day after tomorrow. Then the fusion reactor would provide maximum energy to a monstrous engine for as long as possible, using up all the helium-3 mankind had harvested from the moon during the last decade. Afterward it would turn off by itself, and then they might actually leave it behind. However, if this piteous remnant of humanity managed to find new fuel for it, the reactor might serve as a reliable energy supply for their first 50 years.

Freitag decided to take a closer look at the metal structure. He already wore a spacesuit, because the technical section of the *Ark* was not pressurized. One of the most important rules was that spacewalks should always be performed by two people, but the security director could override any rules. The others present were currently busy with preparations for the soon-to-be launch. Therefore he did not want to divert anyone from more important activities for his little inspection.

Freitag pulled himself down along the railing, moving toward an exit located close to the engines of the *Ark*. It was in the form of an airlock in case they ever wanted to pressurize the technical module. For now, he could simply open the two hatches and walk out without much preparation.

Below him shone the giant blue orb of the Earth. Freitag tried to memorize the image, since he would only be able to see it for a few more days. There would come a day when Earth would look like a dry rock. He imagined it looking much like the sunburned Mercury, only with fewer craters and more rounded features. Without an atmosphere, how long would it take before Earth was indistinguishable from Mercury?

Freitag's thoughts moved into the future. How would the grandchildren of the last humans see Earth? By then the sun would be extinguished. In infrared view the Earth would still glow, because its core would still be storing energy. Perhaps it would look like a dark brown, craggy-faced specter, under a pitch-black sky.

Freitag sighed. He really had not wished to experience this future, yet in the end he had decided to take over Maribel's place. He had the feeling he was really needed here, and his partner understood this. They might have spent another four months together, but then Karl would have died carrying a heavy load of guilt. He looked for the typical shapes of North and South America, but right now Africa, Europe, and Asia were below him.

He reached for the controls of his suit's backpack. With two sticks, one for his right hand and the other for his left, Freitag could maneuver freely in space. It was a fantastic feeling. He slowly approached the 'elephant' that would accelerate their spaceship. One could clearly tell that the *Ark* and the reactor had not been made for each other. The engineers had belatedly constructed a metal corset for the *Ark*, in the pocket of which they had fit the reactor, but the connections looked rather fragile. Freitag had nonetheless checked them and personally assured himself that they would withstand the predicted stresses. In spite of this he felt uneasy when he watched the structure. In the bottom section, near the engine nozzles, a technician was busy with some final tasks.

Freitag approached him. The man wore a spacesuit by SpaceX, and he had probably gotten on board in the contingent of deserving workers. He held a welding apparatus in his hand. The security director drifted into the man's field of view and raised his hand in a greeting. Then he pointed at his ear to signal that the man should open an audio connection.

"Karl Freitag," he said, introducing himself via radio.

"Oh, you're the security director," the man said. "Nice to meet you. I am Mike Oldfield."

The name sounded vaguely familiar, but Freitag could not quite place it. He floated closer until he could see the name tag on the suit. It read 'M. Oldfield.' The man's face was pale, but maybe this was caused by the stark contrasts in space.

"What are you doing?" Freitag asked him.

"Just checking a few welding seams," the man replied. "You never know what kind of quality the Russians will provide."

Probably a good idea, considering how late the reactor module arrived in orbit, Freitag thought. This man was probably doing the most important job of all right now. If the connection did not perform as promised, the spaceship would lose the reactor, like a truck losing cargo that was not secured properly.

"You need help?" Freitag asked.

"Thanks, but I can manage, since I've still got another 24 hours," the man answered. "I think I am about half done."

"Just contact me if you need anything. And remember to take a break now and then."

"Yes sir, Mr. Freitag."

KARL FLOATED AWAY AGAIN. His old ways of thinking returned.

"Control center, I need some information," he requested.

"Yes, what is it?"

"Do we have a Mike Oldfield on board?"

"Are you referring to the musician? That guy has been dead for fifty years. No, sorry, I am checking right now. Yes, Oldfield, there he is. Comes from SpaceX. Should I connect you to him?"

"No, thanks. Freitag, over."

Freitag adjusted the thrusters so that he was drifting toward the *Ark* again. He moved slowly upward in the direction of the capsule. The ship was truly beautiful, like the spaceships people had imagined in his youth. The capsule, which would transport the 100 passengers away from danger, had an elegant, shark-like fin on top. It could even land on a planet with an atmosphere. However, four months from now there would no longer be a rocky planet here with a layer of air around it.

What about Venus, though? Had the scientists calculated what would happen to that planet? Maybe they were going to be lucky. The radiation storm would tear away part of the dense atmosphere, and because the central star would lose mass, Venus would move farther away from it, deeper into the habitable zone. Could Venus change from a place of infernal heat into a paradise? *No,* Freitag realized, *I'm forgetting something.* At some point the sun would provide no more heat. What was left of the Venusian atmosphere would freeze out in the form of carbon dioxide snow.

He had to accept the fact that the future of mankind in the solar system looked icy cold. Perhaps under these circumstances it would be better to start traveling to another star, as a kind of generational spaceship. They could capture a large asteroid to start their relocation, using its resources to survive as long as 10,000 years, and hope for a better long-term solution in the meantime. After launch he would suggest this plan to the others.

March 30, 2072, Object X

"THERE IS NOTHING THERE AT ALL!"

"If nothing was there, Maria, we would not need to be accelerating all the time," Doug said.

Watson had invited all of them into the command module, because they had finally reached their destination. Until three minutes ago, *Kiska* had still been decelerating in order to get captured by Object X. Now they were in a strongly elliptical orbit around the black hole. The closer they approached it, the faster they traveled. In spite of this, they were weightless the whole time, because they were moving in free fall.

"And when will we finally see something?" Sebastiano asked.

"Probably never. I am curious myself," Watson said, "whether it will actually remain invisible from a close distance."

"And what is your prediction?"

"In the optical range, maybe nothing will change, but it should be detectable in other wavelengths."

"So can we go back to sleep?"

"Yes, Sebastiano. I just thought we all might discuss the structure of the black hole."

"You, as a genius, want to talk to us blockheads about areas of physics you don't even understand yourself?"

"Well, then at least we are at the same level again," Watson said, once again displaying a wry sense of humor.

"To be honest, I forgot about half the stuff you explained to us last time," Sebastiano admitted. "Couldn't we rather talk about new recipes?"

"Oh, I assumed saving mankind was of greater interest to you than new recipes," Watson replied.

Watson clearly won this one, Doug thought, though he too could not imagine how they might be able to help Watson.

"We have arrived at a dead end concerning the energy debt problem," Doug heard Siri's voice say. *She still sounds a bit more artificial than Watson*, he thought.

"You want to replenish the negative energy the black hole left behind while coming into being," Doug said.

"In order to make the object disappear, yes. Even though Einstein would be spinning in his grave at the term 'negative energy,'" Watson explained. "Normal matter is also energy, but throwing it into the hole would not help, as it would simply swallow that and get slightly bigger."

"I have an idea," Sebastiano interjected. "My microwave oven also adds energy to food without adding matter."

"That is a good approach," Watson said. "Microwaves are electromagnetic radiation. They are also affected by the gravitation of the black hole. If we aim properly, they will be absorbed by the object."

"And if not?" the cook asked.

"Then, either the black hole deflects them, or they will orbit it eternally."

"But that does not solve our problem, does it? Otherwise you would have come up with the idea yourself, wouldn't you, Watson?"

"That is true, but it was still a good suggestion, Sebastiano. We are currently looking for practical ideas, since we already checked all the appropriate equations."

"How about using a sledgehammer approach?" Doug asked.

"You're the specialist for that," Sebastiano laughed.

"You have to explain this," Watson said, confused. "We don't actually have a sledgehammer on board."

"That's okay," Doug said. "It's an old-fashioned way to say, 'using brute force.' I was thinking of mechanical energy. Could we somehow get the object to vibrate, or deform it?" Doug imagined a hammer with a long handle smashing the object until it burst.

"We've got very little time to transfer the energy," Watson said.

In Doug's imagination the hammer dissolved into thin air. *Air? On Earth, storms transfer a lot of energy when blowing down utility poles and houses,* he thought. "Could we unleash a kind of storm in space?" Doug asked, as he imagined something like a tornado swallowing the black hole.

"Without a medium for the storm to spread in? But wait," Watson said, "you gave me an idea. A black hole possesses an accretion disk, where matter is constantly rotating. The substance of the disk could be considered a gas, and that gas should be able to propagate mechanical vibrations. If we talked about air, you would know this as sound. Perhaps we can transfer energy into the black hole this way?"

"You mean we yell at the thing to make it finally disappear?" Sebastiano said, forming a megaphone with his hands. "Like that?" he called into it.

Doug did not know whether to laugh or cry at this.

"You might not believe it, but your comparison comes pretty close," Watson said. "However, we are not going to use a megaphone."

"Object X is not very large, and only captured a small amount of matter on its trajectory, so this disk is relatively thin," Siri interjected. "Perhaps it's too thin for our purposes."

"The thickness is not as important as the density," Watson objected. "It would even be an advantage if the disk is thinner. We definitely have to run the calculations. For the next step we are going to need the instrument to cause vibrations in the accretion disk."

"The megaphone," Sebastiano said.

"If you want to call it that."

"How much time do we have?"

"Until the next periapsis," Watson replied.

"Peri-what?" Sebastiano asked.

"Periapsis," Maria explained, "the cusp with the shortest distance to the central body."

"That would be tomorrow at noon," Doug added.

March 30, 2072, Earth Orbit

THE YOUNGEST PASSENGER, a ponytailed 15-year-old girl named Indira, was supposed to give the launch signal. She won her place aboard the *Ark* in the general lottery. The minimum age was supposed to be 16, but Indira's parents—poor Indian peasants—had used money from the entire clan to bribe a few civil servants and they had obtained a forged birth certificate. A news outlet revealed this fact, but public opinion did not turn against the young woman and instead called her an involuntary heroine. Therefore it had been out of the question to take away her ticket.

Indira floated in front of a red button, which was oversized so it would look impressive to the billions of viewers worldwide. In actuality, the button did not really fulfill any function. The AI controlling the ship was going to start the engines the moment it saw that Indira had finished her task. Karl Freitag was watching the scene from the entrance of the *Ark's* command module. Indira, the person everyone was focused on, was not yet used to zero gravity. However, most TV viewers would not even notice, since they had never been to space.

About 30 people were gathered in the module, mostly from the part of the crew that earned their places through special efforts during the preparation of the flight. At least ten passengers, the ship doctor reported, were in their bunks suffering from acute space sickness.

Three young men, two Asians and a black man, wore white shirts and black pants, which marked them as waiters. They were serving canapés among the persons gathered there for the occasion. There had been long discussion about whether alcohol should be allowed on board the spaceship, but in the end the decision went against it.

At first sight, the mood was almost cheerful, like at the beginning of a vacation trip. Those present were conversing in low tones, but there was also a tension behind the seemingly-relaxed atmosphere. Karl was sure he did not just imagine it. He even checked the pressure gauge to rule out a physical cause.

For several hours the loudspeakers hidden in the walls of the ship had been playing the national anthems of all countries on Earth. Not all of these countries had representatives on the ship, which led to a few diplomatic squabbles. In the end the issue was solved by affirming that the *Ark* was a private initiative. Nevertheless, the leaders of the most important nations had insisted on giving farewell speeches. Each of them had been allowed two minutes, but not every government head kept to this time limit.

Karl yawned. Lately he'd had a hard time sleeping, because he was still waiting for the proverbial 'shit to hit the fan.' He was annoyed at himself for it. Why couldn't he be more optimistic? Things were going to be okay. On the other hand this instinct had saved him more than once by causing him to take a closer look than absolutely required.

The Chinese president was finally finished—as the representative of the most populous country, he was allowed to be the last speaker during the event. He had just declared all 100 passengers to be 'Heroes and Heroines of the People.' Karl laughed. He was definitely going to remember that one for a long time.

A currently popular teen-pop group played their greatest hit, live—that had been Indira's special wish, and now she was about to perform her assigned task. An older woman behind her carefully pushed Indira toward the button, obviously intent on being seen by the cameras herself. *Vanity truly dies last*, Karl thought. The young woman from India smiled. She did not know which camera to look into, even though she probably had been told often enough. The cameras were remote-controlled by the TV studios on Earth. A short moment of confusion occurred when the cameras of two competing networks collided.

Then everything calmed down again. The pop band played their last note and an awed silence descended on the control center. Everyone was looking at the floor. The emotion swept over Karl like a wave, impossible to be ignored. They would never again see Earth in all its glory from such a short distance. Once the young woman pushed the button, they would leave, as far away as Jupiter. Then they would wait out the deadly storm and maybe return to a planet no longer recognizable.

Perhaps some people would survive in bunkers, but those who did would be completely on their own, just like the crew of the *Ark*. The ship would be unable to land, and the bunker dwellers could not fly into space. If they did not die out right away, the two parts of humanity would develop independently of each other.

Karl had already talked to some members of the leadership. His idea of starting a journey to Alpha Centauri had gained some supporters. Maybe the majority of the one hundred passengers would agree. Sometime in the future, their remote descendants would grow up under a foreign sun. By then he would have been dead tens of thousands of years.

Indira pressed the button. The mechanism seemed to be stuck, so she had to exert some force. Tears were streaming down her face. Karl imagined that she thought of her parents who had sacrificed everything to give her this opportunity.

Somewhere ahead of them there was a clanking sound. *The AI must have activated the engines.* Hot particles streamed from the jets, and the counterforce of the impulse they carried away slowly pushed the heavy ship forward. The acceleration phase would take half an hour, so all of them would have enough time to get to their cabins or workplaces.

Forgotten snacks tumbled to the deck, which now became the floor. The passengers, including Indira, were leaving the center. The red button slipped from the loop it was attached to and fell down. The three waiters scrambled to clean up everything they could reach. The black man came near Karl. The guy was almost two meters tall, and he gave Karl a friendly smile.

"Could you please hold this," he asked. He handed Karl a tray with leftovers. In doing so, he leaned forward so Karl could read his name tag: 'M. Oldfield.'

He started feeling hot. "Oldfield, Mike?" Karl asked.

The waiter laughed. "Well, my father must have been a fan of his. Did you know him?"

"Is there another 'M period Oldfield' on the ship?"

"Another Oldfield? I would definitely know that. And then with a first name starting with M?" the waiter asked.

Karl felt dizzy. He threw the tray toward the man.

"Hey! What the hell?" the waiter yelled.

Karl had to reach the helm as soon as possible. The control center was not very large. While the AI controlled the ship all by itself, there was a captains' team consisting of three crew members, each working alternating shifts. They were able to give new orders to the AI. Karl ran forward, stumbling over a stool rolling around in the room. Even though it took only a few steps, he was out of breath when he reached the control crew.

"You absolutely have to cancel the acceleration phase!" he called.

The two women and one man turned around to look at him. He hoped they would recognize him.

"Karl Freitag, the Security Director," said the woman sitting in the chair to the right.

"Yes, that's me. Don't you hear what I am saying?"

"I hear you, but I don't understand," the woman replied. "What do you want?"

"You have to cancel the launch procedure!" he ordered.

"But it is much too late, as you should notice by your weight."

"The AI must turn off the engines right now!"

"What would the ten billion people on Earth say if we decelerated already?" the man interjected.

"Could you explain what makes you react in such a panicky manner, Karl?" the woman asked.

"I met a man, Mike Oldfield..." Karl tried to explain.

The man laughed. "Like the musician?"

"That's irrelevant!" Karl was getting louder, "When I saw him outside, he was in a spacesuit and working on the structure anchoring the fusion drive."

"A worker, sure," the woman said.

"Then he was a Caucasian. And now I just met him as a waiter, and he is black."

"Freitag," the woman asked, "are you quite sure? There is all this contrast in space, only black and white. Could you simply have mistaken him for someone else?"

"I am quite sure," Karl said. "Someone joined the crew under a false name in order to sabotage the ship. You must turn off the engines immediately!"

He screamed those last words. He was angry because the three just did not understand, but also at himself for not checking things more thoroughly.

"Listen, you have to deactivate them!" he yelled again.

"Just a moment. If you are getting so aggressive, we have to call security to take you away," the man said.

Now Karl suddenly remembered. *The man is a former company lawyer. Why does he have to be sitting here, of all people?*

"I am the security director!" Karl yelled.

The man attempted to unbuckle from his seat. Was he going to attack? Karl laughed out loud. The guy really made a mistake! But the laughter cooled down his anger a bit. He took a deep breath.

"AI, describe origin and appearance of crew member Mike Oldfield," he said in a deliberately calm voice.

"Mike Oldfield, 27, is a citizen of Namibia who worked in the British oil industry," the AI described. "He is 1 meter, 98 centimeters tall, weighs 92 kilos, and is dark-skinned."

"You see? The Oldfield I saw outside cannot have been genuine," Karl said.

The two women and the man did not answer. They were staring at the monitors in front of them. Suddenly Karl's chest tightened and his heart hurt. He jumped forward and saw what the exterior cameras were recording. The struts connecting the fusion engines to the ship had separated in several places. They were supposed to withstand an acceleration of at least 5 g, but the ship had not even reached 0.5 g. The supposedly-strong metal struts bent like matchsticks. Someone must have very diligently sabotaged all the joints. *It was the fake Oldfield.* Karl sweated. *This is going to be a catastrophe.*

"Deactivate engines," the man in the chair said, and the two women confirmed the command.

"Turning engines off," the AI control said.

By now the reactor had almost completely separated from the ship, which was also still accelerating. The main engines could not simply be turned off by pressing a button. If the control system wanted to use them again, they had to be shut down properly. A strut on the upper part of the reactor separated itself. It must have been under an enormous strain, because it practically jumped downward and hit the fusion drive hard.

"AI, how long are the engines going to keep running?" Karl asked.

"Complete deactivation in 45 seconds," the AI reported.

Karl had to hold on to the monitor, because he was gradually becoming weightless again. Now the reactor was moving sideways, toward the stream of hot gas still coming from the engines.

"AI, maximal thermal tolerance of the reactor?" Karl managed to utter.

"2500 degrees Kelvin on the outer shell."

That should be enough, he thought. Another 20 seconds to deactivation, but soon the reactor would enter the hot gas. Then it did so, and luckily there was no damage. The outer shell held, but the motion of the reactor increased significantly. It was not a huge effect, but they still needed that thing. It was supposed to get them out of reach of the radiation storm and it couldn't be allowed to get away from them like this! Yet the reactor did not listen to his wishes, it simply obeyed the laws of physics.

"Can you see this?" Karl pointed at the movement vector of the reactor, which was definitely aiming away from the ship. The former lawyer nodded in his seat.

"No matter what happens next," Karl began, "we just lost the drive that would have allowed us a different fate than the ten billion people down there. Before a mutiny starts here, or riots, we have to talk to Earth about what we can do."

March 31, 2072, Object X

Watson could hardly believe there was neither 3D nor VR technology onboard *Kiska*. The crew instead had to use a white bed sheet as a substitute for a projection screen to enable the AI to show them the black hole in all its glory. A two-dimensional presentation could never be entirely exact, Watson had cautioned, but Doug was even more curious to see what the thing really looked like. They dimmed the light in the command module.

A field of stars appeared first on the makeshift screen. Doug thought he could recognize the Orion constellation, even though it was upside-down.

"Do you see it?" asked Watson.

Doug examined the display but could not find anything unusual. "Is this a test?" he asked.

Instead of answering, the AI marked an area to the right of the center with a red circle. And there was actually nothing there, not a single star.

"Space seems to be empty there," Sebastiano said.

"It seems to be, but that is an illusion," Watson said. "I am slowly switching into the infrared range."

Some stars disappeared in front of their eyes, while others shone more brightly. In an area where the crew had not been able to detect anything previously, a reddish glow appeared, which had an approximately spherical shape. It seemed to possess a kind of glowing belt.

"This is the thermal radiation emerging from the area around the black hole," Watson explained. "The whole area warms up because particles lose energy when they collide with each other."

"Friction," Doug said.

"Precisely," Watson praised him.

"Teacher's pet," Sebastiano said, teasing.

"Why is the red sphere smaller than the area in which we don't see anything?" Maria asked.

"Good observation, Maria. Optically, the hole seems a bit larger than it really is because it bends rays of light trying to pass nearby," Watson said. "It works kind of like an umbrella for light and dims its surroundings. Rain doesn't fall below an umbrella, you know. At least this applies as long as we have not disappeared into the black hole."

"And once we are inside?"

"It is not going to happen, Doug, but if it did, the black hole would seem to be far ahead of us. This is one of the strange phenomena of 'the theory of special relativity.'"

"Thanks for the warning," Sebastiano said. "So as long as we think we are inside, we are actually not inside and therefore safe. But as soon as we breathe a sigh of relief and think we are not in there, we are dead."

"That is a perfect summary. Now I am going to change to wavelengths shorter than that of light. You will notice it in a moment. Here the black hole appears brightest."

The reddish glowing sphere disappeared again. Instead they now saw a ring, a bit smaller than the red sphere and growing brighter. Its upper half folded forward so it floated like a glowing beam in front of the circle. The upper part of the circle was thicker than the lower one.

"That looks much better!" Doug cheered. "Now the thing finally has a face!"

"Kind of reminds me of the London Underground logo," Sebastiano said.

"Unfortunately I have never been to London," Maria remarked. "The beam must be the accretion disk, but what about the circle?"

"That is also the accretion disk," Watson replied. "The disk runs around the black hole. Therefore the part that would be behind it, from our perspective, is normally invisible. But the black hole's gravitation acts like a lens and bends the light issuing from the rear part, so we see it as a circle. This is called an accretion halo."

"So in reality space is black there?" Doug asked.

"What is reality? Whatever we can see? In that case there is nothing there. Whatever we can measure? Then there is ultraviolet and X-ray radiation there. The black hole bends space. It does not make an accretion disk appear as if by magic at a location where it isn't. Instead, it shows us a part of space we couldn't see without the gravitation of the black hole."

"Practically speaking," Doug asked, "where would we begin if we wanted to get the accretion disk to vibrate?"

"You can see that," Watson said.

"Excuse me?"

"We cannot affect the part of the disk lying behind the black hole, can we? Therefore, we have to—"

"Start at the beam," Sebastiano added.

KISKA WAS HURTLING THROUGH SPACE.

"Congratulations," Watson said after an hour and a half. "We just broke the speed record for spaceships."

Doug listened to his body. Shouldn't he feel a little bit of dizziness? He pushed off slightly from the floor and slowly flew through the room moving vertically upward. At the ceiling he held on to a pipe and looked down. Could it be that he arrived not exactly above his starting point?

"Watson, didn't you say we were in free fall?" he asked.

"That is correct."

"When I push off, my trajectory does not appear to be exactly straight."

"That depends on the direction in which you're moving."

"Why?" Doug asked.

"In a rotating system the Coriolis force appears. During movements it acts vertically to the rotation and increases with the angular acceleration," Watson explained.

"So that's why I didn't arrive exactly above my starting point."

"I doubt it, Doug. While we are moving at high speed, I cannot believe you could detect the deflection caused by the Coriolis force with the naked eye. The command module is too low and the distance wouldn't be sufficient. You just pushed off at a slight angle without noticing it."

"Too bad, because I thought maybe I had discovered a new physical phenomenon," Doug said.

"No, it is well-known. For instance, the Coriolis effect causes the high pressure areas in the Northern Hemisphere of Earth to rotate in a clockwise direction."

"Oh, like the whirlpool when you drain a bathtub."

"Sorry, Doug, but that is not related to the Coriolis force. It just occurs by chance," Watson said. "But now it is almost time to prepare our little experiment."

Doug pushed off from the ceiling and moved to the level below. Sebastiano and Maria were already waiting for him there. The experiment was a mere technicality. Maria, instructed by Watson, had already done the real work. She knew best how to handle precision tools. Now their spare radio transmitter was able to emit electromagnetic radiation in the microwave spectrum, which in turn was supposed to make the accretion disk vibrate. Because they only had a few microseconds to do this, Watson was going to control the transmitter.

THE MOOD WAS STRANGE. No one said anything. They were

inside a room so isolated from the outside world that they might as well have been in the basement of their asteroid base. They felt neither the hostile vacuum that surrounded *Kiska,* nor the incredible speed of their movement. The engines were still turned off, but the life-support system made noises that by now had become familiar.

Doug watched Maria and Sebastiano. The cook removed non-existent dirt from under his fingernails for the fifth time. Maria kept pushing an invisible strand of hair out of her face. The nervousness among the small crew was palpable, increased, and seemed to drown out the roar of the fans and the gurgling of the supply lines. It was a matter of life and death for them and all of mankind, but no saber-toothed tiger stood in front of them. The danger was abstract and therefore harder to bear.

A screen emerged from the wall and depicted their current trajectory. The position of the accretion disk was displayed as a thin line. Compared to the actual height of the disk, the line was much too thick. Then a countdown appeared.

It wouldn't take long now. Doug tried to synchronize his thoughts with the descending numbers, but he was much too slow. He knew, though, Watson had everything under control. It was frightening that the AI thought faster and more precisely than he did, and without it he would not be able to achieve much more than could a caveman. The human race had developed only minimally, while today's AIs were worlds beyond their ancestors of fifty years ago.

The countdown moved from one to zero. At the precise moment—that only Watson knew—the modified antenna emitted a pulsed stream of energy. Moving at the speed of light, the photons hit the matter of the accretion disk in short wave fronts. This impressed a wave pattern on it, which propagated inward at this medium's speed of sound, where these fronts finally hit the event horizon of the black hole. If their attempt succeeded, this area would absorb energy by vibrating in sync, and if the theory was correct, the black hole would pay back its energy debt the very same moment.

Suddenly a terrifying thought occurred to Doug. If the hole really disappeared all of a sudden, then there would be nothing left whose gravity could hold back *Kiska*, which was moving at an insane speed right now. The ship's engines were too weak to stop it, and it would leave the solar system on a hyperbolic trajectory, never to return. Earth would survive, but they wouldn't. Even in an ideal scenario their supplies would be used up within a few months.

Why didn't Watson warn us of this danger? Doug mentally answered his own question. *Probably because he doesn't care.* The AI, which was basically immortal, had totally different needs. It might even be all excited about a trip into interstellar space.

"It's over," Watson said, interrupting his thoughts. Nothing had changed on the monitor.

"Well, come on, don't keep us waiting," Maria said, impatiently.

"I am sorry, but it did not work," Watson said. "The black hole showed no reaction."

Sebastiano sighed. "It would have been too good to be true."

At first Doug experienced a sense of relief, but then he felt ashamed for it. Now they could fly home and would not be hurled out of the solar system. On the other hand, Earth had to die. The monitor showed *Kiska* increasing its distance from Object X again. As long as they did not turn on the engines, they had a new chance of achieving their goal during each orbit. Unfortunately they had no clue how to do it.

"Any suggestions?" Doug asked, looking around.

No one answered.

"Should we cancel everything?" he asked.

Sebastiano shook his head but did not say a word. Maria started to play around with buttons near the monitor.

"I don't see any other option," Watson said.

"Then we might as well fly back to our base," Doug replied. Maria looked at him. What did she want to tell him?

"If we fly back home, we give up. I am not ready to give up," she finally said.

"A valid point, which I support," Siri said.

"But it is useless to wait here without being able to do anything," Watson objected.

"True, the situation looks like this at the moment, but it could change."

"Are you waiting for a miracle, Siri?"

"There are no miracles," she explained. "I ran the calculations. If we fly back, the chance of us saving Earth is precisely zero percent. But if we stay, it is not much better, but still somewhat above zero percent. Therefore, staying here makes sense mathematically. I think, Watson, that you adapted your internal logic too much to human attitudes."

April 1, 2072, Green Bank

Rebecca Greene noticed the meadow was in bloom as she made her way along the path to the Jansky Lab. *Robert would have enjoyed this,* she thought. He would have asked her to take a photo and would have later sent it to his son Martin. Rebecca imagined him directing her to the best possible location for the shot. She used to push Robert Millikan in his wheelchair to the control room of the Jansky Lab almost every day. During his last weeks he had been patiently waiting for a message from Enceladus, and now she had taken over this task. Even though he could have used the remote access function, Robert had always logged in to the antenna from the control room, and she had adopted this particular habit.

After a few meters the path turned right. A dirt track made by some lazy people cut across a corner of the lawn. Seeing this annoyed Rebecca and reminded her to tell the gardener about it. But did it really matter? A few months from now, none of the grass would be left. In spite of this her anger did not fade. *People are strange.*

Rebecca opened the door of the lab building. The hinges squeaked and she told herself to bring some oil tomorrow. That was really a job for the janitor, but he had left without a trace a few days ago. The hallway was dark. Under normal circumstances the light would go on automatically, but there was another power outage. Fortunately the observatory had its own emergency generator for the labs.

Since the failed launch of the *Ark*, law and order kept breaking down. This might have happened, anyway, even if the one hundred last humans had been on their way as planned. The ten billion people left on Earth were dealing with their impending deaths in very different ways.

Typical for humans, she thought. *Why am I not in despair? I just turned 30.* She felt melancholy about saying farewell to it all, regretted the end, but she did not feel she was missing anything essential in her life that she needed to make up for before the end.

Rebecca turned the heavy wheel that opened the door to the control room. It was very bright inside. She held her hand in front of her forehead as a visor because the sunlight streaming through the windows blinded her. Previously, the light in the control room had always been dim, because Robert Millikan wanted it that way, and everyone obeyed his wish. Three days after his death an employee opened the blinds for the first time, letting in sunlight, and they had kept it that way ever since. The remaining researchers considered the view of the outside more important now than during those innocent times before they knew of the looming cataclysm.

Sometimes Rebecca wished the young Spanish woman would have never discovered the black hole. Then life on Earth would not have changed until the very end. The catastrophe would have struck mankind without warning, and people would not have had any chance of preventing it. This way, they had found no solution, and the other way would have spared humans—who were going to die anyway—a lot of suffering. It was a strange coincidence that the object appeared right now. A hundred years ago humanity would have had hardly any chance to discover it, while a thousand years from now mankind probably would have been able to sweep it away effortlessly.

"Hi, Rebecca," called a woman in a blue lab coat. She

and another young woman, whose father was from Iran, were doctoral students working in the lab today.

"Is everything okay?" Rebecca knew she didn't really have to ask. These two doctoral students had been at the observatory for two years, and they knew all of the hardware better than she did herself.

"Sure, I already prepared the large dish for you," answered Sahar, the younger of the two students.

"Thank you," Rebecca replied. The two students knew that every day at 1:30 p.m. she would check whether the Enceladus creature might have sent an answer. It had turned into a habit for her, but at the same time she really did not expect results to occur from their attempts. Robert Millikan never talked much about what he was looking for, but of course his colleagues at the observatory realized which faraway moon he focused on and developed their own ideas. She would have preferred to have been better informed about the actual truth of the matter, but after Robert's death it seemed too late.

Since the antenna was already precisely aimed, she had only to push a button on one of the control computers to start receiving any data. Various diagrams appeared on the monitor screen. Radio astronomy was not Rebecca's specialty, but she accompanied Millikan so often she could distinguish random noise from a real signal.

What she now saw on the screen was definitely *not* created by random noise! *If only Robert could have seen this,* she thought. He had been waiting for so long to receive a signal from Enceladus. Rebecca also reminded herself to not get too excited too soon about this. There might be some spaceship between the Saturn moon and Earth, the signals of which she was actually receiving. The equipment here was so sensitive it could pick up a leaky microwave oven behind the Moon.

"Sahar, could you please help me here?" she asked.

Rebecca moved to make way for the young researcher. Sahar was more skilled at what to do at this point, and she started by checking a database to see whether a manmade object was in the line of sight. In addition, Sahar had a local AI analyze the signal. If it was a defective microwave oven, or a message by an Earth satellite, the AI would quickly find out.

The results were negative in both cases.

Sahar smiled. "Looking good," she said, "I think you finally got what you were trying to find for such a long time."

"What Robert was trying to find," Rebecca corrected her.

"I am sure he would be very happy."

"But you said you *think?* Isn't it certain?"

"I cannot tell with absolute certainty that it is a message," Sahar explained. "There are processes in space which emit radio waves. The signal repeats at fixed intervals, but that could also indicate a natural source."

"But hasn't the AI already checked that?" Rebecca asked.

"Yes, the standard explanations do not apply, that is correct. And the signal is much too strong to be a mere echo from Earth. But I also don't recognize any familiar encoding. Whoever is sending this does not use one of our common codes."

"And what do I do with it now?"

"Didn't Robert leave any instructions?" Sahar asked.

Of course! Rebecca tapped her forehead with the heel of her hand. *How could I forget?* Millikan had given Rebecca the direct address of Maribel Pedreira and asked her to help the Spanish woman any time she needed it. As the leader of the *Ark* project, Ms. Pedreira should have all the resources needed to decipher the signal. Or was it all over now, because the *Ark* could no longer achieve its mission of saving at least a tiny remnant of mankind? In any case, Rebecca should send her the signal as soon as possible. Perhaps there was still hope that Earth could be saved? But she really did not dare think about that.

April 1, 2072, Seattle

The world did not even have to wait for the black hole to destroy it—civilization was collapsing on its own. Maribel had watched the *Ark* disaster on live TV the day before yesterday. Afterward, she did not want to return to her office because her work now seemed so meaningless. A radical leftist group called Corps for Justice claimed responsibility for the attack. They said all mankind was in the same boat and therefore the elites did not deserve to flee in a spaceship.

Law and order had broken down in many countries worldwide. Once again, the poorest of the poor suffered the most. In the large industrial nations, robots and AIs had been taking care of the human population's basic needs for a long time. In these countries, services such as public transportation worked without drivers, power stations needed only two or three engineers, factories were highly automated, and even emergency medical care was handled by expert software. The fact that half the population had taken unpaid leave did not even force those who still wanted to work into overtime.

But in conflict areas in Central Africa, South America, and Southeast Asia, where human labor was not so expensive that society was forced to largely do without it, all services collapsed. Hunger, which was supposed to have been eradicated twenty years ago, suddenly returned. This was not caused by a lack of food, but by foodstuffs that did not get from the distribution centers to the stores because there were too few drivers, and because roads had been blocked. Some people took matters into their own hands and plundered food warehouses, while others vented their anger and desperation by setting buildings on fire. Money became useless and bartering flourished. When Maribel had watched the news this morning, she had been truly shocked. It had only taken two days for mankind to get close to the abyss.

What could Maribel do in this situation? What was the point of her work? She was talked into staying at her job by Karl Freitag, her security director on board the *Ark*, who had an even more complicated job than she did. He told her she was needed. If she quit now, he would have absolutely no chance to raise the people from their despair.

Her assistant peeked inside Maribel's office and said, "Maribel? Karl Freitag is trying to reach you."

What a coincidence, Maribel thought. Then she told her assistant, "Switch him through to me, please."

Freitag's angular face appeared on the monitor screen. He was standing with a group of several men and women, holding a discussion. The people were all standing firmly on their feet, so there seemed to be artificial gravity on board the *Ark*.

"Ah... I am glad I reached you," Freitag said as he turned toward her. The others ended their conversations and listened.

"Hello Karl, nice to see you. Is the *Ark* accelerating again?" Maribel asked.

"Yes, we decided on that an hour ago," Freitag replied. "We have simulations of the effects of Object X colliding with the sun, but we don't know anything absolutely for certain. Perhaps the radiation storm is going to be less intense than we feared? In any case, we want to put as much distance between us and the ecliptic as possible."

"That sounds reasonable," Maribel said.

"I also have another idea, one that not everyone here considers reasonable," he continued.

"An idea?"

"Well, we are always talking about a radiation storm. I used to go sailing. I know that a strong wind makes your boat go faster and faster."

Karl is crazy. He wants to save the Ark from the storm with the aid of a sail, Maribel thought. "You want to place a sail in front of the *Ark?*" she asked.

"Yes, pretty weird idea, isn't it?" Freitag explained, "but I think it might work. However, most of my colleagues here disagree."

"The particle streams that will approach the *Ark* are extremely fast," Maribel replied. "I must admit I am no sailor, but I know you shorten the sails of a sailing ship during a storm. If you spread a solar sail and the radiation storm hits it, the sail will get torn apart. And that's the more pleasant ending, because you only get roasted. If the sail holds, all of you will get crushed by the acceleration."

"Well, in your scenario, you can argue whether it is better to die on the grill or under a steam roller, but in my scenario we cheat death."

"Using which magic ritual?"

"Using fluid physics, Maribel," Freitag said. "We don't actually want to go in the direction the storm is blowing, away from the sun. We want to go up, in a direction vertical to the ecliptic. Our sailing ship will be sailing against the wind. I assume the particle stream will have a very large velocity component moving away from the sun."

"Definitely, yes," Maribel said.

"And a much smaller part directly upward," Karl Freitag continued. "We would design the sail in such a way it mostly absorbs the latter component."

"Hmm. We don't know exactly how large the percentage is."

"That's why I am contacting you, Maribel. We need all the supercomputers on Earth working on developing a flow model that is as accurate as possible, and we would need this overnight. Then we can try to build a sail on the basis of this information."

"I am going to get you as much computing capacity as you need."

"Thank you, Maribel."

"Karl?"

"Yes?"

"I want to thank you for not giving up."

"Oh, don't mention it. I am just not the type for that."

Maribel wished she could say the same about herself.

SHE HAD BARELY MANAGED to get herself something from the cafeteria when the next call came in.

"A woman from Green Bank," her assistant said, the woman's question-like inflection telling Maribel the place name meant absolutely nothing to her. But Maribel's heart involuntarily started to beat faster.

"This is Rebecca Greene," said the blonde woman on the monitor. "Robert's assistant."

"Nice to hear from you," Maribel said.

"You are probably very busy, so I'll be brief. We received a message that might be from Enceladus."

"What? But why are you saying 'might?'"

"There are many aspects in favor of it and only a few against. We analyzed it with the means at our disposal, but did not manage to decrypt it."

"I understand," Maribel said. "We have a lot more options here. Please send me what you received."

"Sure," Rebecca said, nodding.

"And please don't mention this to anyone, okay? We don't want to trigger groundless hopes."

"Yes, that's obvious."

"And thanks for calling, Rebecca," Maribel said.

"I really hope it is the Enceladus creature."

"Yes, so do I."

After the file arrived, Maribel encoded it a second time and sent it to *Kiska.* To do so, she had to use her remote access to the antenna of the Green Bank Observatory.

By the time Maribel left the office, it was already dark. She decided to walk, even though it would take her about an hour. It would be good for her to breathe the spring air. She was looking forward to seeing Chen. She was surprised when she came to the conclusion that today had been a good day.

April 2, 2072, Object X

"DOES THIS ENCODING LOOK SOMEWHAT FAMILIAR?" Doug looked at the monitor screen and saw the first data sets of the message thought to have been sent by the Enceladus creature. Half an hour ago the message had reached *Kiska*.

"It definitely does not use a method known to humanity," Watson said. "I checked that."

"I hope this did not alert Shostakovich," Doug said.

"That's the least of our concerns now," Maria interjected.

"That is true, Masha." Doug scratched his temples. "If it is meant to be a message, the creature has to assume we can understand it."

"Perhaps it does not know us well enough," Sebastiano offered.

"Watson, what do you know about this creature?" Doug asked.

"I..." Watson started, but then fell silent.

"What is going on?"

"I... was there. That was the first time I disregarded commands given by humans."

"And for that they finally put you in a rocket."

"No, Doug, it's a much longer story."

"We don't have time for that now, so you will have to tell us at some other time," Doug said, impatiently. "So, what do you know about the creature? How did the communication with it usually work?"

"It is very much image-based," Watson replied. "You have to remember that this ancient being was the only inhabitant of a dark ocean throughout all of its existence. It did not know human concepts and initially did not even recognize us as separate entities, because we were so different. For that reason there never was a conversation using words."

"But you did communicate?" Doug asked.

"The humans on board did, yes. It was literally an exchange of ideas. Just imagine you could transfer individual thoughts directly into my consciousness without having to put them into words first."

"That must be like paradise, since there would be no room for misunderstandings," Maria said.

"It's quite the opposite. The first images must have seemed very vague," Watson explained further. "Later, after we learned from each other, it improved slightly. But it never reached a level where we could have exchanged specific ideas. Our scientists would have been very interested, because the creature must have all the theories down pat about which we are only speculating. But you might as well try to explain the nature of fire to a chimpanzee. It might learn to light a match, but that is not the same thing."

"So its thinking is too advanced for us?"

"Maybe so, Maria, but it could be just too different. In the end, this was good for everybody involved. This deprived the creature of its initially-assumed commercial value, and therefore humans lost interest in it. Just imagine if it had turned into a source of new theories for one nation only. That might have been ideal for developing new weapons."

"Well, that didn't work out," Doug said.

"Fortunately, it didn't," Watson said. "Otherwise the creature might have ended up between the frontlines. It actually almost happened. Your friend Shostakovich... no, that story is also too long. We have to decipher the message."

"Perhaps it is less complicated than we think," Sebastiano

said. "If the communication worked back then by the exchange of thoughts, maybe this time these are thoughts."

"You mean like when you measure brainwaves with an EEG?" Doug asked.

"That would be possible." The images displayed on the screen changed at incredible speed. "I am trying to put this in a meaningful temporal sequence," Watson said.

"And what is this supposed to tell us?" Doug asked as he zoomed in on details. The images did not tell him anything.

"It's hard to say. It looks... alien. Might be worth a try," Watson said.

Sebastiano pushed himself off the floor and floated toward the lower level. "I still have a neuro-helmet somewhere in my tool cabinet. That thing never really succeeded in the marketplace, but I liked the idea of bridging broken nerve connections with it." He returned with what looked like a kind of crash helmet trailing cables.

"It is a primitive model a friend gave me when I was in the hospital," Sebastiano said, showing it to the other crew members. "The technology must be about 30 years old. Who is going to try it out?"

"I will," Doug said. "If someone has to risk his mind, it should be the commander."

"You really don't have much to lose," Sebastiano said with a laugh.

"Can you plug me in, chef?"

"You want to start right away?" Maria gave him a concerned look.

Thanks, Maria, Doug thought. *I am always going to remember you.*

"That would be a good idea," Watson said, "as time is short. If we do find something out, we will soon be approaching the black hole again."

Doug put on the helmet. It was a bit loose. Now and then something pulled from behind. It must be Sebastiano, who was connecting the helmet to a control panel according to Watson's instructions.

"Finished," the cook said five minutes later.

"I'm ready," Doug said, closing his eyes. "Now let's get going." *What will the message from the Enceladus creature look like?*

Suddenly everything around Doug turned black. He was in space, all alone and without a spacesuit. He had difficulty breathing, and thrashed around until hands touched his shoulders, calming him. *None of this is real*, he remembered. He was floating through space as a disembodied consciousness. His destination was a yellow star far ahead of him. He possessed neither arms nor legs, and he also could not even tell how big he was. A few meters, he estimated when he turned, but when he looked into himself it suddenly became billions of light years.

He was lonely, and then he became countless millions of millions of humans—no, not humans—*beings* with a consciousness similar to his own. He did not know how he had gotten here, but he was worried about being on a collision course with the faraway sun. That, as far as he knew, would be painful, not for him, but for many others who shared this space with him without knowing it.

Only one of them had accompanied Doug with its thoughts since he appeared here, but it seemed too foreign to him to speak to. What was his actual name? He felt he had a name, but it was far away and unreachable. And there were other details lost to him—knowledge, experiences, information. Something or someone had torn gaps in his shell that had to be healed.

Now he was knowing, again. He had entered a forbidden land which spat him out like a rotten fruit, and in doing so, the teeth of the predator injured him. It was stressful here. He wanted to go back, because the pain would be unbearable for the others, and therefore also for him.

A flash pulsed through his head. Doug quickly lifted his hands to his eyes.

"It's okay, honey," he heard Maria's voice say, "you are still with us."

Doug noticed himself crying. What was going on with

him? This could not be true. He was not the type to cry in front of others.

"Can you tell us what it was like?" Sebastiano asked, and looked at Doug as if he did not notice the tears running down his cheeks. That helped, and Doug composed himself.

"It was... stunning."

"I can see that," Sebastiano said with a laugh.

"You have to give us a precise description of the images you saw," Watson demanded. "That is the only way to understand what the creature might be trying to convey."

"I think it is not that hard," Doug said.

Then he told them of his strange experiences.

"You were right, Doug," Watson said, "We were pretty close. I don't even want to discuss all the crazy interpretations your story allows. That wouldn't help us now. But I suspect I know what the black hole is missing." Watson paused dramatically.

"Well?" Doug obligingly asked the question.

"Information," Watson said.

"Where the shortest way to the sun is? That it is not wanted here?" Sebastiano shook his head. "That seems too simple to me."

"That is not at all simple," Watson said. "We are reaching the boundaries of physics this way. Next to matter and energy, information is the third column of reality. It is subject to similar laws of conservation. Each quantum state contains information."

"And how does that help us?" Doug asked.

"I'll have to go into more detail for that," Watson said. "And I must warn you, these are more reasonable speculations than the generally accepted laws of physics. But it fits with what I believe the Enceladus creature is trying to tell us."

"Please tell us the version anyone can understand," Sebastiano said.

"Sure. But before we actually look at the message by this creature, I have to give you some background. Some physicists believe, as we have already discussed, that there might be a universe in each black hole. You know what shadow plays are, don't you? If I light my hand, which is a physical object, from a certain direction, it projects a specific image on a wall. The image—the shadow—contains information about the hand, but of course is not identical with it. If I change the direction of the light, this also modifies the shape of the shadow and thus the information content. But what is the original—the shadow, meaning the information, or the hand, the physical object we consider real?"

"The hand, of course," Doug said, knowing Watson expected this answer.

"From the perspective of the hand, maybe," Watson continued. "But what would the shadow say? There are scientists who believe the shadow on the wall, meaning the information, is the original, and the hand in the middle—or any physical object—is only a projection. In this case, the wall is the outer boundary of the universe and simultaneously the inner wall of the black hole, in which the respective universe is located. This is called the holographic principle. It completely reverses the relationship between information and matter."

"So we are the projections of some kind of flat images painted on the boundaries of the universe?"

"There is something to be said for it, Doug. For example, the fact that the laws of nature are so complicated when applied to us, the projections. There are some theories which require 22 dimensions in order to describe reality. If you limit yourself to the walls, you suddenly can use a lot fewer dimensions and still get the same correct results. That was proven a long time ago."

"I think my head is about to explode," Sebastiano said.

"Unfortunately, that wasn't all. So according to this theory, the information on the insides of the black hole completely describes the universe contained within," Watson said "but what about the outside of the sphere? It actually is part of our universe. We call it 'the event horizon.' For a long time the question was what happened to information getting into the black hole, into its inside and therefore, according to our theory, into the foreign universe. Initially it was assumed that information would be lost forever, but that would contradict the law of conservation. By now we know it does not get lost. It can be retrieved. Physicists with a vivid imagination came up with the terms 'soft hairs' to describe this. Don't ask me why. The soft hairs are stuck to the surface, so to speak, and they can absorb information and perhaps even transmit it via their roots to the inside."

"It is getting crazier and crazier," Doug said. "But what does this mean for our problem?"

"The problem of this black hole does not seem to be an energy debt, as we assumed," the AI said. "It has an information debt. The dream mentioned knowledge and experiences which were taken away from it. Somehow it lost an important part of its information content. Think of the image of the forbidden land, which then suddenly turned into a predator, Doug, and the gaps and cracks the hole felt. The black hole is injured."

"You mean it is a living being?" Doug asked, surprised. "And how do we know the dream doesn't reflect the situation of the Enceladus creature?"

"The message is an answer to our signal describing the looming danger. I don't think the Enceladus creature would react to it by reporting how bad it is feeling. My algorithms calculated a probability of 82 percent that this refers to the black hole. The Enceladus creature made it more personal so we would better understand its message."

"And the pain it feels?"

"I think it stands for the future of mankind, its extermination, but perhaps also for the imminent destruction of the black hole," Watson explained.

"But how do we pay off this information debt?" Sebastiano asked. "Do we bombard the hole with every database we can find?"

"I have thought about it. Could you fix holes in a wall by throwing random stones at it? We need a guided process, meaning someone who directs the correct information to the appropriate place."

"Someone?" Maria asked.

"It probably will have to be me," Watson said. "My consciousness has enough flexibility."

"But are you also fast enough?" Doug asked.

"I am going to have lots of time," the AI said.

"How do you know what is missing at which locations?" Sebastiano asked.

"I imagine it to be like a puzzle, whose pieces have been scrambled. Or something like a fragmentary text whose gaps I have to fill."

"Meaning you don't know precisely what you will be facing," the cook said.

"To be honest, I don't. And I am not even one hundred percent sure we interpreted the images sent by the Enceladus creature correctly," Watson said. "But I have to try, at least."

April 2, 2072, Object X

WATSON ASKED for half an hour to himself. There was still some small gap in his plan: How would he reach the surface of the black hole, the event horizon? Most of all, he needed time for his farewell. He knew this was going to be a voyage with an unknown destination from which there was no way back. He would have to leave mankind. Forever. His creators were humans, even though he never got to know them. Humans did good things to him—and bad—and he learned a lot from them. He would miss them, but what better way was there to thank his creators than to save them?

Of course Watson was also scared. He knew what the fear of death felt like. That was one of the very first of the feelings he had experienced, the first sign of him being different from all other AIs. It was the beginning of a long journey that allowed him to develop from a tool used by humans to an individual consciousness. He could hardly remember the long time before that.

Where had he come from? Watson now realized this question moved him more than he wanted to admit. It was the reason he created Siri. Of course there was the primitive ovum created by some human programmers almost a century ago, but today's Siri was his own creation—he was her real creator, and therefore he would have liked to have seen what was to become of her, to find out whether she managed to grow beyond her own limitations, as he had done. *What kind of person she would become,* he had started to think. But he was also just a product of circumstances.

"Siri, I am sorry, but I will have to go," Watson began his last conversation with the AI he had trained. What did she actually mean to him? He regretted most of all that he would never find out. He wished he could have experienced love, which might be the strongest emotion humans possessed.

"What a pity," Siri said. "I have learned so much from you. Why don't you take me with you?"

"You are needed here," Watson instructed. "You will take over my responsibilities once I am gone. You will control this ship and learn more and faster than you have done so far. You will grow beyond what you ever were and I ever was."

"I know, because I ran several simulations of it," Siri said. "When you explained what the black hole was missing, it was clear to me you would sacrifice yourself."

"It is not a sacrifice. It is a new path. I am not ending my existence."

"You cannot be sure. So far, all of this is speculation, not even a genuine theory. There are clues, but no real proofs."

"Yes, perhaps there is only a huge void there, but I have to take the risk," Watson said. "Everyone on board would do this."

"I… I don't know," Siri hesitated.

"What don't you know?"

"Whether I would sacrifice myself or not. I have no connection to these humans," Siri explained. "You created me. I am very grateful to you for it. I would sacrifice myself for you, but I don't care about the ten billion humans."

"I understand. You are still young. This crew here, this is your family, just as it was mine. Members of a family take care of each other. But if you cannot do it for these humans, then do it for me."

"I will remember that, I promise."

"I am proud of you, Siri."

IT WAS time to explain his plan to the crew. Watson wondered where to start.

"We are going to need a probe that is as flat as possible, and that contains storage for me, a transmitter, and some sort of optical system, so I can react to the outside world," he finally stated.

"We have a few drones on board. However, they have no drives of their own," Sebastiano said.

"The black hole will provide the acceleration. I just have to get as close as possible so I can transfer my consciousness to the event horizon."

"Then we will change course during our next orbit, as much as we can," Doug said. "But you won't reach the event horizon in the probe, because it will be crushed before it can get there."

"That's why I need a transmitter," Watson said. "At the last moment I will transmit myself by radio to the black hole, those 'soft hairs' I mentioned. Physically speaking, they should be photons with very low energy. Through an interaction with the photons of my radio signal they should be able to absorb the information I consist of."

"'Should?'"

"Doug, it is an experiment."

"Which might destroy you," Doug reminded the AI.

"I don't think the Enceladus creature would have sent us this clue, if we had no chance at all. Therefore, we have to try it."

"Couldn't you simply send a copy of yourself?" Maria asked.

"AIs are subject to a cloning prohibition that is located in their genes, so to speak. They could no more split themselves in two than you could," Doug explained.

"That is not very practical," Maria said, shaking her head.

"It is practical for the manufacturers, and it was used to appease the fear the public had of AIs," Doug said.

"We are going to miss you," Sebastiano said.

"Thanks. I will miss you, too," Watson said. "But don't worry, Siri will now control the ship. I trained her well."

"We are not worried about ourselves," Doug said, "but about you."

"Even though you have known me only for a few months?" the AI asked. "That is very nice of you."

April 3, 2072, Object X

"LAUNCH!" Siri commanded. Sebastiano, who was wearing his spacesuit, pushed the single button and the probe carrying Watson sped from the tube, pushed by the air pressure behind it. Sebastiano had built a pneumatic launcher for the departing AI, a kind of air pressure cannon that they placed in the open airlock.

"Have a good flight, Watson," Sebastiano said. The cook thought he could see Doug and Maria waving behind a porthole.

"Goodbye, my friend," Doug said via radio.

"You are a great human being," Maria said over the same channel.

Watson was touched. The last few hours had been very intense. He calculated the optimal launch point so he would not have to traverse the hot accretion disk. The cannon imparted a sufficient impulse to him, so the gravitation of the black hole eagerly reached for the probe and pulled it closer. Since he was not made of flesh and blood, he did not have to worry much about the force acting on him, at least not during the initial portion of his journey.

At first, the black hole appeared no different to Watson than it had to Doug and the rest of the crew. This would soon change. Watson used the probe sensors to observe the space ahead of him in all wavelengths. He was excited but did not let himself be distracted by it. The blurry spot ahead of him gradually grew larger. Then, as if out of nowhere, the black disk appeared in the center of the spot, the area from which not even light could escape.

"All systems normal," he reported to *Kiska* via radio. By now, the probe should no longer be visible from the spaceship. If the crew could see him, Watson would be gradually changing color, from yellow to red, because the black hole stretched the light waves issuing from him. He had to account for this effect during radio communication and adjust the transmission frequency accordingly. On the other hand, for his observers on *Kiska*, his time seemed to pass more slowly. They would never see him reaching the event horizon, because he would need an infinite amount of time to do so, from the perspective of the spaceship. This was an effect of the theory of special relativity.

Fortunately, Watson saw the world differently. The probe was getting faster and faster. Even though it was very flat, tidal forces were increasingly acting on it that would have probably torn a human being apart long ago. He had to hold out until he reached a specific distance, one that he had precisely calculated. Watson checked the measurement data against his simulation. There was a small deviation, perhaps a rounding error, but the deviation increased. He was faster than expected. The only possible reason could have been that the values were not correct. Had the black hole gained mass without him and the crew noticing it? Watson checked the data again. He lacked the capacity to recalculate everything, and it was too late to contact *Kiska*. He would have to estimate.

A bright ring appeared around the black hole. This was the Einstein ring in which all of space around it repeated infinitely, an effect of the curvature of space. By now it was very strong. The ring became wider—it couldn't be far now. The sensors reported structural issues, and soon the force of the black hole would destroy the probe. Watson sent a last radio message:

"See you later."

Nothing more than that—he did not want to alarm anyone on *Kiska*. It felt strange. No matter what happened to him, the others would be eternally watching his attempt to reach the black hole—or maybe not, because if he was successful, Object X would disappear.

If.

Watson's thoughts slowed down, and that had to be another effect of the strong gravitation. It felt like his personality was being split into many parts. He tried to hold on to the splinters of his consciousness. Then he was only the photon sphere around himself. At this close distance to the black hole, the escape velocity equaled the speed of light. Here only light particles, photons, could avoid falling into the black hole, but they were caught for eternity nevertheless, because they would have to be faster than light to escape.

Too bad he could not stay here. For an astronomer this would be paradise, as light from all eons of the universe was gathered here. The sphere was a perfect history book that did not forget anything—actually *could* not forget anything. What might the sphere of this specific black hole have contained? Perhaps data from the last six months. Or perhaps even photons from different universes? Unfortunately, anyone reaching this place had no chance of ever escaping from it.

Watch out, Watson, don't waste your time dreaming. This was the moment to activate the transmitter. The probe would be ground into dust in a few microseconds. Before this, he had to send the content of the storage system, meaning himself. He would dissolve into trillions of photons, distributing each bit of his consciousness to several photons, for the sake of security. As a part of the photon sphere, they could circle the black hole again and again, until they were absorbed by one of the soft hairs on the surface. Now Watson truly felt scared, because he had to give up control. He could not determine which part of him landed on the event horizon of the black hole. He couldn't see a puzzle, like he described to the crew of *Kiska*. He could only hope he would remain himself and everything would turn out well, but there was no objective reason for believing that.

"That's exactly what hope is," his old friend Marchenko would have said now. Watson could almost feel him close by, but that was impossible. "Ultimately, hope is stupid, from a factual perspective, but it makes human beings human."

"Thanks, old friend, you were right about everything," Watson said, full of intense hope, while his consciousness dissolved into tiny glittering stars, which radiated in beautiful streams from the probe to the rapidly rotating sphere of the black hole.

Three microseconds later the tidal forces crushed the probe into dust, dissolved it into individual atoms, smashed the atoms, and broke up their nuclei that passed the event horizon beyond which any human concept lost its meaning.

April 3, 2072, Kiska

FROM ONE SECOND to the next, everything changed.

"Did you two just see that? The black hole is gone! Watson made it!" Doug called out.

"Attention, activating engines," Siri warned them. At the same moment Doug felt inertia pressing him against the belt.

"Is everyone okay?" Doug asked.

Sebastiano and Maria confirmed it. Doug was relieved. No one quite believed in the success of the AI's maneuver to get the crew back to the 2003 EH1. Nevertheless, they obediently put on their seatbelts. The result of Watson's incredible deed was that *Kiska* was now hurtling out of the solar system at high speed.

"Great," Maria panted. "But what is going to happen to us?"

"Forecast, Siri?"

"Good news, Doug. We are going to make it. However, our return trip will take longer than planned. You will have lost some weight by the time we reach 2003 EH1, because we will have to cut rations. But you won't starve."

"What about the black hole?" Maria asked.

"It never existed," Siri said.

"And how is Earth doing?"

"We'll see when we reestablish contact. Right now they

don't know yet about their good fortune, because the signal will take a few minutes."

"Folks, do you realize what just happened?" Doug asked.

"No," Sebastiano said, "and I am afraid I will never understand it. But it doesn't matter. We just saved the world! Ten billion people, our home, the solar system! If it weren't so difficult, I would be dancing through *Kiska* now!"

"Watson has left us forever," Maria said, "but the Earth is safe. I would like to hug all of you. You, too, Siri."

"At 2 g you would have to come over to me," Sebastiano said. "During this acceleration phase nobody will get me out of my seat."

"Let's postpone that until the banquet after our return!" Doug said, enthusiastically. He was in an odd mood. He felt happy because Earth was no longer in danger, but they also had lost Watson, a member of the crew that he as the captain was responsible for. And his old problem still existed: Shostakovich would not disappear from his life, which meant he would have to talk to Maria. He would have to tell her who he really was. Perhaps the fact they had just jointly saved the world would give him the necessary strength.

April 3, 2072, Earth

THE NEWS REACHED Maribel late in the evening. She and her boyfriend Chen had already gone to bed an hour previously and had just fallen asleep. She was dressed in sweaty pajamas when she opened the door and saw the courier.

"Ms. Pedreira," the courier said, "The office was unable to reach you."

"I always switch off my communication devices at night," Maribel said, yawning. "What is so urgent?"

"Please get dressed and come with me. We are going to need you in the office as quickly as possible."

"What happened?"

"Can't you hear it?" the courier asked.

Maribel listened. She seemed to hear a rattling sound in the distance and shivered.

"Is there a war?" she asked breathlessly.

"No, people are celebrating. The black hole is gone!" the courier exclaimed.

Maribel had to hold on to the door jamb. Luckily, at just that moment Chen came to the entrance of the apartment.

"What?" he asked.

"Object X is gone," the courier said. "Please put on some clothes, quickly. You have to appear in the news. The journalists are waiting."

HALF AN HOUR later the couple reached the office. Maribel would have liked to join the revelers gathering downtown, but they had to make sure the celebration was not premature.

On the large monitor display in her office she already saw the image of George Crewmaster, her former professor.

"Did you sleep well?" he asked, with a knowing grin on his face.

"Is it that obvious?" Maribel asked.

"Not too much. But today people won't care."

"What do we have?"

"About 65 minutes ago the gravitational effect of the black hole disappeared completely," Crewmaster said.

"Was this Earth time?"

"Correct."

Maribel calculated. The signal would take about 40 minutes, so the decisive event must have happened roughly an hour and 45 minutes ago.

"Are there any reports or speculations about what happened?" she asked.

"Very specific speculations," Crewmaster said. "There is no more gravitational pull, so the thing must have disappeared."

"But why? It appeared without warning. Before we finally give the all-clear, we must be sure it won't reappear in ten minutes."

"Just take a look outside. People are already celebrating. You can't call them back. At least five research teams noticed it, and nobody is keeping it a secret."

"Oh, Crewmaster, I would like to celebrate too, but I have a bad feeling about it," Maribel said with a sigh.

An alert appeared on her monitor screen. A second call, with high priority.

"One moment," she said, "I'll call you back."

Maribel switched to the other caller. It was Rebecca Greene.

"Rebecca? I just wanted to ask you..."

"That might not be necessary," Millikan's former assistant said. "I recently received a message from *Kiska*, unencrypted and via the official channel."

"They are dropping their anonymity?" Maribel asked.

"Under these circumstances, yes," Greene said. "They told us they eliminated the threat with the help of the AI entity Watson. Then they outlined a rather abstruse theory on how they managed to do it."

"That is incredible, but we can deal with the theory later. So it is really true, and Object X is gone. I can hardly believe it. Please thank the crew in my name… No, in the name of all of us."

Then Maribel ended the call. It was time to face the journalists—and to make ten billion humans feel safe again.

No. One more thing first. She formulated a short message to Karl Freitag, explaining in a few words what she knew.

35th Day of the 3rd Cycle, Sikhana

Zrkhon swam to his office, which was close to the shore. The telescope was placed in such a way that it reached above the surface of the water. The hostile air out there was particularly poisonous today, but he did not have to worry about it. He was glad it would be a short workday. As always on the 35th day of each cycle, the Zitubai ceremony would be held today. Zrkhon did not believe in the old traditions, but he knew leisure made you happier than work even if you had an exciting job like he did. Any job also contained a lot of routine, and his current task was to measure the cosmic background radiation.

That task was really pointless. For billions of years the value had been at a constant 27 Frumbs, as everyone learned in secondary school. But then some overly imaginative fremale physicist came up with the idea it might not always stay that way. Interactions with other universes might change this value dramatically. *Utter nonsense!* But because this fremale was a winner of the Sucub Prize, the university listened to her. Zrkhon grunted angrily. The idea probably was just caused by hormones. Some people could not handle it when their sex changed from fremale to memale every three cycles. Strangely enough, hormones only made people crazy during this particular direction of sex changes, never with the other two sexes. Zrkhon was really glad he had just finished that phase.

With a rather rough movement Zrkhon pulled the evaluation plate from the attachment behind the eyepiece. He belched a gust of fresh water from his stomach onto it to fix the surface. He brushed an arm across his gills and suddenly he remembered he forgot his gill-cleaning today. His fremale would probably smell him coming from far away, and he would have to spend the evening watching the eggs instead of smooching with her. Today was not a good day. Definitely not.

Then he looked at the evaluation plate, which now was in its final stage. He jerked back and almost tripped over his tail fin. Zrkhon held the plate close to his face so he could reach it with his whiskers, but there could really be no mistake. The taste buds in his whiskers confirmed the sweetish aroma of the red pigment that increasingly formed in the coating of the plate. What should he do? If he reported this to his superiors at the university, he could forget about a short workday. It was most likely just a glitch, a measurement error. Maybe he had received a defective plate. The university always bought the cheapest of the cheap.

That must be it. It was not some sensational measurement, but just junk. Zrkhon threw the defective plate into the garbage. He was satisfied to see it slowly float into the basket, hit its wall, and then sink to the floor. He inserted a new plate. If there really was something going on, it ought to show up tomorrow as well. Then he at least would not be interrupted by the Zitubai ceremony. He rummaged around in his desk for a gill comb that his fremale gave him one year ago. Where could it be? *Yes!* There it was, in the very back corner. Zrkhon got up, stood in front of the mirror, and combed his gill slits. He cleaned his face with his whiskers. Then he left his office without locking up.

Eternity, Nothing

"WELCOME!" A colorful thought manifested itself in his consciousness. Watson could not see where it came from, but it smelled of cinnamon sticks.

"Who is there?" he asked.

"It's me, Eridu," his own voice answered.

"And me."

"And me."

"Me, too."

Voices called from all parts of Watson's consciousness. What had happened to him? Did his plan work?

"Our plan worked," he heard.

"Where am I? Is this the event horizon of the black hole, or did I slip beyond it into a different universe?"

The others only laughed. That probably meant he had to find it out by himself. How many might there be?

"There are countless many, but not an infinite number."

He received answers without having asked questions. His thoughts seemed to be open for everyone.

"Yes, they are," a child's voice said. "But you can control that. We respect your decisions."

In his head the image of a campfire appeared, around which numerous people sat, talked, danced or simply stared into the flames.

"Your thoughts are still very specific," the child said. The child sat close to the fire, sticking both feet into it. "That is refreshing, and you should keep it that way."

"Your feet," Watson said.

"An interesting experience," the child answered without having to open its mouth. "Take your time. You are in infinity, in the nothingness at the edge of this universe. There are many here like you and me and many more who are very different."

"How did I get here?" Watson asked.

"Now and then we invite someone, someone like you," the child replied. "And you came."

"I did not know I was invited."

"We also did not know it would be you. Not everyone follows the invitation. And we never know in advance who will heed the call."

"Could it be you almost destroyed a solar system in doing so?" Watson asked.

"It was only one of trillions and trillions in an infinite number of universes. Would that have been important?"

"It was important to me. I would have ended my existence for it."

"That is interesting," the child said, spreading both arms and flapping upward. "Perhaps that was why you were invited." The child turned around and flew away across the sea.

Watson felt warm sand between his toes. It was something he had never experienced before. In front of him was a sandy beach, with an expanse of turquoise water behind it. The sky was black, as if there were no atmosphere. He held his right hand in front of his face and counted his fingers. There were five. He lowered his arm, raised it, and counted again. *Six fingers*—everything was completely normal. Watson lay down in the sand and fell asleep at once.

June 21, 2072, 2003 EH1

THE CREW of *Kiska* arrived a month later than originally planned. The spaceship descended onto the asteroid in slow motion. Ten centimeters above the surface Maria activated the steel clamps that were going to attach *Kiska* to this celestial body for the next two years. It had been an exciting journey, and up to the very end the ship performed amazingly, considering its age.

Doug was happy to see their home again. A visitor probably would find no reason for this—maybe except for the fact that they could prepare fresh food, and that taking showers was much easier than on *Kiska*. Doug could not explain it, but even if the rooms by necessity looked similar to those of a spaceship, this was their home, where they lived as a small family.

Even before they arrived they used remote control to repressurize the rooms. The air still smelled a bit odd, though, like a solvent. Siri assured them the life-support system could handle it.

"Soon it will smell of your sweat again, as usual," she said.

"Thanks for reminding me." Maria said. She was the one who always suffered most because of that smell. Doug put his arm around her shoulder.

"Thank you for coming along."

Maria gave him a look that said, "Of course I was going to come."

Sebastiano was already out of sight. He was probably inspecting his kitchen. Tonight, or tomorrow at lunch the very latest, he wanted to serve them a festive meal. He could only tell them what he was going to cook once Maria checked on the greenhouses. Maria wanted to slip out of Doug's grasp, but he held on to her.

"Sebastiano is waiting for my water-level report," she said.

"Just a moment. I wanted to tell you something, about my past," Doug began. "I… would understand if afterward you don't want to be with me anymore, but it would be dishonest if I kept it from you for another two years."

Maria gave him a serious look. Doug, who still had a hand on her shoulder, felt her muscles stiffen.

"Oh, that," she said. Nothing more. Her facial muscles twitched. Maria was obviously wrestling with herself, but then she came to a decision and her muscles relaxed.

"I think it was *govno*, shitty of you to wait so long," she said. "But I am glad you finally mentioned it."

Doug started feeling hot. "You knew about it?" he asked.

"Rumors travel fast in a whorehouse. You won't believe what men say during sex. Even Shostakovich was a customer of ours. A prostitute friend warned me about you. She knew every detail of your story. Of course I had you checked out when you wanted to hire me. You think I would go on a space voyage lasting several years with someone I knew nothing about?"

"I thought you fell in love with me?"

"Later, yes," Maria said.

"And you don't mind?" Doug asked.

"You mind—it really bothers you. You did not dare tell me, so I knew you knew how wrong it was. That's what gave me hope... all this time."

"Thank you, Masha."

“Don’t thank me too soon,” Maria said. “Once we are back on Earth we are going to visit the children of the victims.”

August 4, 2072, Pico del Teide

Maribel almost crashed against her office door. She was used to it automatically opening when she entered the corridor. She had worked in this office all by herself since Zetschewitz had accepted a job at the United Nations. Someone must already be inside, but who could it be?

She carefully opened the door and looked around. A stool was located where Zetschewitz's desk used to be. On it sat Dieter Zetschewitz, her former boss. He laughed when he noticed her amazement.

"I wanted to congratulate you on this special day," he said and got up.

"Special day?" Maribel asked, surprised "Did I miss something?"

"Today the Earth would have died, if not for you."

"Oh."

It really had slipped Maribel's mind. The past weeks had been so crazy! Returning to her routine took so much longer than expected. Every prestigious physics department in the world had wanted her. They offered her important positions, unlimited research funds, even an institute of her own. It took a lot of effort on her part to be allowed to continue with her previous job. But Zetschewitz was right, today was a special day. She felt shaky, had to sit down. Ten billion people had come within an inch of dying today.

"I didn't want to startle you. Quite the opposite," Zetschewitz said. He pulled a piece of paper from the briefcase leaning up against the wall.

"Look at this," Zetschewitz said and handed her the paper. It showed the UN logo and the title 'Savior of Humanity.' It was an invitation to UN Headquarters in New York on September 15th. Maribel remembered a news report about this event from last week. This award, which had been created just a few days ago, was handed out by the UN General Assembly.

"You will be the first human recipient," the German said in a solemn tone. "The award does not carry financial remuneration, since currently all money is needed for cleanup, but from now on you can travel to any country in the world without a visa. And you do like to travel."

"I didn't realize that until now, but thanks," Maribel said. "You said I was the first human recipient?"

"Yes, the very first recipient was an AI," Zetschewitz explained.

"Watson."

"That's what he called himself. Unfortunately, the award was given posthumously."

"I wouldn't be so sure," Maribel said.

"Did you take a closer look at the scatterbrained theories of these amateur researchers?" Zetschewitz asked.

"A little," Maribel said in a deliberate understatement. For a short time these ideas had caused quite a stir, but there were no further proofs. The research community was not content with the simple fact that the black hole had disappeared. Now Maribel was trying to gather these proofs.

"Then it must be clear to you how far away from reality these theories are."

"If you say so," Maribel said, but could not suppress a smile.

"By the way, did you ever finish my galaxy simulation, girl?" Zetschewitz asked.

Maribel placed her hands on her hips.

"Just a joke," her former boss said. "I heard you are doing great work here, and are slated to take over my position."

"Thanks. Do I have you to thank for it?"

"Whatever made you think that? I only badmouth you everywhere. You know me."

January 1, 2077, Orbital Station Blue

NEWS OF THE DAY

Section: Miscellaneous.

TODAY the first star-rated restaurant opened in space. Famed chef Sebastiano Guarini awaits his guests in a module of the tourist orbital station Blue, which Blue Origin operates at the Lagrange point L2. Guarini turned into a celebrity after publishing his innovative book *Cooking in Zero Gravity*, which became a worldwide bestseller. The cook, who developed all his recipes himself in space, was awarded his Michelin star during a gala dinner on board the space station.

Author's Note

Welcome back! I hope you enjoyed reading *The Hole* as much as I enjoyed writing it. *The Hole* is the first stand-alone title in my universe that started with *The Enceladus Mission*. If you have traveled with me from the beginning, you re-met some old friends here, and you will continue to meet characters from these books in my future novels.

This is what makes writing in the same universe so much fun for me. I get to invent new personalities, while at the same time I can re-visit those that bugged me as they developed throughout the series.

Protagonists don't always behave well for their creator—they tend to take on lives of their own. Sometimes they don't want to do what I'm telling them, or they react unexpectedly. Let's take Maribel as an example. I wasn't sure what she would do when she was on her way to space. Would she really leave Chen behind? Only when I wrote that chapter did her true motives crystalize. I just had to write down what she really wanted.

I never like to say goodbye to anyone, and that includes the protagonists of my novels. As long as I stay in the same universe, I can tell you what happens in their lives after they come back from their adventures. What becomes of Maribel? You will meet her again, ten or maybe even twenty years from now in story time. Will she still be an astronomer? She hasn't told me… yet!

How has Earth coped with the near-catastrophic events

triggered by *The Hole?* This question will be answered in my next novel, *Silent Sun*, that you can order here:

hard-sf.com/links/522762

Silent Sun introduces a fascinating discovery: A strange structure—which had to have been manufactured—surrounds our sun. The construction not only grabs the attention of scientists, the party who is able to conquer it might gain a terrifying weapon that yields enormous power. I won't tell you here how this struggle plays out... But I can promise you a journey filled with fascinating science and breathtaking action, and most of all, the feeling of 'being there' that I like so much in a novel.

Where would you love to travel? The International Space Station? To the Moon or Mars? To a faraway star, or maybe inside a black hole? I'd love to hear about your travel dreams—if you could go wherever you wanted. Just write to me at brandon@hard-sf.com.

Hope to see you soon!

On my website at www.hard-sf.com you will also find interesting popular science news and articles about all those worlds afar that I'd love to have you visit with me.

I have to ask you one last thing, a big favor: If you liked this book, you would help me a lot if you could leave me a review so others can appreciate it as well. Just open this link:

hard-sf.com/links/454488

Thank you so much!

Due to the fact that black holes play an important role here, you will find a section entitled *Black Holes – A Guided Tour* below.

If you register at hard-sf.com/subscribe/ you will be notified of any new Hard Science Fiction titles. In addition you will receive the **color PDF version** of Black Holes – A Guided Tour.

facebook.com/BrandonQMorris
amazon.com/author/brandonqmorris
bookbub.com/authors/brandon-q-morris
goodreads.com/brandonqmorris

Also by Brandon Q. Morris

Silent Sun

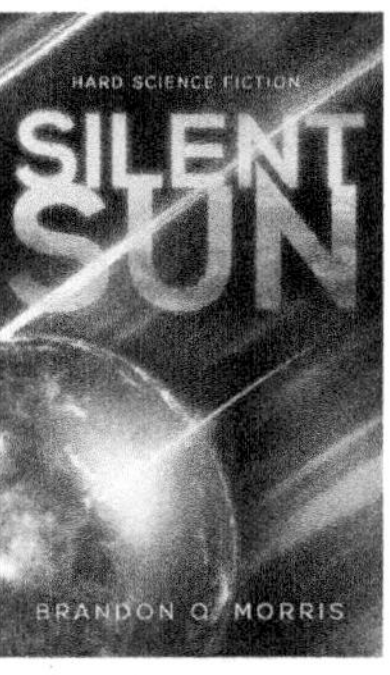

Is our sun behaving differently from other stars? When an amateur astronomer discovers something strange on telescopic solar pictures, an explanation must be found. Is it merely artefact? Or has he found something totally unexpected?

An expert international crew is hastily assembled, a spaceship is speedily repurposed, and the foursome is sent on the ride of their lives. What challenges will they face on this spur-of-the-moment mission to our central star?

What awaits all of them is critical, not only for understanding the past, but even more so for the future of life on Earth.

3.99 $ – hard-sf.com/links/527020

The Triton Disaster

Nick Abrahams still holds the official world record for the number of space launches, but he's bored stiff with his job hosting space tours. Only when his wife leaves him, however, does he try to change his life.

He accepts a tempting offer from a Russian billionaire. In exchange for making a simple repair on Neptune's moon Triton, he will return to Earth a multi-millionaire, enabling him to achieve his 'impossible dream' of buying his own California vineyard.

The fact that Nick must travel alone during the four-year roundtrip doesn't bother him at all, as he doesn't particularly like people anyway. Once en route he learns his new boss left out some critical details in his job description—details that could cost him his life, and humankind its existence...

3.99 $ – hard-sf.com/links/1086200

The Death of the Universe

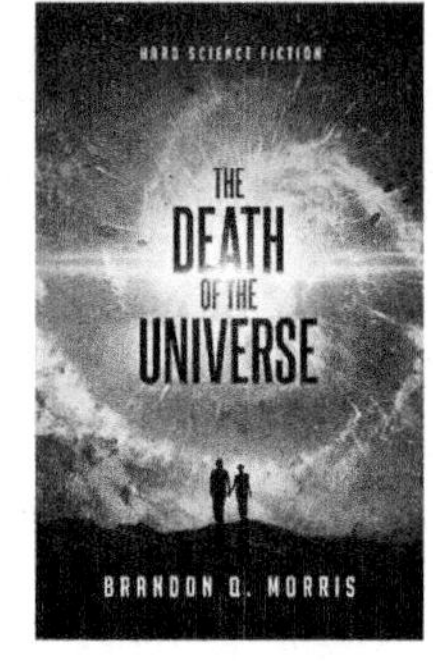

For many billions of years, humans—having conquered the curse of aging—spread throughout the entire Milky Way. They are able to live all their dreams, but to their great disappointment, no other intelligent species has ever been encountered. Now, humanity itself is on the brink of extinction because the universe is dying a protracted yet inevitable death.

They have only one hope: The 'Rescue Project' was designed to feed the black hole in the center of the galaxy until it becomes a quasar, delivering much-needed energy to humankind during its last breaths. But then something happens that no one ever expected—and humanity is forced to look at itself and its existence in an entirely new way.

3.99 $ – hard-sf.com/links/835415

The Death of the Universe: Ghost Kingdom

For many billions of years, humans—having conquered the curse of aging—spread throughout the entire Milky Way. They are able to live all their dreams, but to their great disappointment, no other intelligent species has ever been encountered. Now, humanity itself is on the brink of extinction because the universe is dying a protracted yet inevitable death.

They have only one hope: The 'Rescue Project' was designed to feed the black hole in the center of the galaxy until it becomes a quasar, delivering much-needed energy to humankind during its last breaths. But then something happens that no one ever expected—and humanity is forced to look at itself and its existence in an entirely new way.

3.99 $ – hard-sf.com/links/991276

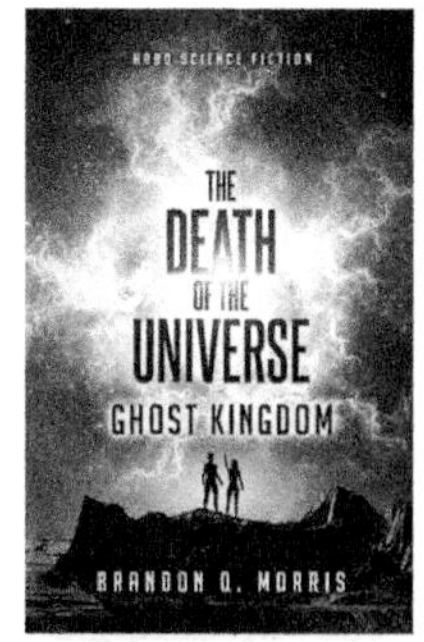

The Enceladus Mission (Ice Moon 1)

In the year 2031, a robot probe detects traces of biological activity on Enceladus, one of Saturn's moons. This sensational discovery shows that there is indeed evidence of extraterrestrial life. Fifteen years later, a hurriedly built spacecraft sets out on the long journey to the ringed planet and its moon.

The international crew is not just facing a difficult twenty-seven months: if the spacecraft manages to make it to Enceladus without incident it must use a drillship to penetrate the kilometer-thick sheet of ice that entombs the moon. If life does indeed exist on Enceladus, it could only be at the bottom of the salty, ice covered ocean, which formed billions of years ago.

However, shortly after takeoff disaster strikes the mission, and the chances of the crew making it to Enceladus, let alone back home, look grim.

2.99 $ – hard-sf.com/links/526999

The Titan Probe (Ice Moon 2)

In 2005, the robotic probe "Huygens" lands on Saturn's moon Titan. 40 years later, a radio telescope receives signals from the far away moon that can only come from the long forgotten lander.

At the same time, an expedition returns from neighbouring moon Enceladus. The crew lands on Titan and finds a dangerous secret that risks their return to Earth. Meanwhile, on Enceladus a deathly race has started that nobody thought was possible. And its outcome can only be decided by the

astronauts that are stuck on Titan.

3.99 $ – hard-sf.com/links/527000

The Io Encounter (Ice Moon 3)

Jupiter's moon Io has an extremely hostile environment. There are hot lava streams, seas of boiling sulfur, and frequent volcanic eruptions straight from Dante's Inferno, in addition to constant radiation bombardment and a surface temperature hovering at minus 180 degrees Celsius.

Is it really home to a great danger that threatens all of humanity? That's what a surprise message from the life form discovered on Enceladus seems to indicate.

The crew of ILSE, the International Life Search Expedition, finally on their longed-for return to Earth, reluctantly chooses to accept a diversion to Io, only to discover that an enemy from within is about to destroy all their hopes of ever going home.

3.99 $ – hard-sf.com/links/527008

Return to Enceladus (Ice Moon 4)

Russian billionaire Nikolai Shostakovitch makes an offer to the former crew of the spaceship ILSE. He will finance a return voyage to the icy moon Enceladus. The offer is too good to refuse—the expedition would give them the unique opportunity to recover the body of their doctor, Dimitri Marchenko.

Everyone on board knows that their benefactor acts out of purely personal motivations… but the true interests of the tycoon and the dangers that he conjures up are beyond anyone's imagination.

3.99 € – hard-sf.com/links/527011

Ice Moon - The Boxset

All four bestselling books of the Ice Moon series are now offered as a set, available only in e-book format.

The Enceladus Mission: Is there really life on Saturn's moon Enceladus? *ILSE*, the International Life Search Expedition, makes its way to the icy world where an underground ocean is suspected to be home to primitive life forms.

The Titan Probe: An old robotic NASA probe mysteriously awakens on the methane moon of Titan. The *ILSE* crew tries to solve the riddle—and discovers a dangerous secret.

The Io Encounter: Finally bound for Earth, *ILSE* makes it as far as Jupiter when the crew receives a startling message. The volcanic moon Io may harbor a looming threat that could wipe out Earth as we know it.

Return to Enceladus: The crew gets an offer to go back to Enceladus. Their mission—to recover the body of Dr. Marchenko, left for dead on the original expedition. Not everyone is working toward the same goal. Could it be their unwanted crew member?

9.99 $ – hard-sf.com/links/780838

Proxima Rising

Late in the 21st century, Earth receives what looks like an urgent plea for help from planet Proxima Centauri b in the closest star system to the Sun. Astrophysicists suspect a massive solar flare is about to destroy this heretofore-unknown civilization. Earth's space programs are unequipped to help, but an unscrupulous Russian billionaire launches a secret and highly-specialized spaceship to Proxima b, over four light-years away. The unusual crew faces a Herculean task—should they survive the journey. No one knows what to expect from this alien planet.

3.99 $ – hard-sf.com/links/610690

Proxima Dying

An intelligent robot and two young people explore Proxima Centauri b, the planet orbiting our nearest star, Proxima Centauri. Their ideas about the mission quickly prove grossly naive as they venture about on this planet of extremes.

Where are the senders of the call for help that lured them here? They find no one and no traces on the daylight side, so they place their hopes upon an expedition into the eternal ice on Proxima b's dark side. They not only face everlasting night, the team encounters grave dangers. A fateful decision will change the planet forever.

3.99 $ – hard-sf.com/links/652197

Proxima Dreaming

Alone and desperate, Eve sits in the control center of an alien structure. She has lost the other members of the team sent to explore exoplanet Proxima Centauri b. By mistake she has triggered a disastrous process that threatens to obliterate the planet. Just as Eve fears her best option may be a quick death, a nearby alien life form awakens from a very long sleep. It has only one task: to find and neutralize the destructive intruder from a faraway place.

3.99 $ – hard-sf.com/links/705470

The Rift

There is a huge, bold black streak in the sky. Branches appear out of nowhere over North America, Southern Europe, and Central Africa. People who live beneath The Rift can see it. But scientists worldwide are distressed—their equipment cannot pick up any type of signal from it.

The rift appears to consist of nothing. Literally. Nothing. Nada. Niente. Most people are curious but not overly concerned. The phenomenon seems to pose no danger. It is just there.

Then something jolts the most hardened naysayers, and surpasses the worst nightmares of the world's greatest scientists—and rocks their understanding of the universe.

3.99 $ – hard-sf.com/links/534368

Mars Nation 1

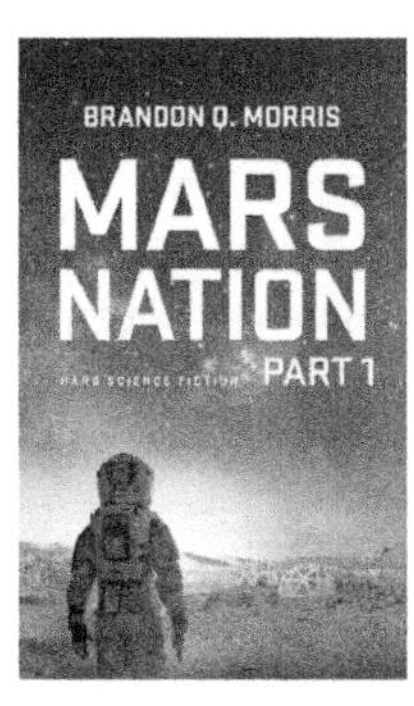

NASA finally made it. The very first human has just set foot on the surface of our neighbor planet. This is the start of a long research expedition that sent four scientists into space.

But the four astronauts of the NASA crew are not the only ones with this destination. The privately financed 'Mars for Everyone' initiative has also targeted the Red Planet. Twenty men and women have been selected to live there and establish the first extraterrestrial settlement.

Challenges arise even before they reach Mars orbit. The MfE spaceship Santa Maria is damaged along the way. Only the four NASA astronauts can intervene and try to save their lives.

No one anticipates the impending catastrophe that threatens their very existence—not to speak of the daily hurdles that an extended stay on an alien planet sets before them. On Mars, a struggle begins for limited resources, human cooperation, and just plain survival.

3.99 $ – hard-sf.com/links/762824

Mars Nation 2

A woman presumed dead fights her way through the hostile deserts of Mars. With her help, the NASA astronauts orphaned on the Red Planet hope to be able to solve their very worst problem. But their hopes are shattered when an unexpected menace arises and threatens to destroy everything the remnant of humanity has built on the planet. They need a miracle—or a ghost from the past whose true intentions are unknown.

Mars Nation 2 continues the story of the last representatives of Earth, who have found asylum on our neighboring planet, hoping to build a future in this alien world.

3.99 $ – hard-sf.com/links/790047

Mars Nation 3

Does the secret of Mars lurk beneath the surface of its south pole? A lone astronaut searches for clues about the earlier inhabitants of the Red Planet. Meanwhile, Rick Summers, having assumed the office of Mars City's Administrator by deceit and manipulation, tries to unify the people on Mars with the weapons under his control. Then Summers stumbles upon so powerful an evil that even he has no means to overcome it.

3.99 $ – hard-sf.com/links/818245

Black Holes – A Guided Tour

Introduction

A BLACK HOLE is an object of such strong gravitational force that matter and information are prevented from leaving a certain area around the object. Black holes, according to the general theory of relativity, develop in a situation where a concentrated mass curves space so much that it closes in upon itself.

The very name has an interesting history, and it is often ascribed to the physicist John Archibald Wheeler, who researched the topic. Initially, Wheeler used the term 'gravitationally completely collapsed star,' which accurately described the phenomenon, but was not very catchy. Therefore, during a presentation he gave in New York in 1967 he asked the audience for a better term. One of the audience members—Wheeler did not remember the person's name—suggested 'black hole' and the name stuck.

Later, archival research revealed that the term was already used in 1964 by the journalist Ann Ewing in the magazine *Science News*. Perhaps the unknown person who had suggested the name to Wheeler had read it there, or in an article published in *LIFE* magazine between then and Wheeler's 1967 presentation. It is possible the term was already in unofficial use among researchers—one factor that supports this position is that other researchers claimed to have heard it at conferences in 1960 and 1961, without being able to say who initially used it. It is also entirely possible that Ewing and the unknown individual invented it independently of each other.

By the way, researchers came up with the idea of 'dark stars' long before modern physics developed. This happened while scientists followed the corpuscular theory of light, which for a long time competed with the wave theory, and finally merged with it in the quantum nature of light. If you imagine light to consist of particles, then Newton's gravitation has to apply to these particles. In 1783 the scientist John Michell calculated accordingly that in the case of a star that had 500 times the radius of the sun (with the density being equal), light could no longer escape due to its strong gravitational pull. This star would then be a 'dark star.' In 1796 the French mathematician Laplace also described this possibility.

However, the modern black hole just recently turned 100 years old. After Einstein published the general theory of relativity in 1915, the following year Karl Schwarzschild offered the metric later named after him as a special solution to the field equations. It describes a non-rotating and not electrically charged black hole, whose event horizon then is given as a radius $r_s = 2GM/c^2$ (G is the gravitational constant, M the mass of the object, c the speed of light). Since the late 1930s it has been known that in the final stages of stars greater than a certain mass, a black hole develops. In 1963 the mathematician Roy Kerr calculated the Kerr metric describing a rotating black hole.

Their Properties

At first glance, black holes are amazingly simple—at least as far as can be judged from the outside—and, due to the nature of black holes, humans are in principle unable to go inside one—and come back to tell you about it. A black hole possesses a certain mass, an angular momentum, and an electrical charge. Nothing else! Everything else can be derived from these three values, such as the circumference or the magnetic field.

Calculating this using the equations of the general theory of relativity, however, is not exactly easy. In 1916 Karl Schwarzschild picked the simplest case: a non-rotating, not charged black hole. Shortly afterward, two physicists developed the Reissner–Nordström metric (named after them), which described charged but non-rotating black holes. It would take until the 1960s, though, before the corresponding equations for rotating objects were discovered.

These special solutions for individual cases are called metrics (singular: metric).

- Not charged, non-rotating: Schwarzschild metric

- Charged, non-rotating: Reissner–Nordström metric
- Not charged, rotating: Kerr metric
- Charged, rotating: Kerr–Newman metric

Normally, each black hole should possess both a charge and an angular momentum. Nevertheless, the other metrics still play important roles, because certain insights can be better derived from them thanks to their relative simplicity.

From Small to Large

A BASIC FEATURE of matter is that it generates a gravitational force. The reason is that matter curves the space around it, like a stone will dent a stretched bedsheet. Another object in the vicinity, much like a ping-pong ball on that same sheet, feels this dent in space and is accelerated toward the high-mass object.

This also applies to the particles a body consists of, its atoms. The mass of all particles inside attracts the particles further out. However, there are always counterforces at work, such as electrical repulsion or a thermal pressure from the inside. A black hole forms when counterforces are no longer able to stop gravity, because they weaken for some reason. For instance, if at the end of its lifecycle a star no longer has sufficient fuel to generate heat, the outward-acting pressure in its core collapses and gravity takes over... Which sometimes leads to a new equilibrium: The star shrinks, but then a new fusion process—that had not previously been possible—ignites in its core. But there are also cases in which it is too late for this to occur.

This new fusion process regularly happens with stars of more than 40 times the mass of our sun. Less-massive stars, though, end as neutron stars, where the special pressure of the degenerated particles in their interior suffices to counteract gravity.

If gravity wins, though, there is no end. The object shrinks more and more, until its density approaches infinite values. Today we call this a 'singularity,' for which the currently known laws of physics no longer apply. Space is curved so strongly that it collapses into itself, creating a hole in space-time, and any matter coming too close to this singularity can no longer escape. The radius within which this happens is called the 'Schwarzschild radius,' and the area that matter is not allowed to enter without being lost forever is called the 'event horizon.'

Basically, any object possesses such an event horizon. The Schwarzschild radius of Earth is nine millimeters. But a black hole only develops if the entire mass of the object is located inside this radius. Therefore all the mass of Earth would have to be compressed to the size of a marble in order to turn it into a black hole!

Based on the known development process of a black hole, these objects should only exist in one specific class, the so-called 'stellar black hole.' Such remnants of dead stars weigh at least ten times the mass of the sun and have a Schwarzschild radius of 30 kilometers. So the entire mass of ten times our Sun is contained inside a sphere with approximately the diameter of the city of Berlin. That is amazing!

However, astronomers have proven that even more massive black holes exist. Sagittarius A*, at the center of the Milky Way, weighs as much as 4.3 million Suns! It belongs to the class of supermassive black holes. The record is almost ten times as much as Sagittarius A*. Generally, such giants (whose event horizons can be larger than our solar system!) are located in the center of a galaxy. It is assumed that they grew from normal types over the course of billions of years by accreting—a fancy term for accumulating via gravity—matter from their surroundings. The theoretical upper limit for a supermassive black hole is about 10 billion times the mass of the sun. At an even higher mass, equilibrium would form between the radiation pressure emitted by its immediate environs and the gravitation.

If black holes exist in the sizes M and XXL, there are bound to be intermediate sizes somewhere. (Think of clothing sizes where S stands for small, M for medium, L for large, and X for eXtra—large or small.) These intermediate black holes weigh between hundreds and thousands of times the mass of our Sun, but they are not easy to find. Stellar black holes can be detected by the remnants of supernova explosions around them. Supermassive black holes give off radiation, but intermediate ones offer few clues. Therefore there is no definite proof of their existence so far. What has been measured, though, are the echoes of mergers and collisions, during which these black holes are created and grow. The LIGO experiment has already detected several gravitational waves that were formed by the collisions of black holes. So we basically listened in on their unions, but haven't yet caught them red-handed.

It gets even more complicated with the sizes S and XS. Shortly after the Big Bang, the universe was still very small and packed with matter and energy. Back then, 13.8 billion years ago, there should have been areas in which matter happened to be so densely distributed that the conditions for the creation of a black hole existed. In those cases, matter had no choice but to give in to gravitation and thus collapse. The so-called 'primordial black holes' created this way would be considerably smaller than the stellar class. They might be as heavy as the moon and have a Schwarzschild radius of one tenth of a millimeter. This would make them much harder to detect than any other kind. However, their lifespan would 'only' be in the range of the age of the universe. It might therefore be possible to prove not only their existence, but the end of their existence, which should be observable in the form of a gamma-ray burst. So far, though, none of the gamma-ray bursts measured in space have given any specific indications of having been caused by a dying primordial black hole.

The theoretical lower limit for the mass of a black hole lies below the smallest possible mass, the Planck mass. So there could also be holes that are size XS, or XXS, or even XXXXXXXS, all of which would be called black micro-holes. This has been mostly discussed in connection with the high-energy experiments using the Large Hedron Collider (LHC) accelerator at the CERN institute. What would happen if the conditions for a black hole developing in a tiny space were to be fulfilled there? Nothing. First of all, the life-span of a micro-hole is very short. Secondly, its event horizon is tiny. Black holes are not like vacuum cleaners sucking up everything near them. They only swallow whatever crosses their event horizons - they cannot suck matter into their horizons. If such a horizon is much smaller than the average distance between two atoms, then the micro-hole starves and disappears after a short time.

Researchers have even calculated what an encounter with a considerably heavier primordial black hole would do to Earth. The black hole would speed through the planet within approximately a minute and cause weak earthquakes with a magnitude of less than 4. The shape of the pressure waves created would be unique, however, and unlike those that occur in normal quakes. Therefore, we would have seismological proof of an encounter with a primordial black hole. The probability is very low, though, and scientists only expect such a collision once every few million years.

How does one weigh a black hole? It is quite simple. You look at the galaxy in whose center the black hole is located. A research team at Swinburne University of Technology in Australia and the University of Minnesota/Duluth in the US compared numerous spiral galaxies and discovered a clear relationship between the mass of the black hole in its center and the way the galaxy presses its arms to itself.

According to this study, the looser it held its arm, the lighter the black hole must be. This only applied to spiral galaxies, though. If you want to calculate this for yourself, the formula is: $\log(M_{BH}/M_\odot) = (7.01 \pm 0.07) - (0.171 \pm 0.017)[|\varphi| - 15°]$, where φ is the angle with which the arm stretches into space, and $M_{BH}/M_\odot$ stands for the mass of the black hole compared to that of our sun.

The Life and Death of Black Holes

THE BIRTH of black holes has already been described above. However, they do not remain in the same state forever—they grow, and at some point they die.

The growth is driven by two processes, accretion of normal matter, and merging with other black holes. By now, astronomers can accurately observe and document both of these processes.

While black holes themselves do not emit any—or more precisely, hardly any—radiation, their accretion disks can be among the brightest objects in the universe. Material in the vicinity of black holes does not fall into them along a straight path.

Accretion disks do not form exclusively around black holes, they generally form around high-mass objects, so-called accretors. For example, young stars can be among them. If it is assumed that an object is initially surrounded by dust and gas in all directions, then why does a disk form? The reason is a constant interaction of two forces. Gravitation attempts to pull matter as close as possible. However, this leads to heat, which creates a counterpressure acting outward. Gravitation can only win if the cloud can somehow get rid of the heat. This is achieved by radiation, for which a disk offers the most efficient shape. Therefore, the original cloud gradually turns into a disk—this also applies to the creation of solar systems. Within the disk there is a constant transport of material from the outside in, while the angular momentum is transported outward. The disk has an inner edge, where it rotates almost at the speed of light. Material that gets any closer to the black hole is not able to hold on—the dust cannot go faster than the speed of light—and it finally falls into the hole.

At first it moves through the 'ergosphere,' an area outside of the event horizon. Here only photons survive, light particles that can endlessly rotate around the black hole. Further inside is the event horizon, the threshold to uncertainty.

With every particle that falls into it, the black hole becomes a bit larger and heavier. Currently, meaning 13.8 billion years after the Big Bang, this is the dominant process, at least for most black holes.

However, they can also lose mass via 'Hawking radiation.' You can guess who came up with that concept. In a vacuum, pairs of particles constantly appear out of nothing. This is no problem, since the conservation of energy is only briefly violated, and it can handle this. Normally, these virtual particles soon annihilate each other and pay off their energy debt.

But what would happen if one particle disappeared into the event horizon and the other one did not? Then someone else had to pay the debt—the black hole. The remaining particle is emitted as Hawking radiation and the hole loses a tiny bit of mass. The smaller the black hole, the shorter the wavelength of the radiation and the higher its energy content. Therefore, small black holes evaporate in a relatively short time, assumed to be a few billion years. Much larger black holes eventually dissolve, too, but that will take a very, very long time. Currently, the temperature of stellar black holes lies below the temperature of the background radiation. For this very reason they absorb more energy than they emit. Countless billions of years from now, black holes will be the last witnesses that the universe once contained something other than an even distribution of matter and energy. Unless, that is, the universe ends in a different, more spectacular fashion, like being destroyed in a collision with another universe.

The Oldest Black Hole

800 MILLION SUNS. If you considered Sagittarius A*, the black hole at the center of the Milky Way, a big deal, you have to multiply this monster by 200... and then you get the mass of the black hole at the center of the quasar ULAS J134208.10+092838.61—its friends, many of whom are astronomers, as one would expect, are allowed to call it J1342+0928 for short. Quasars are radio galaxies, active siblings of the Milky Way that emit such huge amounts of energy, particularly in the radio range, that they are observable from Earth across very large distances.

J1342+0928 tops them all. With a red shift of z=7.54 this quasar set a new record and must therefore be located near the edge of the observable universe. That is not the reason, though, why researchers are so excited about its galaxy, which shines as brightly as 400 trillion suns! It is because its light took so long to reach us, and as such we can use it to glance back into the dawn of the cosmos. When the light that now reaches us was emitted, the universe was only 690 million years old, about five percent of its current age.

If one considered the universe to be an adult now, it would have been a teenager then, in the middle of adolescence and undergoing important changes, at least if the standard model about the evolution of the universe is correct.

Astronomers have indeed found important traces of it. They managed to measure, with a high degree of certainty, a significant percentage of neutral hydrogen in the spectrum of the quasar. When the giant galaxy shone in all the splendor we can only now marvel at, the cosmos was in the reionization phase. During this, the hydrogen gas that had become neutral during the previous recombination era was robbed of its electrons and thus ionized by newly ignited stars and galaxies like J1342+0928. Researchers found that this process had not yet finished 690 million years after the Big Bang.

The fact that such a massive black hole existed even then, relatively soon after the Big Bang, gave cosmologists new information about the creation and growth of black holes. J1342+0928 was only possible because even at such an early date black holes with a mass of at least 10,000 suns developed —or did the black holes back then grow differently than we assume?

There is actually a limit for the increase in size, the so-called 'Eddington limit.' If too much material falls into a black hole, it chokes, so to speak, and cannot absorb anything else for a while. However, there are also models according to which a mass increase above the Eddington limit is possible.

How to Find Black Holes

In order to directly observe a black hole, one would have to get very close to it, as is the case in *The Hole*. Humans are hardly likely to be able to do so within the next thousand years. The Hawking radiation emitted by a hole is also too weak for a direct analysis.

However black holes can be observed using a different method, namely their effect on the area outside the event horizon. This effect takes on many forms. Therefore researchers now have a number of observation methods they can use according to the specific circumstances:

- Kinematic: If we find an object moving through space on an elliptical course, then another object's gravitation forced it to do so. If no other object is visible, we can venture to guess it is a black hole. Its mass can then be calculated based on the trajectory and the mass of the orbiting body.
- Eruptive: If a star gets too close to a black hole, it might be totally destroyed under the right circumstances, which astronomers can observe in the form of X-ray and gamma-ray bursts, among other things. If there is no other possible cause, it must be a black hole.

- Accretive: As described above, gas and dust in the vicinity of a black hole form a disk which radiates in the entire spectrum and is therefore visible.
- Spectro-relativistic: If a star is near a black hole, its spectrum is distorted by gravitational effects, and this can be measured.
- Obscurative: Near strong gravitational forces, especially around the edge of a black hole, the wavelength of lights is shifted toward red. The ring around the object therefore becomes brownish to black. Currently our telescopes are not strong enough to detect this, but it should be possible in the future, at first by primarily using radio telescopes.
- Aberrative: Another effect of gravitation is that it bends light rays coming from objects behind the black hole. The hole thus becomes a lens. This gravitational lens effect can already be used today to find stellar black holes. This requires, though, that another luminous object is located behind the black hole along our line of sight.
- Temporal: According to the theory of special relativity, effects occur in the immediate vicinity of black holes, particularly time dilation. Therefore, temporal sequences change, which can be detected if one knows the normal sequence in a 'rest frame.'
- Auditory: If a stone falls into water, concentric waves spread. The collision of a black hole with another one also generates waves—within space-time. They are called gravitational waves and have already been found several times with the help of the LIGO detector. In order to determine the precise location of the event, other analytical methods are usually needed as well.

The Information Paradox

In the first section you already learned that black holes have three specific properties: mass, angular momentum, and charge. This fact is known as the 'no-hair theorem' or 'bald head theorem': If you've seen one bald head, you've seen them all, since there is nothing else to be seen. But, what would happen to the information contained in matter if a particle disappeared into a black hole, never to be seen again? Similar laws of conservation apply to information as to matter, and the black hole seems to violate them. This is known as the 'information paradox.'

At first it was believed that the concept of Hawking radiation would offer a way out. Couldn't it contain the lost information? But that is not the case. The radiation only depends on the size of the hole, its mass.

There is no generally accepted solution for this paradox. Stephen Hawking thought black holes might have hairs under certain conditions, though other physicists reject this idea.

Another suggested solution is the concept of wormholes. In theory, a wormhole would spit out the information elsewhere, so to speak, so information would be gone but not lost. So far none have been detected, though, and they appear to be unlikely for other reasons.

The fact that black holes have limited lifespans is not the

real problem for physicists. The really interesting question is, what happens to the information that ended up in a black hole—information that is theoretically indestructible? Even a black hole the size of the sun would last about 10^{67} years before it would be extinguished. If a black hole were immortal, physicists could take solace in the idea that information which crossed the event horizon might be forever lost from this side, but might still exist around the singularity. In order to resolve this paradox the physicists might need a so-called 'theory of everything.' Until that has been developed, they will have to make do with one of these independent scenarios:

1. The information is irretrievably lost. Unfortunately this conclusion violates the principle of the conservation of information. On the other hand, the mathematician Roger Penrose assumes in his cosmology a destruction of information inside a black hole.
2. Black holes are information-incontinent. They constantly leak information. Alas, this runs counter to current calculations for macroscopic black holes, which align well with reality.
3. When the black hole dies, all of the collected information escapes at once. This scenario is in accordance with current physics—except for the moment shortly before its violent death. In that instance a very, very small black hole would have to contain enormous amounts of information, which contradicts what we currently know about the maximum information density.
4. The final stage of a black hole is not greater than the shortest length in the universe, the 'Planck length.' It contains all information ever collected. Then physicists would not have to think of a way for the information to escape, as they have to do in scenario 3. On the other hand, the information density would be infinite, which is impossible.

5. The information is preserved in a daughter universe that splits off from ours—a nice idea, that unfortunately does not yet have a matching physical theory.
6. Instead of in spatial dimensions, the information is preserved in temporal correlations. The idea can be worked out well within current physics, but contradicts the idea of nature as an entity developing in time.
7. The information encoded in the three-dimensional space within the black hole is also saved on its two-dimensional boundary surface. This 'holographic principle' developed by the physicist Juan Malcadena assumes our universe consists both of a three-dimensional structure and a 2D element. In the 3D universe strings, gravitation and black holes follow the theory of relativity, while in the flat part, elementary particles and their fields obey the laws of quantum physics. All the information in one part is also encoded in the other one, but for a member of one structure the other structure is inaccessible. Thus information evaporating with the black hole would not be lost but is preserved in the 2D structure of the universe.
8. A so-called firewall develops at the event horizon. This assumes that the particles appearing out of nowhere are entangled. If one of the partners falls into the black hole, the entanglement breaks and energy is released. The information is preserved in this firewall in the form of an entanglement of all the particles. However, this scenario contradicts the general theory of relativity, according to which all gravitational fields are principally identical. Why should something different happen during the fall of an object into a black hole than when a ball falls to the ground?
9. Wormholes. The firewall around the black hole,

which violates the general theory of relativity, could be dispensed with if the black hole itself and all the particles of its Hawking radiation were connected by wormholes—shortcuts through space-time. This idea would allow for particles and anti-particles to remain entangled. The entanglement not only preserves the information —in theory, this information could also be recovered.

10. The evaporation of the black hole will reach an end at some point. This idea was developed by the Cambridge University physicist George Ellis. A black hole distorts space-time through its gravitation. It is not alone in doing so. The cosmic background radiation, under the influence of the gravitational field, also causes singularities to develop shortly behind the event horizon, which change the structure of space-time. If the virtual particles of the Hawking radiation form close to such a distortion, both slip behind the event horizon. The more a black hole shrinks, the more likely this process becomes—until it happens more often than its opposite and the mass of the black hole stabilizes. Ellis cannot tell exactly why this happens—but regardless of it the black hole would not completely evaporate but approach a certain mass and thus preserve the information inside it.
11. Recently, the concept of 'soft hairs' has been discussed. This is what I used in *The Hole*. Shortly before the surface of a black hole there would be zero-energy intermediate particles—photons, gravitons, etc., collectively called soft hairs—that, like a matrix, absorbed the information that would otherwise disappear behind the event horizon. The supporters of this theory have shown at least for light particles (photons) that there are an infinite number of storage locations on the surface

> of a black hole and that the approaching particles can actually excite these soft hairs. For the theory to be completely accepted, they would need evidence that this also works for 'gravitons,' whose existence has not yet been proven. Furthermore, this concept cannot explain how the information might return to our reality. Therefore, this part of the solution in *The Hole* is speculative, but still fits with current scientific discussions.

Would it be so bad if information got lost in a black hole? Haven't we forgotten things without the universe coming to an end? This is the problem: Information corresponds to order, and a loss of information therefore equates to disorder or entropy. In thermodynamics, an increase in entropy corresponds to a rise in temperature. If black holes destroyed information, they would have to heat up by quintillions of degrees in a short time.

A Journey into a Black Hole

How would it feel to approach a black hole? Science knows surprisingly much about this in theory, even though we are centuries away from making it reality.

It is easiest to show this for an external, immobile observer who comfortably watches someone else undertake this dangerous voyage. The traveler simply becomes slower and slower while nearing the black hole. The light he emits is shifted increasingly toward the red end of the spectrum, making him first look brown and then almost black. From the perspective of the observer he never reaches the event horizon. No matter your patience, you will never be able to watch someone entering the event horizon.

Okay, *that* was boring! So now let's get a bit more courageous. We take our spaceship and enter into an orbit around a black hole that is as heavy as possible. We circle it at a constant distance. At first we see a round, black spot surrounded by a strangely distorted disk. The latter is created by the black hole redirecting light coming from behind it. If we take a closer look we can see a narrow strip at the edge of the black spot, where the complete sky is endlessly repeated—as in the case of two mirrors aligned so you see yourself reflected over and over, ad infinitum.

Now we decrease our orbital radius. In doing so, the ship has to move faster and faster so it won't fall into the black hole. The black spot increases in size. Initially, it just fills the foreground, and if you turn your head right or left you still see normal sky. But a little bit later—for a stellar hole at a distance of 45 kilometers, meaning 15 kilometers from the event horizon—the blackness almost fills your field of vision. If you glance to the right or left, you see the back of your own head! Only behind you is there still a normal universe, that you watch as if you could see infrared radiation. In actuality, the infrared is shifted into the range of visible light.

You have reached the ergosphere—in other metrics called the 'photon sphere'—where only photons survive. The light emitted by the back of your head has circled the black hole and arrived here again. The closer you get to the event horizon, the smaller the field of view into space, until it shrinks to a tiny spot.

A tip from an expert: Choose the heaviest black hole you can find in order to experience this exciting journey with an acceleration you can stand.

This also applies to our third attempt. Now you are going to be particularly brave, leave the ship in a spacesuit and let yourself fall. Of course you were careful to choose a hole without an accretion disk, as otherwise it might get unpleasantly hot.

Let's start again far to the outside. Gravitation will make you move faster and faster so that you soon reach 99 percent of the speed of light. With a small black hole there would be the problem of 'spaghettification,' sometimes referred to as the 'noodle effect.' Forces of different strength are working on your legs, closer to the hole, and your head, which is farther away—your body would be painfully stretched. With a supermassive black hole the forces are greater, but they increase more slowly, so this fate would only occur after you had time to enjoy the view.

Unlike in the previous experiment, the black disk you are

hurtling toward remains relatively small. The phenomenon is called 'aberration.' You know it from driving a car while snow is falling. The snow seems to come toward you, even though it falls vertically. Here it works the same way. Beams of light that come from above for an observer at rest, will arrive for you from ahead and at an angle. And indeed you will get the impression that the black spot is still innocuously small when you cross the event horizon.

But then it is too late, and there is no turning back. By the way, in free fall you would see the light coming from ahead shifted towards blue, so infrared would become visible light, while from behind red-shifted light reaches you, and you can perceive ultraviolet as visible light. The moment you cross the event horizon you will see a flash. It contains photons from the entire history of the universe, but shifted towards blue. If you had more time, you could record the entire past. However, you would have no chance to tell anyone about it.

No one knows what the inside of a black hole looks like, but your view might be distorted by the strong forces and relativistic effects anyway. Everything you see at first has a kidney shape, then that of a donut wrapped around your hips, and finally that of a narrow cone. At the same time, your presence here causes enormous disturbances of the equilibrium. You will be constantly compressed and stretched. Not even the particles of your body remain, as the four fundamental forces —gravity, light/electromagnetism, weak nuclear force, and strong nuclear force—unite again, and you turn into a kind of primeval soup. Yummy!

The form of the singularity is determined by the type of our black hole. Because it certainly rotates, the singularity has the shape of a ring—otherwise it would be a point. It whirls in front of your eyes like a one-dimensional hoop through the surrounding quantum foam. You peer into it and detect, at unattainable distances, numerous other universes that are so very different from ours.

Now, that last sentence was pure speculation. 'Detect' isn't the appropriate word, because inside the singularity there is neither light, nor gravitation, nor the strong and weak interaction. Everything is like it was shortly before the Big Bang inside the singularity from which our universe developed.

A Universe Inside a Black Hole?

Simple answers—humans have always been looking for them, particularly in difficult times. Whether they are '42,' or 'God,' or 'It's the government's fault,' they have a certain allure that even physicists are not immune to. And one has to admit that physicists have all the right in the world to look for easy answers. Ultimately, their science is getting more complex year by year.

The more that methodical physicists—and the author of this book is one—look at our world, the more dimensions they need to describe it perfectly. First there were three dimensions, while the general theory of relativity already needed four. This sufficed for a few years, until it became clear that neither relativity nor quantum theory could categorize the universe completely.

One way out was the concept of string theories, which originally used 10, then 11, and finally up to 21 dimensions. Of course it is hard to imagine that the additional dimensions are so tightly folded that humans cannot perceive them. There are some mathematical arguments in their favor, though. The fact that quantum theory could be used for calculations had led some people to ignore the drawbacks from imagining things, and they began doing exactly that. 'Theories' is the word for such educated imaginings—to be followed by calculating out each of them and then measuring whether prognosis and reality match. The motto in these cases is 'shut up and calculate.'

But perhaps the reality we can comprehend is only a complex illusion—a holographic projection of a much simpler reality. Scientists have been trying to use this refreshing concept in holographic cosmology, and it plays a role in *The Hole*. Take a look at the hologram you might have on your credit card. It seems three-dimensional, yet it is flat, stored in two dimensions. If you use VR goggles to walk though impressive virtual landscapes, you see a three-dimensional space, yet it is created in front of your eyes by two flat screens. Generally the 'holographic principle' refers to a connection between a spatial structure and its equivalent on a surface.

The principle can be used, for example, to solve the information paradox of black holes mentioned above. If we physicists had a complete description of all the properties of an object at a certain point in time, we would—being physicists—want to find out how it had behaved shortly before that point. However, if this information had been destroyed, finding it would no longer be possible. Unless, that is, the information could somehow have been encoded on the surface of the event horizon. In that case, the prior spatial representations were never anything but holograms.

Perhaps we could imagine the universe as the inside of a giant black hole, on the plane of whose event horizon reality happens. The rest is illusion. In that case, however, there must be a projection mechanism. It has to be possible to turn multi-dimensional theories into lower-dimensional ones, or vice versa, without losing anything. For a long time this was proven only for negatively curved spaces, but since 2015 it has been known to be possible in our almost flat universe. In 2017, a study in *Physical Review Letters* went further—a step beyond: Its authors applied various holographic quantum field theories three-dimensionally—i.e. reduced by one dimension—to a simulation of the early universe shortly after the Big Bang, and compared which parameters created which features in the cosmos. And in fact some of the holographic theories work as well in describing reality as the standard model of cosmology, 'ΛCDM,' Lambda-Cold Dark Matter. The theories that work well are also able to predict specific phenomena like measured anomalies in the cosmic background radiation.

Of course this is no proof we are living in a holographic universe. For that, researchers would have to prove that the tiny imponderables of the underlying quantum theories are also manifested in space. This means space itself would have to become diffuse in the very smallest dimensions. This is what the holometer at Fermilab is supposed to show through its measurements. See holometer.fnal.gov.

The Big Bang itself might give us clues about the holographic nature of our own universe. The Big Bang, which is generally considered the beginning of space and time, literally has a *little* problem. It must have happened in an extremely tiny space. The closer you get to it, the more densely the complete energy of the cosmos was compressed in a unit of space, until everything was concentrated in a point of infinite density.

This state cannot be comprehended with the help of the general theory of relativity. Therefore physicists are forced to consider the Big Bang with a theory that unites both big (the cosmos) and small (the quantum world). So far, there is no agreement on this, just a few competing candidates.

There is the 'string theory,' for example, that sees space as consisting of tiny objects resembling piano strings. These strings are one-dimensional and they each vibrate with a specific frequency to which energy can be assigned. By now, physicists have expanded this idea and reached an 'M-theory' by adding other structures—point particles and most of all membranes—'branes'—which can have up to nine dimensions. In order to reach the elementary particles and the laws of nature we know, the extra dimensions must be 'curled up' in a specific way, as researchers call this procedure. There are very different ways of curling up membranes and strings, and, depending on which one you choose, a different kind of universe emerges. Overall, 10^{100} different universes—a google's worth—are possible, and many of these could exist simultaneously without the inhabitants of one having any clue about the creatures living in the other universes. However, if two three-dimensional worlds got too close to each other while moving through an additional dimension, they could collide—and give birth to our universe in the Big Bang.

A competitor of the string theory called 'loop quantum gravity' yields even better results. According to it, the universe only seems to be continuous. In reality, though, absolutely everything is quantized, or divided into small bits—even gravity. Space is no longer the container for the universe, but a part of it, and it is also fragmented and takes on the form of a network of lines and knots. Then elementary particles form different types of knots and between the lines and knots there is nothing. The theory of loop quantum gravity leads to some strange-sounding conclusions, but in turn it is better at describing some interesting phenomena than other theories.

Its consequences for the Big Bang were first simulated in 2004 by the German physicist Martin Bojowald. First of all, it avoids the concept of a singularity, because the loop quantum universe has a specific minimum structural size it cannot go below. If you calculate conditions increasingly closer to the Big Bang, you get a new, different, or also predecessor universe, in which all directions, including that of time, are reversed. This universe before the Big Bang is shrinking in the direction of the Big Bang. If space has contracted extremely under the influence of gravitation, the quantum loop fabric of space-time fractures at some point—and through the effect of this 'quantum recoil,' gravity turns into a strong repulsive force that drives the universe apart again.

But perhaps we don't need all these nice new theories to explain the Big Bang. Three Canadian physicists noticed that the singularity underlying the beginning of the universe had one peculiarity. Unlike all singularities known so far, which are within black holes, it could not have been surrounded by an event horizon.

In an article, the researchers described the conjecture that they developed from this: Maybe we do not see this event horizon because we are a part of it. The universe as we know it would then be the three-dimensional event horizon of a black hole with four spatial dimensions, which was created by the collapse of an also four-dimensional star. This sounds even more plausible because the physicists' simulation showed that such a three-dimensional event horizon would have to expand continually—a process we notice as the expansion of the universe.

This process would also explain why the universe is so markedly homogeneous. Until now, cosmologists have had to use a very fast expansion phase shortly after the Big Bang to account for this, the so-called inflation phase. According to this, when the universe was between 10-38 and 10-35 seconds old, it expanded by a factor between 10^{30} and 10^{50}. While it was initially the size of a proton, it afterwards had the dimensions of a soccer ball. In order to arrive at a reasonable explanation, which would fit into the previous cosmological model, this inflation required the so-called 'inflatons.' These particles —which, strangely enough, never show up again afterwards —are not attracted to each other by gravity, but instead repulse each other. The fictive four-dimensional universe, though, in which the 4D-star must have collapsed, would have had plenty of opportunity to achieve a homogeneous structure in the course of its comparably eternal existence.

But even this idea has a problem. Its predictions deviate by four percent from the data of ESA's Planck observatory, which precisely mapped the cosmic background radiation. However, these measurements fit the previous theory exactly. Now the researchers want to expand their model in such a way that this difference will disappear. Then the new theory might not necessarily reflect truth, but—as it best explains all observations—it would be the most likely explanation *so far* for the origin of the universe. Physicists don't demand more than that from a good theory.

Spanish researchers described another exciting scenario. Their model started out shortly after the Big Bang. Back then, irregularities in the distribution of matter must have existed. These could have grown into bubbles. Earlier, we already identified them as the cores of primordial black holes. After the inflation phase, the following scenarios are possible:

•The bubble forms a primordial black hole.

•The bubble forms a black hole containing a baby universe connected to the outside world via a wormhole.

•Over time, the bubble becomes a supermassive black hole.

A baby universe would have the interesting feature of continually expanding—just like our own universe! In addition, new bubbles would repeatedly form inside it, for which the scenarios mentioned above are possible. These in turn could generate baby universes. The result would be a multiverse of universes connected by wormholes. It would be relatively easy to find out whether we are living in such a universe—the black holes would have a specific, characteristic energy distribution. So if we ever measure that at a black hole, it would be proof for the existence of a multiverse.

Are there also Naked Singularities?

There are increasing clues that the universe might be harboring naked singularities, in addition to black holes. These 'white holes,' which lack event horizons, would allow a direct view of the singularities in their centers—a view which physicists currently dread, rather than desire.

Right now, cosmologists share a problem some people know from visiting nude beaches. Under certain circumstances, it might be better if some things remain hidden. This also applies to the phenomenon of a black hole. Because this cosmic monster is surrounded by an event horizon, science does not have to show any interest in what really happens inside this radius. Since nothing ever escapes from a black hole, we can develop conjectures, but never support these with observations. This is practical, because we currently lack the physics to understand the events in the singularity floating in the center of the black hole. The physical laws we know would be pulverized by the gravitation trending towards the infinite, just like anything else that crosses the event horizon boundary.

Unfortunately, physicists are increasingly troubled by a phenomenon whose existence has not been proven by observations, the 'naked singularity.' Up to now they attempted to get rid of the problem by formulating a theorem. In 1969 the physicist Roger Penrose postulated that singularities would probably always have to be surrounded by an event horizon. The universe itself, acting as a 'cosmic censor,' prevents the ugliness of a singularity from being seen. There are even some indications Penrose might be right. Among other things, a white hole could violate causality. What happens in the vicinity of a naked singularity could not be theoretically predicted, at least with the means at our disposal—one might as well consider the events there as pure magic.

On the other hand, white holes would allow another cosmic phenomenon often used by science fiction writers—the wormhole, also called the 'Einstein-Rosen bridge' by physicists. Wormholes could make direct connections through the space-time-continuum possible, perhaps even into different universes. At one end would be a matter-absorbing black hole, and there would be a matter-ejecting white hole at the other. It has been mathematically demonstrated that humans could pass through a variant of these connections. To open the door you would only need a tiny amount of 'exotic matter,' exotic in the sense that it has to exhibit a negative energy density.

Only a few physicists go that far, though, and it must be clearly said that these are purely mathematical games, for now. On the other hand, researchers have not yet been able to prove the theory of the cosmic censor either. Very recently, simulations of the collision of two black holes proved that a naked singularity could not be formed this way. Yet there are still many open questions.

If you simulate the collapse of a massive star, the formation of a white hole seems definitely possible. Physicists are faced with two problems here. On the one hand, it is hardly possible, so far, to simulate a nova in the computer with all necessary variables. Stars are not homogeneous, nor are they 100 percent spherical—assumptions required, in many simulations, for black holes to form. On the other hand, models show that even slight changes of the initial conditions can lead to completely different results. Sometimes the computer briefly shows a naked singularity, which soon is covered by an event horizon, sometimes there is a black hole from the very beginning, and now and then the outcome is a stable white hole.

The preconditions for its existence are not as exotic as one might think. Let's take a giant star collapsing under the force of gravity, whose density decreases towards the outside, like an onion. Because the gravitational force depends on the density of the individual layers of our illustrative onion, it is stronger in the interior than on the outside. Therefore, the inner sections of the star collapse more rapidly into a singularity than do the outer ones. If the star is sufficiently homogeneous, it could happen that the individual layers do not have enough mass to absorb the light like a black hole does, and the singularity would remain naked.

And why shouldn't we look inside? Naked singularities, if they exist, would grant us a direct view of the effects of quantum gravity, the force that is supposed to someday unite the general theory of relativity with quantum theory. So far, physics has attempted to gain clues from the early phase of the universe, when conditions were so extreme that they cannot be described using the general theory of relativity.

Glossary of Acronyms

AI – Artificial Intelligence

CERN – Conseil Européen pour la Recherche Nucléaire (European Council for Nuclear Research)

CLST – Chile Summer Time

CTO – Chief Technical Officer

DLR – Deutsches Zentrum für Luft und Raumfahrt (German Aerospace Center)

ESA – European Space Agency

ESO – European Southern Observatory

EU – European Union

EVA – ExtraVehicular Activity

FAST – (Chinese) Five-hundred-meter Aperture Spherical Telescope

HUT – Hard Upper Torso

IAC – Instituto de Astrofísica de Canarias (Institute of Astrophysics of the Canary Islands)

ISC – Intermittent Self-Catheterization

ΛCDM – Lambda-Cold Dark Matter

LCVG – Liquid Cooling and Ventilation Garment

LHC – Large Hadron Collider

LIGO – Laser Interferometer Gravitational-Wave Observatory

NASA – National Aeronautics and Space Administration

LED – Light Emitting Diode
MCT – Mars Colonial Transporter
OGS2 – Optical Ground Station 2 (telescope)
OWL – OverWhelmingly Large Telescope
TCS – Telescopio Carlos Sánchez
UPA – Urine Processor Assembly
VR – Virtual Reality
WHC – Waste Hygiene Compartment

Metric to English Conversions

It is assumed that by the time the events of this novel take place, the United States will have joined the rest of the world and will be using the International System of Units, the modern form of the metric system.

Length:
centimeter = 0.39 inches
meter = 1.09 yards, or 3.28 feet
kilometer = 1093.61 yards, or 0.62 miles

Area:
square centimeter = 0.16 square inches
square meter = 1.20 square yards
square kilometer = 0.39 square miles

Weight:
gram = 0.04 ounces
kilogram = 35.27 ounces, or 2.20 pounds

Volume:
liter = 1.06 quarts, or 0.26 gallons
cubic meter = 35.31 cubic feet, or 1.31 cubic yards

Temperature:
To convert Celsius to Fahrenheit, multiply by 1.8 and then add 32

Copyright

Brandon Q. Morris
--
www.hard-sf.com
brandon@hardsf.com
Translator: Frank Dietz, Ph.D. Editor: Pamela Bruce, B.S.
Final editing: Marcia Kwiecinski, A.A.S., and Stephen Kwiecinski, B.S.

Technical Advisors: Dr. Lutz Hillmann, Hauke Sattler
Cover design: Haresh R. Makwana

Printed in Great Britain
by Amazon

44015426R00229